SILENT SATURDAY

To Lisa

Helen Grant

SILENT SATURDAY

*Good luck with your
writing!*

Very best wishes,

Helen Grant

THE BODLEY HEAD

SILENT SATURDAY
A BODLEY HEAD BOOK 978 0 370 33241 3
TRADE PAPERBACK 9781 782 30007 6

Published in Great Britain by The Bodley Head,
an imprint of Random House Children's Publishers UK
A Random House Group Company

This edition published 2013

1 3 5 7 9 10 8 6 4 2

Set in 12.5/15.5 pt Minion by Falcon Oast Graphic Art Ltd.

RANDOM HOUSE CHILDREN'S PUBLISHERS UK
61–63 Uxbridge Road, London W5 5SA

www.**randomhousechildrens**.co.uk
www.**totallyrandombooks**.co.uk
www.**randomhouse**.co.uk

Addresses for companies within The Random House Group Limited
can be found at: www.randomhouse.co.uk/offices.htm

THE RANDOM HOUSE GROUP Limited Reg. No. 954009

A CIP catalogue record for this book is available from the British Library.

The Random House Group Limited supports The Forest Stewardship
Council® (FSC®), the leading international forest-certification organisation.
Our books carrying the FSC label are printed on FSC®-certified paper.
FSC is the only forest-certification scheme supported by the leading
environmental organisations, including Greenpeace. Our
paper procurement policy can be found at
www.randomhouse.co.uk/environment

Printed and bound in Great Britain by Clays Ltd, St Ives PLC

For my father, William Bond

Prologue

Holy Saturday, ten years ago

When the screaming got too bad, Veerle ran away.

She had no idea what the row was about, how it had started. It was new and baffling and it gave her a creeping sensation of fearfulness, as though something cold and slimy were slithering over her bare skin.

At first she simply tried not to listen. She pushed back her thick dark hair and put her hands over her ears, and did her best to concentrate on the book in front of her. It was large, hard-backed and entitled *Explorers.* The text was too difficult for a seven-year-old, but Veerle always loved to look at the pictures. The book was open at a double-page illustration of the Arctic, with a fur-clad man confronting a polar bear. Beyond the two figures was a seemingly endless expanse of snow and ice – pure, empty. Silent.

Another scream rose from downstairs and Veerle flinched, her eyes round and shocked. Her hands were still clamped to her ears but it was no good, she could still hear it, and the only thing she could think of was to run away, out of earshot. She jumped up and the book fell unheeded onto the rug.

Veerle ran. She ran out of her room and along the narrow landing, and then down the wooden staircase, her feet clattering on the boards. There was no danger of being heard; her parents were too busy screeching at each other. As she passed the kitchen door, closed in a futile attempt to keep the row from her tender ears, there came another great roar of fury that carried her like a tidal wave down the hallway, running as fast as her legs would carry her, the ends of her red cardigan flying out like wings. She had just enough presence of mind to close the front door carefully without slamming it, and then she was standing on the pavement, with her chest heaving.

She wasn't crying, not yet, but now there were drops of water on her face, running down like tears. Rain was falling, and she had not thought to grab her rain jacket from the peg in the hallway. It was too daunting to think of re-entering the house, the narrow hall that reverberated with anger like the throat of some monstrous beast. Instead she dashed across Kerkstraat, the street of terraced brick houses where she lived, slipped through the gate in the wall, and ran for the door of the Sint-Pauluskerk, the great stone-built church.

It was open; as she slipped into the cool darkness inside, she was greeted by the familiar church smell of stale incense, wood polish and dusty hymn books.

The door did not lead directly into the church interior; instead there was a kind of vestibule, lined with wooden panels. Leaning against the panelling, turning something over in his hands, was a boy, perhaps a year older than she was, skinny and sharp-featured with a shock of untidy dark hair. Veerle recognized him at once, as anyone in the village would have. Kris Verstraeten, of *those* Verstraetens.

The local telephone directory was full of Verstraetens but everyone knew who you meant if you talked about *those* ones – even someone as young as Veerle. She had heard her mother talking about them. Kris was the youngest of five; the oldest was already a jailbird. Veerle actually thought Kris was nice. Unlike his older brothers, he didn't swear at smaller kids or shove them out of the way, and he never laughed at anything she said, even though she was younger than he was. All the same, she hadn't expected to see him here, and for a moment curiosity intruded in spite of her woes. *What is he doing in here?* She opened her mouth to ask but Kris put a finger to his lips, tilting his head to indicate that someone was in the church.

'Look,' he said in a low voice, holding out his hand. Something gleamed in his palm. 'The key to the bell tower.'

Involuntarily, Veerle looked upwards. There was nothing to see, only the shadowy recesses of the wooden capsule that enclosed them, but she knew that the looming height of the tower was directly above their heads, thrusting into the grey sky like a rocket awaiting takeoff.

'It's Silent Saturday, right?' continued Kris. 'The day all the church bells fly off to Rome to get the Easter eggs. Supposedly.'

Veerle nodded, her hazel eyes solemn. She knew the legend, as did all Flemish kids her age.

'Well,' Kris continued, 'I'm going to go up there and see if it's really gone. I bet it hasn't. They just stop it ringing for the day, that's all. I bet it's still hanging up there.'

Veerle heard a tiny metallic *click* as he slid the key into the lock, then a rattle as he turned it. The door swung towards them, light from an upper window revealing a circular stone staircase, the centre of each step worn with the passage of feet over hundreds of years.

Kris looked at her. 'Well? Do you want to come too?'

Veerle thought about it. 'Yes.'

The stone stairs went up and up, spiralling away out of sight. It was like clambering into the whorl of a gigantic seashell. After a dizzying series of turns they reached the top of the stone stairs, and found themselves in the corner of a square room, the floor laid with wooden planks. There was also a worn and cobwebby wooden staircase, barely more than a ladder, running up to an opening in the ceiling.

Kris went up it first, as agile as a monkey. His head reappeared in the hole. 'It's like a ladder. Just hold on with your hands.'

Veerle approached the wooden steps. Kris was right: it was like climbing a ladder, and almost as steep. Halfway up, she began to wonder how she was going to get down again, but by then the floor was a long way below her, and it was easier to go up. When she had almost reached the top, she felt Kris's hands gripping and pulling her up. She flopped onto the wooden floor at the top of the steps and almost immediately sat up again, pulling a face.

'*Bird poo.*'

Kris wasn't looking at her; he was standing up, brushing his hands on his jeans.

'There's another ladder,' he said.

Veerle glanced at it as she got to her feet. It was horribly cold here. The large square windows were not glazed, simply louvred, and in places the wooden slats were broken. The wind came straight through, howling dolefully and plucking at her clothes and hair. The combination of the yawning opening leading to the stairs and the sensation of rushing air was vertiginous; it was like being perched in the crow's nest of a sailing ship, rolling and pitching on the sea. It was daunting to think of climbing up the ladder – and this one really *was* a ladder, there wasn't even a handrail. All the same she didn't want to look like a scaredy cat in front of Kris. She went over and stood by him, ready to do anything he did.

Kris laid his hands on the ladder and pushed. It shifted, and with the movement a cloud of dust and pigeon droppings came down. He slapped his hands together.

'I'm not going up there,' she said.

He shrugged. 'No big deal. Maybe we can see from here.'

He began to circle the foot of the ladder, peering up at the opening in the ceiling above. 'Yes,' he said eventually. Veerle couldn't tell whether he was satisfied or disappointed. He gestured for her to look.

They both peered upwards. At first all you could see was a tangle of cross-hatched beams. Then Veerle leaned forward a little and she saw it. The mouth of the church bell, rimmed with grey-green, with the great round head of the clapper hanging in the centre.

'It's there,' said Veerle. 'It didn't fly to Rome.'

'No,' said Kris disgustedly. He shrugged. 'Let's look out of the window.'

'What for?'

'We might as well. Now we've come all this way up. Maybe

5

we can see as far as Brussels from here. See the Manneken Pis waving at you.'

Veerle began to giggle at that – at the idea of seeing the little statue breaking off from his endless piddling to give her a cheery wave. She followed Kris over to one of the windows.

The wind was very strong here. It made her eyes water. There wasn't much to see, either; even standing on tiptoe she could only just peep over the bottom slat of the louvres. She caught a glimpse of slate roofs, a single chimney, grey sky.

'Boring,' was Kris's verdict. He went over to one of the other windows, the one looking out from the front of the church. Veerle didn't bother to follow him; she knew there would be nothing much to see. There had been a shop, long since closed down, on the corner opposite the church, but it had been knocked down months before and the site had not been redeveloped. Beyond the remains of the foundations there was nothing more interesting than a large expanse of allotments.

'Can we go?' she said.

Kris had his back to her. He was looking out of the window, and when she spoke he didn't turn round. 'Wait,' he said, preoccupied, and then, 'I'm just . . .' His voice tailed off.

Veerle waited for a couple of seconds and then she said, 'Just what?'

There was no reply. Kris's posture was hunched, as though he were concentrating hard on whatever he could see from the window. He seemed to have forgotten Veerle entirely.

'Just *what*?' she repeated insistently, and began to make her way over to him, with an idea of pulling on his arm to make him come away.

'Fuck,' said Kris very clearly.

Veerle's jaw dropped. He turned towards her and she saw that his face had a white, strained look. He put out his hands. 'Stay there. Don't look.'

'Don't look at what?' Veerle tried to get past him. 'What is it?'

'It's – it's Joren Sterckx.'

'Who?' The name didn't mean anything to Veerle. The only thing that interested her right now was whatever it was that Kris didn't want her to see. In spite of the wind and the cold, she couldn't help wanting to look.

She feinted left and then dodged to the right, slipping past Kris with ease. He didn't look as though he had the energy to catch her. He looked as though something essential had drained out of him. He sagged against the rough stone wall and his face was almost greenish.

There was a ledge running along the bottom of this wall. Climbing onto it, Veerle had a good view between the louvres.

Who is Joren Sterckx? What is he doing?

First she saw the foundations of the old shop opposite, fenced off to prevent anyone falling in. She could see a length of red-and-white warning tape twisting in the wind. Beyond the foundations were the allotments. Perhaps half a kilometre behind them was a row of houses, all but lost in the relentless grey rain. Down the centre of the allotments was a dirt track, rutted and muddy, and down this filthy path someone was walking, directly towards the church.

The name Joren Sterckx had meant nothing to Veerle, but she recognized him all the same. She must have seen him dozens of times in the village. He was probably only about nineteen or twenty, but to Veerle he belonged to the ranks of Grown-Ups as clearly as Goliath belonged to the ranks of Giants. Tall, broad-shouldered and hulking, he had heavy, coarse-looking features and small surly eyes that peered out from under an untidy thatch of dirty blond hair. Even under normal circumstances he would have appeared intimidating to a small child, with his great bulk and unsmiling expression. Now he looked absolutely terrifying. His mouth was stretched impossibly wide in a silent howl, and his hair was plastered flat to his head by the pouring rain, and his eyes were screwed into tiny specks. With his blunt wet head and great gaping maw he looked like a man-eating shark.

That was bad enough, but the rest was worse. Joren Sterckx was holding something in his arms, holding it across his body so that each end of the bundle flopped and bounced with every lumbering step he took. He had taken off his jacket and wrapped it around his burden, so now he was in his shirt, and it too was plastered to his skin with wet. You could see the outline of his massive shoulders through the sodden fabric, and the muscles of his meaty arms. The shirt, which had probably been white to begin with, had turned a kind of dirty yellow where it stuck to him – all except the front. The front was red, and it was not a neat, even red with clearly defined edges, as you might get from a panel of crimson fabric; it was a ragged, streaky dark red, staining the shirt from collar to hem and bleeding into the fabric of his jeans.

Veerle knew what the red was but she couldn't take her eyes off Joren Sterckx – his red shirt and his thick arms and the thing he was carrying. She could see that what bobbed and flopped at one end of the bundle were *shoes.* She tried not to look at what was at the other end but she couldn't help her-self. The round, dark object, that was a head, although the way it lolled so limply on the neck meant that the owner of the head was not merely asleep. The red too – that meant something bad for the person whom Joren Sterckx was carry-ing across the allotments, back to the village.

Still she couldn't take her eyes off him. He was coming closer; if he kept going in the same direction, he would come right up to the church. Supposing he came inside? Supposing he knew they were up in the bell tower, spying on him? Anything seemed possible. Joren looked huge to Veerle; he looked unstoppable. Supposing he came up those spiral stairs, with his bloody burden in his arms?

Veerle dropped down below the window onto the filthy floor, heedless of the cobwebs and the bird droppings, heed-less of Kris standing, sick and trembling, beside her. Then she began to scream.

1

The present day

Veerle De Keyser hung upside down, her face in a grimace, every muscle in her body taut, her dark plaits swinging. She tried bracing her toes against a small outcrop, hoping to take some of the weight off her upper body, but her arms were actually hurting, from the shoulders right down to her fingers. *It's only pain*, she told herself, but she wasn't convincing anyone. She could feel tremors running through the muscles. If she didn't make a move soon she would fall off the wall like an overripe fruit dropping from a branch.

'Be careful,' said someone in English close by, and that was enough; her concentration was broken. She managed to hold on for long enough to let her legs swing down under her, and then she crashed onto the mat.

'Don't fall off,' said the voice.

Veerle looked round, a retort rising to her lips, and realized that the remark wasn't addressed to her at all. The speaker was a woman of about forty, slightly plump, pink-faced, with thick blonde hair held back from her face by an unsuitably girlish band. She looked like an overripe child, pudgy, flushed

11

and pouting, compared to Veerle, who was serious, and pale in spite of her dark hair, and slender to the point of wiriness.

English, Veerle surmised. The hairband was part of the uniform: sunglasses pushed to the top of the head in summer, hairband in winter. She wasn't one of the climbing wall's regular customers – Veerle knew most of those by sight, but even if she hadn't, you could tell just by looking at her that the woman wasn't a climber. Those fingernails for a start . . .

The woman was speaking to a bristle-haired, pudgy boy of about eight, who was clinging onto the wall close to the overhang Veerle had been attempting. An escapee from the birthday party taking place raucously on the kids' wall, Veerle judged. Whatever his mother might think, he wasn't in any danger; his chubby feet were only fifty centimetres off the floor with its padded mats.

The child swung round, hanging by one arm, his small eyes scanning the room belligerently. He saw Veerle sitting on the mat flexing her chalky fingers and looking at him, and he stuck his tongue out.

Veerle didn't really care about his rudeness but the woman's words had touched a raw nerve. *Be careful.* How often had she heard *that*? It was a constant litany at home, had been ever since she could remember. *Stay away from the edge of the road, don't talk to strangers, don't go near the lake in the park, don't climb trees. Be careful, be careful, be careful.* Sometimes those two words made Veerle want to scream.

She stood up, rubbing her chalky hands together. On impulse she turned and spoke to the woman in English. 'He can't hurt himself. The mats are really thick.'

She got an appraising look in reply, but that was all. No *Thanks*, no *Mind your own business*. Just a look.

She went over to the boy and said, 'If you want to climb that, you have to use your legs, not your arms.' She hopped up onto the wall beside him. 'If you pull yourself up with your arms, you'll get tired. And you have to stick to one colour. Look, the red ones are quite easy.' She nodded at the holds.

The boy looked at her and then glanced at his mother, calculating whom he could annoy the most. 'I can go higher than you,' he announced.

'Go on then,' Veerle invited him.

'Excuse me,' said the boy's mother. 'Would you please not encourage him?'

Veerle jumped lightly down onto the mat. 'If he swings on his arms, he'll tire himself out. He'll be more likely to fall off,' she said. 'If he learns to climb properly—'

'He's only here for a party,' said the woman stiffly.

'Still . . .'

'Come down from there,' said the woman to the child. 'You'll fall.' She watched the boy make another move upwards. '*Now* look,' she said to Veerle.

Veerle relented. 'Hey, kid,' she said.

'My name's George.'

'George, you want to learn how to traverse?'

'What's that?'

'You go along, not up.'

'That's rubbish.'

'You think? Bet you can't go right round the room without touching the floor.' She gave him a challenging look. 'I can.'

To prove it, she stepped back onto the wall and moved a

13

couple of metres to the right. By the time she stepped back down onto the mat, the boy was already following.

'I can do that too,' he told her.

'That's good,' said Veerle, grinning.

'George—' began the woman.

'Be careful,' finished Veerle with a sigh.

She ignored the venomous look this earned her and padded off to the other side of the room, but her concentration was broken. She started to climb the underside of the arch she had fallen from, but she didn't even get as far as she had the first time. The voice of the woman telling her son to *get down from there, George* and *be careful, George* was impossible to ignore. It echoed around her skull like the throbbing of a headache. Telling herself that it had nothing to do with her, that she had to ignore it and focus, didn't help. She still wanted to go over and shake the woman by the shoulders, ask her why she didn't just keep the kid in a cage at home where nothing was ever going to happen to him. Eventually she dropped onto the mat and went to change back into her street clothes.

It had been snowing earlier that day, and it took her a while to bundle herself up in her winter jacket, jeans and boots. She stuffed her leggings and rock shoes into a rucksack and headed for the exit.

The scruffy reception area was full of children, most of them boys, jumping up and down thunderously on the worn floorboards, their voices full of bluster and bravado. The little boy called George was amongst them, leaping around as boisterously as the rest. His mother stood nearby, chatting unsmilingly with another woman. Her gaze fell on Veerle as she pushed her way through the milling children and she said something to the other mother. Veerle heard the words: '. . . thanks to her'.

'You're welcome,' she said, and that was all it took to tip her day from frustrating to bad.

The woman looked at her with naked irritation in her pale eyes. 'I said *no thanks to you*,' she snapped. 'Don't you speak English?'

Veerle stopped in her tracks and looked at her. 'Yes, I speak English,' she said.

The expression of contempt she got in return was unmistakable. 'I don't think so,' said the woman. She was already turning away, towards the other mother. That might have been the end of it, only then she said something to the other woman, something deliberately half audible. Veerle heard the single word 'stupid' and saw the glance that flickered back at her.

She thought afterwards that if it had not been for that glance, she might have walked away. Instead she stood her ground.

'You,' she said. 'Do you speak Flemish?'

'I don't need this,' said the woman dismissively.

'So, do you?' persisted Veerle. Her heart was pounding now, pounding so hard that she felt dizzy and short of breath.

'I don't see what that has to do with you.'

'You asked me if I speak English.'

'I'm really not interested,' snapped the woman.

'We're in Flanders. Do you speak Flemish?'

Veerle knew she shouldn't be losing her temper, but the way the woman kept trying to brush her off was the last straw. She could feel herself losing her grip on calm as surely as if her fingertips had been peeling off a polished hold on the wall.

'How long have you lived here?' she said.

'I don't have to tell you that.'

'How long?'

'Just go away, will you?'

'How *long*?'

Now the pair of them were almost shouting at each other, and the children were starting to look round, their eyes wide and avid.

Someone came striding towards them, pushing their way through the milling children. With a sinking heart Veerle recognized Bart, the manager. Bart looked like the most laid-back old hippy in the world with his tie-dyed green T-shirt and faded pink climbing trousers and three-day-old stubble, but Veerle wasn't fooled; that shaggy greying head contained a business brain as sharp as that of any suited city business-man. She was outnumbered, she realized; Bart would never side with one seventeen-year-old against a group of over twenty paying customers, whatever the rights and wrongs of the situation.

Two minutes later she was out on the street in the evening dark and cold. The door was swinging back and forth in its frame from the violence of her exit, and back inside the brightly lit exterior Bart was already shepherding the crowd of kids towards the bar area for another round of cola.

'Shit.' She swung her rucksack at the wall. 'Stupid, stupid, stupid.'

She wasn't even sure whom she was aiming that at – the

woman for her infuriating rudeness or herself for rising to the bait. There was no point in raging at Bart; he had a business to run. She thought that he might tolerate her returning to the climbing wall at some future point, as long as there weren't any more rows, but it wouldn't be for a while. Weeks, months . . . next year, maybe. By then perhaps her cheeks would have stopped flaming and she could contemplate going back herself.

For the time being, it was another escape route closed down, another corridor sealed off in the maze that was her life. She stared back at the bright square of light in the door and reflected bitterly that there was nothing for it but to go home.

2

The bus stop was a five-minute walk away, on the other side of the retail park, along pavements that were slick and shiny with the melted remains of recent snow. Christmas lights were strung up across the road, but they didn't strike Veerle as festive any more. There was something faintly depressing about Christmas lights once the festivities were over, the gifts had all been opened, the tree had dropped all its needles. She kicked away brown slush with the toe of her boot. *Happy New Year.*

Inside the pockets of her winter jacket, her hands were clenched into fists. She was in the grip of a feeling so bitter that it was like being caught in the coils of a python; her rib cage was tight with it, her breath came in painful gasps. *Everything's wrong*, she thought desperately. The rudeness of the boy's mother, her own overreaction, and the unstated ban from the wall, one of her only refuges. The situation at home. That was at the core of it; that was the thing that flowed underneath everything else like dark brackish water. Home. Claudine. Hearing *Be careful* half a dozen times every day of her life, and knowing that it was getting worse: her mother's fretting, the restrictions, the perceived threats everywhere.

Sometimes, just existing in that claustrophobic atmosphere felt like struggling inside a clinging net. *How did it get this bad?* she asked herself.

When Veerle finally reached the bus stop she couldn't stand still; she paced up and down under the yellow-and-white De Lijn sign as though testing the limits of an invisible enclosure.

The bus she took back to her own village was not the only one that went from this stop. You could take a bus to Leuven from here, or if you crossed the road you could take one to the nearby airport or to Brussels-North. *Supposing I did that?* Veerle said to herself, pacing. *Supposing I got on a different bus and went somewhere else entirely?* She could see herself doing it, being borne away into the night. Escaping. *I'll take the first bus that comes,* she told herself. *If it's the one home, I'll take that, and if it's to somewhere else, I'll take that instead.*

She glanced at her watch, and when she looked up there was a bus only fifty metres away. It was her normal one, the one that ran to her village, stopping within sight of the house on Kerkstraat. She grimaced, and then stuck out her arm.

On board were five other people, and in the artificial light all their faces looked grey and pouchy. *Bus of zombies,* thought Veerle, but the thought didn't raise a smile. It was too near the truth. Dead inside, dead with boredom, but still walking. She slid into a seat. It was too depressing looking at those faded and dreary faces, so she looked out of the window instead, into the dark.

The bus pulled away from the kerb. It would take about thirty-five minutes to get to her village, since the route took a dogleg through half a dozen other villages first. Shiny wet streets slid past, then a parade of shops, and then the bus was leaving the town again and it was dark on Veerle's side. There was very little to see for about half a kilometre apart from a long stretch of crumbling red-brick wall overhung with bare winter trees, closely clustered together.

Veerle had passed this way every week for years, so she knew what was on the other side of the wall, even though she couldn't see it. Behind the trees was a large area of open parkland, overgrown and unkempt, and in the middle of it was a castle.

The castle had probably been stunning once. The oldest part was built of uncompromising grey stone, but the newer and larger part was of bi-coloured brick, red and white, so gaudy that it might have belonged to the witch in the ginger-bread house. There were towers and a spire and a small arcade, and a big stone canopy supported by columns over the main door. It had been designed to impress, from the gilded weathervane on the tip of the spire to the sweeping curve of the drive, introducing the building like a bow and a flourish.

Look a little more closely, however, and you could see that the castle's glory days were long past. The walls were crumbling, there were slates missing from the roof, and some of the windowpanes had been smashed, leaving dark holes where there should have been gleaming reflections of the grounds. The gravel drive was choked with the dead brown weeds of the previous summer. The castle looked desolate and unloved. Even without the wire fencing over the main gate and the KEEP OUT notices there was nothing to invite anyone inside. It was old, creepy and probably dangerous.

Local people said it was haunted too. Lights had been seen in the castle on dark nights, moving to and fro along the upper galleries. There were tales of a grey cavalier, a pale lady. Restless ghosts. Nobody did anything to refute the idea. It was a convenient way of discouraging children from trying to get into the castle grounds. Go in there and something will *get you.*

Veerle was not afraid of ghosts, but she thought the old building was intriguing. She always looked out for it on the way to the climbing wall, simply because it was something a little different from the uninteresting vista of neat little houses, shops and petrol stations that dotted the route. At this time of year there was nothing to see on the way home. The castle was set so far back from the road that it had vanished in the dark as completely as if it were a stone dropped into inky black water. She still looked, because there was nothing else to do, but she didn't expect to see anything.

The bus was slowing down for the stop closest to the castle – right outside the gate, in fact; so close that the bus stop had KASTEEL printed on it.

Veerle was still gazing into the dark, and suddenly her eyes widened.

I can see something. There's something in *there.*

She leaned closer to the glass, and instantly it fogged over with the warmth of her breath. She pulled the sleeve of her jacket up over the heel of her hand and rubbed at the glass. Now it was clear again and she could still see whatever it was; she wasn't dreaming, there was a *light* in the castle.

It was so tiny, so faint, that she could barely see it; it seemed to flicker too, sometimes vanishing altogether. But her eyes were not deceiving her. There was definitely a light.

A series of possibilities flitted across her mind in a matter of seconds. *Local historian visiting, surveyor checking the property out?* No; they would be carrying halogen torches you could see from a kilometre away, or more probably they would come in daylight. *Kids?* Maybe, though she'd never heard of break-ins at the castle before, perhaps because of its sinister reputation. *A fire starting?* That didn't seem likely, either; the castle was probably too old, too long-deserted to be electrically wired, and there wouldn't be any power even if it were. *So that leaves . . . ghosts?*

Don't be ridiculous, Veerle told herself, but she felt the stirring of excitement. She peered out of the window, and then she glanced at the bus driver. An elderly man had just got onto the bus and was making a drama of looking for his bus pass, which was seemingly nowhere to be found. Veerle saw the driver lean over, saying something. *Don't drive off yet,* she prayed silently.

Suddenly her heart was beating wildly. *I could get off here,* she thought, glancing back out of the window into the dark. *I could get off the bus and go and see what that light is for myself.*

She looked at the driver again. The elderly man had found and presented his pass, and was fussily wedging himself into a seat. Now there was a tall youth in a leather jacket getting on, his face sullen, his jaws working a piece of gum. The driver said something, and the boy began to dig around in his jeans pockets. The driver revved the engine, trying to speed up the transaction. There were perhaps ten seconds left before the bus pulled away.

Ten seconds to decide between adventure or a bus ride to boredom.

Last chance, thought Veerle, and before she had time to think about what she was doing, she was on her feet, heading for the door.

Too late. The rear doors were closing with a sound like an indignant sigh. The bus lurched forward a metre, and then Veerle was pressing on the STOP button, pressing it again and again even though there was no point, and glaring at the driver in the rear-view mirror, willing him to stop and let her off.

He shrugged at her, and for a moment she thought he wasn't going to stop. He let the bus drift on another couple of metres, and then, grudgingly, he braked. The doors opened.

'*Dank u*,' said Veerle, and then she was out of the bus, standing on the pavement, breathing rapidly as though she had been running. The doors closed behind her and the bus moved off, a lighted capsule tunnelling away through the dark.

Veerle watched it go. The wind plucked at her clothing with icy fingers. There was nothing on this side of the road – nothing except the wall with the desiccated skeletons of bushes huddled up to it, and the bus stop. On the other side there were houses but the ones directly opposite were all dark. She felt the night close in. She was alone.

3

You know this is madness, Veerle said to herself as she picked her way along the wall. The strip of pavement by the bus stop had run out and now she was walking on snowy mud and grass. The ground was pitted and studded with stones, and the dried-up remains of brambles looping across the grass threatened to trip her up. *If it's bad out here, it's going to be worse in there.* She could feel her boots crunching through the thin ice that crusted the ruts in the mud. *You should . . . what, go home?*

She was shocked by what an unappealing option that was. To get off the bus in the usual place, to turn the corner and walk up Kerkstraat alongside the churchyard wall, to the brick house with the roller shutters prematurely lowered for the night, like eyelids closed in speechless disapproval. There wouldn't be any lights visible, no golden glow to pilot her home, because her mother, Claudine, shut out the rest of the world as soon as she got home from work, and sealed the front of the house so tightly that no chink of light escaped. So Veerle would walk up the wet pavement to the front door, and then she would ring the bell before she inserted her key into the lock, because her mother liked to

24

know the instant she was home, even if she herself were in the furthest reaches of the house. Then she would go inside and Claudine would come out of the kitchen or the sitting room, her cardigan pulled tight around her skinny body as though she were trying to keep out the cold, her unmade-up face shining in the yellowish light of the hallway, her eyes pale and pink-rimmed yet somehow avid.

Even before Veerle had hung up her coat it would start. Why had she been so long? Had the bus been late? Why hadn't she taken the earliest one? Didn't she realize how dangerous it was travelling around after dark on your own?

There was going to be a scene if Claudine found out about this, and she was almost certainly going to, because Veerle was going to be *very* late home.

The prospect of this, and the equally evil prospect of hurrying home every day like a little kid, and the incident with the woman at the climbing wall, were all thundering around her head like great pieces of flotsam carried on flood water, crashing into each other, splintering, whirling off again into the foaming dark. *No*, she thought. *No, no. I don't want that to be my life.*

She felt an overwhelming urge to break out, to do something reckless. She felt the bite of the chill January air, felt the night all around her like the beating of dark wings. She wanted to run until she was exhausted, she wanted to scream with defiance. It was cold and dark and possibly dangerous, but she was going to go to the castle, break in if necessary, and see what that light was.

A car was coming. Veerle put her head down and did her best to walk along the verge without stumbling. *Look as though you're just out for a stroll,* she told herself. The head-lights swept past, and as the car dwindled in the distance she reached the castle gate.

There were panels of metal fencing across the gateway. They had been fastened together with a length of chain, but the chain was now lying on the ground. The two panels were still overlapping, and a casual glance from a passing driver would not have revealed anything amiss. There were more headlights visible in the distance, perhaps three hundred metres away. If Veerle continued to stand where she was, the headlights would wash over her; someone would notice her standing there. *Now or never.*

She pulled the two fence panels apart and slipped inside. She looked at the panels from the other side, glanced out at the road. *I'm on the other side of the cage now*, she told herself. *I'm not inside, I'm outside. I'm free.*

Silently she turned and began to pick her way up the drive to the castle. There were no lights on this side of the road and it was too dark to see where she was putting her feet, but she could feel grit under her boots; grit and rough spongy patches that were the dead remains of weeds. She moved slowly, allow-ing her eyes time to adapt to the dark. It was easier to see the terrain now that she was no longer under the strong artificial lights of the bus, but still she had to go cautiously. Once she strayed off the gravel and felt pitted mud again under her feet. She stepped back onto the firmer surface of the drive and stood for a moment, getting her bearings.

Up ahead, the castle was a grim hulk, a blacker silhouette against a black sky. It looked entirely shrouded in darkness. Had she been mistaken about the light?

Did I imagine it? she wondered. *Maybe I saw a reflection of the streetlamps behind me or something.* No. There it was again – a yellow light, insubstantial as marsh fire, in one of the upper windows. It flickered and then it was gone.

Veerle felt the pulse throbbing in her throat, a wild beat singing its own song of *Turn round, go home, this is a seriously bad idea.*

She bit her lip. 'This is stupid,' she said aloud, as though the sound of her own voice would reassure her. *There are no such things as ghosts.*

Still she stood there, not venturing any further, tugging her jacket around herself.

It's freezing, it's too dark to see anything properly, and whatever or whoever is in there might be dangerous.

So run on home then. That's what she *would want you to do. Do the safe thing. Run home like a good little mummy's girl.*

That did it. She began walking again, picking her way carefully up the drive.

You wanted adventure. Here it is.

There was the light again, wispy and indistinct, dancing across one of the upstairs windows. *What* is *it?*

When she was so close to the front wall of the castle that she could have put out a hand and touched the bricks, Veerle stopped again, and listened. She could hear the sighing of the wind and the occasional roar of a passing car, but she could not pick out any sound from inside. She began to move stealthily along the wall towards the front door. The door itself was lost in darkness, but the great canopy that overhung it was made of a pale stone that showed up as a lighter patch against the brickwork. She made for that, like a child daring itself to run up and slap the door of a deserted house. She thought she would check the door: assuming it was closed, she had some vague idea that she might be able to climb the stone canopy to peer in at one of the upper windows.

The space under the stone canopy was inky. Veerle felt in her pocket for her mobile phone. She pressed the button, and by the light of the little screen she was able to pick out the weathered wooden panels of the door, some scuffed and faded tiles at her feet, and a drift of dry brown leaves driven in by the wind. The light faded before she was able to take a close look at the door. She pressed the button again, holding the phone close to the wood.

My God. It's open.

She froze, her arm outstretched, holding the lit phone towards the door. It was only open a couple of centimetres. Still, there was something horribly suggestive about that narrow strip of black.

The light faded and the open door was once more drowned in the darkness. Still Veerle kept her face turned towards it; even though it was invisible, the thought of turning her back on it was somehow unpleasant. There was nothing welcoming about the interior of the castle. The front door was open but there was no light or heat bleeding out of it, any more than the warm breath of life comes from a dead mouth. All the old castle exhaled was cold and the smell of dust and decay.

Veerle stood there silently, listening, waiting for the sound that would tell her that a live person was moving around in there. If there were nothing, if the castle, or at least this part of it, were empty of living people, she would step inside for a moment and use the light from the phone to look around.

She leaned close to the door. *Nothing.* Not so much as the light scurry of a mouse crossing the neglected floor. She clasped her mobile phone tightly in one hand and felt for the edge of the door with the other. She pushed; it swung open more easily than she expected, though the long groan from the hinges sounded terrifyingly loud in the dark.

Again she waited, listening for the sound of someone moving away, rapid footsteps in the upper reaches of the castle, or even a rat scuttling away from the unexpected noise. Still nothing. *I dare you to step inside.*

The thought made her heart beat faster and her throat constrict, but still she knew she was going to do it. She would step in, and when she was right inside the castle, her back to the door, she would turn the phone on again and see whatever there was to be seen by its short-lived light. A glimpse would be enough, a secret to be carried away into the tedium of daily life like contraband. *I'll have* done *something for once, something that most people would never dream of doing.*

She stepped through the doorway. It was no warmer in the castle than it had been outside; if anything Veerle thought it was a degree or two colder. There was a hard floor under her feet – tiles, she suspected. She was breathing heavily, unnerved by the sense of unseen but empty space around her. She switched on her phone.

The little illuminated square of screen hung in the blackness. Its light was insufficient to show her the full dimensions of the room in which she stood. She kept pressing the on button with her thumb every time the light went out, and sweeping the phone from right to left, up and down, trying to make sense of the little glimpses of the interior that it gave her. Dusty tiles, sections of wooden panelling, a fragment of patterned wall covering. She was holding the phone up high, at head height, to examine the pattern, when she heard it. The unmistakable sound of something dropping with a brittle *clink!* onto a hard surface.

Veerle didn't have time to think. Her body reacted for her, jumping as though she had come into contact with something scalding. The phone slipped from her fingers and hit the tiled floor, clattering away into the dark. The screen light went out.

Ohshitohshitohshit. Now she was fumbling for the door, her chest heaving with panic, and she knew that she ought to try to keep the noise down, she was panting like a racehorse, but she couldn't help it because there was somebody *in here* with her, in the dark.

Then she heard a rasping sound, and there was light – not a great light, but the light she had seen from outside, small, yellow, dancing and flickering. And in the light she saw it. High up, impossibly high up in the inky blackness, its hollows and lines graven deep by the wavering light. A face.

4

'Stay there,' said the face. 'I'm coming to you.'

No. Oh God, no. Veerle turned and groped wildly for the door. For one moment she considered trying to find her phone, but the urge to flee was too strong. She ran at the door and her shoulder connected painfully with the frame. She let out a stifled yelp.

Behind her, the light was snuffed out as suddenly as it had appeared. Veerle heard the thunder of footsteps. *Stairs.* Whoever it was was running down *stairs.* He moved with the confidence of someone who knows the environment intimately, who does not need to *see* to know where he is going.

Run. Veerle was within arm's length of the door, she *knew* that, but she couldn't orient herself. She saw the distant yellow glow of a streetlamp and ran towards it, but found her hands beating uselessly against glass; she had come up against one of the windows instead of the door. The footsteps were approaching fast across the dusty floor. The next moment she was struggling in the grip of invisible hands.

'Vlinder,' someone was saying. 'Vlinder – are you Vlinder?'

Veerle's nails scraped across leather. She tried to twist, to kick out, but whoever it was evaded the kick easily.

'Calm down,' said the voice. Veerle felt its owner let her go. She heard a rustle and a *click*, and then there was suddenly light – light so bright that it was momentarily blinding. Instinctively she put her hands to her face.

'Are you Vlinder?'

She shook her head.

'Well, who the hell are you then?'

Veerle's eyes were adjusting to the light. She could see the door now, standing open not six paces from where she stood. She would have lunged for it, but the stranger anticipated her movement and grabbed her by the arm.

The halogen torch was shining in her face. It was impossible to see anything behind it.

'Veerle,' she blurted out. 'Veerle De Keyser.'

'*Veerle De Keyser*,' he said, and the surprise in his voice was unmistakable.

He knows me?

'Are *you* Vlinder?' he repeated.

'No, I'm not bloody Vlinder,' croaked Veerle.

Vlinder? Butterfly? What kind of name is that?

'It's me, Kris.'

'I don't know any Kris.'

Veerle dragged her arm out of his grasp. This time he didn't try to grab her again. She didn't try to run, either; it was useless when he had a light and she didn't, and he knew the ground well enough to allow him to sprint downstairs in the dark.

'You're Veerle De Keyser, from the house in Kerkstraat?'

She didn't reply. *How do you know that?* Goosebumps were rising on her arms.

'Don't you remember me?'

'I can't see you.'

He flipped the torch over and handed it to her, handle first. 'We should get away from the window.'

Kris? Veerle was thinking. *I don't know any Kris.*

She could pick up nothing from his voice. It was totally unfamiliar. As soon as he stopped moving she shone the torch at him.

He was tall, lean, dressed casually: leather jacket, dark shirt, jeans. Camouflage for creeping around unlit castles at night. The torch beam moved up from the jacket to his face and she studied his features doubtfully. Unkempt dark hair. Large dark eyes, aquiline nose, a wide mouth with a sardonic pucker at the corner of it. She couldn't place his age accurately. Shadows engraved the lines of his face very deeply; he could have been her own age or fifteen years older.

I've no idea who he is.

'Kris Verstraeten,' he said reprovingly.

Veerle stared at him, and then suddenly she saw it, saw the resemblance.

My God, she thought. *It's him. How long has it been? Ten years? Eleven years?*

She remembered Kris as a thin, sharp-faced boy – that was her idea of him, not this fully grown young man. At seven or eight years of age she hadn't considered whether he was good-looking or not; he was just Kris, just a boy from her village, and she had liked him because he was nice to her in spite of being a year or two older. All the same, she had an idea of what he looked like, and now it was as though the years had taken that idea and stretched and pulled and distorted it. His nose was too big, his mouth was too wide, his brows were too dark. Only his eyes were the same as ever, large and dark and expressive, as though the original Kris, the younger Kris, were looking out of the grown-up face as from behind a mask.

That was her first impression; the second one was that Kris was rather good-looking, when you got used to the changes.

'Turn the light off,' said Kris.

Veerle was still staring at him, but when he moved to take the torch from her she hastily switched it off.

Kris Verstraeten, she was thinking, still half wondering whether she should make a bolt for it, now that she had the light.

'Too bright,' said Kris. 'It would be visible from the road.' He must have sensed her moving nervously in the darkness, because he added, 'I have candles upstairs.'

'Why? What are you doing here?'

'I could ask you that.'

Veerle heard the scraping sound of a match being lit, and then he was holding it up, examining her in the light of the tiny flame.

'Why *are* you here?' he said.

'I was on the bus and I saw a light so . . .' Veerle's voice trailed off. She couldn't think of a way of finishing the sentence that didn't sound either insane or pathetic. *My life is so boring that I thought I'd have an adventure.*

'. . . you came to investigate?' The match was burning down; he shook it out. 'Are you always so public-spirited?'

Veerle felt her cheeks burning. She was grateful for the darkness. 'No,' she said shortly.

'So . . . ?'

Veerle was silent for a moment. Then she said, 'It was just a stupid idea. Next time I'll stay on the bus. I'll forget about this, OK?'

Forget about seeing you, she wanted to say, but that felt as though it was straying into dangerous territory. She was unable to think of a single good reason why Kris Verstraeten should be lurking in a darkened and dilapidated castle; if he had a *bad* reason for being there, then her position was precarious, and if she could get away before this fact occurred to him, so much the better.

'No,' he said. 'Look . . .' He reached out in the darkness and grasped her arm again. 'Maybe you *were* just passing and you just decided on impulse to come in here, but I don't think so. I think you're here for the same reason I am.'

Veerle tried to extract her arm, but this time he simply tightened his grip, pulling her a little closer.

'If you're Vlinder, I need to know.'

Veerle's heart was pounding. For one wild moment she considered saying, *Yes, I am Vlinder*. The impulse was so strong that it was like a taste in her mouth, acrid and nauseating. He *wanted* her to be Vlinder, whoever Vlinder was, she could tell that, and she was not sure which would be more dangerous, to be *Vlinder* or to be *not Vlinder*.

'I'm not,' she said at last. 'I've never heard of anyone called Vlinder. I don't know what you're talking about.'

5

If Kris was unsatisfied with her answer, he didn't say. At any rate he let go of her arm, apparently no longer concerned that she would bolt without replying. Then he went upstairs to find the candles. He refused to switch the torch back on. He took it from Veerle's fingers and it disappeared inside his jacket, out of temptation's way. Then he was gone. She heard his footsteps moving across the floor, and then the creak of the stairs.

Alone in the hallway, Veerle found the darkness chilling – the sense of it pressing in on her, urgent yet insubstantial. If she looked towards the window she could dimly make out the streetlamps lining the distant road, but behind her there was darkness so complete that it could have been the void of deep space.

There could be anything, anyone, waiting there in the dark. She imagined putting out her hand and touching something. A cold still face, the features waxen under her fingers. Or worse, rough hair or scales. *Teeth.*

She put out a hand, trying to reassure herself, groping blindly at the air. *Nothing. Of course.* But just because she reached out and touched nothing at all didn't mean there wasn't anything there. *There might be a bare millimetre between my fingertips and whatever's lurking in the dark.* She drew back her hand with a shiver.

There's nothing to stop me slipping out of the castle, making for the gateway and the road.

She didn't, though. Partly it was the fact that Kris had gone upstairs on his own. *Leave if you want to,* he was saying. *Stay if you want to.*

Partly it was the fact that he wasn't just *anybody,* he was Kris Verstraeten from her village. She felt that she *knew* him somehow, even if the sharp-featured nearly-nine-year-old he had once been had been stretched like taffy into a craggy-looking young man.

Candlelight bloomed at the top of the stairs and Veerle saw what she had seen before: Kris's face, underlit by the flickering flame. Waiting.

When he didn't come down, Veerle went up. She went cautiously, testing the stairs before putting her full weight on them in case they had rotted through. Also, she was in no hurry to reach the top step where Kris was sitting. She wanted to show that she was still being careful, still making up her mind about him.

The stairs were sound enough, although they creaked under her feet. Halfway up, she trod on something that rolled under her shoe. She stopped and felt about with her fingers, trying to locate it, thinking that if she stepped on it on the way down she might fall down the whole flight. Her fingers brushed through dust and then closed over a thin metal cylinder. She ran a finger along it and found the wooden bulb at the end. *A screwdriver. What's a screwdriver doing in here?* She pocketed it anyway and went on climbing.

She stopped within three steps of Kris, but he was already getting to his feet, the candle in his hand. He shielded the flame with his other hand, in a gesture so natural that Veerle guessed he was used to carrying a candle around. *Is he squatting in here?* she wondered. What she could see of the upstairs décor was not inviting. The castle interior must have been magnificent once – she could see that from the carved cornices and the faded remains of the wall coverings. All the same, it was as cold and comfortless as a mausoleum. There would be no heat, no light, no running water. Veerle could not imagine laying her head on the bare boards, listening to the creaks and groans of the ancient building, perhaps feeling tiny creatures crawling over her in the dark.

'Here,' said Kris, indicating that she should follow. There was no choice, anyway; he had the only light. They passed through a wide doorway with a carved wooden frame. Veerle guessed the room was at the back of the castle since Kris went in boldly, right up to the window, with the candle held in his left hand. Outside there would be nothing but trees, although even those were invisible in the dark. Veerle imagined how it would look from outside: the flickering light at the upstairs window, the two faces peering out into the darkness, their features given a yellow cast by the candle flame. Was that how the castle had gained its reputation for being haunted?

'Give me the screwdriver,' said Kris. He did not say that he had seen Veerle pocket it, nor did he express surprise that she had it in her possession. He simply held out his hand, while still apparently examining the window.

Veerle thought about it for a moment, and then she handed him the screwdriver.

She watched him put the candle down on the windowsill and begin to work on the window catch. She watched, and the longer she did so, the more puzzled she became.

'What are you doing?' she asked eventually.

'Mending the catch,' came the laconic reply.

'Why?'

Kris continued working on the catch for a few moments without replying. He opened the window a little way, closed it again, and checked that the catch was working. Then he turned back to Veerle.

'It's part of the deal. Like paying for being here.'

'Paying who?'

He shrugged. 'Nobody. The castle, I guess.' He pocketed the screwdriver. Now he came closer to Veerle, until they were only an arm's length away from each other. Half of his face was illuminated by the candle's soft light, the other was in darkness.

'It's a game,' he said.

'A game?'

'Empty buildings. You spend time there, and you do something in exchange. Mend something. Clean something up. Whatever. It's like . . .' He thought about it. 'Guerrilla gardening, only inside. Guerrilla DIY, maybe.'

Veerle stared at him. 'You break into places and do *maintenance*?'

Something doesn't add up. She looked at Kris's face, at the sardonic twist of his lips, the unkempt hair falling over his forehead, the dark eyes with their watchful expression. She looked at the leather jacket, the jeans and boots. Kris didn't look like an eco-warrior or a rogue furniture restorer. He looked . . .

Dangerous. That was what her mother had called him. Fragments of memory were coming back to her now. Her mother had told her not to play with Kris Verstraeten any more, not even to speak to him, because he was a *bad influence.* That didn't mean much; Claudine thought half the world was dangerous, though she hadn't always been as bad as she was now.

But what was he supposed to have done? She had a vague remembrance of exploring with him; he had known every interesting corner in the village. They had climbed the bell tower of the church once too; she remembered following the curve of the stone staircase, how it had reminded her of climbing into a gigantic seashell. And then they had got to the top, and something had frightened her, frightened her terribly. Had Kris done something to upset her? Was that why her mother had warned her off? Veerle couldn't think what it might have been. He had surely been no more than eight or nine himself at the time. He couldn't have done anything *that* bad.

All the same, looking at him now she couldn't imagine that he would be content with creeping into ruined buildings to repair broken window catches. *There has to be more to it than that.*

'So what about you – do you make a habit of breaking into places?' asked Kris, interrupting the silence.

'I didn't,' Veerle pointed out. 'You'd already done that. The door was open – so was the gate.'

'It's still trespassing.'

Veerle folded her arms and looked at him. She didn't bother to point out the obvious, which was that he had been trespassing too.

Kris leaned towards her. 'Do you want to do it again?' He grinned at her startled expression. 'Joke,' he added.

He's playing with you, thought Veerle, aware that if he had waited another moment before telling her he was joking she would have said yes.

'Look, I should go,' she said, a little stiffly.

'Meeting someone?'

'No.' She wondered if he was asking her whether she was seeing anyone. 'Just home.'

'You want me to walk you to the gate?'

She shook her head. 'To the door would be good.'

Kris picked up the candle again and she followed him downstairs in silence. She still had the uncomfortable feeling that she was missing something. But what could she ask?

She found her phone lying on the tiled floor and pocketed it. When they got to the door, Kris offered her the torch. 'It's risky, but if someone sees you, you could always say you were trying to take a short cut.'

'It's OK, I can manage.'

Veerle put her head down and began to pick her way towards the road. Before she had gone a dozen steps she regretted not saying goodbye, not parting in some more meaningful way. *We used to know each other, after all.* She turned to look back, but Kris had gone. He must have blown out the candle, since the castle was entirely shrouded in darkness.

On the way back to the road she put her foot right through the thin crust of ice on a puddle. Dirty water splashed up and ran down inside her boot.

6

Darkness covers a multitude of sins, some great and some small.

In daylight hours, a crow perched upon the gilded weathervane of the castle, had it taken it into its mind to do so, could have flown south-east for about eleven minutes, over fields and rooftops and woodland, and landed on the shabby roof of a certain nondescript house on a quiet village street. Now it was late at night, and the crows were roosting in the trees; the darkness was for hunters, the medium in which they swam as easily as sharks gliding through the ocean. Owls claimed the chill air, and foxes the tangled undergrowth, and in the house in the village someone else was stirring.

De Jager thought it was time. The moon had dwindled to a sliver, a cheese rind; where there were no streetlights the darkness was impenetrable, the blackness of an ocean floor, five kilometres down.

There was nobody to ask him where he was going when he let himself out of the house. It was an ugly building, blank side turned to the road, but it was convenient; impossible to peer into unless you were brazen enough to trespass in the garden, and large enough to keep things in – things with which other people would have hesitated to share their living space. In appearance it was reminiscent of the house in which he had grown up, but that had played no conscious part in his decision to buy it. It was simply another rather dowdy, anonymous village house, the sort of place your gaze just slid past. He had no history with it, and that was fine. He had no immediate family to share it with either, and that was fine too. His parents lay side by side in a cemetery some kilometres away, under a plain memorial that bore only initials, the family name being instantly recognizable in a way that would attract the wrong kind of attention. A headstone with that name on it was liable to be defaced, kicked over, scratched. Nobody wanted that name next to a loved one's resting place.

He no longer had it on his identity card, either. When he'd come back to the area after his long time away, he'd chosen another name, taken a house in a different village, one where his face was less likely to be recognized. Even after all these years there was a chance that someone, a former neighbour or friend, would see his younger self in his face.

He didn't care about the new name any more than he cared about the drab new house. It wasn't him, in any meaningful way. *De Jager*, that was what he called himself, that was what defined him. *The hunter.* Anything else was convention, the tiger-stripes that allowed him to move through the shadows, stalking his prey unseen.

Tonight the hunter had work to do.

De Jager had rubber boots on, keys, gloves, a scarf that covered his mouth and nose. When he came home that afternoon he had parked the car close to the outbuilding at the back of the house, so there was no need to back it up any further. The trees generally provided a screen from nosy neighbours, but at this time of year the branches were bare so he scanned the next house carefully before he went any further. There was only one window facing his property and the roller shutters were down. There were no lights on, no car in the drive. When he was satisfied that there was no one there he took out the keys and unlocked the outbuilding.

The thing was where he'd left it (*where would it go?*), and although it was time to dispose of it he couldn't resist unfolding the tarpaulin and taking another look.

It was preserved remarkably well. That was because of the freezing winter temperatures. If this had been July it would have been another matter. He studied the dead face. People sometimes compared death to sleep; they said that a dead person looked as though they were asleep. This one didn't look as though she was asleep. He remembered the sounds she had made, the stillborn scream that had turned into a cough, a gurgle. He relished the memories, reliving them with the sensual enjoyment of a couturier fingering expensive fabrics – raw silk and cashmere.

After a while he covered the face again, taking care to conceal it completely in case of prying eyes. He went and opened the boot of the car, then came back and fetched the bundle in its tarpaulin. It was large enough to be unwieldy but he was strong, he had the family build. Good farming stock somewhere back in the past.

He put the thing in the boot and shut the lid. Then he went back and closed and locked the outbuilding. He started the car and drove down the drive and onto the road. There was no other traffic. He turned right and headed out of the village, taking a road that snaked through several other villages and into the town of Tervuren.

The spot he was aiming for was in a stretch of parkland normally closed to cars, but roadworks on one of the streets running into Tervuren meant that traffic was being diverted through the woods that fringed the park. A little while later he was turning in at the gateway in the high brick wall that surrounded it.

At this time of night hardly anyone chose to drive through the park. In the hours of full darkness it was a lonely and sinister journey, car headlights turning the overhanging trees into a bleached tunnel through the blackness, and the massive potholes, concealed by the night, could do serious damage to wheels and axles.

All the same, De Jager kept an eye on the road behind him in the rear-view mirror. There was no sign of anyone else in the park, no headlights, no cycle lamps. He drove carefully through the woods and along the side of the lake.

When he was within view of the chapel, the Sint-Hubertuskapel that overlooked the lake, he pulled in and killed the lights. He sat there for a while, waiting. He wanted to let his eyes adjust to the darkness.

There was a pond at the edge of the woods, the black water overhung with beech trees. That was where he planned to put the thing in the boot. It would be easier than trying to put it in the ground, when the earth was frozen, the vegetation too sparse to cover his work. The lake itself was too open and well-maintained to keep a secret for long, but the pond was obscured by tree branches and a tangle of unkempt bushes. Dank and neglected, it was the perfect dumping ground for unwanted items. There was even a fallen tree, and because it wasn't across the road or in anyone's way it hadn't been cleared away yet.

De Jager judged that if he could put the body into the water under cover of the trees, perhaps even wedge it under the fallen one, it would be a while before anyone spotted it. It didn't really matter if they did; he hadn't left any traces of himself on it. The water would hold them up a bit, anyway, while they hauled out the body and discovered that she hadn't drowned, and tried to work out where she *had* died. No trail leading back to him *there*, either. If they found any carpet fibres on the body they'd match with fibres in a house that didn't belong to him, whose owners had been in Mauritius when the girl died.

When he was sure that there really was nobody around, and his eyes had become accustomed to the darkness, he carried the body in its tarpaulin shroud to the pond. It took some effort to get it down the bank under the trees to the water's edge, but he took his time and eventually he managed it. He unwrapped the tarpaulin; if she went into the water in that he thought there was a risk of air pockets.

He managed to get the body right underwater, beneath a heavy branch of the fallen tree. His legs were wet to the thigh by the time he finished. If there had been more moonlight they would have glistened like sealskin. The water was freezing; he didn't spend any longer in it than he had to. He had checked the place out pretty thoroughly during daylight, so he was satisfied that the body would not be obvious from the track. Somebody would have to go nosing about to see it. He folded the tarp and stowed it in the boot of the car. He changed the boots too. They were new, but they would have gone by tomorrow night, as would the tarp.

As he drove home he was thinking about the girl again, about the night she died, reliving the hunt. He had hunted many times and still it gave him a sense of icy gratification. The planning. The *deciding* who it would be and when. The adjustments, the refinements of technique that made him ever more efficient, a killing machine processing its victims.

The first time he had taken a human life he thought he had reached some kind of summit, an apotheosis of killing: it was not a pet he had slaughtered, some trusting dog or cat, but a human being. Now he looked back upon that first adventure with slightly contemptuous eyes. With more experience, with a steadier hand, it need never have led to the consequences it did. He might never have gone away; he might still have an identity card with his real name on it.

He had learned so much since then. The hunting of this last girl, it had been well-nigh perfect.

He wondered how she would look when they eventually found her, whether it would be easy to identify her. *If the skin was discoloured, would they still see it?* he wondered. The tattoo she had. The one of a butterfly.

That night the temperature dropped again, and in the morning the surface of the pond was covered with a thin layer of ice. The day after that it snowed, this time more heavily, and the wind blew the snow into drifts. It got everywhere, like desert sand, even under the fallen tree, where it covered the ice with a powdery white frosting. Underneath the ice, in the dark water, lay the dead girl, her face pointing downwards, as though at some chill Hades. On the surface, however, there was nothing to be seen at all.

7

The snow kept falling, and covered everything with a white pall. After a day or two it stopped snowing, but the temperature remained low. Those who walked in the park looked forward to getting indoors again. Nobody went near the pond or the lake; dog owners kept their pets away from the water, where the covering of ice was treacherously thin.

For Veerle, the next two weeks slid past without incident. It was as though the scene at the climbing wall, her precipitate flight from the bus and the events of that night at the castle had never been, as though some strange encrusted sea creature had broken the surface of the ocean and then sounded, leaving the waters smooth and undisturbed. The only thing that had changed was that she no longer went to the climbing wall after school.

Veerle didn't tell her mother what had happened; she didn't tell her that she wasn't going to the wall any more either. The thought of all the questions, the feverish seeking after all the details, was too much to contemplate. Besides, she suspected that Claudine would actually be *pleased*. One less hazardous activity for her daughter to indulge in. It made

Veerle feel like taking up something even more dangerous, like BASE jumping.

Claudine's anxious complaints were becoming more and more insistent. Once she followed Veerle to the bathroom and stood outside the door lecturing her about some imagined hazard in a fretful voice, while inside Veerle brushed her teeth and made faces at herself in the mirror. Veerle suspected that Claudine's anxiety was bordering on an illness and wondered whether she should do something about it – try to contact her father or persuade her mother to see a doctor.

'You don't know what you put me through,' said Claudine through the closed door. She spoke in French; she had been born in Namur.

Veerle looked at herself in the mirror. She had toothpaste at the corners of her mouth. *I look like a rabid dog,* she said to herself. She thought that her mother acted as though the whole world were a pack of mad dogs. As though if Veerle were exposed to it she would be infected, there would be no holding her back, she would go mad too.

How did it get this bad? she wondered. When she looked back at the past, well, everybody had less freedom when they were a little kid, your parents kept a closer eye on you, but it seemed to Veerle that Claudine had got *more* anxious, *more* cautious since then, not less. *I used to run around all over the village on my own. I used to go over and play in the churchyard or go to the shop for an ice cream and she didn't have to know where I was every single moment. She's got worse. She's still getting worse.*

'Calm down,' Veerle replied in French. She didn't open the

door. She looked into her reflection's hazel eyes as though seeking some kind of conspiratorial reassurance. *I can't give in to her. I can't let it rule my life. I might as well be in prison if I do.*

Veerle was not afraid of much, but her mother's smothering anxiety filled her with dread. Like the irresistible gravitational pull of a massive planet, it would suck her in and ultimately it would crush her. It was not possible to maintain the form of your own will when subjected to those forces. She would as soon have opened the door to a vampire.

What happened? she asked herself silently. *Why did she get like this?*

She kept to her routine, spinning out the hours of freedom. She hoped that eventually she would be able to go back to the climbing wall, that Bart would forgive or possibly simply forget; in the meantime she filled her spare time by hanging out with people from her class, going window-shopping or eking out a single Coke in the snack bar near the school. If nothing else was in the offing, she went to the public library, which was at least warm.

And she kept an eye out for Kris whenever she was out. She didn't really expect to see him; she thought perhaps the family had moved away from the area. If she hadn't seen him for over ten years, why would she run into him now? But she looked anyway.

Once, she found the local telephone directory and looked up Verstraeten, but that didn't tell her anything either. There were fifteen local listings for Verstraeten, and she couldn't remember what Kris's father's Christian name was. There was no separate listing for *Kris Verstraeten*. Feeling rather foolish, she put the directory away.

For two weeks Veerle saw and heard nothing of Kris, but on the fifteenth day after her visit to the castle, she saw him again.

It was a Thursday afternoon, and she was on the bus home from school. The bus was full of other students, chatting, laughing, jostling with each other for space. Veerle knew most of them, but she wasn't in the mood for chatting; she put her earphones in and gazed out of the window, letting the music wash over her in a soothing tide.

When the bus reached her village she was the last to alight, fighting her way through the packed bodies. She stepped onto the pavement, and then the bus drove off, leaving a cloud of evil-smelling exhaust behind it, and she looked across the road, and there he was.

He was leaning against the high wall that ran around the churchyard. In the black leather jacket and black jeans he stood out starkly against the grey stone with its frosting of snow; he might have been a priest or a demon. It was a shock to see him, here in the street so close to her own house. It was like opening her roller shutters one morning and seeing a tiger walking down the middle of the street, its flame-and-cinder pelt wet with Flemish rain. He didn't belong here, not any more, not since the boy Kris had metamorphosed into this tall, broad-shouldered young man.

Is he here for me? she thought, and something was churning inside her stomach like a swimmer kicking up through muddy water. Then she thought: *Please God, don't let* her *see him.* In no possible alternative universe could she imagine any happy conjunction of Kris and her mother; they were polar opposites, natural enemies.

She hesitated. *Supposing he's waiting for someone else? How stupid am I going to look then?* All the same, she couldn't stop staring at him.

Now he was looking at her, he had recognized her, and he was pushing away from the wall. Veerle was convinced he was going to come over to her. Her heart was thumping as she crossed the road diagonally, moving further up the street; her path took her away from him but at least she was beyond the line of sight of the house if her mother decided to look out.

Kris was moving towards her, languidly at first, but then a little more quickly as he saw her moving away. 'Hold on,' he said.

She was safe now: the solid wall of the house at the corner of the street was between her and anything her mother could see from the doorstep of their home. She turned and looked at him. *Kris. It's so weird, seeing him now when I remember him as a kid of ten or something. He's changed. He's so . . .* She found the word she was looking for and glanced away, not wanting him to see it in her eyes, the way she reacted to him. It might be nothing to do with her, him being here.

'Don't you live on Kerkstraat?' said Kris.

'Yes,' said Veerle succinctly; she didn't want to tell him she was avoiding Claudine.

'So are you going for a walk or something?' His tone was dry.

'No.' She dared not elaborate. 'Why are you here?' she asked, and then wished she hadn't. He would probably say he was waiting for someone else.

Kris shrugged. 'I have something for you.'

For me? She stared at him in spite of herself.

He slid a hand inside his jacket and produced an envelope. 'Here.'

She took it, and turned it over. The address read *Veerle De Keyser, Kerkstraat 6. How did he know that?* But it was no mystery, she realized; even if he had forgotten which house she had lived in from the days when they were both children at the same village school, it was easy enough to find the address in the phone book.

'If you didn't come I was going to put it in the letter box,' said Kris.

Veerle shot him a glance. *Thank God you didn't.* She imagined Claudine picking up the envelope. She had no idea what was inside it, but she already knew that she didn't want to share the contents with her mother. She ripped it open.

Inside was a single sheet of paper, folded twice. She unfolded it and read the words written in a large bold hand.

ENGELENSTRAAT 51
TOMORROW 20.00.
K

That was all it said. No *Dear Veerle*, or any explanation. She looked at Kris, but there was no need for either of them to say anything. It was a challenge. She could take it, or she could screw up the paper, hand it back to him and walk away.

'So?' said Kris. He had his head on one side, and that ironic look on his face.

'I don't know,' said Veerle. She stuffed the letter into her jacket pocket. She waited for him to try to persuade her, but he didn't. 'I'll think about it,' she said.

Later, when she was alone, she took the paper out of her pocket and looked at it again.

Engelenstraat, she thought. It didn't mean anything to her. She knew all the main streets in the village, of course, and it wasn't any of those, so it was probably one of the little residential streets tucked away somewhere at the edge where the houses abutted fields and roads petered out into tracks that meandered amongst greenhouses and vegetable patches.

It doesn't matter, she thought. *I'm not going anyway. He may be gorgeous but he's presuming too much.*

She put the letter into the kitchen bin, but a minute later she took it out again and tore it into little pieces, imagining Claudine fishing it out, reading it. She stuffed the pieces back into the bin. It made no difference, though; she wouldn't forget the message.

8

The following evening Veerle told her mother she was taking the bus to Overijse to see a Flemish film in the theatre there. This was a safe way of ensuring her mother didn't try to come along; her Flemish was virtually non-existent. It didn't stop Claudine trying to persuade Veerle not to go.

She stood in the hallway of the house with her shoulders hunched and her arms folded across her body, as though she alone could sense some chill bleak wind that others could not feel. Her hair had long since turned grey and she kept it cut very short in a mannish style that didn't suit her. Unmade-up, she looked worn and faded, like a doll left out in the rain.

'I won't go to bed until you get back,' she told Veerle in a reproachful voice.

Veerle sighed inwardly, but she kept her expression calm. If she showed any sign of impatience Claudine would only become more distressed.

'Don't forget I have to turn my phone off during the film,' she told her mother. 'So you won't be able to call me.'

She felt as though she were in charge of an elderly child. *Except*, she thought, *there would be some chance that a child might change, and grow out of it*. Claudine was only going to get worse, she suspected. She reminded Veerle of flypaper: once she stuck to you it was almost impossible to free yourself, and the more you struggled, the more she stuck. *I hate thinking about her like that. But – but . . .* It was true, that was the trouble.

She was afraid that if she prolonged her departure Claudine might work herself up to tears, so she left the house as quickly as she could. She went round the corner towards the bus stop, even though she wanted to go in the other direction entirely, just in case Claudine was watching from the doorstep.

She had a pretty good idea what Kris was proposing, so she had dressed in black jeans and boots, a dark roll-necked jumper and a warm jacket. The snow was melting, but the air still had a savage chill. She hung about near the bus stop until the bus had been and gone, and then she doubled back along a street that ran parallel to Kerkstraat.

Engelenstraat, she had discovered, was only about three hundred metres from her own house. She had never been down it; even when she cycled about the village she avoided lanes like that because the cobblestones were vicious: old and irregular and ill-maintained. Not many people lived there; there were empty plots between the houses, which were all at least forty years old. The night she had explored the old castle there had been hardly any moonlight, the moon a sliver like a Mona Lisa smile, mostly obscured by clouds. Tonight there was a bright moon, which was just as well because Engelenstraat had no street lighting and all the houses were dark. In most cases the shutters were down on the doors and windows, and in all probability there was light and cosy warmth on the other side, but even before Veerle got to number 51 she could see that it was not the case there. The house was empty.

There was an estate agent's board outside with TE KOOP printed on it in large letters. This struck Veerle as a hopeless waste of time; this was not the sort of street that had through-traffic, where there was a chance of anyone seeing the board and contacting the agent. She was contemplating the sign from the other side of the road when she saw a dark shape detach itself from the shadows at the side of the house.

She waited until she was sure it was Kris before she went over. It was almost impossible to spend years living in a house with Claudine without paranoid thoughts about your own personal security creeping in, however much you tried to resist. In Claudine's terms, what she was doing was absolutely suicidal – which was part of the attraction, Veerle supposed.

'Hi,' she whispered. She saw Kris smile that lopsided smile, and she knew that there had never been any question about whether she would turn up tonight.

He didn't say anything, just inclined his head to indicate that she should follow. It was a clear night; Veerle could hear the cars on the main road and a dog barking somewhere. Sound carried outdoors; it was best to keep talking to a minimum.

She followed Kris along the side of the house. She thought it had been built in the 1930s or '40s; it was a dull, ugly-looking red-brick building with small square windows, the frames painted white and the shutters let down. You could tell by looking at it that it would be dingy inside, even on sunny days. On a grey rainy Flemish morning the rooms would be like cells.

The main door was at the side but Kris went straight past it and turned the corner. The back of the house was bathed in moonlight. It was no more prepossessing than the front: dowdy brick, too-small windows.

'Here,' said Kris. He laid his hand on the back door with its peeling white paint, and it opened easily.

'How did you do that?' whispered Veerle.

He shrugged. 'I've already been in.'

Veerle scanned the back of the house. There was a lean-to against the wall, and next to it a log-pile that would be easily scaled. About a metre and a half above the roof of the lean-to was a sash window, open just a few centimetres.

She felt exposed here at the back, with the moonlight bleaching the bricks. There were no houses in the neighbouring plots, but the neglected garden backed onto allotments, and on the other side of those there were houses. Anyone who happened to look out of their back window would see her and Kris quite easily. She didn't waste any time asking herself whether she really wanted to go inside; it was good to be out of sight of curious eyes.

The back door led straight into a large kitchen. The window shutters were down but light streamed in through the glass panels in the door. It didn't look as though anyone had replaced anything in this kitchen for decades. The work surfaces were made of Formica so aged that it had passed from merely vintage into archaeological. There was a faint and melancholy smell of damp and neglect.

You could almost hear the house sighing in a martyred sort

of way, thought Veerle. She thought of Claudine and instantly felt guilty.

Kris clearly knew his way about. He led her across the kitchen and into a narrow hallway, and as soon as the door between the rooms was closed behind them he switched on a torch.

The beam travelled over walls papered with an old-fashioned floral design, a tiled floor in a clashing pattern, and the side of a wooden staircase, painted white. There were light patches on the walls where pictures had once hung. The general effect was overwhelmingly dismal.

Why does he do this? thought Veerle. She felt uneasy in this forlorn and decayed environment; it had all the appeal of drinking coffee in a room with a corpse propped up in the corner. More than that, she was baffled by Kris's actions. The castle, yes, she understood that; it had a kind of dilapidated grandeur to it. This place was simply ugly and depressing, the sort of place you wanted to break out of rather than into.

There was a door to the left. Veerle watched Kris go to open it. There would be another dark and musty chamber on the other side, she guessed. To her surprise, however, when the door swung open she saw a soft light coming from within. She stepped forward and peered round the doorframe.

The room was much as expected: a bare floor with tiles of an old-fashioned design, dog-eared floral wallpaper, an empty curtain pole with the rings still on it, like bangles on a skeletal arm. There was a large marble fireplace that must have been grand when it was installed, but now looked outmoded and too heavy for the room. On the marble shelf over the fireplace was a candle standing on a saucer, and next to the candle was a bottle of wine and three glasses.

Three? The room was deserted; there were only the two of them.

'So,' said Kris, holding out his arms to encompass the room. 'Welcome.' He went over to the mantelpiece and picked up the bottle of wine. 'Drink?'

'There are three glasses,' said Veerle bluntly. She didn't move from her place in the doorway. 'Why are there three glasses?'

'Someone else is coming, obviously,' said Kris, grinning at her. He didn't seem bothered by her obvious suspicion.

Veerle watched him as he filled two of the glasses.

I thought it was just the two of us. Who else is coming? She began to think that maybe it wasn't enough that she had known Kris when they were kids, that she didn't really *know* him, this grown-up Kris with his insouciant manner and ironic smile. She glanced back into the darkened hallway, wondering whether she should just try to leave right now.

'Hey, it's just Els,' said Kris, coming over with the glasses. 'Only don't call her that. *Hommel*, that's what she likes to be called. Don't call her Els and you'll be OK.'

He handed Veerle a glass of wine. She took it from him but she didn't try it.

'I thought it was just us,' she said. She was conscious of the darkened hallway behind her; she kept listening for the sound of someone else coming into the house. Els, or Hommel, whatever her name was, and if that was really who was coming. She stepped into the room; she felt better with the floral wall at her back. 'What are we doing here, anyway? Mending window catches again?'

Kris shook his head. 'Admin.'

'*Admin?*'

'If you want to do this, someone else has to agree. Not just me. Two of us.'

'Do what? Break into dusty old houses where nobody lives anyway?'

Kris shook his head. 'Of course not. What would be the point? This place will probably be pulled down as soon as it's sold, anyway. Look at it – it's practically falling down on its own. The castle, that's different – it's worth working on it, and anyway, I wasn't there for that. I was looking for Vlinder.'

Vlinder again.

'Who's Vlinder?'

He shrugged. 'A friend of a friend of a friend.'

'And Hommel?'

'Hommel's a friend.' He didn't seem inclined to pursue it. 'She's coming at nine. We have about fifty minutes to discuss the proposal, and if you don't like it you can leave before Hommel gets here, OK?'

Veerle stared at him for a moment. Then she took a first sip of the wine, watching him over the rim of the glass. His bold dark eyes, his sharp features and unruly hair. The way he leaned against the wall, long-limbed and casual. The taste of the wine filled her mouth gloriously, all blackberries and spices.

'OK,' she said.

'It's not about dumps like this,' said Kris, glancing around. 'It's not about the castle, either, though some people like to do those. Vlinder, for example. She mostly did the old places.'

Did? Past tense?

'So why did we come here then?' asked Veerle.

'To see if you would.' Kris took a mouthful of wine. He didn't sip it the way she did; he took a swallow. 'Look,' he said, 'haven't you ever thought about all the houses there are around here, standing empty? Not just the ones waiting for the demolition ball, like this one. The other ones. The ones rented by bigwigs from the Commission, wealthy business-men. They come for a few years, then they go, and the place is empty for a couple of months. Or they go home to wherever it is they come from for a month in the summer, and leave the place empty. Christmas is the same. The airport is full and the houses are empty. Some of them, you have to see them to believe it. Six bedrooms, four bathrooms, marble everywhere. Some of them have pools. And what they save on rent, because they're not paying it themselves, they spend on all this other stuff. Plasma-screen TVs, state-of-the-art sound systems. All of it sitting there in an empty house.'

'You're saying you break into *those* houses?' said Veerle. 'To do what? You *steal* stuff?'

'No.' Kris shook his head. 'Anyone who does that is out. We . . . enjoy the houses. Watch TV, listen to music, sit in the jacuzzi. Whatever. But there are rules. You clear up after your-self, and you do something for the house.'

'Mend the window catch?' asked Veerle mischievously.

'Maybe. Whatever needs doing.'

'What did you do in the last one you went into?' she asked him. She took another sip of the wine.

'I . . .' He paused. 'I alphabetized the CD collection.'

'You *what*?' Veerle couldn't help herself; she began to laugh. 'You *alphabetized* the *CD collection*?'

'Yes.' Kris was laughing too.

'That's idiotic.'

'There was nothing else to do. The place was a palace.'

'Someone will have noticed.'

'So what? They'll think the maid did it.'

'You're insane,' said Veerle, but she was smiling. Smiling, and thinking. 'And what if I want to do that too?' she said.

'What, alphabetize CDs?' He was smiling back at her.

'No. You know. Enjoy houses. Ones with plasma-screen TVs.' She looked at Kris. 'What would I have to do?'

'Nothing. Hommel just has to agree.' He looked at her idly, summing her up. 'There have to be two of us who agree, that's one of the rules. But don't worry, Hommel won't say no. She won't like it, but she won't refuse.'

Veerle looked down into her glass of wine, seeing a dim liquid shadow of herself in the depths. The wine was almost black in the low light.

'Why did you ask me?' she said.

'Seemed like you already had a thing for creeping around empty buildings in the dark. Anyway, it's more interesting with two. Some people like to go into places on their own – like Vlinder, for example. I like company.'

'Who do you normally take with you?'

'That depends.'

'Hommel?'

'Sometimes. Not any more.'

Ah, thought Veerle. She kept her gaze turned down into the glossy red-black depths of the wine. In the silence she heard something. A door closing. She thought it came from the direction of the kitchen.

Hommel, she thought. Suddenly she was tense again; her body was effervescent with nerves.

She heard the door between the kitchen and hallway open and close. She glanced at Kris, but he was looking at his watch, his dark brows drawn together in a frown.

'Way too early,' he said under his breath.

Footsteps were approaching down the hallway.

'Hommel,' said Kris.

Veerle's first thought was, *She's nothing like her name.* Hommel, Bumblebee – it had made her think of someone rotund, fuzzy-haired. Hommel was nothing like that. She was slender and pale and angular like a statue of a saint; even through the padded jacket and thick jeans she was wearing you could see how thin she was. She had very light blonde hair that was scraped back into a ponytail: practical but severe. The hair was very sleek; the end of the ponytail hung in a point like the tip of a paintbrush. She had high cheekbones and pale unfriendly eyes. The gaze of those pale eyes moved up and down Veerle's body but Hommel didn't bother to greet her.

'Hello, Kris,' she said coldly.

'You're early,' he said mildly.

'Nine wasn't suitable.' She didn't say why. 'We can't all just jump whenever you call us.'

'Do you want some wine?' He held up the glass.

'No,' said Hommel shortly.

'Why not? It's a good one.'

'You're full of shit, Kris.' Hommel glanced at Veerle. 'So this is why you dragged me out here to this dump, is it? Is she the new one?'

'Hommel . . .' Kris assumed a conciliatory expression.

'Don't bother trying to be nice,' Hommel told him. 'The charm offensive won't work on me.' To Veerle she said, 'I hope you know what you're getting yourself into.'

Veerle said nothing. She was beginning to dislike Hommel acutely. *The name Hommel suits you after all,* she thought. *You've got a sting in your tail all right.* She was determined not to rise to the bait, though. She contented herself with giving Hommel a stony look.

'What's her name?' Hommel asked Kris, as though Veerle couldn't speak for herself.

'Veerle,' said Kris. He didn't react to Hommel's angry tone. 'De Keyser.'

Hommel made a sceptical grunt of dismissal, as though she had never heard such a ludicrous name in her life. 'Fine,' she snapped. She pulled the collar of her jacket close around her neck, thrusting her chin out. 'I'm not hanging around here, Kris. I've got better things to do.'

'You agree, then?'

'Whatever. Yes.'

Kris followed her out into the darkened hallway, leaving Veerle alone. She could hear the two of them arguing in low voices as they moved towards the kitchen door. She sipped wine, put her head back and stared up at the ceiling, doing her best not to listen to what they were saying. It seemed to her that on the whole she didn't want to hear what Hommel might be saying to Kris, especially if it was about her; and more than that, she didn't want to hear what Kris was saying back. There was nothing he could say to Hommel about the situation that would gratify both of them. Instead

she gazed up at the ugly and moribund light fittings and the
map of damp patches that disfigured the ceiling.

After a while she heard the door slam and Kris came back
on his own. He was still holding his glass of wine, but something that had been building up in the atmosphere had
evaporated.

The new one. It was obvious what Hommel had been
implying – that Veerle was just the latest in a string of
gullible girls. *Hommel could be the one with the problem*, she
reminded herself. Maybe she wasn't an ex at all; maybe
she was someone Kris had rejected, trying to get her own
back.

Which of them is more plausible? she thought, rubbing her
fingers against the stem of the wine glass. Aloud, she said, 'So
she's OK with it?'

'Not really. But she has agreed.'

'Mmm.'

'She'll get over it. It had to be her, anyway. She's the
nearest.'

Veerle thought about that. 'So this isn't just a local thing,
then?'

'Nope.'

'How far does it go?'

Kris shrugged. 'I don't know. Nobody knows everybody,
that's the point.'

'Who started it?'

'Fred started the circle here. But even he doesn't know
everyone, just the ones in this group, in this area. Fred made
up most of the rules.'

'Who's Fred?'

'He does something in Brussels – runs a gallery or something. He got into it because he loves old buildings. Says he's a purist. He doesn't do the expat houses.'

'You've met him?'

Kris shook his head. 'Hearsay.'

'But why do you need the group anyway?' persisted Veerle. 'Isn't it risky, involving other people?' She thought of Hommel, who clearly held a grudge. 'Why don't you just do it yourself?'

'Exchange of information,' said Kris. 'It's safer that way. If you know the family next door to you are going to be away for three weeks, it's risky to go in there yourself. You're more likely to be recognized by the other neighbours. If the break-in is detected you'll get questions. Better to let one of the others do that one.'

Veerle looked him in the eye. 'What if someone decides to tell? What if I walk out of here and go to the police? It's trespassing, after all.'

'I'm not going to track you down and kill you, if that's what you think.' Kris's voice was ironic. 'I can't stop you, if you want to do that.' He took a mouthful of wine. 'In practice, nobody ever does. You're trespassing too – you'd have to explain that. And we don't steal anything or smash anything up.' He eyed her. '*Are* you going to the police?'

'No.'

They stared at each other. Unspoken messages were travelling between them, but Hommel's hostile mood still hung in the air like a poisonous gas. If Kris had moved closer to her, she would have stepped back.

'What happens next?' she asked, breaking the silence.

'Fred sends you the contact details. You'd better give me your email address.'

He watched her write it on the back of a till receipt, looked at the proffered piece of paper briefly and pocketed it. Then he raised his glass to her.

'Congratulations,' he said drily. 'You're in.'

9

Towards the end of January the temperature rose; the snow gave way to sleet and then to rain. The ice on the lake in the park began to melt. It was still unpleasant to walk in the park – wet and dirty underfoot and cheerless overhead, with the bare and wet black branches of the trees jutting into dreary grey skies. It required a certain hardiness to root oneself out of bed on a Sunday morning to walk the dog.

That was probably the only reason the discovery didn't make more of a stir at the time; it was early and there was hardly anyone in the park. In the south-west corner near the Sint-Hubertuskapel there was only a local man, Johan Bogaerts, who was walking a dog – or, more specifically, his wife's dog. Johan was in a filthy mood because the weather was wet and cold and he hated the dog anyway; it was a stupid thing, small and yappy and wilful. The only thing that prevented him from planting a stout shoe on the dog's backside and punting it into the lake was the fear of what his wife would say and do. All the same, he entertained pleasant thoughts of doing just that as he trudged after the loathed animal. He could see that the white hair of its belly and legs was already brown with mud; that meant brushing the car out after he'd taken the dog home, and bathing the bloody thing, while resisting the temptation to hold it underwater until bubbles and life itself burst forth from it.

Now he saw with annoyance that the dog had started down the bank that led to the pond. It was barking – or rather, it was making the shrill and irritating noise that passed for barking – and forcing its way under the green remains of fallen branches to the water. With the thaw, the wet earth had turned to mud; the dog would be even more filthy than usual. Johan called and whistled, but with a certain sense of futility; the dog did whatever it wanted, regardless of the admonitions of its owners.

'*Klootzak*,' said Johan disgustedly to the dog. Then he went to follow it.

The bank was, he saw to his dismay, steeper and muddier than he had expected. If he went down it himself he would end up just as filthy as the dog, even assuming he managed to keep his footing. He called the dog again. 'Mirko. Mirko.'

Johan raised his voice but the dog still didn't respond, even when he shouted '*Klootzak!*' at it.

It was at the water's edge, barking its hairy little head off and ignoring him completely. Johan opened his mouth to curse it again, and then he saw what the dog was barking at. For a moment he tried to tell himself that it was something innocent – a carrier bag that had blown into the water, a discarded piece of clothing. But even as he struggled down the bank, slipping and sliding, mud coating his trousers, he knew that it wasn't. As he went down, he tried to fumble his mobile phone out of his pocket, intending to call the police, an ambulance, his wife. But he stumbled over a mossy branch and the phone flew out of his hand and landed in the pond with a faint splash.

The bottom of the bank was so slippery that he was unable to avoid putting one foot in the water. It was freezing, and in his mind's eye it was contaminated too, the solution in which a dead thing was suspended like an exhibit in a medical museum. He made a strangled sound and launched himself back onto the bank.

He looked for his phone but it had vanished in the leaden water. Then he looked at the body and he knew that it was down to him, he had to do something. He was as sure of that as he was of anything, as sure as he was that his marriage and his life since had been a complete mistake, that he was going to tell Céline it was the dog or him when he finally got home. *I'm going to have to turn the body over. I have to be one hundred per cent certain that whoever it is is really dead.* He didn't think there was the remotest chance of life in that motionless and submerged form, but he had a duty to find out before he went off for another fifteen minutes to fetch the police in person. He couldn't leave someone to drown if there was the faintest hope of resuscitation. So he took his courage in both hands and grasped the sodden clothing, which moved in the water around the silent form like the gently waving seaweed on a reef. He pulled, feeling the weight of the water trying to suck the body back down out of his grasp, and then he braced himself and heaved, and the body turned over.

Johan looked at the dead grey face and screamed.

10

Veerle heard nothing for six days. She travelled to and from the high school, the bus passing shops where the newspaper headlines outside screamed BODY FOUND IN LAKE. She didn't read up on the details; it seemed prurient somehow, like taking pleasure in someone else's tragedy. All the same, it was not possible to avoid it. Students and teachers alike were talking about it at school, and Claudine sucked up every minor piece of information with an obsessive zeal: suspicious death and bloody mysteries simply served to confirm her view that the world was an impossibly dangerous place to live in. She went after the smallest snippets of news with the morbid compulsion of someone unable to stop picking a scab.

Meanwhile, Veerle kept checking her email account. It was not easy. She couldn't trust her mother not to pry, to look over Veerle's shoulder while she was online, or peep at the screen when Veerle had gone to make herself a coffee. Claudine hated to be excluded; it made her even more suspicious.

Being stalked by Claudine made Veerle feel desperate to make contact with Kris and his group. It was as though she had been wandering for years in some grim labyrinth and suddenly he had opened a door in the wall and said, *Look, here's the way out.*

I wonder if this is how criminals feel, she said to herself. *As though the laws aren't really there, as though they're something made up that doesn't apply to them.* There was a kind of reckless freedom in it. Everyday life, the round of bus and school and going home to Claudine at night, seemed like a façade, a crust that she had broken through. It would never look the same again; she could see the cracks now. She kept herself awake with coffee and checked her emails late at night, when Claudine had gone to bed.

On the sixth day she came home, studied for a while in a listless sort of way, ate the supper Claudine had prepared and went without much hope to check her email account. For once she could expect to work undisturbed: Claudine wanted to watch something on television, a doom-laden documentary of some sort. Inevitably this would supply her with more grounds for fretting, more proof of the evil of the world outside the heavily bolted front door, but Veerle was prepared to worry about that later. She booted up her laptop, went online and accessed her email account.

1 new message.

It was from an address she didn't recognize, and the title read *Fwd: Bird-watching.*

There was a line of text: *Welcome to the world of bird-watching!* Underneath it was a link to a website address, http://www.koekoeken.be, and underneath that were a user name and password. The username was *Honingbij,* Veerle noted wryly. Honeybee. Was someone trying to tell her something, hinting that she was the latest in a long line of successors to the embittered Hommel? She clicked on the link.

When the website came up she thought for a moment that there had been a mistake. *KOEKOEKEN!* shouted the header – *CUCKOOS!* The screen was sprouting wild birds – robins, finches and various other species, not all of which Veerle recognized. There was a paragraph of text which began with *Welcome to the world of bird-watching!* and ended with a list of bird species. The final line read, *Our especial interest is of course the cuckoo.*

At the very bottom of the page were two fields marked *Username* and *Password*.

Someone has a sense of humour, thought Veerle as her fingers hovered over the keys. *Cuckoo. The bird that's in some-one else's nest.*

Then she thought about the username, Honingbij, and decided that the wit was not so much to her taste after all. She entered the username and password, and pressed RETURN.

The flocks of birds vanished and Veerle found herself staring at a message board. Most of the message subjects were similar: *Sighting, Sterrebeek. Sighting, Tervuren.* She opened one at random. *Possible cuckoo sighting, Feb 14–28, Eikstraat 209.*

She exited the message and scanned down the list. There were a number of messages with *Vlinder* in the title. *Vlinder, if you're reading this, please contact . . .*

She might have opened one of those out of curiosity, but another message caught her eye. *Honingbij, welcome.* It had been posted by *Schorpioen.*

She opened the message.

There was an address, and then: *Friday, 21.00. K.*

Kris. Veerle looked at the message for a while. She could hear the sudden blare of music from the sitting room. She supposed the documentary was ending; it sounded like the sort of sombre and over-dramatic theme tune that she associated with the harrowing documentaries her mother liked to watch. In a minute or two Claudine would be in the room, peering over Veerle's shoulder and asking her whether she wanted a hot chocolate or something.

Friday, 21.00. K.

She exited the message, logged out of the Koekoeken site and shut down the laptop. She had just finished when Claudine came in.

'Do you want some cocoa?' was the first thing she asked, and the second was, 'What have you been doing?'

'Looking at a wildlife website,' said Veerle promptly.

'Really?' said Claudine vaguely, losing interest. 'It's amazing what you can do with that thing, isn't it?' She meant the laptop.

'Yes,' agreed Veerle. 'It is.'

11

There was another fuss when Veerle announced that she was going out on Friday night.

'Where are you going?' demanded Claudine suspiciously.

'Someone in my class has a birthday, so we're all meeting up,' said Veerle. She plucked a name out of the air. 'Anna.'

'I didn't know there was an Anna in your class. You've never talked about her.'

'Her family just moved here last term,' said Veerle. She didn't feel guilty about lying to her mother; it was like telling a child something that wasn't strictly true to reassure it.

If I say I'm meeting someone she'll go overboard. She'll want to know who he is and where he comes from and how I know he's OK, and she'll probably decide he isn't OK, whatever I say. Then she'll try to stop me going.

Over Claudine's shoulder Veerle could see the coffee table and the newspaper spread out on it, the headline screaming about the body in the lake, that it was definitely murder. Her heart sank.

If I'm not careful she'll start thinking I'm going to be next and then I won't get out of the house at all, not without a row. And I don't want to row with her.

Veerle sensed that some kind of showdown was coming. At present it was in the distance, like a range of mountains seen on the horizon during a trek through scrubland, apparently never getting any closer; however slowly you walked, one day you would reach them, there was a geographical inevitability to it.

I'm seventeen. I can't let her treat me like a kid, always having to ask permission to go anywhere, always having to tell her where I am every single minute of the day.

Sooner or later she would have to confront it, this situation with Claudine; she knew that.

Not now, though. Now I just have to meet Kris.

'I already said I'd go,' she said aloud.

'Well, you don't have to,' retorted Claudine. 'If she just moved here last term, I don't see why it's so important.'

'Everyone's going.'

'Still . . .'

'It'll look odd if I'm the only one who doesn't.' Veerle looked at her mother. 'I'm going, *Maman.*' Impulsively, she leaned over and put her arms around Claudine, holding her close for a few moments. 'Don't worry,' she said. But she knew her mother would.

It was still very cold outside. She dressed in warm trousers, boots, a thick jumper. In the stuffy environment of the house she instantly felt overheated, and so excited that she was almost nauseous. It was like being kitted out for some staggering physical feat – sub-aqua diving under arctic ice or wing-walking on a bi-plane; the discomfort and the anticipation were almost more than she could stand. She kept thinking about Kris, thinking about him much more than she had intended to.

At half past eight she went to the bus stop. There was a bus to within a few hundred metres of the address Kris had given her. She was early; it wasn't due for another six minutes. She walked up and down as she waited, hugging herself, trying to look neutral while all the time she was bursting with impatience.

You're building this up too much, she told herself. *You'll see him and it won't be like you think.* But it was. When she got off the bus at the other end and walked the short distance to the agreed address, he was leaning against the wall in that loose-limbed way he had, with the dark hair falling into his eyes and that ironic twist to his lips, and she felt something inside her *jump.* He leaned towards her and she felt a pang of anticipation so sharp that it was like being stabbed, but he simply kissed her on the cheeks, once, twice, as friends do when they greet each other.

'Is this the place?' she said hurriedly, to conceal her disappointment.

'No,' said Kris laconically.

'But this is number hundred and nine,' she said, looking at the number on the gate again to make sure.

'I know. But we've just walked up to it in plain view,' Kris pointed out. 'We're going to number seventeen in the next road, but we don't want anyone to see us doing it.'

Of course. Veerle looked at Kris and thought, *It's real. We're really doing this.* She had that feeling again in the pit of her stomach, excitement so strong that it was almost nauseating, like looking down from a high board and knowing you were going to jump. She thought, *If anyone sees me they'll know what we're going to do.* Her skin was prickling with anticipation; her whole body was fizzing with it. It seemed impossible that anyone could look at her and not see it boiling off her in waves.

They began to walk up the street. There was a corner where the street intersected with another residential road; if they vanished from view here there was an even chance anyone who was looking out of their house would think they had turned the corner. The nearest house was shut up as tight as a bank vault, with all the roller shutters down.

Kris glanced around briefly. The street was deserted. He stepped between the front gates of the shuttered house. Veerle followed him down the drive and into a lane at the back, with invisible access to the rear gardens of the houses.

Two minutes later Veerle was standing on the porch of number 17, watching Kris open the door. Her breath was coming in sharp little gusts that were almost painful.

The porch had a Roman-style pediment supported by white columns. Between the columns were planters containing what appeared to be small trees, the foliage clipped into perfect ovoids. All the shutters were down, even the ones on the narrow windows flanking the door. It gave the house a blank look, as though it were some ancient mausoleum, built on architectural principles but with stone panels replacing the windows.

Veerle expected Kris to pick the lock, though she had no idea how to go about it herself. She was surprised when he felt in his jeans pocket and produced a key.

How did he get that?

She had the sense not to ask the question out loud.

Kris opened the door. Inside it was pitch dark, as expected, but Veerle was horrified to see a red light winking away.

There's an alarm.

Kris didn't seem bothered, although he moved quickly. He drew Veerle inside and closed the door. The light switch had an illuminated panel so it was easy to locate; he turned on the lights and went to the alarm control box. Veerle watched as he entered four digits and pressed a button. There was a moment's silence. Then she heard him exhale.

'They didn't change it,' he said. 'I always think they're going to do that.'

Veerle opened her mouth to ask him how he knew what the number was in the first place, and then she looked around, *really* looked for the first time, and totally forgot what she was about to ask.

My God, she thought. *It's a palace.*

The entire footprint of the house she shared with her mother would fit into the hallway of this one. It was *enormous*, a house for giants, an impression only heightened by the size of the artworks used to decorate it. There was an oil painting so big that Veerle had never seen anything like it outside a gallery, and a marble statue so tall that she had to look up into its face. The sheer vastness of it all made her feel somewhat better about trespassing. It was more like being in a museum or a grand hotel than a home, and the people who lived in such a place seemed as remote as beings from another planet. Veerle couldn't imagine them as real people at all, more like elegantly costumed figures in an elaborate tableau. Nobody could possibly come into a hallway like this one at the end of a long day and throw their bag into the corner, kick off their shoes, relax. She stretched out a hand and touched the statue's arm, feeling the cool marble smooth under her fingers, confirming that it was real.

'Come on,' said Kris. He was already opening another door, one that led further into the house. Veerle followed him through a series of rooms, each more luxurious than the last. She gazed about her, wide-eyed. There was a drawing room with cream leather sofas and heavy green velvet curtains, a dining room with spindle-legged gilded chairs and a vast table polished to a high gloss, the white rose bowl placed in the centre of it dimly visible in reflection, like a ghost of itself. The feeling of unreality grew. Veerle felt as though she were walking through a series of theatrical sets.

Finally they reached a flight of steps leading down to a lower floor. Kris stood back to let Veerle go first. From the cryptic smile he gave her she knew there must be something interesting on the other side of the door at the bottom, but even so she couldn't repress a gasp when she saw what it was.

An indoor pool, a great rectangle of sparkling turquoise, underlit so that the water seemed to glow and wavelets of light danced over the tiled walls and ceiling. The owners had clearly aimed to continue the last-days-of-Pompeii theme suggested by the Roman portico and the statuary in the entrance hall; amongst the towering ferns and potted palms lurked classical statues, white-limbed and elegant. It was wonderfully, tropically warm in spite of the chill outdoors; almost as soon as she was inside the pool room Veerle was uncomfortably hot in her outdoor clothing.

She took off her jacket, and then she took off her boots

because it seemed sacrilegious to wander around the poolside in them. The water was deliciously clear and brilliantly turquoise.

It's fabulous. I have to swim.

Kris was already pulling off his clothes. 'There are costumes in the cupboard,' he told her, nodding at a slatted wooden door. He didn't bother, though; he went into the water in his underclothes. After several moments of hesitation Veerle decided to do the same, stripping off her clothes as quickly as she could, feeling self-conscious. She slid hastily into the water. The temperature was perfect, cool but not cold. She swam a few strokes, luxuriating in it.

Kris ducked underwater and came up shaking his head like a dog to get the hair out of his eyes. He laughed at Veerle's blissful expression. She laughed too, twisting in the water, joyful, feeling free, as though unseen chains had fallen away from her. Tonight, in this stranger's house, she wasn't Veerle De Keyser any more, she was Honingbij, simply Honingbij – no family name, no family ties. A rebel. A rule-breaker.

I can do anything I want.

12

After they had finished swimming, Veerle sat on one of the bar stools in the kitchen, while Kris rewired the two-pin plug on the toaster. Like everything else in the kitchen, the toaster was large, shiny and expensive; it had the kind of sleek rounded styling associated with sports cars.

The stool Veerle was perched on was covered in red leather, to match the gleaming red tiles. The work surfaces were all made of black marble. In a small room the effect would have been claustrophobic, like the inside of the smallest cubicle in Hell, but in a kitchen this size it looked impressive, regal. There was an enormous stainless steel fridge, as big as a pharaonic sarcophagus.

In front of Veerle, on the gleaming table top (black lacquer, to match the marble), was a crystal glass of bessenjenever. Kris had brought the bessenjenever in a flask; the glass belonged to the house and would have to be washed, dried and polished before it was replaced in the cabinet. Veerle picked up the glass and took a sip; the rich sweet taste of berries filled her mouth. She watched Kris working. His head was bent over the plug; all she could see was his tousled dark hair. His hands were long-fingered and deft. *How does he know how to do these things?* she mused. *I've never rewired anything in my life.*

'Kris,' she said.

'Mmm.' He didn't look up.

'Where did you go?'

Now he did look at her, one dark eyebrow raised.

'I mean, did you move away? I haven't seen you since . . . I don't know.' She considered. 'It seems like about ten years.'

'We moved to Overijse when I was ten,' said Kris. He shrugged. 'I had to change schools.'

'Overijse – that's not so far away. Didn't you ever come back? It seems strange that we never met before the castle.'

'Not that strange,' said Kris cryptically.

'Why not?' Veerle was genuinely puzzled.

'Don't you remember?'

'No.'

'Your parents. Well, your mother. She wasn't exactly going to invite me in if I came round.'

She hardly invites anyone in, thought Veerle. She gazed down into the richly tinted bessenjenever, considering. She could remember some of her friends coming over when she was younger and still at the primary school in the village. Sometimes she'd visited them too; she had vague memories of a friend's garden, and her dog, a large friendly Labrador, flopping about on the grass. Then there had been that girl who sometimes came over, the daughter of Claudine's friend Melise. *What was her name? Louise or Lotte or something like that, and I remember she was a couple of years older than me and horribly snotty. She came with her mother and I had to amuse her.*

When had things changed? When did the friends stop coming? It wasn't that Claudine refused to let anyone into the house, it was more that she generated a kind of force field of unspoken disapproval that put people off. Who wanted to come and hang out with Veerle if it meant her mother hovering in the background, shoulders hunched as though labouring under a burden, dropping in the occasional chilly question? When Veerle met up with friends, it was usually somewhere other than the house in Kerkstraat.

'It's not just you,' she told Kris. 'She's funny with everyone.'

'Does she tell everyone she'll kill them if they come anywhere near her daughter ever again?'

'She said *that*?' Veerle was open-mouthed. 'But we were just *kids*.'

'Well, that was the gist of it.' Kris looked at her quizzically. 'You really don't remember?'

'Remember what?'

'Silent Saturday. You know, the day the bells fly to Rome. We went up the bell tower.'

'I can sort of remember that . . . I remember something scared me.' Veerle rubbed her arms uneasily.

'*Something*?' Kris's eyes widened. 'It was Joren Sterckx. It was the day they caught him. We were up in the tower and we saw him coming across the fields.'

Veerle stared. She could feel the first stirrings of apprehension fizzing about inside her, like wasps in a bottle. She couldn't taste the bessenjenever any more; suddenly her mouth was too full of saliva and she had to swallow.

She said, '*Joren Sterckx*? The murderer?'

Kris nodded, his dark eyes serious. 'You went crazy and

started screaming the place down. Mum was cleaning in the church and she heard you and came up. She couldn't get you to stop – you were hysterical.'

'I can't believe this. We saw *Joren Sterckx*?'

'Well, he lived in the village.'

'I know, but . . .' Veerle put down her glass. Her brow furrowed as she struggled to remember. It was no use; she might just as well not have seen Joren Sterckx for all the recollection she had of it. She could remember ascending the bell tower, and she could still recall the overwhelming feeling of terror that had seized her, but when she tried to summon up a memory of the killer himself, it slipped out of her grasp and twisted away into the darkness with the sinuous ease of a fish darting down into the black depths of the sea. The feeling unsettled her; she envisioned her seven-year-old self overshadowed by some savage menace she was completely unaware of.

'It's . . . weird,' she said finally. 'It's like I've seen Dracula or the bogeyman or something and I can't remember.' She shook her head. 'So what happened next?'

'Mum didn't believe us. Well, not at first. She looked out of the window and you couldn't see him any more. He'd gone. And you were still howling. In the end she had to practically carry you downstairs. When we got outside the police had arrived and your mother was already on the doorstep looking for you with a face like thunder. I guess it gave her a fright, their finding a kid dead and her not knowing where you were.'

'And she blamed it on you? She told you to stay away or she'd kill you?'

Kris looked at her for a moment without saying anything. Veerle could read nothing in the level gaze of his dark eyes. Then he said, 'She grabbed you by the arm and she slapped you. Really hard. And Mum got cross, because she never hit us, even though people were always saying it would have done Denis good if he'd had a hiding now and again.'

Veerle's eyes widened. *She hit me. I was afraid, and she hit me.* A hard little knot of something – anger, shock – was forming inside her, a jagged fragment she could choke on. She felt a faint sense of unreality too. *Kris's mother told Mum off for mistreating me?* She looked down, away from Kris, angry with and ashamed for Claudine in equal measure.

Kris went on, 'She told your mother not to hit you, you'd had a fright, and your mother lost it and, well, amongst other things, she said I'd better keep away from you, or . . .'

'She'd kill you.' Veerle grimaced.

Kris shrugged. 'We moved away anyway. That was the year my parents split up, and Mum took us and went to Overijse.'

'It's not so far,' said Veerle. 'You'd think I would have seen you.'

'Maybe you weren't looking.'

No, thought Veerle. *Maybe I wasn't.* So much had happened in the intervening time; those were the things that stood out in the landscape of her memory, like the debris of wrecked ships revealed by low tide. Her own parents' divorce; that couldn't have taken place more than a year or two after the bell-tower incident. Her father moving away, back to Ghent, where he had been born. Claudine's mother, Veerle's grandmother, dying in the hospital in Namur. Veerle's uncle, Claudine's younger brother, had died too, in a car accident. If she had wondered where Kris had gone, what he was doing, the curiosity had faded out somewhere during all that upheaval.

And Claudine, what had those years done to her? Veerle was shocked by what Kris had told her. *She hit me.* The revelation was as raw as the red mark of a slap on her skin. All the same, she began to see that there could be more to it than a simple moment of uncontrolled temper.

Was that it? Was that the moment she started to be afraid? When there was a killer on the streets of our village, one of the worst killers, a child *killer, and she couldn't find her seven-year-old daughter? How long did it go on – the hunting, the calling for me, the sick feeling in the pit of her stomach? How long?*

Veerle had been angry with her mother; now she felt a kind of horrified pity. *Ten minutes, twenty minutes – it doesn't matter,* she thought. *Maybe it's never stopped for her.* She shivered. The idea chilled her, and it didn't really help; she still had no idea how to deal with Claudine's paralysing fears.

She picked up her glass and took a sip of the bessenjenever, savouring the rich sticky sweetness, an antidote to dismal thoughts.

'I looked out for you,' Kris said, interrupting her reverie.

'You did?' It took Veerle a moment to realize what he meant. *After he moved away.*

Kris was nodding. 'We drove through sometimes, and I always looked out.'

Veerle imagined a battered car passing through the village – the Verstraetens had never had anything new or respectable looking – and Kris staring out of the window, looking for her seven-year-old self, a small girl with a pale, serious face and two dark plaits.

'Did you see me?' she asked.

'No.' He was smiling at her.

She looked at him thoughtfully, as though she could sketch the boy he had been – her friend – in the person sitting before her now.

'Do you still live there?' she asked him. 'Overijse, I mean?'

He nodded. 'For now.'

'And what do you do? I mean, when you're not breaking into houses?'

When he told her, she was surprised. 'You're training to be a *gardener?*' Then she thought about it, and wasn't so surprised after all. She couldn't imagine Kris stuck in an office or a bank for five or six days a week for the rest of his life.

'You?' he said.

'School.' She made a face. 'And sometimes the climbing wall. And now, housebreaking.'

She watched Kris as he bent over the plug again, working deftly to reassemble it.

'So how did you get the key to this place?' she asked eventually.

'I know someone.' For a moment Veerle thought that was it, he wasn't going to tell her anything else. But then he said, 'Some places, the old ones, you can get into those without keys and codes. There's a broken window catch or a back door that isn't locked properly. Other places, there's a member of the group who has a key. Anne – she calls herself *Kreeftklu*, Hermit Crab – waters plants for people when they're away. She has keys for about fifteen houses. And there's this Dutch guy Fred knows. He calls himself Egbert, though that's probably not his real name. He's obsessed with lock-picking – used to belong to some lock-picking club in Holland.' Kris shrugged. 'Fred told me they chucked him out because he wasn't content with lock-picking contests. He was breaking into places for the hell of it, and they thought he was going to get them all into trouble, so they told him to get lost.' He had finished screwing the plug back together; he turned it over critically, checking that it was perfect, and then pocketed the screwdriver. 'Egbert does the ones nobody else can do,' he said. 'The ones with modern locks, when we can't get the keys.'

'This house, is it one of Anne's?' asked Veerle.

'No.' Kris shook his head. 'This place is one of mine. I've got a cousin who manages a cleaning company, sending maids into people's houses. He's got all the keys in his office, and all the code numbers stored on his office PC.'

'He gave you the codes?'

'Didn't need to. Jeroen's not exactly the brains of the family. He's great at bossing the girls around, and crap at thinking up passwords.'

Veerle couldn't help laughing at that, and then Kris was grinning too, and as she looked at him she nearly forgot what they were saying. She made a valiant effort to continue.

'I thought you said you didn't do the places you knew yourself? I thought everyone in the group swapped that information, so nobody could trace you?'

'They do.' Kris shrugged again. 'Mostly. There are one or

two places that I keep for myself – like this one. It's too good to pass on to anyone else.'

'Special,' said Veerle. *And he brought* me *here*. The thought made her want to hug herself.

Then she remembered what Hommel had said to her the night they had met. *I hope you know what you're getting yourself into*. To Kris she had said, *Is she the new one?*

When Veerle had met Hommel, the girl had seemed so icy that it was a wonder the air hadn't crackled with frost every time she spoke – but then maybe she had a *reason* to be like that with Kris.

Am I making a fool of myself? Am I the next throwaway girl?

If she really thought that, perhaps the best thing would be to walk away before she got hurt. Say *Thanks, Kris, it was fun, but I'm not going any further*. But she looked at him and she knew she wasn't going to do that.

She thrust all thoughts of Hommel and her insinuating remarks away, like a necromancer dismissing a demon.

I'm not stopping.

13

A week later news came, and it was unwelcome.

Veerle was standing on the corner of the street with her mobile phone clamped to her ear. The snow had mostly gone but nevertheless it was a freezing February evening and there was a sharp wind. It was unpleasant to stand outdoors, but Veerle had no intention of going inside and letting her mother overhear every word of the conversation. Once she turned and glanced at the house on Kerkstraat as though she expected her mother to be peering round the doorway, like a moray eel glaring out of a crevice. There was no sign of Claudine, however; no doubt she was shut up inside with her shoulders in that permanent hunch and her cardigan pulled tightly around her body, as though she could never escape from the chill, indoors or out.

'Valérie Renard,' said Kris's voice in Veerle's ear. 'Valérie Renard was Vlinder.'

Veerle stared at the building on the other side of the road, a dull-looking apartment block. She had a vague memory of a time long past when there had been an ugly space like a missing tooth where that building now stood.

Valérie Renard, she thought. There couldn't be a person in

93

Belgium who hadn't heard that name by now. *The girl in the park – the one they found in the pond.*

'Really?' she said at last. 'I mean, are you sure?'

'Yes.' Veerle heard Kris exhale, as though he were tired. 'Gregory was the one who introduced her. He's been away working, otherwise we'd have known before.'

'Someone else must have known her,' Veerle pointed out, as though she were contradicting Kris, trying to argue that the thing could not have happened. She had never met Vlinder, had only heard her name, but even that tenuous connection made the girl's death more shocking. It made her *real*.

'Fred,' said Kris. 'But he's off somewhere buying up stuff for his gallery. Spain, I think.'

Veerle shivered; the wind was icy. 'It's horrible,' she said.

She was thinking about the messages she had seen on the Koekoeken website, the muted condolences. *RIP Vlinder. Vlinder, we'll miss you.* None of them had mentioned Valérie Renard by name, as though even in death Vlinder's anonymity had to be preserved. And so she had asked Kris, and this was the result.

'Sorry,' said Kris. 'I wasn't going to tell you over the phone.'

'That's OK,' she said automatically. She was still staring at the apartment block, without really taking it in. There was a light on, a rectangle of yellow against the grey exterior wall, and inside you could make out the owner of the flat moving about in the kitchen. Cooking the evening meal, maybe opening a bottle of wine. Life was going on, as it always did. A girl was dead but nothing stopped because of it.

Poor Vlinder. Nobody knew exactly when she had died. Her family would not even have a date to carve into her gravestone.

'Veerle?' said Kris in her ear. 'I have to go. I'll see you tomorrow.'

'I know.'

'Eight-thirty at the tram stop, OK?'

When the call had ended she closed her phone and turned reluctantly towards home. She wished she could have talked to Kris for longer, although she was not sure what she would have said. *I didn't know Vlinder personally, but . . .* Veerle shook her head. *I feel as though I did know her. She wanted adventure too . . . She wasn't afraid to break rules. She was special. And now she's gone.*

She could imagine what Claudine would say if she knew what Valérie Reynard had got up to her in spare time. *Doing dangerous things like that, forbidden things, it's no wonder she ended up dead.*

But Valérie – Vlinder – had been found in a metre of filthy freezing water, not in a deserted house.

It had nothing to do with the Koekoeken, thought Veerle. *Nothing at all.*

14

The next night Veerle had a stroke of luck: Claudine went to visit her friend Melise. She took her time getting ready, fussing over the supper and turning the place upside down looking for a magazine she had promised to lend her friend, and trying to decide which jacket to wear. She seemed so reluctant to actually leave Veerle alone that Veerle began to be afraid that she would suggest they both went, saying, *You can come along and amuse Lotte* – or Louise, or whatever her name was – as though they were two small girls again.

In the end Claudine departed, and as soon as Veerle was sure that she had really gone and was not coming back for anything, she began to get ready to go out herself. She was not sure how long she would be out, and if she got home later than Claudine it would inevitably mean a scene of some kind, but she would deal with that if it came to it. At least she could escape from the house without Claudine clinging onto her like a drag anchor, wanting to know whom she was meeting and exactly when she would be back.

You know, she thought as she stood in front of the hall mirror zipping up her jacket, *you're going to have to tell her about Kris sooner or later. Kris – the boy she said she'd kill if he ever came near you again. Even if that was ten years ago.* She made a face at herself. *Later, then.*

A couple of minutes after that she was stepping out into the darkness, her breath visible in the chill evening air. She pulled the door shut behind her with a sense of relief, and hurried to the bus stop. She couldn't help glancing up at the dark bulk of the Sint-Pauluskerk as she passed. Most evenings there was a light burning in the vestibule, illuminating the little stained-glass window above the main door so that it shone out like a single kaleidoscopic eye. Tonight, however, the old church was shrouded in darkness.

Silent Saturday, thought Veerle. Even though any precise recollection of that day was elusive, contemplating the bell tower still gave her a feeling of unease. It was not just the knowledge that she had seen Joren Sterckx with her own eyes, thus playing an infinitesimally minor role in the darkest day her village had ever known; it was the image that kept unfurling in her mind: a terrified seven-year-old child, her screams of fright cut off with a slap that sounded like the flat retort of a gunshot. There was just no getting away from it: *I was scared half out of my wits, and she hit me.* When she looked at it like that, she didn't feel so bad about keeping Kris a secret.

She was still thinking about this when the bus reached the tram stop at the edge of Tervuren. Kris was waiting on the platform; anyone who saw him greet her would think they were just another young couple on their way into Brussels for the evening. *A romantic evening out*, thought Veerle, and suddenly Claudine was forgotten. She almost laughed aloud. *A romantic evening of housebreaking.*

She was still smiling at that when she came up to Kris, so

when he leaned over and kissed her almost casually on the mouth she was taken by surprise. Then they were walking away from the tram stop at a brisk pace, ducking between the trees that separated the platform from the street behind it, and she put her fingertips to her lips in the dark as though she could capture the brief pressure of Kris's kiss on them.

She glanced at him but he wasn't looking at her; he was scanning the street, his aquiline profile silhouetted against the amber light of the streetlamps. It was a very long street, dead straight and broad, and laid with carefully maintained cobbles. It was also very well-lit, so that there was little possibility of them melting into the welcome darkness. One side of the street was lined with trees that screened the tram line from the road, but on the other side stood a series of expensive-looking villas, their balconies and gables and turrets defended by high gated walls and hedges.

The street was deserted; perhaps a hundred metres away Veerle saw the sleek black shape of a cat flit across the cobbled road and disappear into the shadows under the trees, but otherwise everything was still. Kris touched her arm and they began to move down the street.

Veerle's heart was thumping. She wanted very badly to keep looking around, to see whether anyone was watching them. She imagined a face at an upper window of one of the splendid villas, or a security camera whirring and clicking as it followed their motion. *Don't turn round. It looks suspicious.* She put her head down, increasing her pace to keep up with Kris's long legs. *You haven't done anything wrong, remember?* Her lips twisted. *Not yet, anyway.*

She could not remember ever walking along this street

before, in spite of the fact that it lay a few metres off her bus route to high school. There was no reason to come here, not unless you owned one of those enormous houses; there were no shops or restaurants in this part of the town. You could have gated off the whole area, grown a ten-metre thicket of thorn bushes around it like the castle where *Doornroosje*, the Sleeping Beauty, dreamed away a century, and most of the population would have no cause to notice.

They came to the end of the road and turned right, up another street that ran off at an acute angle. Far ahead, a gleaming car slid almost soundlessly across an intersection and disappeared down another street.

'Here,' said Kris briefly, and they turned a corner. Now they found themselves skirting a high wall of white stucco capped with black tiles. Close to the wall was a great beech tree, its bare branches and twigs a roadmap against the yellow glare of the streetlamps; when they were safely in its shadow, Kris stopped and laid a hand on the wall.

'In here,' he said. 'There's a gate further up we can get over, but we have to be quick, OK? That's the riskiest bit. Once we're on the other side, nobody's going to see us.'

Veerle stared up at the wall, assessing it. She supposed it was perhaps two and a half metres high. She glanced at the beech tree too, but there was no hope of using that; if there had been any lower branches they had been sawn off. *The gate, then.*

'OK,' she said, and before Kris had time to react she was off, cutting gracefully along the side of the wall, keeping as close to it as she could. When she reached the gate she could have laughed out loud.

Easy. The most ill-coordinated beginner could have scaled it. Compared to the small, narrow and sloping holds on the climbing wall, the iron gate with its decorative curls and flourishes was as straightforward as a ladder. She was only slightly hampered by wearing outdoor boots. She placed the toe of the right one on what looked like a metal ivy leaf and then she was moving swiftly upwards with the speed and fluidity of a lizard darting up a wall.

When she got to the top, she couldn't resist it: she swung herself up onto the top of the wall and then straightened, balancing at her full height on the black tiles. She allowed herself the indulgence of a satisfying glance at Kris's astonished face, but that was all; no point in remaining in such an exposed position for longer than necessary. Then she moved quickly back to the gate and climbed down the other side.

She was waiting in the lee of the wall when Kris came over the gate, dropping carefully onto the gravelled drive. He opened his mouth to say something and then shut it again.

'That was fun,' said Veerle, delighted. She was filled with a joyous excitement that made her want to run whooping through the enormous gardens. Instead she began to follow the gravelled drive, running lightly along the strip of grass at the side to minimize the sound of her steps. The drive curved sharply through a screen of towering shrubs and then suddenly the house was in view.

'Wow.' Veerle stopped in her tracks, and for a moment she was almost unaware of Kris at her shoulder. The last house had been big, but this one was simply jaw-droppingly huge. Even now, at night, when the only illumination came from the moon and the streetlamps beyond the walls, you could see how staggeringly sprawling the house was; how every aspect of it had been designed to impress, from the colonnade that ran the length of the ground floor to the rounded turret that lent the building a distinctly manorial air. As if this were not impressive enough, there was a kidney-shaped ornamental lake in front, the waters sparkling black like hematite, and in it the dark bulk of the house was reflected, as stately as the Taj Mahal.

So fabulous was it that Veerle felt a little of her confidence drain away. *A place like that can't possibly be left empty and undefended. It has to be bristling with alarms and security lights.* Indeed, she could make out the red wink that meant an armed burglar alarm.

'This is insane,' she said under her breath.

'No, it's not,' said Kris's voice in her ear. She felt him touch her shoulder. 'It just needs a little care. Look, it's one of Jeroen's places. I've got the keys, and the alarm code. We just need to make sure we get in without setting off all the lights.'

Veerle gazed at the house. 'What happens if we set them off?'

'Maybe nothing,' said Kris. 'Maybe no one sees them, or maybe they think there's a fox in the garden or something. But it's best not to. There are about a dozen lights on that place, big ones. Believe me, if they go on, the place is going to be lit up like Zaventem airport.'

Veerle heard his breath coming in rapid gusts. *He's as hyped up as I am,* she thought.

'How do we avoid them?' she whispered.

'We go to the side of the house, there,' said Kris, pointing.

'There's only one window on that wall, and it's on the second floor, so they didn't bother mounting lights there. Then we keep really, really close to the wall when we go round the front. Theoretically we'd set the sensors off but the one to the right of the door is on the blink. It goes off if you walk along the front of the lake but it doesn't pick up anything close to the wall.'

'How do you know *that*?'

'How do you think? By setting it off. The first time I spent half an hour hiding under a laurel bush, thinking the police were going to turn up.' Veerle felt rather than saw him shrug. 'Nothing happened, though. Maybe they have a lot of false alarms. Cats, or night birds. Who knows? But we should try not to set the lights off, just in case.'

'OK.' Veerle tried to inject as much confidence as possible into her voice. All the same, when they started towards the side of the house she was conscious of her own pulse racing and her breath sawing in and out. They crossed the gravel and as they raced over the grass, aiming for the side wall, she was half wincing, expecting the lights to dazzle her at any moment. The moment never came; safely in the lee of the house where the darkness was at its most impenetrable, she felt paving stones under her feet and then her fingers touched the rough texture of the house wall. She could hear Kris moving beside her, and then he brushed past.

'Come on.'

At the corner of the house they paused.

'Stay very close to the wall,' Kris reminded her. A second later, he had started for the door.

Veerle put her back to the wall and moved crab-wise along

the front of the house, her boots whispering across the paving stones. She counted her footsteps, trying to judge how far she had come, how far she still had to go. She tried not to think about the lights going on. *We made it this far. They're not going to go on.* But still she kept imagining them bursting into brilliant life, revealing Kris and herself flattened against the façade of the house like two sideways-on figures in an Egyptian temple carving. *Twenty-nine, thirty* . . . A few steps further and she stumbled over a low step. They had reached the door.

Panting like a racehorse, she stood on the step and listened to the clink and rattle as Kris pulled the house keys out of his pocket and fitted them into the lock. Then the door was opening, and she almost fell into the house after him. The moment the door had closed behind them Kris hit a switch on the wall.

'Let there be light,' he said ironically, and there was.

15

The sudden brightness was dazzling. It made Veerle screw up her eyes. Whoever had decorated this house was into light, lots of it; it was like being on an operating table. Her ears were filled with a high-pitched beeping. Dimly she was aware of Kris brushing past, aiming for the burglar-alarm control panel. It was a relief when the sound stopped, cut off mid-note like a mezzo soprano surprised by a slap in the face.

When Veerle's eyes had adjusted she looked around. The last house had reminded her of a museum, with its classical statuary and enormous oil paintings. This one looked like something out of a glossy interior design magazine. The lobby was huge, and the vast expanses of wall were painted in a shade of raspberry, the kind of colour people chose to show off the fact that their house was big enough to take it; in a small place it would have been stifling. The paintwork was picked out in white and there was a large gilded console table against the far wall, with a huge gold-framed mirror hanging over it. It was the sort of thing Marie-Antoinette would have chosen, had she been propelled forward in time to the twenty-first century. She could see Kris reflected in it, his back to her as he closed the control panel. His reflection turned and grinned at her.

'What do you think?'

'Nice,' she managed to say, and then both of them were laughing at the understatement.

Kris went to each of the large windows that flanked the door, and examined the roller shutters. When he was satisfied that they were tightly closed and that no chink of light could escape and reveal their presence in the house, he came over to Veerle and took her hand.

'Come on,' he said.

He began to pull her to the left, towards the gleaming white-painted staircase that curved round to the upper storey. This was something new; in neither of the other houses had they ever gone upstairs.

Veerle put out her other hand and touched the handrail. It was perfectly, silkily smooth – as flawless as everything else in this modern palace. She put her foot onto the bottom stair, gazing upwards.

I feel like we're trespassing. And yet it was the same as at the last house; it was impossible to take this place seriously as someone's home. It looked as though it had been created for a photo shoot or a film in which all the characters were incredibly wealthy people – men with commanding expressions and a patrician touch of grey at the temples, stick-thin women in taffeta dresses and diamonds. She let Kris lead her up the stairs, trailing her hand along the rail.

The first-floor landing was covered with a carpet whose pile was so deep that Veerle imagined it would be like wading through grass. She stood on the top step and removed her boots; trampling across that expanse of velvety cream would feel like sacrilege, not to mention the difficulty of removing the tiniest speck of mud.

The first room they passed was a bathroom decorated in black, white and gold, with a large free-standing ceramic bathtub in the centre of the room. Veerle wanted to stop and stare at it, at the gold fittings and the gleaming tiles and the huge glass chemist's jars full of bath crystals, but Kris pulled her onwards.

The room he took her to was not a bathroom or a bedroom but a dressing room. Veerle had thought that she was getting over her astonishment at the way people lived in this type of house, but now she was stunned all over again. Whoever owned the adjoining bedroom had a walk-in wardrobe bigger than her own room at home. The doors were mirrored, and seeing herself standing there with her stockinged feet on the luxurious carpet, she thought that she looked like what she was, a housebreaker. She didn't fit. She looked like an urchin, the survivor at the end of a disaster movie, who has stumbled back into civilization, grubby and unkempt.

Kris didn't waste time looking at himself in the mirrors. He slid open the nearest door. '*Voilà*,' he said ironically.

There was a row of outfits hanging there, most of them in protective clear plastic wrappers; the owner evidently didn't bother with anything as pedestrian as washing and ironing the contents – simply sent them all out for cleaning. Through the plastic Veerle could see that most of them were dresses: day dresses, cocktail dresses, evening gowns in a range of jewel-bright colours accented with gold embroidery or beadwork. Veerle lifted one of them out and gently pulled up the plastic cover. It was an evening dress made of heavy raw silk the colour of garnets, with a fitted waist and thin straps designed to leave the shoulders bare. Veerle had never touched such an expensive piece of clothing in her life, let alone worn one. She glanced at Kris.

'You mean, *put it on?*'

He shrugged. 'Why not?'

Because it's not mine, she could have said, but she didn't. There was still a sense of unreality about the house and its contents. Besides, the dress was so beautiful, the cloth almost seeming to glow, that she couldn't resist the temptation. She began to unzip her jacket.

Kris wandered out of the room. 'See you downstairs,' he said laconically.

Fifteen minutes later, when Veerle came down the curving staircase, carefully holding up the hem of the red dress, he was waiting for her at the bottom. She gasped, and then she began to laugh. Kris made her an ironic bow. Evidently he had located the wardrobe of the man of the house; he was kitted out in evening dress, including a black bow tie. Somehow the formal wear just made him look more disreputable than usual. With his sharp features and tousled dark hair, he looked more like a jewel thief than a count or a diplomat. The evening clothes suited him though; they showed off his lean build and broad shoulders.

As Veerle descended the staircase she couldn't take her eyes off him.

She had found shoes to match the garnet-coloured dress, and by some miracle they were her size, though she still wondered how anyone could bear to wear them for a whole evening: the heels were almost unmanageably high and the toes pointed and narrow. She hadn't been able to do very much with her hair, simply twisted it into a knot and secured it with a clip, but she had completed the outfit with a sparkling necklace and matching earrings. Veerle was no expert regarding jewellery but she thought the stones were real diamonds.

Kris offered her his arm. Veerle had to bite her lip to stifle another laugh but she took it. They proceeded through white-painted double doors into the drawing room, which was painted leaf green; clearly the decorator was a fan of strong colours. The electric lights were low and Veerle was surprised to see that there were flames leaping in the grate, before realizing that it was a modern gas fire, turned on or off at the touch of a button. Two big green leather sofas faced each other across a large square coffee table made of antique wood. On the coffee table stood a bottle of champagne and two crystal glasses.

'Champagne?' Veerle let go of Kris's arm and went to take a closer look. 'You didn't bring that.'

Kris came over and picked up the bottle. 'There are seventy-two more bottles like this in the cellar. They won't miss one.'

'I thought we weren't supposed to take anything.'

Kris was already removing the foil over the cork, un-twisting the wire. 'You think they're going to notice?' he said. When she didn't reply he shot her a quizzical look. 'I can come back tomorrow and replace it if it really bothers you,' he said.

Veerle turned away, on the pretext of admiring the opulent décor. She was not sure what to think. *This is new. We didn't just come in here to look around and do some small job in return.* She glanced down at herself. She was dressed in the lady of the house's evening dress, wearing diamonds that didn't belong to her, preparing to drink pilfered champagne.

So what? said a voice at the back of her mind. *Look at this place. Do you really think anyone who lives in a house like this is going to notice a single bottle of wine missing from over seventy bottles? Anyway, why should one family have all this? Whatever the owners do, whether the head of the house is a diplomat or a business magnate or a general, nobody needs this much all for themselves – this much space, this much gilding, all those clothes, the wine . . .*

There was a soft popping sound as the cork came out of the bottle.

Seventy-two bottles, thought Veerle. She turned, the silk dress rustling as she did so, and watched Kris filling the two crystal glasses. Again she had that feeling of unreality. *Who lives in a house like this, with black-and-gold bathrooms and walk-in dressing rooms full of ball gowns and a cellar full of champagne? It's a dream,* she thought, *and you can't steal from a dream.*

She took the glass Kris offered her.

'*Santé,*' he said with a grin.

Veerle sipped the champagne. It was cool and very dry. She looked at Kris over the rim of the glass, at his sharp features, his bold eyes, his rumpled dark hair. There always seemed to be the hint of a dry smile hovering about his lips.

She recalled the brief pressure of those lips on hers and felt a flare of heat in her face. She knew she wanted him to do it again; she knew he *was* going to do it again. Whether it was a good idea or not – that was another matter entirely.

She recalled Hommel's cold resentful face, Claudine's faded anxious one: signposts with BEWARE written on them. There was danger here or, if not actual danger, risk, as though she had been contemplating a climb whose upper reaches she could not see from ground level. There might be a fabulous view from up there, but equally you might be heading for a fall, the sort where they had to collect the pieces in a basket.

All the same, when Kris's dark eyes met hers, she didn't look away. As he stepped towards her she put down her glass of champagne and her heart was thumping. *Last chance to walk away.* She didn't take it, of course; Veerle never backed off a challenge.

16

The heavy gilded clock on the mantelpiece chimed eleven. Veerle was curled up on one of the green leather sofas, leaning against Kris. He had his arm around her; his hand felt warm on the bare skin of her arm. Music drifted through the air from the house's expensive sound system, a tumbling cascade of rich soft notes.

Veerle could feel the effects of the champagne and the soporific dancing of the flames in the hearth. She was happy and rather drowsy. *I could stay here for ever*, she thought dreamily. *It's perfect. Perfectly, perfectly . . . perfect.*

All the same, the sound of the clock chiming roused her. She was hardly aware at first of counting the strokes: . . . *nine, ten, eleven . . .*

Eleven o'clock? Oh God. She sat up.

'Oh no,' she said aloud, looking down at the garnet-coloured dress, at the creased silk.

'Don't worry,' said Kris lazily. He seemed entirely unperturbed. 'We can iron it. I'll have to do the shirt anyway.'

'It's eleven o'clock,' said Veerle. 'The last bus is in forty minutes.'

He shrugged. 'Let's stay the night.'

111

She gaped at him. 'Kris . . . I can't.'

'Why not? We can leave before it gets light. If we went at seven it would still be dark enough.'

'It's not that.'

'Stay then.' He put his arms around her.

Veerle bit her lip. She didn't want to say, *It's my mother*. It sounded childish. On the other hand, she knew perfectly well what would happen if she didn't get home soon. *She'll panic, never mind the fact that I left her a note. Supposing she calls the police or something?*

Considering where she and Kris were, at this moment she couldn't imagine how she would deal with *that*.

That wasn't the only thing, of course. Even if there had been no Claudine waiting for her at home, would she have done it? *It's too soon*, she thought, and then, *Maybe he really just means: stay over here. A room each. But—*

'I really can't.'

He didn't ask her why again like she thought he would. Her hair had come down; he pushed it back from her face with both hands and then he began to kiss her again, on the sensitive spot close to her jaw line.

'Kris . . .'

Suddenly it was so sensitive that it was ticklish. She pushed him away, but they were both laughing now, and the awkwardness had passed.

'I'll walk you to the bus stop,' Kris told her. 'I can come back and fix things up here.'

'How will you get home?'

'Maybe I'll stay over,' he said. He raised one dark eyebrow but he didn't press her.

* * *

Veerle went back upstairs to change into her street clothes. The dressing room adjoined an enormous bedroom with a king-sized bed in it, so she laid the red dress out on that. Against the crisp ivory Egyptian cotton of the bed linen the garnet-coloured silk stood out like a bloodstain. Veerle glanced at it as she pulled on her jeans, wondering whether Kris would really manage to make it look as good as new. It looked sadly crumpled to her eyes.

The party's over, she thought. The relaxed dreamy mood she had enjoyed downstairs in front of the leaping flames on the hearth had given way to a nervous restlessness. *Got to get ready, got to get moving.* She was acutely aware of the hard smooth lump that was her mobile phone in the front pocket of her jeans. She was almost afraid to switch it on.

She pulled her T-shirt over her head. *Going to have to run for the bus.* If she missed it – well, she didn't want to think about that. She shrugged on her outside jacket as she ran down the glossy white staircase.

Kris was waiting near the bottom. He had changed back into his black jeans and leather jacket; his lean silhouette stood out like a charcoal sketch against the dazzling white paintwork. Veerle would have liked to run into his arms, but she didn't trust herself; if she was going to make the bus they had to get moving.

Kris killed the light, and then they slipped out of the front door and ran back the way they had come in, dodging the security light sensors. When they reached the gate, Kris scanned the road for prying eyes, but it was deserted. They climbed over and dropped onto the pavement on the other side.

Safe, thought Veerle. *If anyone sees us now, so what?*

She dusted her hands on her jeans, and then they set off along the street. Veerle was as acutely aware of the phone in her pocket as if it had been red-hot, but still she did not dare to drag it out and switch it on.

I'll do it when I'm on the bus, she told herself. She shivered a little in the chill night air in spite of the rapid pace. *If she asks me who I'm with I can truthfully say nobody.*

When they got to the bus stop, Veerle glanced up the street and saw that the bus was already in sight in the distance.

'Three minutes early,' she said. *And if we'd been any later I would have missed it.* Best not to think about that.

Just before the bus pulled in, Kris leaned over and kissed Veerle briefly on the lips. 'I'll phone you, OK?'

Then she was climbing onto the bus, into its warm, well-lit interior, and when she turned to wave he had already melted away into the shadows.

She slid into a window seat, feeling in her pocket for her mobile phone. Before she switched it on, she held it in her hands for a few moments, trying to relish the evening with Kris for a few seconds more before the feeling slipped away from her like a dream on waking.

I won't believe it tomorrow, she thought. She remembered coming down the flawless white staircase, and seeing Kris standing at the bottom of it, dressed as though for a night at the opera. She had laughed, but she had liked the sight of him all the same, the way the expensive formal clothes suited his lean frame and saturnine good looks. Her fingers strayed to her neck, touching her now bare ear lobe. *I wore diamonds.*

Even while the threat of Claudine's inevitable outburst

hung over her like the bruise-dark clouds of an oncoming storm, she wanted to linger in that fabulous dream. *Where will we go next time?* She smiled into the darkness. *A fitness fiend's house with a sauna and a jacuzzi as well as a pool. Or an aristocrat's town house, full of gilded furniture and paintings of stern ancestors in oils glaring down at us.* Then she thought, *Anywhere, so long as it's with him,* and she could have laughed out loud for joy. Even the prospect of facing Claudine no longer seemed so daunting. Veerle switched on the phone.

23 missed calls.

Instantly that intoxicating feeling of excitement was gone, as thoroughly as if someone had thrown a bucket of icy water over her. For several seconds Veerle simply sat and stared at the screen with its ominous message as a chill feeling of dismay washed through her.

23 missed calls.

She touched the screen, scrolling through each of the messages in turn as the bus tunnelled through the night, but she didn't need to read the details of each one to guess that they were all from Claudine.

I left her a note, Veerle thought desperately, but she knew that that was about as much use as putting a sticking plaster over the stump of a severed limb.

When the phone rang, she was so startled that she almost dropped it. She didn't have to look at the display to know who it was.

The driver of the 830 bus heard the phone ring too. The rumble of the bus drowned out most actual conversation, but you could always hear mobile phones ringing; the pitch and timbre seemed designed to be as irritatingly obtrusive as possible, the electronic equivalent of very vocal nagging. There was only one passenger on the bus: the pale, dark-haired girl in the window seat. He heard her say something into the phone.

Half a minute later something came hurtling down the aisle of the bus and clattered into the barrier at the front. Instinctively the driver braked, peering down at the projectile. *A mobile phone. That girl.* With a rising sense of indignation he slowed the bus almost to a stop and turned in his seat to give the girl an earful. Then he saw the expression on her face, and in spite of his annoyance he held his tongue.

17

De Jager stood in the February cold and dark, in the darker shadow of a tree, and studied the front of the house. The tree was too tall, too overgrown; it should have been cut back, or perhaps cut down altogether – it overshadowed the left side of the house. For De Jager, however, its presence was ideal; it provided him with cover, and it helped to screen the portico from the street. Not that anyone walked down this road; everyone drove, in sleek expensive cars, engineered to such a peak of perfection that they were almost soundless. Most didn't even get out to open their gates; they were remote-controlled. De Jager had had to take care when he arrived on foot; if he had been seen, he would have been far too notice-able, a peasant strolling along on his own two feet.

De Jager had not come to hunt. He knew that the house was going to be empty for two weeks and he was not expect-ing anyone to visit it tonight. He had come to assess the territory, to gauge how best the hunt might be carried out. He had the code to the burglar alarm, but he didn't have a key, so he had two options. He could try to find some way into the house without a key – a window that might be opened with a little effort, or a door that was not very secure. Once, he had got into a house by slipping under the unsecured garage door and then through a connecting door to the house that someone had forgotten to lock. People were remarkably stupid about home security, he had discovered. Of course, it might be that the owners of this house had checked and locked every door and window before they left, that there were no broken window catches or other weak points. Then he would have to fall back on his other option, which was to let the target open the door, and then make his move before they were able to get inside and close it.

He preferred the first option. There was considerable pleasure to be had in the anticipation, the waiting in the darkened recesses of the house. Hearing them enter it, thinking that they were alone. It was less risky too. If he tried to force his way into the house alongside his prey, there was bound to be a struggle. Things might get broken – things that would be missed if he simply took them with him. It could be messy, requiring hours of meticulous cleaning. Far better to be waiting for them inside the house, to take them unawares.

This place would present a challenge, he could see that. It was not the sort of house whose owners left it unsecured. Every visible front window was shuttered. He meant to go and look at the back of the house, but he lingered in the black shadows under the tree for a moment, contemplating the building, imprinting it on his mind.

Those few moments of delay were significant; the ripples that spread from them travelled far further than he could ever have imagined, like an earth tremor with him at its epicentre. If he had stepped out from under the tree he might have been visible at the moment when she walked up to the house. He could so easily have done so; he barely heard her coming because she was wearing those boots on her feet, the sheepskin ones that all the young women of her age were wearing at the moment, flat and soft. No heels to click on the tiled pathway.

She was about eighteen, fairly tall and slim – you could see that she was slender in spite of the padded jacket she was wearing and the long scarf wound around her neck. She had light hair – blonde or light brown; it was hard to tell because of the yellowing effect of the streetlights – done up in a sort of sloppy ponytail, half up and half down, casually chic, and long silvery earrings of some ethnic design which swung backwards and forwards as she moved. She was pretty in a spoiled sort of way – slightly round face, pouting lips, and a way of holding her chin up that implied that she knew every-one was looking at her but she simply couldn't be bothered with it, with the attention. She had a bag over her shoulder, a voluminous leather bag, and she was fumbling with it as she strode up to the house, probably trying to get a key out.

De Jager watched her in silence from the black heart of the shadows. He was amazed and impressed by her insouciance, arriving on foot, marching up to the deserted house in the dark as though she owned it. She never looked behind her once, never checked to see if anyone was looking. She didn't even try to stick to the shadows, instead moving boldly through the yellow light cast by the streetlamps.

He did consider melting away into the night, leaving her to whatever she planned to do. He was not prepared, after all; he didn't have any of his usual tools with him, and the car was parked two streets away. Fetching it would mean leaving the house and returning again, all of which was risky. He knew from experience what could come of impulsive, unplanned action. It led to mess, it led to discovery, it led to being away for a very long time indeed.

He could just let her go inside, and then he could leave. No harm done.

He hesitated, though. If she was here now, it wasn't likely she would come again. It was now or never, prepared or not.

He took a step forward, still turning the matter over in his mind. In that instant she slid the key into the lock, and as she did so she glanced behind her, and now in the jaundiced light of the streetlamps she saw him. Her eyes widened.

De Jager flew at her with the savage speed of a falcon diving for its prey. He collided with her with such force that it carried them right inside the house. They landed on the hard floor of the hallway with De Jager on top of the girl. There was no time for finesse. He grasped the ends of the scarf wound around her throat and pulled it tight, choking her. She realized what he was trying to do, and in spite of her shock she began to fight him, bucking and kicking.

De Jager did not panic. He was confident that he could overcome her, but at the same time he was aware of the open door and the persistent beeping of the alarm system. If he did not tackle them, in a minute or so the alarm would be alerting the entire neighbourhood and he would be in full view of the open doorway.

He made a decision. He gave a truly savage yank on the scarf in the hopes of subduing the girl, and then he got up to deal with the door and the alarm. He closed the door first, then struck the illuminated light switch with the heel of his hand, drenching the hallway with light so that he could locate the alarm control box. He was punching in the code when he heard a sound behind him and realized that the girl had staggered to her feet and was trying to escape.

Verdomme, he thought. It was all going wrong. Now he began to feel real anger. The actual hunt – that brought him a strange pleasure but it had nothing to do with any emotions towards the prey. It never had. His hands never shook when he took a life. But this girl – she was messing the whole thing up. If he wasn't careful she was going to break something or leave traces he couldn't remove if he cleaned all night. He went after her.

She heard him coming and panicked – that was the only explanation. She ran into the kitchen, which was exactly where he would have driven her if he had had the choice. She didn't think to go for the knife block or a rolling pin, though. She made for the back door, which was stupid, because it was locked, and anyway, it led into the back garden, which was almost certainly pitch dark and fenced in. The kitchen was large and decorated chiefly in shades of green and blue, which was good because white was a pain to clean up; but there was a large free-standing unit in the middle of it, which was bad because it gave the girl something to hide behind. She was huddled by the back door, struggling with the lock; De Jager suspected that in her panic she had actually bent the key.

She was crying with fear, babbling, and although he had no real interest in whatever limp defence she was trying to put up for herself he registered that she was speaking English. Not Flemish, nor French. He had some inkling then that she was not who he had thought she was, but it was too late. She had seen his face quite clearly.

After he had dealt with her, and the house was silent again apart from the sound of his rapid breathing, he paused for a moment. De Jager had the sense of being watched, although there was nothing to hear, nothing to see. He raised his head and scanned the kitchen. Most of the windows were tightly shuttered; there was only one circular window, too small to be a break-in risk, that was uncovered. He gazed at it, at the reflective blackness of the panes throwing back a splintered likeness of his own face. At last he went right up to the glass and stared out into the dark. Nothing.

He stood there for a few minutes, and when he was satisfied that there was nobody there, he turned away, dismissing the thought from his mind. He had work to do.

18

If the driver of the number 44 tram had bothered to take a close look at the slim, dark-haired girl who climbed aboard at the terminus, he might have been taken aback at her stormy expression, at the glittering in her eyes that threatened tears. But the driver was preoccupied with thoughts of his own; he glanced back once at the girl to make sure she punched her ticket – *Bloody students*, he thought, *always trying to get a free ride* – and then went back to staring morosely out of the front window.

Veerle sat down with her back to the driver. There were few other passengers on the tram, for which she was grateful. There had been a titanic scene with Claudine before she left; only the danger of being late for her meet-up with Kris had forced Veerle to be brutal and leave in spite of her mother's protests.

I'm never going to be able to keep her happy, she thought dismally. *Not unless I stay home all the time, never go anywhere.* She leaned her head against the window of the tram and closed her eyes. *It's just turning into her-or-me.*

That was just it: trying to carry on with her own life and reason with Claudine was like trying to swim while carrying a lump of lead; you had to let it go or drown. When she'd slammed the door on her way out of the house she'd felt a pang of guilt so sharp that it was like a physical injury, and yet she knew it was necessary, like the pain of an operation. All the same, she had spent the bus journey from the village fighting back tears. Veerle hated crying.

The tram lurched reluctantly into life and began to rattle through the darkened woods. Veerle gazed out into the darkness and thought, *Should I try to contact Dad?* She bit her lip. *I just don't see what he can do. She hates him so much, I can't imagine her listening to anything he suggests.*

Ce salaud de Gand, that was what Claudine called him; that bastard from Ghent. She didn't even call him *Geert* or *your father*. There was no way she was going to let her ex-husband interfere in her life. But Veerle herself felt out of her depth; she couldn't begin to work out how to deal with her mother.

The tram crossed the big road intersection at Quatre-Bras and plunged back into the woods again. After a stretch of darkness, lights became visible, twinkling through the screen of trees. Veerle rang the bell and the tram began to slow. It drifted past the two greenish metal statues that faced each other across the road, and came to a halt at Oudergem Woud. There was nothing here, no reason to alight during the hours of darkness; in daytime people stopped here to go walking in the woods, but now it was so dark that you couldn't have seen your hand in front of your face in there. She and Kris would have to walk the rest of the way. There was a stop much closer to their destination, but Kris didn't want to risk someone noticing them getting off there.

The tram was rattling and swaying away from her, the comfort of its lights receding, before she saw Kris. He was standing under one of the chestnut trees that lined the grassy island in the centre of Tervurenlaan, almost invisible in the shadows, but when he spotted her he began to amble forward with easy grace.

Hastily Veerle wiped under her eyes with her fingertips. She felt an impulse to run over, fling her arms around him and let the events of the whole horrible evening pour out of her in a passionate torrent.

Don't, she told herself. *Don't let her ruin it.* She looked at Kris and she was aware of the blood singing in her veins and the breath shivering in and out of her mouth like the silvery movement of the breeze through the naked trees. It was not just that he was good-looking in a sharp-featured, saturnine way – good-looking enough to make her stomach do a lazy roll every time she saw him. He seemed *rare*, improbable, a creature with no place in the monotony that was everyday life. She might as well have glimpsed a unicorn disappearing round the corner of a concrete underpass or found a glowing phoenix feather discarded on a city pavement. She couldn't imagine doing ordinary things with him – going to the cinema in Leuven or hanging out in the pizzeria in Tervuren. She'd never even seen the place where he lived. She didn't *believe* in it. Kris might have been a visitor from another dimension altogether; he hacked through physical obstacles and rules alike with the abandon of an adventurer carving his way through thick jungle undergrowth with a machete. When they stepped into whatever adventure he had planned for the evening, she was determined not to take Claudine with her. She walked to meet Kris, and when she turned her face up to his her eyes were dry.

Kris put an arm around her and they began to walk down the middle of the grass, where the shadows of the trees were deepest. Where the woods ended, the road opened out into a boulevard lined with villas that bordered on the frankly palatial. Some of them were foreign embassies, with security gates and national flags. Veerle didn't think that even Kris had the brazenness to break into one of *those*.

They followed the road until they came to a left turn.

'That's the street,' said Kris in a low voice as they strolled past it. Veerle knew the routine now; she didn't expect him to walk boldly up it. He led her another twenty metres further, to a smaller turning. A glance behind them to make sure there was no one watching, and then they were walking down a narrow path between high laurel hedges. Some of the houses, including the house they were aiming for, had security fences at the back. They cut through the garden of the house next door, which was less well defended, and then squeezed through the tall shrubs that marked the boundary between the two properties.

In the yellow light from the streetlamps Veerle had her first clear view of the house they were planning to enter. It took her breath away. *It's huge*, she thought. Three storeys of white-walled elegance, with contrasting dark roof and gable tiles of such a high sheen that even in the murk of night they gleamed like gunmetal. Veerle's gaze took in the high windows, the glossy front door, the balcony that ran round part of the first floor, but mostly the sheer extravagant *size* of it. Her pulse began to race at the thought of what they planned to do, the outrageous idea of actually entering this palace and exploring it. Owning it, if only for an hour or two.

The other side of the house was partly shaded by a tall tree, but the route to the front door was less protected. Kris moved swiftly and silently across the lawn, minimizing his exposure to the streetlights. When Veerle caught up he was already standing in front of the door, the key in his hand. It was a couple of centimetres from the lock when he froze.

Veerle waited for him to unlock the door, but still he stood there, his body tense, the key held a finger's span from the lock. She was on the point of saying something when he grasped her wrist and pulled her towards the concealing shadow of the tree.

'What's going on?' whispered Veerle, and then she felt Kris's finger lightly touch her lips, warning her to be quiet. In the darkness he was little more than a silhouette but he was so close that she could feel the warmth of his breath on the side of her face.

For a moment he said nothing, and then: 'Something's wrong.'

'What?'

'I'm not sure.' Briefly he was silent, and then he said, 'There's a light on.'

Veerle stared at the house, but as far as she could see it was entirely dark, the shutters tightly closed.

'Where?' she whispered.

'The little window, to the right of the door.'

She looked, and now she thought she could see something. The roller shutters were down there too, but whoever had closed them had neglected to let them down to their full extent. There was a perforated space between two of the slats, light appearing through the tiny holes so that it looked like a string of little yellow beads.

'Maybe it's on a timer,' she suggested.

'No,' said Kris in a low voice. 'They never leave lights on when they go away.'

'Maybe they did this time.'

'No.' She heard him exhale, considering. 'There's something up. We shouldn't just go in.'

Veerle bit her lip, studying the house. *Is there someone at home after all? But the shutters are all down, the garage doors are closed.* There was no sound from the house, but that didn't mean anything. The shutters would muffle any noises from inside, and in this February chill none of the windows would be open. The house might be completely empty, as it was supposed to be, nothing moving except perhaps a dust mote or two drifting on the stagnant air. Or there could be someone inside, snugly enclosed in their shuttered fortress, within a hand's reach of the telephone. *How can we be sure?* she thought. One thing she did know: she had no intention of just giving up and going home, not if there was any chance of carrying out their plan. She looked at the façade of the house as a mountaineer looks at a peak that has never been conquered.

'Kris—' she began.

'I'll go round the back and look,' he said, pre-empting her.

'I'm coming too.'

'You go round the other way.'

Silently they split up. Kris headed back the way they had come; Veerle kept to the shadows under the tree until she was able to slip round the other side of the house. Her heart was thumping as she picked her way through the darkness. She could tell by the feel of the ground under her feet that there were paving stones on this side of the house, which was good, in that she was not leaving footprints in earth or mud, but which made it essential to tread softly. She had been outdoors for a while now, and in spite of the excitement she could feel the cold beginning to bite; she had to avoid audibly shivering too.

After a minute or two her outstretched hands met the bars of a gate; she pushed gently, and to her surprise it swung open. The hinge was well-oiled but even so there was a faint scraping sound which made her freeze for a few moments, listening.

Nothing. She had no idea where Kris had got to now. The house remained dark and silent. She passed a window, the shutters tightly closed, no chink of light visible.

Up ahead she could faintly discern the end of the wall. It took her a moment to realize that there must be a light source at the back of the house, since she could see a lighter patch contrasting with the dark bulk of the wall. She paused. It wasn't bright enough to be a security light, she could tell that.

Maybe they did just leave an inside light on a timer.

She took another couple of steps.

Or maybe someone's in there.

She stared at that point where the blackness of the shadowed wall met the light patch beyond, a perfect vertical horizon.

The owners are in Burma right now. She shook her head. *They're supposed to be in Burma. So Kris says.*

Was this another test? She knew the consequences if they were caught trespassing on a property like this one. It was light years away from fooling about in a dilapidated castle that nobody seemed to own, with nothing inside it worth stealing and no one keeping an eye on it. This house probably had an alarm that went straight through to the local police station, and an owner with enough influential connections to make sure that Kris and Veerle had the book thrown at them.

Stop thinking like that. You'll psych yourself out.

Veerle made herself keep going, padding along the side of the house as quietly as she could. When she got to the corner, she waited for a few moments before peering round it.

The back garden was clearly enormous, even though much of it was swallowed in shadow. The dim light that came from the back of the house showed a broad paved area, edged with a glittering black rectangle – an ornamental pond. Beyond the paved area there was an expanse of lawn stretching away until it was lost in darkness. There were enormous shrubs too, some of them taller than Veerle, the sort you could only afford to have if your garden was the size of a football pitch.

The light was coming from a circular window in the centre of the wall – the only one small enough not to require shutters, Veerle guessed. It was barred anyway, so nobody could have climbed in that way. She didn't think the light was on in the room behind the round window; it wasn't strong enough for that. It was coming from somewhere deeper inside the house. This gave her the confidence to approach the window.

When she was within a few paces of it she ducked to the

side and peered obliquely through the glass. She was gazing into a large and well-equipped kitchen; she could make out the shapes of fitted cupboards and a tiled central island, and the silhouette of the mixer taps over the sink. The light was coming from a doorway on the other side of the kitchen, so that everything was backlit. It looked *cold*, she thought; uninhabited. There was nothing on any of surfaces, not even a single mug or glass waiting to be washed, not a lone fork or a food carton sitting there. No lights winking on any of the expensive chromed gadgets. The bottles on the shelf above the sink were lined up with obsessive neatness. In the half-light the room had the lonely look of a mortuary. The light never changed, never flickered as it would if someone had passed between the lamp and the kitchen door. *Nobody home,* Veerle thought.

Carefully she moved across the window, to try to get a view of the other side of the kitchen, perhaps a peep through the open door at the lit area beyond. Now she could see the end of the central island, and the bulk of an enormous American-style refrigerator. She could also see a strip, perhaps thirty centimetres wide, of the room beyond the door, although afterwards she could not have described it in any detail. Instead her gaze was irresistibly drawn to something on the tiled floor; something protruding from behind the bulk of the island and clearly visible in the light from the doorway.

A hand.

Without thinking, Veerle ducked away from the window. She pressed herself against the wall, her heart thudding.

Did I really see that?

A hand, palm up, fingers half bent, the wrist disappearing

behind the island. That one glimpse she had had of it was so deeply imprinted on her mind's eye that it had to be real. And if it was . . . there was someone inside the house, all right. But whoever it was was lying on the kitchen floor, completely motionless. *As still as death.*

Maybe I mistook what I saw. Maybe it was something else altogether. But she couldn't think what else it could have been. *Too big to be a doll's hand. A glove? No.* She couldn't have confused that half-curled, solidly three-dimensional object with the flaccidity of an empty glove.

Unwillingly she crept back to the window to look again. *It'll turn out to be something stupid, like a mop-head. Or there won't be anything at all, because you imagined it.*

But when she peered in, there it was, still motionless on the floor tiles, as ominous as a spider. Quite clearly a human hand; she could see the silvery gleam of a ring on one of the fingers.

She slid her hand into her jacket pocket, searching for the smooth shape of her mobile phone. Even as her fingers closed around it, she was moving further to the side of the window, straining to see just a little more of the owner of the hand.

Ambulance, she was thinking. *I should call an ambulance.*

Now she could see something else, if she craned so hard to the side of the window that her temple was pressing against the frame. A curl of hair. The top of someone's head.

Even as she pressed the button to turn the phone on, she had visions of what would happen when she called 112, her mobile phone number appearing on a screen in an emergency call centre somewhere. She'd be traceable, instantly, and here she was standing in a stranger's back garden, with no good reason to be staring in through their kitchen window in the middle of the night.

Supposing it's just a drunk sleeping it off? I could get myself in more trouble than I've ever been in my whole life. Her fingers hovered over the screen. *But if someone's collapsed, I need to call the ambulance now. They could die if I don't.* She bit her lip, focusing on the tiny screen. She touched 1, hesitated, looked up, and there was Kris moving swiftly and noiselessly across the paving stones towards her. His appearance was so sudden that she jumped.

When he was within a metre of where she stood, he put out a hand and plucked the mobile phone right out of her fingers.

'What do you think you're doing?' he whispered fiercely. 'You can't call anyone.'

'There's someone in there,' she hissed back.

Kris glanced at the window but didn't really look inside. 'Then we have to leave. Now.'

'I mean, on the floor. I think she's hurt.'

'*Verdomme*. Are you sure?' Kris's body language had been tense, straining to make a getaway. Now, suddenly, he was still. He didn't move to go, nor did he hand her phone back.

'Yes, I'm sure,' whispered Veerle. They stared at each other in the dark. 'We have to call someone,' she added. 'I can't just pretend I didn't see her.'

'You *shouldn't* have seen her,' Kris pointed out. 'We're not supposed to be here.' Still he didn't move.

'We could call from a phone box,' suggested Veerle.

'Do you know where there is one?' said Kris in a low voice.

'No.'

'Well, neither do I.'

Veerle bit her lip. 'We can't just leave her.'

Kris shook his head. 'Look . . . maybe you were mistaken. There's probably nobody in there at all.'

'There *is*—' Veerle's voice was rising.

'Keep your voice down,' whispered Kris urgently. 'We'll look, OK?'

Cautiously they approached the circular window, moving slowly and silently as though tiptoeing through a tiger's den while the fanged and clawed occupant lay sleeping. Veerle went to the right, Kris to the left, both of them hugging the wall.

From her side, Veerle could not see the patch of floor where the hand lay at all. She leaned her head against the wall, watching Kris's face outlined in the dim light from the window, and waited for him to say that he had seen it.

Kris stared through the window for several seconds, pressing himself against the frame as Veerle had done, in an attempt to get a clear view. He seemed dissatisfied with whatever he could see; after a few moments he risked moving to the centre of the window and gazing boldly in. Then he turned towards Veerle and she saw him shake his head.

He must have seen it. He must. Veerle was beginning to feel reckless herself. She moved closer, up against him, trying to see what he could see, although she knew that the pair of them must be visible from inside, their pale faces pressed almost against the bars.

Now she could pick out the central island again, and if she pushed Kris aside she could glimpse the edge of the open doorway. As she craned to the side, the floor by the island came into view.

There was nothing there. No hand. No curl of hair.

It's not possible. Veerle felt as though she were going mad. *There was a hand there. There was someone lying there, on the floor tiles. I know there was. I saw that hand.*

She stared and stared at those empty tiles, as though the hand would suddenly materialize there again, motionless, the fingers slightly curled, the silver ring gleaming in the light from the doorway.

'Come on,' said Kris in her ear.

She turned a baffled face to him. *I did see it.*

'We'd better forget it for tonight,' he said in a low voice, and her heart sank.

He thinks I imagined it.

She looked away, back into the half-lit kitchen, willing the hand to be there again, proving that she hadn't gone mad, wasn't seeing things. And saw a movement.

Behind the central island something appeared for a split second, then vanished with the lightning speed of a gecko disappearing into a crack in a wall.

Veerle ducked away from the window, pulling Kris with her, and leaned against the wall, her heart thudding.

What the hell was that? she was thinking. She had had no time to take in anything other than a dark, indistinct shape, visible for a mere instant before it disappeared behind the unit.

'Did you see that?' she hissed, but she knew the answer even before he shook his head. Kris had been looking at her, not at the window. Wondering whether she had entirely taken leave of her senses, whether she was always seeing things that weren't there. Now he was probably convinced of it.

I have to take another look, risky or not. She stepped back to the window and peered through.

The glass was thick and the window well-sealed so there was not a single sound from inside, nothing to warn Veerle of the presence of the person behind the expensive bulk of the kitchen island – a person who now rose from what had surely been a stooped or kneeling posture with ominous slowness, like the thick muscular uncurling of a python. First the head came into view, blunt and close-cropped, and then the shoulders, broad and powerful, silhouetted against the light from the open doorway.

It was as well for Veerle that the man had his back to her; for a few seconds she was unable to move, simply standing with her knuckles pressed to her mouth, swallowing the scream that had threatened to burst out of her. If he had been looking her way, he would have had a perfect view of her white face, the dark eyes huge and horrified, staring through the glass. As it was, she stood there paralysed, watching him begin to turn towards her, until Kris took her by the shoulders and dragged her to the side of the window, out of sight.

She might have made a run for it then, made for the side of the house, but Kris pulled her close. Motionless, they clung to each other, trying not to make a sound. Veerle could no longer see anything inside the kitchen, but the window threw a long faint oval of light on the ground, and as the pair of them watched, they saw it flicker. Someone was approaching the window.

They pressed themselves back against the wall, until the person in the kitchen would have had to lean right out of the window to see them, and watched as the shadow of whoever it was grew in size until it had almost eclipsed the light. *He must be standing right up against the glass,* Veerle thought. *Close enough to press his face against it.* She felt almost sick with tension. If Kris had not had his arms around her she thought her legs might have given way beneath her, she might have collapsed.

She imagined the man gazing out into the night, scrutinizing the darkness, trying to pick out the tiniest movement. More than anything she wanted to run, to put a good long distance between herself and the lit window, yet she made herself stay still. A single flicker of movement, a single faint shadow was all it would take to alert the man to their presence.

The man remained at the window for some time, and then abruptly he moved away.

'We should go,' said Kris in Veerle's ear.

He took her hand and they ran.

19

When they emerged from the path behind the houses onto Tervurenlaan, Kris and Veerle slowed to a walk. There were no other pedestrians in sight, but there were still occasional cars passing and there was no point in drawing attention to themselves by running full pelt along the street. Veerle was grateful for an opportunity to assess the damage done by running across a huge and unknown garden in the dark. By some miracle the pair of them had avoided the chill black waters of the ornamental pond, but Veerle had run into a low stone wall with an impact that had left her hip throbbing, and there was a rip in the sleeve of her jacket. She was panting, her breath visible on the frigid air under the streetlights.

'Are you OK?' asked Kris.

Veerle nodded. She had to resist the temptation to look over her shoulder, to check that nobody was coming after them.

You're supposed to be just passing by, she reminded herself. *Try to look innocent.*

For a moment they paused and stood there in silence, listening. Veerle could hear a car moving along a street somewhere out of sight, and the dry rattle of wind through the skeletal branches of a tree. Other than that there was only her own breathing and Kris's. No sound of anyone crashing along the path after them. No shutters opening or doors slamming.

Veerle didn't dare comment on the silence from the house they had just fled, feeling as though it might somehow jinx them. She could not shake the feeling of being watched, of being under the scrutiny of unseen eyes.

Kris shook his head. 'Nothing.'

They began to walk again, heading back towards the tram stop. Kris slipped Veerle's mobile phone out of his pocket and handed it back to her.

'That's the first time that's ever happened,' he said. 'Someone in the house.'

Veerle looked down, turning the mobile over in her hands. She pressed the button, and when the screen illuminated, there was the 1 she had punched in, intending to call 112.

'Kris . . .'

When he glanced at her, she didn't know what to say. She was thinking about what she had seen through the kitchen window, the hand lying motionless on the floor, the lock of hair curling across the tiles.

The person who stood up behind the kitchen island had close-cropped hair, I'm sure he did. And even though I didn't get a good look at his hands, I'm pretty sure they wouldn't be slim, with rings on.

She bit her lip.

What did I see?

Was it possible that there had been two people there all along, the owner of the hand (who she was convinced was female), and the man who had stood up and come to gaze out of the window?

Or am I imagining things? She wondered whether she could absolutely swear to it that the hand she had seen was a girl's or woman's. That the curl of hair was really hair and not the tail of a shirt or a shoelace or some other thing that she hadn't properly identified.

'Who were you going to call?' asked Kris. 'Police?'

'An ambulance,' said Veerle.

'Well, the guy wasn't hurt,' said Kris.

'I know.' Veerle was silent for a moment. 'But I'm not sure it was him I saw on the floor.'

Kris shrugged. 'Who else could it have been?'

'I thought it was a girl.'

'Thought it was, or sure it was?' When Veerle didn't reply, Kris put out a hand and touched her shoulder. 'Look, maybe there *was* a girl. Maybe it was his girlfriend or his wife or whatever. Maybe they like fooling around on the kitchen floor.'

But the hand was dead still, thought Veerle.

'Or maybe it was *his* hand you saw,' finished Kris. 'Who knows?'

I don't know, thought Veerle. *I really don't know any more.*

She cleared the 1 from the display. Then she switched off the phone and slipped it into her jeans pocket.

Forget it, she told herself. *It's the only thing you can do. You don't know what it was you saw, and you shouldn't have been there seeing it in the first place.* All the same, there was something about the scene that was bothering her, something more than the fear of being discovered and reported to the police.

It was nothing more than the echo of a memory, faded and

indistinct, a recording from the ancient past lost in hiss and crackle.

They were approaching the tram stop at Oudergem Woud; Veerle could see the twin bronze figures facing each other across the intersection as though guarding it. A glance down the track showed a tram in the distance; Veerle thought that it had stopped at the next station down the line. All the same, it couldn't be more than a very few minutes before it reached them.

She wished they had longer together. *What happens now?* she thought. She remembered Kris plucking the mobile phone right out of her hand. *What do you think you're doing? You can't call anyone*, he'd said. The memory gave her a cold sick feeling in the pit of her stomach. Supposing he decided that she was too much of a risk, too prone to losing her head and doing something stupid like alerting the authorities to their presence on someone else's property?

Then there was the troubling question of what he would have wanted to do if there had been no doubt that someone was lying inside the house, hurt or sick.

Would he really have walked away, saying that we shouldn't have been there anyway? Saying that the person inside hadn't lost anything by our refusing to call for help, because officially we weren't there?

She imagined him striding away from the window on his long legs, melting into the darkness, and herself standing there by the illuminated circle, looking from the window to Kris's retreating back.

Would I have run after him, or stayed and made the call?

'Hey,' said Kris, seeing her serious expression. 'I told you, that's the first time that's ever happened. I've been in dozens of houses and there's never been anyone at home before.'

Veerle looked at him. She didn't want to ask him what he would have done. 'I'm not worried,' she said.

'Good,' he said, and slid his arms around her. 'Next time it will be somewhere special.'

Next time, she thought with relief, and when his lips met hers she pushed away the thoughts that had been troubling her. She put her arms around Kris's neck and kissed him back, closing her eyes. *Next time.*

20

On Sunday evening Veerle logged on to the Koekoeken website and found a cluster of new messages waiting. Claudine had gone to mass – not in the Flemish Sint-Pauluskerk opposite their house, but at a French-speaking church in a district some twenty minutes' drive away. She had made a number of bitter remarks to the effect that she could not imagine what her daughter would get up to while she was gone, but in the end she *had* gone, pulling her sober-looking best coat tight around her skinny body. Veerle could work on her laptop undisturbed, which was just as well because when she opened the last of the new messages she actually gasped, something that would have brought Claudine running in an instant, ears twitching.

First there were a few messages mourning the passing of Vlinder, as sorrowful as bouquets placed at the site of an accident. Someone had posted a set of dates and an address in Sterrebeek. Kris had posted a message about the house he and Veerle had visited. *Avoid*, it said, and was signed *Schorpioen*. He didn't give the reason.

The last message was also from Schorpioen and it was specifically for Veerle; the subject heading was *For Honingbij*.

It's your turn, Honingbij, read the message. *You find the next location. Tell me when and where.*

Veerle sat and stared at the words on the screen.

No. He has to be joking.

She read the message again.

Me? I don't have any 'locations'. I can't do this.

She felt an almost sickening mixture of panic and apprehension, as though she were a nurse assisting at an operation and the head surgeon had suddenly handed her the scalpel, saying, *Here, you do it.*

I can't.

She closed the laptop without logging out of the site, then got up and began to pace about the room. *I can't, I can't,* she kept telling herself, but she knew that that was not good enough. It wouldn't get her off the hook.

It was the obvious development, she should have seen it coming. No one could be admitted to a group like the Koekoeken if they didn't contribute something. Kris had stuck his neck out for her – the first two houses he'd taken her to had been the most luxurious she had ever been inside, houses whose owners would certainly have pulled every string they could to get the maximum penalty applied to Kris if they ever found out what he had done. The last one had been just as palatial, and while they hadn't actually made it inside, they'd come closer to being caught than ever before.

He's taken insane risks.

She bit her lip.

Now it's my turn to prove myself.

She knew that was the way it worked. Otherwise Kris ran all the risks and she just went along for the ride.

But I don't have keys to any luxury houses; I don't have a cousin who runs a maid service; I don't have a talent for picking locks. There's no way I can come up with somewhere for us to meet.

Restlessly, she paced the room.

So forget it then, she told herself savagely. *Tell him you can't come up with anything.*

She made another circuit of the table, glancing at the closed laptop as though it were an unexploded bomb.

Don't see him again. That's what it means. Stop seeing him.

She surprised herself with the sharpness of the pain that idea gave her, a pang so acute that it was almost physical.

I can't do that. I can't give him up. Not now.

It was an impossible conundrum. Eventually she sat down and opened the laptop again. She re-read Kris's message and then she typed a reply.

I'll let you know.

It was very much later that evening that the idea came to her. Claudine had returned from mass, exchanging the sober coat for one of her limp-looking cardigans, and had cooked a meal for the pair of them. Afterwards, she stood at the kitchen sink washing the dishes by hand, and Veerle dried them. They said little to each other. Claudine passed the occasional remark about this or that person she had seen at church, but Veerle couldn't think of much to say in return. Her head was too full of Kris and the challenge he had set her. She stood shoulder to shoulder with her mother, polishing the plates, and looked at the kitchen window, the view of the street outside hidden by a blank wall of roller shutters.

Veerle had never been able to understand why Claudine would prefer to look at a stack of roller slats instead of Kerkstraat and the outline of the Sint-Pauluskerk jutting skywards. Now she wondered whether her mother disliked the view, whether she looked at the church and the bell tower and thought about Silent Saturday, all those years ago.

There was a heap of papers lying on the kitchen work surface close to the draining board – publicity for local supermarkets – and the uppermost one was for a chain of pet stores. There was a picture of a little white dog on the front, its head on one side, its eyes bright.

It looks just like Toulouse, Veerle thought. *I wonder who's looking after him,* and it was then that it came to her – the answer to the question of where to take Kris.

Toulouse was Tante Bernadette's dog. Tante Bernadette was not really Veerle's aunt; she was Claudine's aunt, Veerle's great-aunt. She was in her eighties, a spry, skinny, active old woman; at any rate, she had been, until she had suffered a stroke. Now she was in a nursing home somewhere and it was doubtful whether she would come home again. Toulouse, presumably, was in the care of a kennels or a friend of Tante Bernadette's; meanwhile, the old lady's flat on the edge of Brussels stood empty, awaiting either its owner's return or the auctioneer's hammer.

We have the keys.

Veerle's gaze slid to the little row of hooks screwed to the wall by the kitchen door. As well as her own keys and Claudine's there were a few others: one for the garden shed, a spare set of car keys, and a couple of keys on a fob decorated with a fragment of Brussels lace sealed in clear plastic, the sort of thing you could buy in any of the tourist traps in the city. Those were the keys to Tante Bernadette's apartment. Claudine had had them for years, just in case the old lady should fall ill and need someone to come in.

Veerle stared at the keys hanging there. They were so close that she could have reached out with her right hand and plucked them from the hook.

Are you serious? asked a voice at the back of her mind. *You'd take those keys while its owner is lying in a nursing home, recovering from a stroke, and you'd go into her home without permission?*

The voice droned on, but Veerle would have been more inclined to listen to it had it not had a distinct hint of Claudine's disapproving, complaining tone in it. She chafed under it, restive as a penned animal.

Claudine finished washing the last of the cutlery and let out the water. Then she went out of the room, bearing the two glasses they had used back to the cabinet in the sitting room, and Veerle put out her hand and took the keys. She held them in her palm, looking at them, at the worn metal of the keys themselves and the discoloured plastic of the fob with its scrap of lace suspended inside. Then Claudine was coming back; Veerle heard the scuff of her slippers on the tiles in the hallway, and without thinking she stuffed the keys into her pocket.

'Are you all right?' asked her mother, peering at her.

'Why wouldn't I be?' said Veerle calmly.

'You had a strange look on your face,' Claudine told her.

Veerle shrugged. 'I'm fine,' she said as cheerfully as she could.

As soon as possible, she escaped, on the pretext of going upstairs for a bath. With the bathroom door closed and the hot water thundering into the tub, she felt she could effectively shut Claudine out. She could think.

She took the keys out of her pocket and put them on the end of the bath, where she could see them.

Is it really so bad, going to Tante Bernadette's flat? she asked herself. *She's never going to know you were in there, not if you're careful – and anyway, why shouldn't you be? You're her great-niece. You might be checking the pot plants, making sure the heating is turned up enough to stop the pipes freezing.* An image flashed across her mind at that moment, of herself and Kris in the old woman's apartment, Kris moving about amongst the spindly and fussily feminine furnishings like an invading soldier prowling a museum, and she felt a sudden pang of guilt. All the same, some reckless part of her, the part that wanted above everything else to be with Kris again, kept on arguing relentlessly for the idea. *Tante Bernadette was young herself once, wasn't she? If you could ask her permission, maybe she'd be amused by the idea. She was supposed to have been gorgeous when she was young; she must have had admirers of her own once.*

Veerle got into the bath and lay in the hot water, eyeing the bunch of keys as though it were some live and dangerous thing, a poisonous creature that might bite her. Just a couple of little pieces of metal, a few centimetres long, worn and tarnished, nothing magical about them at all, and yet they had so much power. They could open doors into two possible futures: one in which she returned them unused to their hook in the kitchen, and walked away from Kris and his dangerous games; and one in which she used them to let the pair of them into Tante Bernadette's flat, thus stepping not only into someone else's property but over another kind of line.

When she had finished in the bathroom she slipped the keys into the pocket of her dressing gown. She had no intention of leaving them lying anywhere where Claudine might see them, might be reminded that they had the keys. When she got into bed at last, she slid them under the pillow, where she could easily touch them in the night, reassure herself that they were still hidden there.

Kris, Kris... she thought, and then: *What am I going to do?*

She lay awake for a while, gazing into the dark; she thought that when she finally went to sleep the presence of the keys might disturb her, that she might sleep as badly as the princess in the fairy tale who had a pea under her mattress. But when sleep came it was deep and dreamless.

21

Veerle allowed herself twenty-four hours in which to consider the question. On Monday morning when she took the bus to the high school, the key to Tante Bernadette's apartment was in the pocket of her padded winter jacket. The pocket was deep, but still Veerle had to keep putting her gloved hand down inside it to check that the keys were still there, that she still had the opportunity to return them to the hook in the kitchen if she decided to do so.

The day dragged by. Veerle found her attention drifting away from the lessons.

All she could think about was Kris; Kris and the question of Tante Bernadette's apartment. At lunch time she went to the canteen with the usual crowd from her class, but she was conscious of a new barrier between herself and the others, as though there were a thick sheet of glass between them.

If they only knew . . . But she couldn't tell them.

Lisa, who was a friend of Veerle's, dug her in the ribs with an elbow and said, 'What are you dreaming about?' but Veerle shrugged and smiled and said, 'Nothing.'

If I tell her about Kris she'll want to know all about him, and then she'll want to know how we met, and worst of all she'll want to meet him.

She tried to imagine introducing Kris to some of her school friends and she simply couldn't do it.

Anyway, how would I do it? She glanced around the table – at Lisa, who had turned to say something to someone else, and Lisa's boyfriend Matthieu, who was talking animatedly through a mouthful of chips, and all the others. She couldn't take them all to meet Kris, not even if it were somewhere relatively safe like the old castle. Certainly not to anyone's actual *house*. You only had to look around the table at all those phones, all those thumbs dodging about the tiny buttons sending texts back and forth, think about all those inbuilt cameras. If any of her friends got so much as a sniff of what she and Kris were up to, it wouldn't be a secret for more than a nanosecond.

The other option, of course, was to bring Kris to meet them somewhere neutral like the snack bar where they sometimes congregated in the late afternoon. Veerle knew she wasn't going to do that either. Aside from the inevitable questions and the need to construct baroque lies to conceal the truth, she just couldn't imagine meeting Kris in such a *normal* setting. He didn't belong in this world – the one filled with coursework and routine and people you saw every day, doing the same old things. If Lisa or anyone else asked her what she was thinking about again, she'd say the same as she just had. *Nothing.* Because that was the only thing she *could* say.

That feeling came over her again – of there being an invisible but insurmountable barrier between her and everyone else. Sometimes she could feel the drag of her normal life, trying to pull her back in like an undertow. Sitting in the canteen with its chipped tables and scuffed plastic chairs and the curling posters on the walls and all those familiar faces, she could still have been the old Veerle, the Veerle of six or seven weeks ago, trailing around the high school with the rest of them and dreaming of her next trip to the climbing wall.

Things aren't really the same any more though, are they? I can't just sink back into the old routine, not properly, not today. I've got a decision to make.

She could feel Tante Bernadette's keys in her jeans pocket, digging into the top of her thigh. She had transferred them there from the pocket of her outdoor jacket, feeling some superstitious need to keep them close, as though letting them out of her sight might somehow endanger her secret.

What am I going to tell Kris? she wondered. But she already knew.

That evening when Claudine was in the sitting room watching television, Veerle went back on to the Koekoeken website and posted a message for Schorpioen. *Friday*, she suggested. *9 p.m., Montgomery. At the tram stop.* She didn't post the actual address; at some future point she supposed she would have to supply the details of a location open to everyone, but she would worry about that later. There was no way she was going to make Tante Bernadette's home public property.

But those places you and Kris have visited, those are people's homes too, objected the voice in the back of her mind. She did her best to quash it.

Friday, 9 p.m., she thought.

22

'No,' said Claudine. She was trembling, but her voice was firm.

'What?' said Veerle. She could hardly believe her ears.

'You can't go out.' Claudine stood in the hallway of the house on Kerkstraat, with her arms folded and her cardigan – it was a pale mint-green one this time – pulled close around her body as usual, as though she were trying to swaddle herself against the harsh atmosphere of life in general. Her face was pale, surrounded by its corona of short-cropped greying hair, but there was a vivid intensity to her faded eyes. She meant business.

'Don't be ridiculous,' said Veerle. She tried to push past Claudine to the door, and found herself being pushed back.

'Ridiculous?' repeated Claudine, her voice rising.

The two of them glared at each other. Now Veerle was trembling too, with annoyance and shock. 'I'm going out,' she said.

Claudine appeared not to have heard her. 'Ridiculous?' she said again. 'You think I'm ridiculous?'

Veerle could envision the great swell of indignation that was building up inside Claudine, as though it were some vast rolling wave, a towering tsunami of emotion that was curling high above her head, waiting to crash down on her with savage force.

'No,' she said at last. 'I didn't mean it like that. But *Maman*, I'm going out. You can't stop me.'

'I'm your mother.'

'I know. But I'm not a little girl. I'm *nearly eighteen*.'

'You live in *my* house—'

'Not for much longer,' snapped Veerle angrily, before she had time to think about what she was saying. She felt a terrible stab of guilt as she saw her mother's face crumple. In spite of the grey hair, the tired face, Claudine looked like a terrified child. *How can you do this to me?* said that look, and it went straight to Veerle's heart.

It wasn't just the fact that she thought Claudine would have some sort of collapse, it was the knowledge that her mother really was almost helpless without her. She had never learned Flemish, she couldn't read official letters or conduct her own business at the administrative centre in Tervuren. Leaving her would feel like abandoning a small child in a strange town.

But you have to go one day, said a hard little voice at the back of her mind. *What about university? One day you'll be gone. She has to get used to that. And anyway . . .*

Now she was coming to it, the real reason she was going to go out, whatever Claudine said or did.

. . . I have to see Kris. She did her best to push away that feeling of creeping guilt. *I'm just going to meet someone. That's not a crime. It's what people do.*

'Look,' she said, rubbing her face with her hand as though

trying to massage away a headache. 'I have to go. It's nothing you have to worry about, *Maman*. I'm just meeting a friend.'

But Claudine had already turned her face away. This time when Veerle pushed past her she didn't try to stop her. She simply stood there, not looking at her daughter, with her shoulders hunched and the dowdy cardigan pulled as tight as a bandage. A picture of reproach and misery.

Veerle could feel a tight little knot of anger way down inside herself. She knew that Claudine was trying to apply the pressure, to make her stay home, to prolong the scene. She could have taken her by the skinny shoulders and shaken her until her teeth rattled.

At the same time she felt a truly terrible pang of pity for her mother, as she would for any lame and hopeless creature. She swallowed her anger, leaned over and kissed Claudine's papery cheek. Claudine showed no reaction other than to close her eyes, as though shutting out the sight of her disobedient daughter.

Veerle pulled away and looked at those closed eyes, at the face that was like a marble statue of a martyr, at once suffering and unyielding, weak and yet hard as stone. She touched her mother's arm gently. 'I'll see you later, *Maman*,' she said. 'I'm going to be quite late, but don't worry. I have my phone, OK?'

There was no reply.

Veerle turned and left the house, shutting the front door gently behind her. She kept calm until she had reached the end of Kerkstraat and turned the corner. Then she stood at the bus stop with her hands over her eyes, fighting back tears, thankful for the cover of darkness.

23

By the time she changed from the bus to the tram, Veerle had recovered a little and even begun to feel resentful towards Claudine. *She can't keep treating me like a kid.*

All the same, she could not shake off her mother's influence as easily as that; Claudine seemed to hover close to her, like a pale ghost. If Claudine had reacted so badly to Veerle's going out, how much worse would it be if she knew whom Veerle was meeting? She could almost hear the words of fear and worry that spilled from those thin lips.

Verstraeten? Not one of those Verstraetens?

I told him to keep away.

Men. You can't trust them.

Your father, ce salaud de Gand . . .

Veerle knew it was no use listening to that voice; it was the voice of a sickness that ran as deep as cancer, rotting everything away from the inside. To Claudine, the world was a terrifyingly dangerous place, its inhabitants divided into helpless victims and stalking monsters.

In a way she's right, thought Veerle. *We had one of those monsters in our own village. Joren Sterckx. But I can't live like that, always looking over my shoulder. It's not really living at all. It's like being in prison.*

There was no joy in life for Claudine, she thought. The best that could be hoped for was a degree of safety, to be achieved by constant vigilance, by withdrawing into the fortified cocoon that was home.

She stared out of the tram window, but it was dark outside and they were passing through the woods now; there were no lights. All she could see was her own reflection, her pale face with its large hazel eyes gazing solemnly back at her, the glossy dark hair parted at the side.

She shivered. *It will be all right,* she told herself. *You'll see Kris on the platform at Montgomery and you'll forget all about her and her worries.*

She couldn't relax though. The twenty-minute journey to Montgomery seemed to take for ever. When the tram veered down into the underground station she was on her feet, fingers drumming a restless beat on the pole by the door.

Veerle saw Kris even before the tram had come to a halt. He was leaning against the tiled wall, clad as usual in black: leather jacket, jeans, boots; hands in pockets, head tilted to one side, dark hair falling into his eyes.

She got off the tram and went towards him, her heart pounding in her chest. She looked at him, at his sharp features, his bold eyes, the wry twist at the corner of his mouth, and felt a rush of nerves so strong that it was exhilarating. Stage fright. *Can I possibly carry the whole thing off? What if someone catches us entering the flat?* What if Kris rejected the offering – would he do that? *I can't take him any-where that has a private swimming pool or a lobby as big as a cathedral, that has seventy bottles of champagne in the cellar.*

She went up to Kris and he put his arms around her. There were people pushing past them, hurrying to get onto the tram, to find a seat before they had all gone. More than ever Veerle had a feeling of swimming upstream, going against the flow. What would they think, all those commuters scurrying home after their week's work in some ordinary little office, if they knew what she and Kris were up to?

Kris's lips were warm on the side of her temple near the hairline. He said, 'Do we have to take the metro?'

'No,' said Veerle into the front of his leather jacket. 'We can walk from here.'

They took the stairs up to street level. There was a kind of sickly twilight created by the streetlamps and the dozens of car headlights. In the distance Veerle could make out the great triumphal arch of the Jubelpark.

Most people were driving to their destinations but there were a few pedestrians hurrying along Tervurenlaan, heads down as though the frigid night air were a barrier they had to push against. There was no logical reason for anyone to take particular notice of Veerle and Kris, and yet Veerle was anxious that they would somehow draw attention to themselves. She was torn between the urge to *run* to Tante Bernadette's place, to get off the streets as soon as possible, and the opposing desire to put off their arrival as long as she could.

'Down here,' she said to Kris, and they turned into a side street between two imposing nineteenth-century apartment buildings, their tiny but perfectly manicured front gardens guarded by black railings. The route to Tante Bernadette's took a dogleg down several smaller streets.

Kris said very little as they walked. He had an arm around Veerle's shoulders and sometimes he toyed with the ends of her dark hair. He seemed relaxed, even a little preoccupied. It was Veerle who felt almost sick with tension. The keys on their plastic fob were warm, the temperature of blood, because she kept sliding her hand into her pocket to clasp them, to check that they were still there.

Long before they reached the apartment building she was looking for it, her gaze seeking it out. There was a low stone balcony on the second floor, where the flat was. It usually housed a profusion of flowers spilling out of their pots, but now there was nothing. Either someone had cleared them away when Tante Bernadette went into hospital, or perhaps she had done it herself when autumn came. Their absence threw Veerle, and while she was trying to make up her mind whether she was really looking at the right building they had come right up to the front door.

She couldn't help glancing up and down the road, although she knew it probably made her look furtive. Apart from her and Kris the street was deserted. In the yellow light of the streetlamps the ornate façades of the buildings had a strangely artificial look, as though they were a stage set, convincingly depicted but with nothing of substance behind the walls. This thought gave her courage; she fumbled the keys out of her pocket and approached the green-painted front door.

She had tried three times to slide the key into the lock before she realized what had happened, and even then she didn't want to believe it.

No, she thought. *No.* She fumbled with the keys. *I've tried the wrong one – I've been using the flat key, not the outside door key* . . . But even before she tried the other key she knew it wasn't going to work. She could see by the yellow light of the streetlamps that the lock had been changed. It was new and very shiny, as though it had been lifted off the shelf of a hardware store that very afternoon and fitted to the street door.

'*Verdomme.*' Just for a moment she allowed herself the luxury of despair. She sagged against the shabby green paint of the door, letting her forehead rest against the wood. She felt like pounding on the panels but she knew it wouldn't do any good, might even attract unwanted attention. The street was deserted at present, the circles of yellow lamplight as still as limpid pools, but she didn't want anyone twitching at their curtains, peeping out to see who was making a racket down below.

Then she looked at Kris and said, 'Change of plan.' She turned to stare up at the balcony above, and let her gaze slowly drop to the ground floor of the building, assessing what she saw.

The balcony of Tante Bernadette's apartment looked a horribly long way up if you stood right underneath it.

I've climbed higher, Veerle reminded herself. *Not without a rope, you haven't,* argued a voice in the back of her mind, but she ignored it. If she started to think like that she would never even get off the ground. *I can do this.*

There were very few potential holds on the ground floor of Tante Bernadette's apartment building; Veerle could see that just by looking at it. The floor above, the first floor, was considerably better; there was a kind of oriel window with rounded stone columns between each arched section. At the point where each column began to curve up and over, there were carved stone projections that looked sturdy enough to take at least part of her weight. If she were able to climb high enough to stand on one of those projections, she could reach the bottom edge of the stone balcony of Tante Bernadette's apartment. She thought that if she could get a good grip on that, she wouldn't need to worry too much about footholds; she could smear her way up the stone façade. Once she was on the balcony there would be no problem at all about getting into the apartment. The folding shutters were ancient and one of the window catches was broken; it had been broken ever since she could remember, so it was unlikely that Tante Bernadette had done anything about it in her infirm state. Besides, nobody expected intruders on the second floor. Not with a drop of some metres onto a stone pavement – assuming, that is, that you missed the railings.

Don't think about that.

The big problem, thought Veerle, *is how to get to the first floor.* The bottom of the oriel window created an overhang with little of substance underneath it. The ground-floor flat was dark but unshuttered, so a swinging foot could easily go through a windowpane, with disastrous consequences. The lack of shutters bothered her too. Supposing there *were* somebody home: they only had to wander into the front room to see her silhouetted clearly against the light of the streetlamps.

The adjacent building held more possibilities. There was a flight of stone steps leading up to the front door, and along-side it a broad bay window with sturdy stone supports. Veerle was pretty sure she could get from the top of the steps onto the nearest stone pillar, and from there onto the top of the window. After that she had only to traverse the width of the window and she would be able to climb over onto the oriel next door. She stared up at the stonework and she could almost *feel* the route, feel the stone under her fingers. *I can do it.*

She glanced down at her boots. Normally she climbed in rock boots; climbing in street shoes was going to present a few difficulties of its own, but at least these boots had profiled soles. Quickly she knelt down and tightened the laces.

'Veerle?'

She stood up and for a moment she gazed into Kris's face. Her heart was beating savagely fast, as though she had been running a sprint race. *I can do this.* The anticipation, the excitement, the fear were intoxicating. Suddenly she felt truly alive, tingling, as though every pore in her body were opening to the cool night air. She couldn't wait to start climbing.

'Wait here,' she said. She'd have to climb quickly, because she was going to be doing it in full view of the street and anyone who chanced to come down it.

She didn't wait to hear what Kris had to say; she turned swiftly and ran to the steps of the next-door apartment block, as lightly as a cat. She stuffed the keys to Tante Bernadette's apartment back into her pocket, thrusting them down as far as they would go to make sure they didn't tumble out if she took a swing. Then she was on the stone steps, grasping the black-painted iron railings with her hands and fitting the toe of her boot into one of the spaces between them, putting her weight on the narrow crossbar. She pushed up, and now she was able to climb onto the top of the railings, steadying herself on the corner of the bay window.

Feeling secure, she couldn't resist glancing mischievously at Kris, but she had hardly focused on his face, noticing with some satisfaction his raised eyebrows, when she felt her foot slipping on the painted surface of the railing. All the struts were cylindrical, and thickly coated in glossy black paint; she had thought the tight fit of her boot between the uprights would stop her slipping, but now she realized to her horror that it wouldn't. Her foot began to slide backwards, and all of a sudden she was fighting to keep her balance, a sick cold feeling of terror washing over her as she pictured herself going over, legs shooting out from under her, torso or maybe – God forbid – her face coming down on the spiked ends of the railings with the finality of a cleaver hitting a side of beef. The splintering cracks as the points hit ribs, the sickening sound of them sliding into her flesh. Her eyes. *Oh God.* For several seconds she teetered there, while adrenalin fizzed through her veins like an electric current, and then she flung out an arm and grabbed one of the ornate posts that supported the building's little porch. The metalwork dug painfully into her hand but she arrested the slide.

She was hunched over now. She made herself straighten up – carefully this time, not wasting any of her attention looking at Kris. *You won't impress him if you spill half your internal organs on the pavement. Concentrate, for God's sake.*

It was not difficult to do so. The shock had had the sobering effect of a dousing with freezing cold water. Veerle balanced on the railings with her fingers curled around the porch post, waited until she was sure that she was secure, and then stepped over onto the little stone lip that ran around the base of the bay window. She began to look for holds. If she could once get her fingers over the matching rim at the top of the window she would have little difficulty in getting up there; the biggest problem was finding a toehold that would enable her to reach that high. For once, however, Fortune had smiled: the stone column that ran up the corner of the bay window was badly chipped in several places. It was no harder than climbing some of the routes at the wall.

In a few moments Veerle had scaled the window and was crouched on the top, her breath coming in shallow gasps. She stood up and moved with great care along the top of the window; it looked solid enough, but you could never tell. A bay window was not designed to bear fifty kilos of active human being moving unevenly over its upper surface. She tried to keep to the edge where she knew the top was supported by the windowframe.

At the other side she was able to step easily across to the oriel window, where there was an obligingly placed stone lip. She could rest her forehead on the cold glass and peer into the darkened room within, trace the dim shapes of furniture. But there was no time to waste. The chill night air was beginning to bite; very soon her fingers would be stiff. She did not look down at Kris; she concentrated everything on the problem in front of her. The riskiest part would be getting high enough to put her weight on the stone boss at the neck of the window arch. Once she was there, the rest would be easy.

She would have to scale one of the stone columns between the windows; they were too far apart for her to attempt to bridge a pair of them.

She ran her fingers over the stone, feeling for cracks, for places between the slabs where the mortar might have come out.

A car purred down a parallel street and she froze, clinging to the windowframe. There was no sound at all from Kris down below her.

Verdomme, she thought. *Get a move on. Someone will see you, or your fingers will freeze off.*

She put her head back and scanned the window arch, and as she turned to the left she spotted a metal strut protruding from the wall. She put out a hand and touched it; it was firmly fixed. She supposed some past owner of the apartment had had a hanging basket of flowers there or some such thing. The basket was long gone – *don't think about it plummeting from the hook and exploding on the paving stones!* – but the bracket was firm enough. She placed her left boot on it, stood up smoothly and then it was right toe on the nearest stone boss, fingers hooked over the upper rim of the oriel, and she was swinging herself up onto the balcony above.

She stood there for a moment drawing the chilly night air into her lungs, but she didn't waste time looking down or waving at Kris; the less attention she drew to herself the better. She forced the ancient shutters apart without too much difficulty, and to her relief the window catch was still broken; she was easily able to open the window and step inside.

24

The apartment had a doleful smell about it, a mixture of old furniture polish and the ashen scent of stale coffee grounds. It was cool and almost silent, the only sounds the ticking of a clock and the whisper of Veerle's own breathing. She took a few moments to let her eyes adjust. Familiar items of furniture gradually solidified out of the darkness: an over-stuffed upright armchair with claw feet; a marble-topped table; a gilded console bearing a Chinese vase.

Veerle went through to the hallway and felt for the old-fashioned light switch. Then she dragged the keys out of her pocket and went to open the front door. To her relief, the key to the apartment seemed to fit perfectly well; she supposed the downstairs lock had been changed since Tante Bernadette's departure, perhaps at the behest of another tenant.

She checked that the stairway was deserted before venturing down to let Kris in. She opened the street door, taking care to keep part of her body inside the doorframe to prevent it swinging shut and locking her outside again.

'Kris?'

He materialized from the dark shadows under the oriel

window and slipped into the lobby beside her. He was grinning. He put his arms around her, pulling her close, and said, 'How did you do that?'

'Shhhh,' Veerle warned him, but she was smiling back.

They went upstairs, treading carefully, saying nothing but listening for the sounds of doors opening, of footsteps on one of the landings – anything that might signify a nosy neighbour on the lookout. They heard a radio playing behind a closed door, but otherwise there was no sign of life. They made it to the second floor without encountering anyone, and Veerle let them into the flat.

She was biting her lip, torn between smiling at her successful ascent of the building's façade and anxiety about Kris's reaction to the flat. When she closed the door behind them she was acutely aware that it wasn't opulent like the places Kris had shown her. In fact, she was pretty sure Tante Bernadette hadn't redecorated since about 1955. Everything had a worn and slightly faded look, from the antique gold and cream striped wallpaper to the fraying runner on the hallway floor. At the end of the corridor was a sagging dog basket, the wickerwork chewed, the cushion inside leaking its stuffing. Toulouse's basket. That gave Veerle a pang. If whoever had taken the little dog hadn't taken his basket along, perhaps he had been re-homed or, worse, euthanized.

Kris moved past her, further into the apartment. Veerle followed him, hand to her mouth, chewing her knuckle. *Let him like it. Let it be OK.* She was half expecting him to turn round and say, *This is just some old lady's place. It doesn't count.* Or *What a dump.*

Then she heard him say, 'Amazing.' He disappeared into the

sitting room. Veerle went after him and found him standing in the middle of the Persian carpet, looking around with evident appreciation at the antique furniture: the gilded salon chairs with their graceful legs and upholstery the colour of dusty roses, the ormolu mantel clock, the oil painting over the fireplace. She felt a rush of something like gratitude.

'This place is like a museum,' Kris was saying, touching the ormolu clock with his long fingers, almost caressing the little gilded figures that decorated it. 'Look at this.' He was holding a little alabaster statue, holding it with both hands to avoid the risk of dropping it. He began to pace the room, stopping to examine things here and there. A Japanese lacquered box. An antique silver rose bowl. 'This is amazing,' he said again, shaking his head.

Veerle sagged against the doorframe, overwhelmed by a curious mixture of feelings: the inevitable down that followed the adrenalin of the climb up the front of the building, relief that Kris liked the apartment, and a seeping sense of unreality at the sight of him wandering about in it, picking up Tante Bernadette's things and examining them. The apartment didn't feel entirely *real* to her; it was as familiar as the lines on her own palms, but without its garrulous ancient occupant it felt strangely empty, as though it were already a memory, and Tante Bernadette already nothing more than a string of words chiselled into a marble headstone. Seeing Kris prowling about in it was even stranger; it was as though he had suddenly strolled across one of her childhood memories, an incongruous and slightly ominous presence in his black leather jacket and jeans.

Eventually Kris looked her way. 'Hey, are you OK?' He came over to her.

'I don't know,' said Veerle. 'I feel strange about being here.'

Kris put his arms around her, pulled her to him. 'It's different, isn't it?' he said. 'When you're the one who's found the place.' He looked down at her, and his expression was serious for once; that ironic smile that always seemed to be lurking at the corners of his mouth was nowhere to be seen. 'That's why you have to do it.' He touched her face with the same care as he had caressed the little figures on the ormolu clock. 'Everyone has to do it. Nobody gets to go along for the ride.'

She gave him an uncertain smile. 'So did I pass the test?'

'Of course.' He leaned over and kissed her.

Veerle closed her eyes. She could feel Kris's lips on hers, his fingers in her hair. But she could also detect the smells of the apartment: that furniture-polish smell and the lingering memory of coffee and something sweet and powdery, the old-fashioned perfume of an elderly lady. The ormolu clock chimed the half-hour, silvery notes that seemed to shiver on the air. She would hardly have been surprised if she had heard Toulouse come running in, his claws clicking on the polished floor.

When Kris broke the kiss at last, she said, 'Are we going to do something for the flat? I don't know . . . repair something?'

'Of course,' he said, but he didn't move. His fingers were still in her hair, twisting the strands. She thought that he was going to kiss her again, and if he continued doing that she was really not sure where it would lead; in the setting of Tante Bernadette's apartment this was not a comfortable thought.

'Let's look,' she said, pulling away. She moved towards the doorway into the kitchen and Kris followed. They went into nearly every room, although when Veerle opened the door which led into Tante Bernadette's bedroom, with its high bed covered with a padded pink satin counterpane, she shut it again almost as quickly, feeling as though they were invading.

In the sitting room they found an antiquated gramophone player, so old that it was housed in a kind of wooden cabinet with little feet. There were cupboards at either side for storing records, strange brittle things in dog-eared cardboard sleeves. Not only had Tante Bernadette not heard of MP3s, she hadn't even progressed to CDs.

Veerle fished out a record with a jolly-looking cover. *Charles Trenet*, she read. *Boum!* The name didn't mean anything to her, but she decided to try the record anyway.

It took her a few attempts to start the record player. It didn't seem to have buttons, mostly dials, and you had to lift the stylus up and put it onto the record yourself. Then there was a hiss and a crackle and a brief musical flourish before a cheery male voice launched straight into a song. Veerle listened with her head on one side. She couldn't help smiling; the music was so ridiculously bouncy and cheerful. And loud. Tante Bernadette was evidently getting deaf; the volume was turned right up.

Kris had wandered over to the other side of the room to examine a black-and-white photograph of Tante Bernadette taken around 1960, looking a little like Audrey Hepburn in a tunic dress and sunglasses. Now he came over to Veerle and he was smiling, a real smile, not just that sardonic little twist of the lips that always gave him a slightly mocking air.

Suddenly she could see her Kris, the one she remembered from her childhood, the shock-headed ten-year-old who had always been nice when the bigger boys were horrible to her, and had once dared her to climb the bell tower of the Sint-Pauluskerk.

'What is it?' he asked her, nodding at the gramophone.

Veerle showed him the record sleeve. The vocalist had started on something about deer making bleating noises and she was trying very hard not to laugh. 'I'm sorry,' she managed to say.

Kris put his arms around her. 'No, it's brilliant. It's like travelling back in time.'

Veerle tilted back her head to look at him. 'You take me to rich people's houses and I take you to nineteen-fifty?'

'Exactly.'

'You think this was cool even in nineteen-fifty?'

'Maybe—' began Kris, but got no further.

Even above the music they heard it. *Knocking.*

Both of them froze. Then Kris reached out almost casually and lifted the stylus off the record. Charles Trenet fell silent halfway through a line, and for a moment all they could hear was the faint sound of the turntable revolving.

Then it came again: a persistent tapping on the front door of the apartment.

'Bernadette?' said a voice through the door.

Veerle and Kris looked at each other with horror on their faces. Veerle raised a hand, showing her palm to Kris. *Stay here*, she telegraphed. Then she slipped out into the hallway of the flat, treading as silently as she could on the worn runner. The knocking had ceased and for a few moments there was silence. Veerle approached the door very carefully and pressed her right ear to the wooden panel.

When the knocking started up again on the other side she nearly jumped out of her skin. She clamped a hand over her mouth as if to prevent the screech that nearly burst out of it. She glanced back at the sitting-room doorway and saw Kris standing there watching.

Stay calm, she told herself. *Don't lose it.*

'Bernadette?' said the voice again. It was high and a little quavery; *an old lady voice,* thought Veerle. Some crony of her great-aunt's from another apartment, most probably.

Why did I put that record on? she asked herself. *That was stupid – stupid!* She wondered whether there was any possibility that the person outside would simply give up and go away. She didn't think so, though; the nervous tremor in the voice indicated that its owner was one of those fussy types who wouldn't give up easily. *Like Mum.* Veerle knew perfectly well what Claudine would have been like in a similar situation; she would have been imagining every possible freak accident and debating whether to call out the emergency services.

'*Bernadette, tu es là?*'

No, she's not here. Just give up and go away. But somehow Veerle knew she wouldn't.

There was silence for perhaps a minute, during which time Veerle remained with the side of her face pressed to the wood, listening. Then she heard a shuffling sound in the hallway outside, and a second voice, a male voice, spoke in French.

'I can't just break down the door.'

'Well, I definitely heard someone inside,' said the old-lady voice. In a higher-pitched, louder tone she added, 'Bernadette? Bernadette, is that you in there?'

'It was probably number one, downstairs,' said the man in a grumbling tone. 'Always so much noise.'

'It wasn't. You think those two play anything the rest of us would want to hear? It was Bernadette's favourite song. It definitely came from here.'

'Well, maybe she came home early and she was listening to it.'

'Then why doesn't she open the door?'

'She doesn't want to be bothered?' suggested the man.

'It just stopped, suddenly – as though someone didn't want us to hear it. Something's wrong, I tell you.'

Then the man said something that made Veerle's breath catch in her throat.

'Well, you have a key, don't you?'

Oh God. They're going to open the door.

'Yes,' said the female voice, slightly huffily. 'But it is upstairs in my apartment. I would have to fetch it. It may not be easy to find.'

Let it be lost, please God, thought Veerle. Her heart was beating so wildly that she was afraid she would faint.

'Easier than shouldering the door down,' said the man. There was some further discussion and then he said, 'I will wait here while you fetch it.'

Veerle did not wait to see if there were any more protests from the woman. How long would it take her to fetch the key? *Ten minutes if we're lucky and the old bat can't find it; a minute and a half if she puts her hand on it right away.* She sped back down the hallway, flicking off the hall light switch as she passed it. If the man was really waiting right outside the door, he might see the thin rim of light around the doorframe vanish, but that was too bad; they were in trouble now anyway, whatever happened.

'She's getting a key,' she said to Kris in an urgent whisper, pulling him into the sitting room.

'Who?'

'Some nosy neighbour.'

Veerle began to move swiftly about, switching lights off. 'She's going to be back any minute. We need to be out of here.'

'Well, let's go.'

'There's a man outside the front door.'

'Is there another door?'

'No.'

There was a silence.

'There's only one way out,' said Veerle eventually.

Kris opened his mouth to argue, but realized that there was really nothing to say. They were staring at each other in the dim light when they heard voices in the hallway again.

'We have to go *now*,' said Veerle, opening the window that led onto the balcony.

Kris followed her out. Veerle closed the window as best she could from the outside, and drew the shutters across it.

When she turned to Kris, he was standing with his back to the wall, his expression unreadable.

'Kris,' she said, going up to him, 'we can't stay out here. That window doesn't shut properly. Anyone with eyes in their head will notice it, and then they'll look out here. We have to climb down.'

She was making it sound as though it were nothing, she knew that, whereas in fact climbing *down* was a lot harder than climbing *up*, and neither of them had the right footwear.

Kris just looked at her. Over his shoulder Veerle noticed that a light had gone on in the apartment; she saw a thin line of yellow flare up between the panels of the shutters.

'I'll go first,' she said. 'It's easy – there was one difficult bit but there's some sort of metal thing sticking out of the wall. You can put your weight on that – I did it on the way up. You're taller than me, anyway – you can reach further.'

Heavier too, so more chance of that metal strut giving way. She didn't say that.

'Just follow me, use the same holds as I do, and—' She had been about to add, *For God's sake don't fall onto the railings*, but she caught herself just in time. 'Take your time, OK?'

She went to the stone parapet and climbed over. Now she was standing with her back to the street and the empty expanse of chill night air, as exposed as a diver about to perform a backflip. The first move was the worst; she had to put most of her weight on a single stone boss while she looked for the metal bracket to step down onto. When she had done that, and safely reached the bottom of the oriel window, she crossed onto the top of the bay window next door and looked up.

Kris had followed her over the parapet and was clinging to the bottom rim of it with grim determination. He remained in that position for so long that Veerle began to fear that he would lose his grip, that his fingers would become numb from the cold and peel off one by one. She squeezed her eyes shut, trying to block out the sudden vision of him plummeting from the window onto the sharp tips of the railings below, the terrible bursting sound as the iron points tore into his flesh. *Stop it.* She made herself open her eyes again, and now he was standing on the metal bracket, and it was holding his weight. She could see one half of his face by the amber light of the streetlamps. His expression was grim.

The shutters of Tante Bernadette's window remained closed, but Veerle wondered how long it would be before it occurred to the old lady's concerned neighbours to check the balcony. It was a relief when Kris reached the bottom of the oriel and stepped over onto the top of the bay window beside her.

There was no time to waste congratulating themselves on getting that far, however. Veerle could not stop herself glancing upwards, waiting for the light to stream out of the shuttered window above. Darkness so far. She led the way down the side of the bay window, taking great care this time as she placed her foot on the railings. Kris was visibly more confident now that they were nearly at street level; his boots hit the stone steps of the next-door apartment only half a minute after Veerle's.

Not a moment too soon; with a clatter the shutters of Tante Bernadette's front window opened and someone came out onto the stone balcony. Neither Kris nor Veerle looked up, however, and when whoever it was looked down, all they would have seen was a young couple who had apparently emerged from the next-door apartment block coming down the steps hand in hand and strolling away up the street.

'*Nom de Dieu*,' floated down quite clearly through the frigid night air, and Veerle guessed that the owner of the quavery voice was getting an earful from her male side-kick for wasting his time. She realized that she had left Tante Bernadette's keys in the apartment, but it didn't very much matter. She could not imagine herself ever going back there again, and remembering the grim expression on Kris's face as he clung to the outside of the building she thought that he would not be in a hurry to do so either.

Now that they were safely out in the street, she was terribly tempted to laugh. The thrill of having escaped by the skin of their teeth filled her with a savage joy. As they turned the corner she looked at Kris and her eyes were shining.

'I wish we could do that again,' she told him.

'You're crazy,' he said.

A couple of minutes later a middle-aged lady on her way home with two Delhaize supermarket bags full of groceries was forced to step into the road to avoid a young couple who were standing entwined in the middle of the pavement kissing each other so enthusiastically that they didn't even notice she was there.

Young people of today, she thought to herself as she trudged past them. *Shameless.*

25

In the first week of March Egbert decided to do another house. He hadn't visited the Koekoeken website for a while. With Egbert, everything went in waves. He'd be obsessed with something for a month, and then he'd drop it and start something else. Just lately it had been an online empire-building game. When he'd started playing it, he'd been staggered by its depth and complexity, the fluid beauty of the graphics. *Fucking awesome*, he'd posted on a web forum under his online name, *Horzel*. He'd spent every single spare moment on it – and eventually realized that it wasn't that awesome after all. It wasn't the *ultimate* game. Nothing ever was.

The trouble was, Egbert's *klootzak* of a boss had caught him playing it during working hours. OK, Egbert had to concede, he'd caught him playing it more than once. And he was not happy.

Egbert's view was that if you employed technical virtuosos you had to understand that they weren't just going to sit there from nine to five like good little galley slaves. It riled Egbert that Paul – sorry, *Meneer De Bock* – didn't get that. He ranted at Egbert for ten minutes, and then he gave him a verbal warning.

While Paul was ranting, Egbert tuned out. He pretended he was listening to white noise. He heard the bit at the end all right, though. He would have liked to punch Paul in his self-satisfied, *stupid* face, but he didn't want to lose the job. All that justifiable frustration made him feel twitchy, though. He thought he'd go and take it out on a house somewhere. Someone else's house.

Maybe this time he wouldn't repair anything. That was a crap idea anyway, and he'd only gone along with it because if he hadn't agreed, he wouldn't have been accepted into the group. Egbert thought it would be a lot more fun to break into a place with a decent amount of expensive hardware in it, and customize it a bit for his own amusement. There were a few places like that amongst the houses visited by the Koekoeken. Expats with more money than sense, who got someone in to set stuff up for them because they didn't know how to do it themselves (*Idiots*, thought Egbert). Then half the time they didn't use it anyway.

Egbert could think of at least one place he'd love to do. A little work could screw up their multiroom AV nicely. Ultimately pointless, since nobody would know it was him, but in a way that made the exercise all the more beautiful; he would be doing it just because he could.

When Meneer Klootzak De Bock had gone for his usual long lunch, Egbert logged on to the Koekoeken website and checked out the locations that were available. Several of them were useless – Egbert had no interest whatsoever in ancient properties with barely a phone line in them – but he found one he recognized, one that would be perfect for his evening's entertainment. He made sure to signal his interest in it, thus warning everyone else off. He didn't want some stupid idiot turning up at the same time.

Two evenings later he went to the house. It was on a quiet residential street in Sint-Genesius-Rode, south of Brussels, not far from the main road that ran alongside the Zonienwoud. He took a tram and a bus and then walked the rest of the way. He didn't worry about anybody noticing him; he dressed nondescriptly and kept his head down. There was never anyone walking about on that particular street at night anyway; they drove in and out in their expensive cars but they didn't actually *walk* anywhere. All the same he glanced swiftly around before he started on the gate. The street was deserted. There was a car parked on the grass verge perhaps a hundred metres away, but the lights were off and the engine wasn't running.

The lock on the gate was so simple that it was almost insulting. Egbert rolled his eyes. *Morons. Why do they even bother locking it?*

When he was on the other side he closed the gate again and then turned to look up at the house. It was the sort of place that sent estate agents into paroxysms of delight. Egbert thought it looked like a stack of kids' building blocks. Tall and white and flat-roofed with enormous floor-to-ceiling black-framed windows and so many different levels that it made you dizzy to look at it; it might have reminded Egbert of one of Escher's impossible architectural drawings, if he had taken an interest in art (which he didn't). There was a balcony high up above him with a black railing to match the black windowframes, and something else that looked like a blocky turret.

There were no roller shutters on any of the windows, which were made of reinforced glass for security. This meant that it was risky in the extreme to put on any lights. Instead, Egbert was armed with a Maglite torch; thanks to the towering laurel hedge screening the house from the road he was pretty sure that didn't represent much of a risk of detection.

He made short work of the front door locks, and that put him in an even worse mood. *Too easy.* He could never understand why his former friends in the lock-picking club back home in Holland had made such a fuss about his predilection for breaking into houses. These people were so stupid they *deserved* to be broken into.

All the same, he was surprised when he found the alarm system was already off. No buzzing, no flashing lights. He walked right across the spacious hallway and it didn't trigger so much as a single beep. *Not just stupid, but careless too.*

He didn't switch on the Maglite straight away. It was a moonlit night, and with those enormous windows he could see pretty clearly. First of all he went into the living room and poured himself a very large measure of the expensive whisky in the drinks cabinet. The glass was large and very heavy. Like everything in the house, it was outsized. Egbert stared out of the huge windows at the vast expanse of moonlit garden and wondered whether the owners were like that too; he imagined a family of giants – Americans, Texans maybe, with broad fleshy shoulders and bellies to match and calves like ham hocks. A lot of Dutch people were tall too but Egbert wasn't. He told himself that he despised that kind of physical robustness. The sooner it was possible to upload yourself into cyberspace entirely, the better. Then they'd see who was the giant.

He wandered back into the hallway, taking the glass with him, and started up the staircase. The first time he'd come here, he had found the experience unnerving. Like the rest of the house, the staircase was aggressively modern; it was constructed of some kind of burnished metal, and when you ascended it, the steps gave back a kind of metallic echo that made it sound as though someone were coming up after you. Now, of course, that didn't bother him. He knew he was alone.

He ignored the bathroom with its gleaming jacuzzi and the master bedroom with the water bed, and headed for the study, slipping the Maglite out of his pocket. He put the whisky down on the carpet for a moment. *Time to party.*

He actually had his hand on the door knob when he heard it. Downstairs, a door closed.

Shit. It dropped from him in an instant, that feeling of smug invincibility, like a tawdry cloak sliding off his narrow shoulders and puddling on the floor. Suddenly his heart was beating so wildly that he thought he might throw up. The Maglite fell from his grasp and rolled away somewhere in the dark. He dropped to his hands and knees on the thick, expensive carpet, knocking over the tumbler of whisky as he did so. He felt the liquid under his clutching fingers, soaking into the pile. *I'll have to clear that up*, he thought in some remote, detached part of his mind, the part that was not short-circuiting with fear.

He did his best to listen, but it was difficult to hear anything other than the sound of his own ragged breathing shivering through his teeth. *Calm down*, Egbert told himself, but the mere knowledge that there was something he needed to stay calm about was like throwing petrol onto the flames of his rising panic.

In the instant of silence between the drawing in of one breath and its release, he heard the distinctive sound of someone stepping onto the metal staircase. *Oh shit. This cannot be happening.*

He could hear the individual footsteps on the stairs now, ringing out forcefully against the metal treads like the blows of a hammer on an anvil, each followed by that tinny metallic echo. Whoever it was *wanted* to be heard, and that meant they knew that Egbert was up there. That this could not mean anything good was clear; people with respectable intentions do not stalk wordlessly through a darkened house, as Egbert himself very well knew.

The sound of the approaching tread galvanized him into action. He got to his feet, forgetting the spilled whisky and the lost torch, and looked about him, searching for an escape route. Not the study; that was a dead end. He went towards the master bedroom instead; there were two doors leading off that, one of them into a dressing room and the other into a bathroom which had a second door leading back onto the landing further down.

In his panic he managed to run into the doorframe with a thud that the person coming up the stairs must have heard. Too late to worry about that, however. Whoever it was must know he was here; the thing was to stay one step ahead. He fumbled his way around the doorframe and staggered into the master bedroom.

It was completely dark in here; thick drapes covered the windows. Egbert had a rough memory of the layout of the room from previous visits, but now he was unable to think clearly, unable to think of anything but getting away, and he blundered into a chair in the darkness.

When he straightened up he was disorientated. He felt the smooth surface of a desk or dressing table but he had no idea where in the room it was or which way he was facing. His fingers brushed a trailing flex. *A lamp.* For a split second he hesitated. If he turned on a light, his location would be completely obvious. On the other hand, he was now completely lost. Another half a minute of flailing about in the darkness trying to fight his way past pieces of furniture and he would have lost his chance of escape altogether. He ran his fingers up the flex until he found the little button and pressed it.

Nothing happened.

Egbert pressed the button again, pressed it several times with feverish urgency. The light remained obstinately off. He tugged at the cable. It seemed to be firmly plugged in, because there was no give in it. *Shitshitshit.* He couldn't believe his evil luck. *The bulb must have blown.*

He began to move across the room in the dark, holding out his hands in front of him, straining all the time for the sound of those footsteps on the stairs. Now he could hear nothing, which meant the person was on the landing carpet. Egbert lunged forward, and felt wallpaper under his palms. He moved sideways, keeping the contact with the wall, feeling for the bathroom door.

He touched the light switch almost at the same moment that he felt the edge of the doorframe. Instinctively he pressed it.

Nothing.

Finally it dawned upon Egbert that there was no light because the power was off completely. It was more than just a blown bulb. He heard a furtive tread entering the darkened bedroom and he seriously doubted it was the electrician. He tore open the bathroom door, stumbled inside and slammed it shut behind him, fumbling for the lock.

He really thought he might throw up. The taste of bile was acrid in his mouth. He managed to twist the lock shut, and then he staggered away from the door on legs that felt as though they would give way beneath him. The bathroom had a huge slanting skylight in the ceiling through which the moonlight poured, silvering his terrified reflection in the big rectangular mirror. He heard as much as saw the stealthy turning of the door handle. In another moment it would occur to whoever was on the other side of the door that he had locked it, and that the only way to get at him was to go back through the bedroom onto the landing.

Egbert fled through the other door.

As he ran for the head of the staircase he glanced behind him, and what he saw nearly dropped him in his tracks from sheer fright. Part of the shock was the fact that he didn't really believe the evidence of his eyes, not one hundred per cent. His knees were suddenly weak beneath him and part of him wanted to let them give way, to let himself crumple to the floor and bury his face in the elegant modern shag pile carpet, because what he was seeing couldn't possibly be there.

Instead he somehow managed to force himself forward and start down the stairs, but fear made him clumsy, and he lurched this way and that, jarring himself painfully on the metal banister. He wasn't really *seeing* the staircase leading down to the ground floor anyway, because his mind was still full of what he had just seen coming after him.

A hunter. An honest-to-God hunter. Egbert knew it was crazy but that was what he had seen, outlined against the huge window at the other end of the landing. The guy had looked about two metres tall – that might be fear magnifying him in Egbert's mind but he was *big* anyway, broad-shouldered and muscular, and he was absolutely armed to the teeth: there was something hanging at his side and something else that looked horribly like a crossbow slung across his back – but that wasn't the worst thing, because that was the jaunty little hunting hat perched on his head. The weapons were bad enough because nobody wandered around a darkened house at night with a private arsenal on their back just for the fun of it, but it was the hat that signalled the guy's *intentions*. He was hunting, and Egbert was the quarry.

It was kind of ironic in a way because Egbert had been in this position a thousand times already, but online. He'd had countless fights like the ones in *The Matrix*, he'd lost dozens of avatars to monsters and zombies and guys just like the one who was following him down the stairs right now, guys who were armed to the teeth and more than a little bit crazy. He'd practically rolled in digital body parts. The gorier the better. Handgun? Cool. Machine gun? *Awesome.*

Now he was discovering something new: that there was nothing awesome at all about weapons when they were real ones and the other guy had them all. As he fled down the stairs he was gibbering with fear.

He ran straight for the front door, but it wouldn't open.

It could have been something as simple as the guy pushing a bolt across but there wasn't time to stop and find out. He darted through an open doorway into the living room but there were no outside doors here, just the huge floor-to-ceiling windows.

He ran over to them anyway and banged on the glass, but it was that reinforced stuff. From outside you probably couldn't even hear him thumping on it. He suddenly had a very clear image of how he must look from the other side, of what someone would have seen if they had been standing there in the garden: a pale, terrified face with an open mouth like a dark circle, screaming noiselessly, palms slapping the glass without ever making a sound. But there was nobody out there. The lawn was silver in the moonlight and as flawlessly blank as a bowling green.

Egbert stopped banging on the glass and ran for the far door. He was not thinking clearly now; the house had become a maze to him. He forgot everything he had learned on previous visits.

The door led into a hallway with a set of stairs at the other end, leading down into the basement. There was no other way out. He wrenched open a door on the way down the hall; inside was a home gym, the dim shapes of a treadmill and exercise bicycle and weights machine visible in the gloom. *Nowhere to hide.* He didn't bother to close the door, but ran on down the hallway.

The stairs at the end descended into a black pit. The basement had no windows to admit moonlight, and without electric lights it was utterly dark. Egbert wasn't particularly suggestible when it came to dark places, and he was a lot more frightened of what was behind him than he was of the black basement. He went down the stairs as quickly as he could, holding onto the handrail for guidance.

It was cold in the basement, much colder than it had been on the ground floor. It was like stepping outdoors. For a few moments it disorientated him. He imagined a huge underground cavern, stretching out for metres in all directions, arching overhead like the dome of a cathedral.

Egbert stretched out a trembling hand and touched the cool matt surface of a wall. Instantly the darkness contracted around him to the width of a coffin. Now he felt claustrophobic. He had to suppress a rising feeling of hysteria as he felt his way along the wall. After a few moments he stopped and listened. His mouth was horribly dry.

There was no sound of anyone coming after him down the stairs. What was the guy doing?

A moment later he found out. There was an audible *click* followed by a hum as the electricity came back on.

Egbert tried to make himself think rationally. He no longer cared two straws whether anyone *outside* the house saw a light go on or not. The question was whether it would give him any advantage to turn the lights on or not. He could run from his pursuer more quickly if he could see where he was going, but he'd be instantly visible too. He glanced back towards the stairs and saw the lighter patch at the top, faint as a sketch. There was no one there, not as yet. He decided to creep onwards in the dark, in the hopes that he could find a hiding place.

The first door he came to was locked. He turned the handle twice, stealthily, but the door was not going to open.

He did his best not to think about what would happen if every single door down here were locked, if he were wandering further into a blind alley.

When he reached the second door, he hardly dared try it. It opened though, on the first attempt. The floor in here was tiled – he could tell from the slippery polished feel of it under his shoes. There was a slight slope to the floor. Egbert guessed that it was a shower room. He reached out and touched the wall and was not surprised to find tiles there too.

He closed the door very slowly and carefully, listening all the time, terrified of making any sound that would give away his location. Once the door was closed, the darkness was so absolute that it almost hurt to look at it, or look *into* it. Egbert located the door lock by touch. There was no key; it was a simple lever that turned to the side. It was stiff, and he didn't dare work at it too forcefully in case it made a noise. It turned about forty degrees and then it wouldn't go any further without a struggle. Egbert let go of it. He huddled against the wall, listening fearfully, shrinking away from the door. If he kept silent, if he kept the light off, if the lock held, he might just escape notice. It was a faint hope but it was the only one he had. He pressed his knuckles to his mouth and tried very hard not to whimper.

De Jager came down the stairs very slowly and carefully. He had plenty of time, after all. There was no other way out. He knew that the first door on the corridor, the one that probably led into the garage, was locked. He had tried it himself earlier in the evening. The prey had almost certainly gone through the second door, which led into the wet room.

De Jager padded up to the closed door and listened. Sure enough, he heard a tiny sound that might have been a smothered gasp or a sob. He let himself savour the moment before he opened the door.

The wet room was the perfect place as far as he was concerned; it could have been made for killing. Run both taps for twenty minutes and most of the mess would have gone down the drain. No need for anything as clean but inherently laborious as strangulation; he could indulge himself this time.

He went over to the illuminated switch on the wall and turned on the corridor light. When his eyes had adjusted to the sudden brilliance, he drew his favoured weapon from his shoulder and approached the wet-room door. His spirits rose, as they always did at such a glorious moment. He wrenched at the handle, jerking the useless lock open. Then he flung open the door and turned on the light, blinding Egbert, who was huddled against the tiled wall. While the pupils of Egbert's eyes were still trying to contract to bring the dazzling brightness down to a tolerable level, De Jager shot him at point-blank range with the crossbow.

26

'You know, it's the first day of spring,' said Veerle.

She was lying on an old picnic blanket on the floor in one of the high-ceilinged upper rooms of the old castle where she and Kris had met – *or re-met*, she reminded herself. Veerle was lying on her back, staring up at the ornate carvings on the ceiling. In spite of the cobwebs and the dust motes drifting through the pale sunshine, the ancient castle still retained a certain kind of beauty, like a very handsome old lady still holding herself with poise and grace in spite of her years. Directly above the spot where Veerle was lying there was a carved wooden head and she was trying to decide whether it was supposed to represent a lion or a bear.

Kris was lying next to her on his stomach. He had a can of Coke but he wasn't drinking it.

'March the twenty-first,' he said thoughtfully. He was staring out of the window at the trees clustered behind the castle. First day of spring or not, the branches remained resolutely bare, spreading like a fine net across the pale sky. All the same, you could feel the spring coming. It was suddenly warmer and lighter. Warm enough to picnic in the old castle's unheated interior, even if the picnic was only a packet of tortilla chips and a couple of cans of Coke.

'Yes,' said Veerle, rolling her eyes. 'March the twenty-first. First day of spring.'

Kris glanced at her, grinning. 'I know. My powers of detection are amazing.'

'Your powers of pointing out the obvious are amazing.'

'I was thinking.'

Veerle rolled onto her side, propping herself up on an elbow. She assumed a serious expression, although her eyes were bright with mischief. 'So what were you thinking?'

'I was thinking that if Horzel doesn't get in touch with Fred soon, there's going to be a meltdown. It must be nearly three weeks.'

'Who's Horzel?'

'His real name is Egbert,' Kris told her. 'He's the guy who's into lock-picking.'

'I remember, you said.'

'I don't really know him. I don't know his surname or anything.'

Veerle flopped back onto the rug, gazing up at the ceiling. 'So why do you care whether he gets in touch with Fred or not?'

'I don't. It's just odd.' Kris drummed his fingers on the worn wooden floorboards, his face pensive. 'Look,' he said, 'nobody knows anybody in the group any better than they have to. OK, there's whoever invited you to join, and there's anyone you ask to join yourself, and everyone has to get the nod from Fred. Some people like to do the houses with someone else, like we do, but never more than two. It doesn't make sense to get to know the friends of friends and the friends of friends of friends. It just means more trouble for everyone if someone gets caught. If you don't know anyone, you can't shop them. That's why it's all nicknames.'

'OK,' said Veerle, shrugging.

'So Egbert, I don't really know him personally. But I know someone who knows him.'

'I still don't see why you're interested in whether he contacts Fred or not. I mean, like you say, nobody knows anybody else all that well. Maybe he's just gone on holiday or something.'

'Egbert's close to Fred,' said Kris. 'He sounds like a bit of a pain but he's useful because he can get into anything, anywhere.' He rolled onto his side, facing her. 'Fred might have invited him personally, I don't know. Anyway Fred's on some kind of mission to save old buildings . . . or maybe he photographs them or something. You know, record it all before it falls down. And when the security is too tight Egbert gets him in.'

Veerle glanced at him. 'So you think Egbert would tell him if he went off?' For the first time she felt a twinge of unease. 'Look,' she said, 'it's probably nothing. Maybe he owes Fred money or something.'

'Maybe,' agreed Kris, but without conviction. 'It's just . . .'

'Just what?' Veerle asked him.

There was an infinitesimally small pause before Kris said, 'I'm not hearing back from Hommel, either.'

Oh. Hommel.

Suddenly there was a feeling of cold dismay in the pit of Veerle's stomach, as sour as guilt. She kept her gaze fixed on the carving high above her and thought about what to say.

She was still thinking about it when Kris said, 'We just talk now and again.'

'OK,' said Veerle carefully.

'But she's not replying.'

She's pissed off at you, thought Veerle. She let out her breath in a long sigh and waited for Kris to go on.

He was shaking his head. 'I don't know,' he said. 'Maybe I'm chasing ghosts. Seeing a pattern where there isn't any pattern.'

'What pattern?'

'People just suddenly dropping off the radar.'

Veerle stared at him. *No*, she thought. *Egbert, that's a bit odd, maybe. But Hommel . . .* She had a feeling she knew why Hommel hadn't been in touch. *She's playing hard to get. Maybe she thinks she can get you to come running after her.* She didn't say that, of course. She said, 'Maybe she's gone away somewhere too. She doesn't tell you everything, does she?'

'No,' said Kris reluctantly. He put one lean hand into his dark hair, tugging at the unruly strands. 'But' – he hesitated – 'it's not just them.'

'Well, what is it then?'

'Vlinder.'

'Vlin—' Veerle started to say something, something along the lines of *Vlinder? No, it couldn't possibly have anything to do with Vlinder*, and then she stopped. The uneasy feeling that had been stealing over her coalesced into something more solid, as though something were curdling inside her.

She remembered very clearly the night she had met Kris, here in the castle, and how he had asked her persistently whether or not she was Vlinder, because Vlinder had gone silent and nobody knew where she was.

And now someone's asking the same questions about Egbert.

Just thinking about what had happened to Vlinder – *Call her Valérie*, she reminded herself. *She had a real name, not just a nickname* – well, it made her feel cold all over. Slaughtered by some unknown person in an unknown location, and then dumped into an icy lake to hang suspended in the glacial water like a cut of meat in a freezer. They didn't even have a definite death date for her.

This Egbert guy, he's probably just gone off somewhere, she told herself uneasily. Aloud, she said, 'It has to be a co-incidence. What happened to Vlinder – that doesn't happen every day.'

Kris shrugged. 'Look at the papers.'

'Well . . .' Veerle was struggling to think of some way of proving that there couldn't be a connection. 'What are the chances of something like that happening to two people we know? Well, sort of?'

'I don't know,' said Kris grimly. He sighed. 'Maybe it's nothing. But it's not just two of them.'

'Hommel,' said Veerle. She took a deep breath. 'Look, she's probably gone away for a few days or something.'

'I'd know,' said Kris.

'You'd know? I thought—'

'I said, I know.' Kris was looking at her sideways, and she could see a slightly amused expression in his eyes that was more irritating than the knowledge that he was still in regular contact with Hommel. 'I know she's probably just gone away or something. I'm probably being paranoid. Anyway,' he added casually, 'I've learned something else today.'

'What's that?'

'You're jealous.'

This was so undeniably true and yet so inadmissible that Veerle was outraged. She sat up, an indignant expression on her face. 'I am *not* jealous.'

She tried to cuff Kris but he parried with his arm. Then they were struggling together, and laughing, and then Kris was kissing Veerle and she was kissing him back and the topic of Egbert was forgotten, as good as packaged up and fired off to the planet Mars.

Later, when she was sitting on the bus home with a smile on her face and the memory of Kris's kisses still warm on her lips, Veerle did think about Hommel again.

Playing hard to get, she told herself. *Or with a bit of luck, maybe she's run away with Egbert.*

27

She's crazy, thought Veerle. *My mother has finally gone crazy.*

She was in her bedroom in the house at Kerkstraat. There was a little white clock on the wall above the door and the clock told her that it was 7.33 p.m. The bus would be leaving in three minutes, assuming that it was on time. Veerle was dressed for her evening with Kris: jeans, boots (you never knew what you were going to have climb over or indeed through), a shirt and a black jacket. Her dark hair was pulled back from her face and fastened in a loose knot. She had a small torch in her pocket; she even had a screwdriver of her own now – one with interchangeable heads stored in a space in the handle. She was, in fact, one hundred per cent ready to leave the house. And she couldn't open the door.

She thought she could even identify the exact moment when Claudine had locked it. Veerle had been standing in front of the mirror applying eyeliner and she'd heard a stealthy tread on the landing outside. The door was closed because after the bitter exchange she had had with her mother earlier in the evening Veerle wanted to retreat into her own space. She didn't want to argue with Claudine any more and if Claudine saw her getting ready to go out, the whole thing would inevitably start up again. So the door was closed, and when she heard her mother padding along the landing Veerle didn't react, other than to frown at her own reflection in the mirror. Somehow it was worse that Claudine was creeping about like that than it would have been if she had come stamping along the landing screaming reproaches. Lurking silently on the other side of the closed door was somehow a little pathetic. It was not as though you could move along that landing without other people hearing you, anyway. The old house had so many creaky boards that walking along the landing was like playing a harmonium.

For a period of several minutes Veerle had been painfully aware of her mother's silent presence on the other side of the door. Then there had been a small but audible *click*. At the time Veerle had thought her mother was trying the handle, and had glanced at the door, inwardly praying that this was not the harbinger of another round of arguing. But the door had remained stolidly closed, and now she knew why. Claudine had locked her in.

She planned it too, thought Veerle. Normally the key was on the *inside* of the door, and since Veerle had been the first to reach the room after the row, evidently Claudine had been up *earlier*, when Veerle was out, and removed the key.

She's finally flipped, Veerle said to herself. She tried the door again, but it wouldn't budge, and she had a horrible feeling that the sound of her rattling it or banging on it would simply have gratified her mother in some unpleasant way. She put her ear to the battered wood and listened, but all she could hear was her own breathing.

'*Maman?*'

Silence. Then she heard a door closing downstairs, and a few seconds later the sound of the kitchen radio blaring into life.

Verdomme.

She glanced at the clock again. *I'm going to miss the bus now, that's for certain.* She could see the bus stop in the town quite clearly in her mind's eye – the white and yellow De Lijn sign and Kris standing underneath it, looking at his watch. The image was so sharp that she could almost – almost – have stepped right into it, spoken to Kris, touched him. But she wasn't going anywhere, not unless she could find a way out of this room.

I'll have to text him, she thought, and then for the first time she could have screamed with frustration, *really* screamed. Her mobile was downstairs on the little table in the hallway, charging.

Now she was angry. She went to the door and hammered on it with the flats of her hands. '*Maman! Maman!*'

She no longer cared whether Claudine got some unhealthy satisfaction out of hearing her. She wanted to get *out*. She screamed at her mother for a full minute and when she stopped to listen, her throat feeling scoured and dry, the kitchen radio was still blaring away to itself like a lunatic and there was no other sound from below. No reaction from Claudine.

Veerle kicked the door as hard as she could, but although it relieved her feelings it didn't help her get out. Then she went to the window. She had some idea that she might be able to get out that way, remembering her hasty departure from Tante Bernadette's apartment. Climbing *down* was always going to present more of a challenge than climbing *up*, but she was desperate.

When she looked out, however, she knew it was useless. She was a good climber, she knew that without any false modesty, but you'd have had to be Spider-Man to get down the front wall of the house without dropping off and breaking your neck. Unlike Tante Bernadette's apartment block, which had all manner of archaic and useful architectural features, the front of Veerle's house was pretty much a blank slate, without even a drainpipe within reach of her window. She looked sideways too but neither the bathroom window to her left nor the neighbour's window to the right were close enough to reach; and neither of them had a windowsill you could really stand on. She stared down at the street for a moment and then she drew her head back in and closed the window.

She went and sat on the bed and put her head in her hands, overwhelmed with angry despair. *Why, why did I leave my phone downstairs?* She could power up her laptop and *email* Kris, but she couldn't even call him right now to let him know she wouldn't be coming. She wondered how long he would wait for her at the bus stop in town.

How long before he gives up and goes off on his own? What is he going to think?

She raised her head and looked with savage fury at the stuffed toy rabbit sitting on her pillow. Claudine had given it to her years ago, and whenever Veerle tried to relegate it to the back of the wardrobe her mother put it out again.

She wants to keep me a little kid.

Veerle picked up the rabbit by the throat and threw it across the room.

Verdomme. Verdomme!

28

At 11 p.m. Claudine unlocked the door. Veerle was sitting on her bed, still wearing her boots and jacket, as though there was some faint chance that she might go somewhere. She had left the window partly open too, in spite of the cold air that seeped in with the darkness. With everything closed tightly the room felt too much like a prison. There was a gentle breeze that sucked the light curtains in and out, as though the night itself were breathing.

In spite of the soft rubbing of the curtain material she heard the click as the key turned in the lock. She didn't bother to get up right away. *What's the point?* She knew that the last bus had gone nearly an hour ago. She sat on the bed hugging her knees and waited for the creaking of the floorboards that would tell her that her mother had moved away down the landing.

When she finally heard her mother's bedroom door close, she got up and crossed the room. The door opened easily to her touch. Claudine had left the landing light on, but she remained closeted in her room.

Veerle went downstairs and retrieved her mobile phone from the table in the hallway, slipping it into the pocket of her jeans. Then she went into the kitchen, switched on the light and opened the fridge. She hadn't realized until that moment how hungry and thirsty she was. She found a wedge of apple tart in a bakery box, and wolfed it straight from the cardboard, not bothering to find a plate. She poured herself a tall glass of orange juice and drank that too. She looked in the fridge again and found a chunk of Chimay cheese, and ate it while wandering around the kitchen.

She didn't like to sit down; she'd spent too many hours sitting upstairs waiting for Claudine to open the door. She pulled her mobile out of her pocket and switched it on, dreading to find either that Kris had called a dozen times or that he had not called at all. The screen lit up.

Two missed calls.

She checked, and both of them were from Kris's number. There was no message though, and no text.

Veerle glanced at the clock. Quarter past eleven.

To hell with it. I'm calling him.

She wasn't entirely reckless, though; before she entered his number she went into the darkened hallway and listened. Silence. She supposed Claudine was still in her room. All the same, when she went back into the kitchen she quietly closed the door. Then she went right to the other end of the room and leaned against the wall with its faded paper, a design of squares overlaid with sunflowers that had probably been cheerful once. She entered the number and listened to Kris's mobile ringing.

It occurred to her too late that perhaps it might be unwise to call him this evening, that maybe he had gone to the house they had planned to visit without her. If he was climbing over someone's garden wall at this very moment, the last thing he wanted was an electronic riff blaring out of his pocket. While she was debating whether to hang up, Kris answered the phone.

'Veerle?'

She could hear a kind of rushing sound behind his voice, as though he were outdoors somewhere with the wind blowing, or perhaps it was the sound of distant traffic.

'What happened?' he asked. 'Are you OK?'

'Yes, I'm fine.'

'I thought maybe you'd vanished into thin air like . . . Egbert.'

Veerle closed her eyes. *Hommel*, she thought. *You were going to say Hommel.*

She pushed the thought away.

'No,' she said. 'I'm at home. I couldn't get away.'

There was a pause. Veerle bit her lip. It was simply impossible to explain the whole thing with Claudine over the phone, especially when they were in the same house; she didn't *think* her mother could hear anything from upstairs, but the possibility was off-putting. It was more than that, though. She'd never really talked to Kris about Claudine.

The thing she had with Kris, it wasn't *about* that – the everyday crap: school, home, problems with your parents. It was about stepping right *out* of that life for a while, shrugging it off like a particularly dowdy and restrictive piece of clothing. She couldn't imagine ever bringing him home to meet her mother, even if Claudine had been an easier, more sociable person, any more than she could imagine introducing him to her school friends. There was simply too much that would always have to remain unsaid. So she had kept the two things apart, Kris and her other life.

Now, however, she could see that they were on a collision course.

I can stop her locking me in again, thought Veerle. *I'll just hide the key. I'm never letting my mobile phone out of my sight again either. But I still have to explain why I didn't turn up tonight. And I can't just say, my mother locked me in my room. It sounds crazy.*

'It's difficult,' she said into the mobile. Then she told him what she wanted to do.

29

The next morning Claudine wouldn't look her in the eye. Veerle came downstairs with her school bag slung over her shoulder and went into the kitchen to grab a slice of bread and butter, and her mother was in there already, standing by the coffee maker. When Veerle came into the room, Claudine turned her back with an audible sniff.

She's angry with me, Veerle realized with incredulity. *She probably thinks I ought to apologize.*

There was no way she was going to do that, so instead of the bread and butter she took a cellophane-wrapped sweet roll with jam in it out of a packet in the larder and walked out of the house. She could eat it on the bus if she kept out of the driver's line of vision.

It was a mild dry morning. Spring was in the air, and it was already fully light. Veerle unwrapped the roll and broke off a piece as she walked to the bus stop. She was thinking that spring and eventually summer were going to present some interesting challenges for her excursions with Kris.

It won't be so verdomd *cold any more, but nor will it be so conveniently dark in the evenings.*

The bus was four minutes late, and she had eaten the whole

roll before she climbed on. It was nearly full. She showed her bus pass to the driver but he wasn't interested; all he wanted to do was offload his rowdy passengers at the high school in the town.

Veerle looked down the bus and saw Lisa sitting almost at the back, along with a couple of other girls from her class. She began to push her way down the aisle. It was difficult because there were so many people and bags in the way, and a couple of boys from her year were deliberately obstructive, dodging this way and that when she tried to get past.

Veerle sighed. She supposed this was inevitable; she hadn't exactly been running with the crowd recently. In the end she shoved her way past them with an ironic 'Sorry' when her elbow caught one of them in the ribs. She ignored the remarks that followed her down the bus to where Lisa sat.

There was nowhere to sit so she simply leaned over, pulling an envelope out of her school bag. 'Lisa, will you give this to Mevrouw Verheyen?'

Lisa took the envelope, turning it over to look at the name on it. 'What is it?'

'I'm not coming in this morning. Hospital appointment.'

'Hospital?' Lisa looked up at her, squinting in the early sunshine.

Veerle shrugged. 'Just a check-up.'

'Hmmm. Are you sure you're not bunking off?'

'Quite sure.' Veerle wasn't rising to the bait. 'Will you take the note in for me, then?'

'OK.' Lisa sounded bored. 'Are you coming in later?'

'Maybe. It depends how long the appointment takes.' Veerle dared not prolong the conversation. 'Look, I have to get off the bus at the tram stop. I'll see you later, OK? Or maybe tomorrow.'

She fought her way back down the aisle to the doors. The boys didn't get in her way this time, but they still made a couple of comments, just loud enough for her to hear. Veerle wasn't really listening, though. She was wondering whether Mevrouw Verheyen would suspect the same thing too, that Veerle was simply bunking off for the day. *I hope she won't call the house*, she thought.

Writing the note hadn't presented a problem; since Claudine didn't speak Flemish, let alone write it, the school were used to Veerle composing her own sick notes and Claudine signing them. The only bit of forgery involved had been the signature, and Claudine's was a scrawl anyway; she wrote the way she spoke, in a wavering, nervous-looking script that was easy to reproduce.

If they phone, though . . .

It was a relief to get off the bus. Veerle stood on the pavement and watched it pulling away in a cloud of evil-smelling fumes. Lisa coasted past, but she was already deep in conversation with someone and didn't glance out at Veerle.

Don't forget to deliver the note, Veerle willed her silently. Then she turned and crossed the road to the tram stop. She went and stood right under the shelter, making herself as inconspicuous as possible; the last thing she wanted was for a teacher driving past on their way to school to notice her standing there. She looked at her watch.

I'm going to be hours early.

Veerle was trying her best to keep anxiety at bay but it was like being attacked by a pack of small but irritating lapdogs;

as fast as she kicked one away, another one would come darting in from a different angle.

What's he going to think when I tell him what's going on at home?

She saw herself turning into a kind of Cinderella-in-reverse, shedding the glittering plumage of the thrill-seeker who could scale the front of apartment blocks and morphing into just another girl with messy home-life problems.

But what option do I have? she thought. *I have to explain why I stood him up.*

He sounded different when I asked him to meet me today; maybe he's annoyed with me.

And then there was the question of Hommel . . . Veerle grimaced.

The tram ride seemed to take for ever, and at the other end she had to walk. The address Kris had given her was surprisingly urban considering what he did during the working week; she looked at the grimy old buildings and scruffy shops, wares spilling out onto the pavement, and wondered where there could be any plants growing. But Kris had said they were doing some work for the council; perhaps they were trying to coax a few flowers into bloom amongst the cigarette ends and drinks cans that sprouted like weeds in the municipal flowerbeds.

She spent a bit of time browsing in the shops but in the end there was nothing to do but go and wait for Kris. The place he had suggested was a little café and bakery squeezed in between a dry cleaner's and a tobacconist's. The trade seemed to consist mainly of people coming in to buy pastries or coffee in polystyrene cups to take away; Veerle was the only

customer who elected to sit down, so she had a choice of
tables. She considered sitting by the front window where she
could look out at the street, but the thought of carrying on a
private and possibly awkward conversation while framed in
the café window like a couple of Jan Klaassen and Katrijn
dolls in a puppet theatre was not an appealing one. She chose
a table near the back and ordered an iced tea.

The minutes ticked by with agonizing slowness. *Lisa will
have given that note to Mevrouw Verheyen by now.* Veerle
sipped the iced tea and watched the door.

At the back of the café the light was dim but outside the
morning was suddenly sunny, so that when Kris finally
appeared it was as a dark silhouette against the bright
rectangle of the glass front. It took Veerle a moment to be
sure it was him, and when he slid into the seat opposite her
she was dismayed. His face was grim.

'Hi,' she said, keeping her tone light.

'I took an early break,' said Kris. 'I've got half an hour.'

They looked at each other. Veerle was acutely aware of the
strangeness of the situation. *We never meet anywhere like this.
A normal place. We never go to Quick for a burger or take the
bus to Leuven to see a film or hang out at each other's houses. It
feels weird sitting here together at a table in an ordinary café.*

It was though she had suddenly found herself sitting opposite a fictional character, someone from a book or a film.

The solitary waitress came out from behind the glass-
fronted counter and took Kris's order. When she had gone,
Veerle said: 'Did you do the house last night?'

Kris shook his head. 'No.' He looked as serious as she had
ever seen him. He was dressed pretty much as he always was,

the familiar black leather jacket slung over a work shirt, but when she looked down at his hands she saw that the nails were grimy with earth.

He's going to end it, Veerle thought suddenly with horrifying clarity. She felt a sickening lurch in her stomach. *Maybe Hommel's moved back in already.*

An appalling thought occurred to her. *Supposing he called her when I didn't show up?*

She had to push on anyway. 'I'm sorry about last night.' She took a deep breath. 'Look, it's my mother. I think she's actually sick or something.'

Then it all came pouring out. The fretting that had turned into worrying that had turned into obsessive anxiety. The health scares, the security scares, the letting down of shutters and locking of doors before night had even fallen. The fact that Veerle seemed to have less freedom, less privacy – now, at the age of seventeen – than she had had all those years ago when she was only seven and Kris was nine. The questions, the constant questions. And finally the attempt to stop Veerle going out altogether, by locking her in her room.

The waitress came with Kris's coffee and went away again and Veerle barely noticed. She didn't cry – she hardly ever cried and hated it when she did – but the words poured out of her, as hot and irresistible as tears. There was a reckless compulsion to it; she suspected she was burning her boats with Kris, exposing the sickly underbelly of her life, but she couldn't seem to stop herself.

She looked down into her iced tea while she was talking, and then she looked sideways at a faded photograph of the Atomium on the café wall, and then she looked over Kris's shoulder at the dazzling rectangle of window. When she finally finished talking she looked at Kris and she was amazed.

The grim expression had gone. He was listening to her very carefully; his face was grave, but some dark cloud had lifted. Then he sat back, thinking about what she was saying, and although he still looked serious his posture was relaxed, his shoulders were down, his fingers were toying with the coffee spoon. He looked . . .

Relieved.

Now he was leaning towards her across the table and was asking her something about her mother, about whether she had talked to anyone else about her, like maybe the GP, but she wasn't listening one hundred per cent because she was cradling a new realization as though holding a newly hatched fledgling in her hands.

He's relieved because he thought I *was going to end it.*

It was not possible to fully savour the implications of this in the midst of her woes, any more than it is possible to look up from the desert floor where you lie prone under the shadows of circling vultures and lose yourself in admiration of a butterfly that lands a hand's reach away. She still had a big problem: the fact that her mother was rapidly turning into her jailer and she had no idea what she was going to do about it. Still, she felt a small and sudden surge of happiness, because now she knew.

He was afraid of losing me.

Kris had stopped speaking; he was waiting to hear what she would say.

Veerle shook her head. 'I haven't told anyone before now.

I mean, she wasn't always this bad. It's been getting worse for a long time and you get used to it, you don't realize how insane it all is. But anyway, I don't know who I'd tell. I suppose I could try the doctor.'

'What about your father?'

'She hates him. There's no way she'd listen to anything *he* said. She calls him *ce salaud de Gand*.'

'Harsh.'

'I guess so. I never see him – I mean, *she* won't ever see him so neither do I. He could be a total bastard for all I know.' She shrugged. 'I haven't seen him since I was about eight.'

'Look.' Kris held her gaze. 'You could move out. You don't have to stay with her.'

Veerle sighed. 'I still have to finish school. I couldn't afford to live on my own while I'm doing that. And anyway . . . I couldn't just leave her, not while she's like this. She doesn't speak Flemish, she can't read her own letters, she can't even renew her own ID card at the Administratief Centrum. She has a job, but only because the woman who runs the business is a French speaker. If she lost it she couldn't even read the job ads.'

'Why doesn't she move back?'

'To Namur, you mean? I just don't think she could cope with the move – all the paperwork and everything. I suppose my dad did that when they bought the house.'

'Veerle' – Kris's voice sounded urgent – 'she's going to have to cope without you sooner or later. You can't stay there for ever.'

'I know. It's just . . . she's never been as bad as this before. I really think she's actually . . . sick.'

'Then she has to get help.'

'I know.' Veerle smiled at him ruefully. 'I suppose I'll try the doctor. Look, I didn't mean to get into all this really heavy stuff. I just wanted you to understand why I couldn't come last night.'

'Do you think she'll try it again?'

'No. I took the key out.' Veerle fished in her pocket and flourished it in front of him. 'It's the only one. She can't lock me in again . . . well, not unless she nails the door shut.'

'Well, keep your phone with you, OK?' Kris looked at her seriously. 'If she does anything like that again, you can always call me.'

They exchanged a glance, and although no further words were spoken on the topic of Claudine, something passed between them, as fleet and intangible as a nerve impulse passing along a neural pathway.

Outwardly nothing had changed. Veerle did not expect that they would meet like this again, in the prosaic environment of a café, he in his work clothes and she carrying her school bag, any more than the bear and the wolf can meet on a city street. The next time they met it would be in the old castle, or in an expensive suburban villa full of strangers' photographs. That was their natural domain, the place where they existed together most intensely.

All the same, something is *different.*

It was though they had stretched out to each other and broken through some gossamer barrier.

It's her, thought Veerle. *Mum. She's not standing between us any more.*

The half-hour was up, and Kris had to go back to work.

They paid for their drinks and embraced briefly on the pavement outside the café, and then Kris was striding away down the street, and Veerle was watching him go, with her fingers to her lips and her eyes shining, silently repeating the words he had murmured into her hair before parting.

30

Oh my God. It's that *house.*

Veerle froze with a forkful of pasta on the way to her mouth. Her jaw dropped, her eyes widened in shock. A pasta twist dropped back onto the plate unheeded as she stared at the television screen.

It can't be. It just can't be.

But it was. She began to fumble for the remote control, wanting to turn up the volume, before realizing that Claudine had it. She made herself sit still then, not wanting to draw attention to herself, but she simply could not stop staring. The shock of recognition was like an icy wave flooding the labyrinthine spaces of her body, overtopping every defence, lapping into every corner.

They must know, she thought, not stopping to define *them* clearly to herself, and her mouth was dry with the acrid taste of panic, as bitter as bile. A searing sense of injustice swept over the glacial sense of shock, a fresh wave breaking over the ebbing remains of the first. *We didn't even go inside that one. We didn't* do *anything!*

She gazed at the screen, at the fancy villa very clearly visible behind the windswept RTBF presenter. She could remember the night she and Kris had visited that house, could remember it with painful clarity. Walking from the tram stop at Oudergem Woud, trying to make themselves inconspicuous. The large tree in whose deeper shadow they had concealed themselves. The elegant portico and the door flanked with the little windows, one of them with the imperfectly closed shutter whose chinks had revealed the light on inside. She could even spot the corner of the house, and although you couldn't see what was round there, she remembered the path and the wrought-iron gate. If Claudine had turned to her suddenly and said, *What a lovely house, I wonder what the back garden is like?* Veerle could have told her that too.

It has a beautiful ornamental pond, but there's a stone wall right in the wrong place, and it hurts like hell if you run into it in the dark.

She'd had the yellowing bruise for ages. Absently she put her hand to her hip and rubbed at the spot through her jeans.

She was terribly tempted to leap up, to make an excuse to escape to her room, to call Kris, to ask him what on earth they were going to do, but she made herself sit still and listen to the presenter. She had to know what *they* knew.

As she listened, it gradually dawned on her that there was trouble all right, but it was somebody else's trouble, and she and Kris had skirted it like explorers picking their way around a green swamp filled with venomous snakes. The matter of their having trespassed in the villa's garden one night paled into insignificance; indeed, she began to think how ridiculous it was that she had thought all this might be for that – the television reporter's earnest words, the shots of the house, the little inset of a face she didn't recognize.

A girl had vanished, and not just *any* girl, it would appear, but the almost-grown daughter of the wealthy director of an international company headquartered in Brussels. The company's logo appeared briefly on the screen, as though the girl were some valuable corporate asset that had been stolen.

The girl was missing, and she had been missing for weeks; the earnest television report, the pleas for information, were simply the flowering of an affair whose roots ran backwards in time, back into the chill and darkness of February. She hadn't gone missing from Brussels, though, and that was the complicating factor, the *Zandmannetje* sprinkling his psychotropic dust in the investigators' eyes. Although the family lived in Belgium, they were British, and the girl had been studying at a university in England since the previous autumn. There was some problem though; she had decided she didn't like the course any more or had been slipping behind with her studies, and after a heavily loaded meeting with her tutor she had simply dropped out of sight, failing to show up for her lectures and tutorials. After a time the lumbering machinery of the university had realized that she had actually gone, left, and was not simply curled up in her room in an almighty snit. Attempts had been made to contact her family, but her parents were on a two-week holiday in Burma and it had taken a while to track them down and for them to fly home.

Even then, the initial search had tended to concentrate on Great Britain. The house in Belgium was closed up during the family's absence and there was no reason for anyone to think that Clare – that was the girl's name, Veerle learned – had gone there. Someone was employed to water the house plants in the family's absence and he or she had seen nothing un-toward at all, no sign that anyone else had been inside the house.

One of us, Veerle realized with a sense of shock. *The person who waters the plants is one of the Koekoeken.*

That wasn't the worst of it, though. It was bad enough, yes, because if the police decided to lean on the plant-waterer hard enough, he or she could blurt out everything, drop every single one of the Koekoeken in it up to their neck. But what was a million times worse, the thing that was making Veerle feel suddenly sick with foreboding, as though her entire body were clenched in a spasm of cold horror, was the thought that the girl, Clare, *had* been inside that opulent villa; that it was Clare's motionless hand she had seen out-stretched on the kitchen tiles.

She didn't *want* to believe it, because apart from anything else, if it was Clare she had seen, lying so terribly still on the kitchen floor, then she and Kris and the rest of them were standing at the rim of something appalling – an abyss, a black hole whose gravitational pull would suck all of them in.

Veerle sat with her plate of pasta cooling on her lap, her gaze fixed on the television screen, and tried to reason it out, but she kept coming back to the same horrific conclusions. *The house was* supposed *to be empty when we visited it; the owners were in Burma. Only a handful of people had access to it, and one of them has vanished. Someone was lying on the floor when I looked in through the window that night, someone who wasn't moving . . . If it wasn't Clare, who else could it be?*

She couldn't think of a single satisfactory alternative. She remembered Kris suggesting that perhaps what she had seen was one half of a couple. *Maybe they like fooling around on the kitchen floor.* That was possible, of course, but everything still pointed to Clare; Clare who was missing. Kris had the key to the house that night, which meant none of the other Koekoeken had it, not unless one of the others had made a secret duplicate, and when you looked at that possibility against the likelihood that Clare herself had come back to the family home and let herself in with her own key, well, it was a no-brainer.

So what was she doing lying on the kitchen floor? And who was the man? That was the crux of it. She had tried to see that scene in the kitchen in another way. Perhaps Kris had been right: perhaps it was the man's hand she had seen.

I don't think so, though.

At the time, she had almost come to doubt the evidence of her own eyes, and it had been easier, safer, to think that she had seen something with an innocent explanation. Still, she could remember the horror that had welled up inside her when she saw that motionless hand; the way she had instinctively reached for her phone to call for an ambulance – would actually have done so regardless of the consequences if Kris hadn't stopped her. She had started entering the number, she remembered that, so at the time, what she had seen had convinced her of its urgency, no matter how muddy the memory had become afterwards.

Whatever I saw happening, it wasn't good. If the hand belonged to Clare, well, Clare had vanished, but apart from that undeniably sinister fact there was that feeling she had

had that night, something ill-defined and just out of her grasp.

The echo of a memory.

Wrongness, she thought now. The horror she had felt when the man had risen into view from behind the kitchen unit was more than the simple shock of seeing someone where there should have been no one. She had felt the *wrongness* of the situation.

Oh God, what did we witness?

It was no use, she couldn't sit here any longer. *I have to contact Kris.*

She knew that it would upset Claudine, but she still had to do it.

Veerle had chosen to spend the evening with her mother, watching television in the stiflingly dull atmosphere of the living room. She had thought that it might pacify Claudine, that it would paper over the cracks, work as a kind of trade-off. *Hey, I go out alone sometimes, but we still have our safe little evenings at home, same as ever, just the two of us. OK?*

Neither she nor Claudine had broached the subject of Veerle having been locked in her bedroom. Her mother was still a little stiff with her, but Veerle now suspected that she was ashamed of herself, rather than angry, and as the evening had progressed in its reassuringly uneventful way, Claudine had gradually unbent. She had cooked something she knew Veerle liked, and had gone so far as to ask her questions about school and her friends.

Veerle had fed her mother some tame titbits of inform-ation in much the way that she might have offered scraps to a timid animal – an outline of the last Dutch assignment, a description of a friend's mother's new car. Nothing alarming. She had felt Claudine relaxing, felt that things had returned more nearly to normal than they had for some time.

Now I'm going to ruin it by going off upstairs and shutting myself in my room. If she chooses to listen outside she'll know that I'm calling someone. Even if she doesn't, she isn't going to like it.

I can't help it. I have to call him.

She put the unfinished plate of pasta on the floor and got to her feet.

31

'Kris? It's me, Veerle.'

Veerle was standing by the window in her bedroom, looking down at the street below. She had chosen the spot because it was the furthest point from the door, which was firmly closed. She didn't *think* her mother was listening in – in fact Claudine had gone into the kitchen in a state of dudgeon and started washing up with a staccato energy that was perilous to the crockery – but she didn't want to take any chances.

'Have you seen the news?' she asked.

'Yeah. Have you seen the message from Fred?'

'What message?'

'He's told everyone that the house is off limits. Extinct. He's crapping himself.'

Veerle sagged against the windowframe, putting her free hand to her forehead.

'Are you still there?' asked Kris after a moment.

'Yes.' She exhaled slowly. 'I was just kind of hoping that I'd made a mistake – that maybe it wasn't the same place or something.'

'It's the same place, all right.' Kris sounded grim.

'Fred recognized it?'

'No, he only does the old ones, remember? He has this thing about restoring them. Someone else tipped him off, and now he's panicking, scared as a weasel.' Kris paused. 'He's not the one who has to worry, though. He's never been near the place.'

'Shit.' Veerle closed her eyes. 'Look, we didn't go in. It's not like we've been all through the house leaving fingerprints on the doorknobs or anything.'

'*You* haven't,' said Kris succinctly. 'Me, I'd better hope the maid polishes everything properly.'

'But . . .' Veerle was fighting to think of some way of warding off the horrifying possibilities that were suggesting themselves. 'Even if you'd left stuff all over the place, they wouldn't come looking for us, would they? If you're not on their records already, then prints and stuff don't tell them anything.' She said *they* because she didn't want to say *the police*.

'As long as the girl who waters the plants keeps her mouth shut,' Kris pointed out. He sighed. 'She probably will. If she tells anyone about the extra key and all the rest of it she'll drop herself in it, not just us. I'm guessing she won't tell the police anything.'

We hope. Veerle was silent for a moment. She was gripping her mobile phone very tightly; her palm was slick against the plastic casing.

'But should *we*?' she said finally.

'Should we what?' said Kris, and then he realized. 'Talk to the *police*, you mean? No. No way.'

'Kris . . .' Veerle massaged her brow with her fingers, as though trying to work away a headache. 'There was that hand.'

'The hand on the floor? But you didn't see whose hand it was. It could've been anyone's.'

Veerle felt an insane desire to laugh at that. She said, 'It was a woman's hand – or a girl's. I'm sure of it. Anyway, who else would be in the house if it wasn't that Clare girl? They said everyone else was away.'

'I don't know. Anyone. If the house had been empty, *we* could have been in it.'

'We had the keys,' Veerle pointed out. 'So it can't be any of the other Koekoeken, not unless someone has a second key.'

Kris thought. 'Look, supposing it *was* Clare's hand you saw. So what? They already know she's missing, and they're already investigating whether she came back to Belgium or not. If she did, they'll find out. Telling them we saw a hand won't do anything, if we can't confirm it was her.'

'There was the man.'

'Whose face we didn't see,' Kris pointed out. 'We can't identify him either.'

There was a long pause.

'I suppose not,' said Veerle reluctantly. She stared out of the window. The streetlamps were just coming on. A man was passing the end of Kerkstraat walking a little dog. Everything looked normal. Reassuringly normal.

'Veerle?'

'I'm sorry,' she said. 'I just feel as though we ought to help them find that girl, if we could. But you're right, we couldn't tell them anything useful.'

So why do I feel so bad about keeping quiet?

32

Egbert made a journey, his first ever visit to Wallonia, the French-speaking part of Belgium. Egbert had never shown an interest in this region of his adoptive country, nor was he likely to do so now. He travelled in the boot of a car, his darkened and tainted features concealed under a tarpaulin shroud. He travelled until he had passed out of Flemish Brabant and into the province of Namur; indeed his journey took him past the birthplace of Veerle's mother, Claudine. He continued onwards, into the Ardennes, travelling along ever smaller and narrower roads, until he was passing through forest.

There were places in this region that thronged with tourists, stretches of river patrolled by plastic kayaks, picturesque hiking trails. The haunts of the living. Egbert had done with those for ever. His destination was a lonelier one, a stretch of unkempt forest pierced by a single winding road. The leaves of the trees and bushes lining the road were grey with the dust of traffic that simply passed through on the way to somewhere more interesting: the next boathouse, the next town where the weary walker or mountain biker could quench his thirst with a cold beer and turn his face to the sun.

There was a track leading off the road and into the woods, so little used that it was almost concealed by the overhanging foliage. It was deeply rutted; as the tyres bounced over the gouges in the earth, Egbert's dead limbs jumped and jerked as though an electric current had passed through them. His head lolled.

When the car stopped and the engine died, there was a second or two of absolute silence. Then there was the sound of the car door opening and closing, the muffled crunch of footsteps on the mulchy ground, and shortly after that, the grunt and strain and thick hacking sounds of someone turning the earth. A gouge, a furrow, and finally a shallow grave.

The boot of the car was opened, the tarpaulin drawn back, and the sunlight that filtered down greenly through the clustering leaves illuminated the skin of Egbert's face for the last time. The marks of passing time were clearly visible; soon Egbert's own mother would not have recognized him.

Presently he lay in the makeshift grave, nestled in the earth like some strange unhealthy tuber. The weary spadework began again. At last the rich dark soil closed over Egbert's sunken features as though he were slipping slowly down into black water, overwhelmed, drowning.

After the soil came some mossy branches and leaf mulch. Now a casual passer-by, if such a person ever ventured into this part of the woods, would be unlikely to notice anything at all.

In life, Egbert had prided himself on his ability to enter forbidden places unseen, to come and go undetected. Now at last he had achieved the ultimate: he had vanished altogether.

33

Kris and Veerle met at a house in Everberg, an upmarket village which required two bus journeys to reach from Veerle's home. The house was large and very modern and ill-defended; the alarm was not working at all. It had a pool, although it was smaller than the one in the house to which Kris had first taken Veerle, and a sauna; but better than that, it had a large basement with a home cinema. It even had padded chairs like the ones you found in real cinemas, up-holstered in deep blue plush fabric.

Veerle liked the house, and not just because of the home cinema. She was glad that they had selected a property far away from the villa she had seen on the news.

She didn't want to think about that villa, about the circular window at the back, and the light that had poured out of it that night, making a paler patch on the close-cropped lawn. She *had* thought about that house almost constantly when the news first broke, but Kris was right: even if she had contacted the police, she could not give them enough inform-ation to identify the people she had seen inside, assuming that there really *were* two of them, and she hesitated to take a step that would implicate so many unknown others.

Fred did the right thing, she told herself, trying to swallow the unease that rose in her like nausea. He had warned everyone off the villa, had declared it permanently off limits, had sealed it off from the Koekoeken network as neatly and finally as a surgeon performing an amputation. *It has nothing to do with us any more.*

. . . And if that was Clare you saw, and you could have saved her if you'd made that call? Better not to think about that, unless you wanted to stagger around with a burden of guilt, and wake up at night thinking *What if . . .* It was too late anyway, she realized.

Veerle came out of her reverie and saw that Kris was sorting through the ranks of DVDs. She went over and stood beside him and started looking at the spines of the plastic covers herself. Nearly every one of them was in English, with no Dutch soundtrack or subtitles. She supposed the owner had ordered them all from Great Britain.

They live in a bubble, Veerle thought. It didn't make her feel any more empathy for the people whose house she was invading. How could you trespass in someone's space if they weren't really *there*?

It's weird, she mused. *These people always either live in the past, hankering for the place they left, or live in the future, yearning for the day when they'll return. Never in the present. If I had a house like this, I'd enjoy it properly.*

She picked out a DVD. 'What about this?'

It was a horror film, an extravagantly trashy story about a group of teenagers being picked off one by one in improbable and grotesque ways.

'Nice,' said Kris, looking over her shoulder. He leaned in

almost casually and kissed the side of her neck. Veerle shivered pleasurably, her eyes closing, wanting him to do it again, but Kris was already taking the DVD out of her hands, opening the plastic box to extract the disc inside. Veerle's eyes followed him but she went to sit down on one of the blue plush seats.

When he started the film, she almost jumped. The rumble from the speakers was so loud that it was like listening to an aeroplane landing. Kris adjusted the volume and turned down the lights, and then he came and sat next to Veerle, putting his arm around her, pulling her towards him.

On the screen, horrible things were starting to happen, mouths gaping open, eyes wide with terror, screams, fire. Blood. Veerle wasn't looking at it. Her face was turned to Kris's and his to hers. They were bathed in the colours pouring out of the screen – white glare alternating with the golden bloom of explosions. Kris put out a hand to touch Veerle's face and his skin was tinted the colour of flames. The screen went black for an instant and Kris's face, so close to hers, was lost in brief darkness, as though a great wing were beating between them.

I think I love you, she thought, and on screen someone died.

She gave herself up to the pleasure of being kissed by Kris, but she was not oblivious to the film; she was consciously ignoring it. She hadn't picked that one at random, either. She had seen an earlier one in the series; she knew what it was about. A string of freak accidents, utterly improbable but theoretically possible events. The plot didn't just go out on a limb, it tiptoed out to the very end of the branch, to the slimmest twig, until the whole thing was bending under its weight and a single step further would make the whole thing snap.

The thing was, *Claudine* thought like that. She would knock on Veerle's bedroom door half an hour after both of them should have been asleep: she had been lying awake wondering whether Veerle had fallen asleep with her laptop on the bed – all because she had read about someone who had done that, leaving the machine plugged in at the wall, so that some part of it had heated up and set the bed linen alight. When she used the dishwasher, which was rarely, she still washed up the cook's knives by hand because she had heard of a person who had slipped on their kitchen tiles and fallen onto the upturned blades stacked in the cutlery holder. And if she went down with an illness, she never suspected anything as harmless as a cold, she always went directly to fretting about tumours and heart defects and killer viruses.

If Claudine could have been induced to watch this particular film – which was impossible; the mere suggestion would have horrified her – Veerle thought that she would have *recognized* the world she knew, a world where circumstances combined in baroque ways to try to get you. Being cheerful and confident, or indeed happy, or hopeful, or *young*, just seemed to Claudine to be asking for trouble, daring the massed forces of darkness to finish you off in some unimaginably nasty way.

If it had been possible to talk to Claudine about it in a rational manner, if the discussion would not inevitably have led to a venomous row, Veerle would have told her, *No, I can't accept your view of the world, I can't live in a place that feels like a vast grey labyrinth with traps waiting round every corner. I can't spend my whole life worrying about stuff that might never happen. I want to do, and see, and be. I want to be free.*

So she let the horrors on the screen wash over her, she turned her shoulder to them and put her arms round Kris's neck and kissed him back, not just because she knew she loved him, but in defiance of Claudine and everything she stood for.

34

When the film was over they went upstairs and wandered through the expensively decorated rooms. There was little they could do for the house; everything appeared to be recently decorated and superbly maintained. Eventually Veerle opened the enormous American-style refrigerator and discovered that the owners had forgotten to clean it out before they went away on holiday; she removed the mouldering head of lettuce and the tomatoes, which were so soft and rotten that they were bursting open, and put them in the compost bin in the garden.

When she went back inside, Kris was leaning against the heavy marble worktop in the kitchen. He said, 'Did you do anything about your mother?'

Veerle didn't reply right away. She went to the sink and began to wash her hands under the gleaming chrome mixer tap.

'I tried seeing the GP,' she said. She looked at the water running over her hands, how clear and sparkling it was, like liquid diamonds, and wished she didn't have to keep thinking about Claudine.

'And?'

'It didn't really help.' She turned off the tap and shook her hands over the sink. 'She said she'd really need to see my mother. She said if Mum was depressed she could help her get treatment.' Veerle sighed. 'She suggested I try to persuade her to make an appointment.'

'Are you going to?'

'I've tried, but . . .' Veerle shook her head. 'She'll go when she thinks she's actually ill – you know, physically; in fact she's never out of there, thinking she's got this or that. But she doesn't think there's anything wrong with the way she's behaving. She still thinks she was right to lock me in my room. She says it's for my own good.'

'Shit.'

'I knew she'd be like that. I told the doctor it wouldn't be any use. Then she started asking me all this other stuff, like did I think I was in any danger, or did I think Mum was a danger to herself.'

'What did you say?'

'No.'

'Veerle, she locked you in your room.'

'I know . . . but she didn't hit me or anything.'

'You said she tried to stop you leaving the house once before, and shoved you.'

'Yes, but I wasn't in any *danger*.'

'Look . . .' Kris thought for a moment. 'What about your dad?'

'I haven't seen him for years, and anyway, she wouldn't listen to him. He's the last person.'

'I mean, if she gets a lot worse. Could you move in with him?'

'I don't even know him any more,' said Veerle. 'And anyway, he lives in Ghent.'

Kris shrugged. 'Ghent – it's not the moon. And it would only need to be for another year or so, until you finish school.'

Veerle was silent.

'You don't want to leave her,' said Kris, 'do you?' He came over, put his arms around her. 'Look,' he said, 'she's going to lose you in the end anyway. Unless you stay there for the rest of her life she's going to have to cope without you in the end.'

Veerle leaned against him. 'Sometimes . . .' she said. *Sometimes . . .*

I hate her.

She didn't like the feeling that was churning up inside her. She didn't even want to be having this conversation.

If I spend my whole time with Kris going over what has happened in the past and what my mother might possibly do in the future, I'll be as bad as the people who own this house, living in luxury but always wanting to be somewhere else. I want to be with him, really with him, enjoying what's happening now.

'Sometimes what?' asked Kris.

'I don't know,' she lied. 'Look, I'll think about calling my dad. I'd have to find his number somehow, and I don't think she'll listen to him even if he agrees to talk to her, but I'll try to call him.'

She nuzzled in close to him, brushing her lips against his skin, hoping that he would kiss her again, that they could recapture the feeling she had had while they were watching the film – of a defiant joy so intense that it was almost savage.

When Kris didn't immediately respond she was slightly piqued.

He put his head back, looking at her very gravely. She could tell that he was going to say something serious.

No, she thought. *I don't want to talk about* her *any more.*

But he didn't want to talk to her about Claudine.

'Veerle . . .' He paused. 'We need to talk about Hommel.'

Oh God. He might just as well have thrown a bucket of icy water over her. Veerle took a step back, staring up at him, her face a blank mask, waiting to go one way or the other, follow the signposts to anger or upset or – *please God* – relief, because he wasn't going to say he was back with her.

He must have seen the thoughts that were darting through her mind, as swift and spiked as venomous fish.

'No . . .' he said. 'I mean, she's still missing.'

Still missing. Veerle had no love for Hommel but Kris's words sent a chill through her. *Missing. Like Egbert was missing . . .*

'How do you know?' she asked, trying to keep her voice neutral, not wanting to believe it.

'I tried to contact her. Look, it's not just me. Other people have been trying to get hold of her. Nobody seems to know where she is.' Kris shook his head. 'Something's wrong. I thought at first it was me; that she was pissed off at me. But something *is* wrong. The other person who's trying to get hold of her, Koen – he wants to get a key back from her. Some place over in Wezembeek.'

Veerle was conscious that Kris was no longer trying to hug her; he was holding her by the upper arm, holding her quite firmly as though he didn't want her to get away – as though he really wanted to persuade her of something.

'Veerle, she took the key to go over to this place and that was the last anyone heard of her. Koen wants the key and he's been trying to contact her for ages. He's tried the web forum and she's not replying to anyone, so he got in touch with one of her other contacts who knows her personally – not me, someone else. He got her mobile number and he called that, and she never answers. It doesn't even ring, it goes straight to the messaging service, and she never calls back.'

'Email?'

'She's not replying to that either.'

'Maybe she doesn't want to be contacted,' said Veerle doubtfully.

'She'd still have returned the key,' said Kris. 'She knows Koen's never going to stop pestering her for it if she doesn't.'

Veerle looked at him very carefully. 'You have her landline number, right? Why don't you call her at home?'

'I tried,' Kris told her. 'I even went round. Her *klootzak* of a stepfather wouldn't tell me anything.' His face clouded with anger. 'He just told me to fuck off. He wouldn't let me in, either, so there's no way of knowing if she was there or not.'

'Well, maybe she was,' said Veerle. 'Maybe she didn't want to see anyone.'

'Or maybe she's gone, and he's just so glad to see the back of her that he doesn't want to ask why and where,' said Kris. 'They don't get on, mainly because he's such an *eikel*.'

'Surely he wouldn't just ignore it though, not if she'd disappeared,' said Veerle. She was a little shocked.

'She's over eighteen,' said Kris. 'It's not like she's still studying or anything. There's nothing to stop her going, not if she wants to.'

'Well, maybe she *has* just gone off,' suggested Veerle.

'She would have said something.'

'Maybe she didn't *want* to tell him where she was going, if she hates him that much.'

'Him, yes, she wouldn't tell *him*, but she would have said something to the rest of us.'

To you, you mean.

Veerle looked away from him, as though she had taken a sudden interest in the pots of utensils on the work surface, or the expensive chrome coffee maker. It was tempting to feel angry about Kris's concern for Hommel; she was aware of the subtle pull of indignation, plucking at her like the current that leads more and more urgently into the centre of the whirlpool.

But what if something really has happened to Hommel – something bad? That was the thing, wasn't it? It was the *terrible* thing, the elephant in the room, the stinking corpse under the floorboards. She thought of Vlinder, suspended in the icy water. She thought of Clare, whose hand she might – or might not – have seen. An image flashed across her mind, of the rotten tomatoes breaking open as she dropped them into the compost bin, spilling their soft innards, and she felt a tinge of nausea. *We can't ignore this.* She thrust the beginnings of anger aside as though she were kicking away a nipping dog.

She said, 'Is there anyone else we can ask, who might know where she is?'

'There's her mother,' said Kris. He sighed, leaning back

against the marble work surface. 'But I can't call her at home in case the *klootzak* picks up the phone, and I can't really catch her at work.'

'Why? What does she do?'

'She's a hairdresser. Women only. But it's not just that. She's completely under his thumb. It's one of the reasons Hommel hates him. He's got her totally cowed, creeping around like a mouse. There's no way she's going to talk to me, especially if she knows he's already told me to get lost.'

'Hmmm.' Veerle knew what she was going to say even as she was still appearing to think about it. This was going to mean crossing another barrier, this time actively interfering in the life of another Koekoeken member, but recently she had stepped over so many barriers that she was beginning to feel like a monster in a movie, brazenly rampaging its way through cities, knocking down everything in its path.

'I suppose,' she said to Kris, 'that *I* could talk to her.'

35

Before Veerle went to see Hommel's mother, there was another difficult conversation she had to have.

It had not taken her long to get hold of her father's address and telephone number. She had planned to search for him online in the White Pages, or go through Claudine's little bureau in the dining room, looking for divorce papers, or perhaps call older relatives or friends of her mother's to see if anyone knew of Geert De Keyser's whereabouts. She was not very optimistic about the last of those options since she'd had no contact with any of her father's relatives and she suspected that Claudine's family in Namur would feel much the same about Geert as her mother did.

All the same, she had picked up Claudine's address book from the hall table, where it always lay next to the telephone, and flicked through it. Veerle rarely handled the address book; all her own friends' details were stored on her mobile phone or her laptop. The book struck her as terribly old-fashioned and also highly reminiscent of its owner. It was bound in artificial brown leather and had a kind of dog-eared, run-down, apologizing-for-itself look about it. It even smelled a little musty and unloved.

She looked under D and K, and even finally G, but there was no entry for Geert De Keyser, and she was about to put the book down again when she noticed that there was a piece of paper in it, folded in two and inserted between the last page and the back cover. On impulse she pulled it out of the book and opened it, and discovered with a tiny thrill of surprise that it was a letter from her father – a short and businesslike one, something about sending documents – with an address and telephone number in Ghent at the top. Evidently Claudine had saved it for future reference, but had not wanted to commit herself so far as to give her former husband his own entry in the address book. It was a small gesture of repudiation, a way of relegating Geert to the outer darkness beyond the wall she had built, keep-like, around herself.

Veerle looked at the date at the top of the letter; it was eight years old.

He might have moved by now, you know.

There was no harm in trying, though. She copied the telephone number into the address book in her mobile phone; if she used the landline and the call came up on Claudine's Belgacom bill, she could imagine the scene that would ensue. Then she waited for an opportunity to call. She could not imagine doing it in a snack bar or, worse, in the park, where she would have to shout against the sound of the wind and distant traffic and dogs barking. Instead, she waited for Claudine to go out.

Now, for once, her luck was in, and Claudine *had* gone out, departed for an appointment with her French-speaking dentist. It was late enough in the afternoon that Geert De

Keyser might reasonably have arrived home from work. Veerle went upstairs to her room, and even though she knew that Claudine was out, wouldn't be back for at least an hour, she closed the door. She was not sure what she felt about what she was about to do. She was purposely making herself *not* think about it too carefully, because if she did that she might talk herself out of calling at all, or she might dial the number, and then, when Geert answered, find herself entirely unable to say a word to him. She wasn't even sure what she *was* going to say, but simply hoped that the right words would come at the time.

She sat on the bed and began to tab through the names in the mobile's address book, but before she had even got as far as D she was on her feet, restless, pacing about in the limited space between the bed and the desk.

De Keyser Geert, she read. She hadn't shortened it to *Pa* or *Papa* because she wasn't sure yet whether that was what he really wanted to be. He might tell her that he wasn't interested, that he couldn't help. He might be resentful at the intrusion, or angry because she had never contacted him before; or if he was the bastard Claudine made him out to be, he might be shockingly rude and dismissive. She touched the green CALL icon and waited, trying to quell the unpleasant fluttering in her stomach.

The phone rang seven times before she heard the *click* of someone picking up at the other end.

A female voice said, '*Met Janssen.*'

'Um . . .' For a moment Veerle almost hung up. Then she said, 'I'm trying to contact Geert De Keyser.'

She half expected the brusque-sounding female voice at

the other end to berate her for being stupid; she'd said *Janssen* after all, and Veerle was asking for *De Keyser*.

Instead there was a pause and then the voice said, 'Who is speaking, please?'

'It's Veerle.'

'Veerle who?'

'Veerle De Keyser.'

This time there was a longer pause. 'Wait, please.' There was a *clunk* as whoever it was on the other end of the line put down the receiver.

Veerle bit her lip. *He's there.* The anticipation was almost more than she could bear. She felt uncontrollably jittery; she couldn't stop herself roaming the room. She turned and saw that Claudine had replaced the stuffed rabbit on her bed. Veerle went over, swept it up with one hand and shoved it into her wardrobe, still keeping the mobile phone clamped to her ear.

'Geert De Keyser,' said the phone in her ear.

Veerle jumped so hard that she almost dropped it.

'Hello?' said her father. Veerle was surprised at how unfamiliar his voice sounded. She had no proper recollection of it, and yet . . .

I thought I'd recognize it.

'Hello,' she said. 'It's Veerle.'

'Veerle? From Kerkstraat?'

'Yes. Veerle, your . . . Claudine's daughter.'

She heard him draw in a breath.

'Has something happened?' he asked.

'No,' said Veerle. 'Nothing's happened.'

Again there was silence on the other end of the phone, a silence so complete that Veerle wondered momentarily

whether her father had simply set down the phone and tiptoed away.

Finally he said, 'I'm sorry. This is so unexpected. I don't
know what to say. How are you?'

'I'm fine,' said Veerle.

'And Claudine? I mean, your mother?'

'She's . . . I don't know how she is,' said Veerle. She put up
her free hand and smoothed down her dark hair with it. She
said, 'I feel funny doing this. Calling you.'

'That's fine.'

'Who was it who answered the phone?'

'That was Anneke, my girlfriend.'

'Your girlfriend,' repeated Veerle. *Now I really feel weird. He
has a girlfriend.* She couldn't imagine her mother ever having
a *boyfriend.*

'Yes.' Her father paused. 'Are you sure nothing's happened?
Is Claudine there?'

'No, she's out. I waited until she'd gone out before ringing.'
Veerle took a deep breath. 'It's about her. I didn't know who
else to ring.'

'Is she sick?'

'No . . . well, at least, she isn't ill exactly, but it's the way she
behaves. She's been kind of . . . weird, and I think it's getting
worse.'

'How?' asked her father, so Veerle told him.

She told him about the way her mother worried excessively
about herself and Veerle. The probing, anxious questions she
was always asking. The rows they had had. The way Claudine
tried to stop Veerle going out, to the extent that she had
finally locked her in her bedroom.

She did her best to describe it all as dispassionately as she could. She knew that Claudine would view Veerle's phoning her father to tell him all this as some kind of terrible betrayal akin to wartime collaboration. She wanted to be sure that she was at least being fair to her mother, so she tried to keep her feelings out of it, to bite back the hot indignation that threatened to pour out of her in torrents of angry words whenever she thought about that evening spent under lock and key, unable even to phone Kris.

All in vain. Her father listened to it all carefully and patiently, she had to give him that. But at the end the first thing he said was, 'Look, it's bound to be difficult. She's in her fifties now, and you must be . . . sixteen now, right?'

'Seventeen,' said Veerle heavily.

'It's normal not to get on with your parents when you're seventeen,' her father went on. 'You want to go out, she wants to know where you're going, you don't want her poking her nose in . . . It's normal, believe me.'

He's not taking me seriously.

Veerle pressed a hand to her forehead. 'She locked me in my room,' she said, and then to her horror she heard her father actually chuckle.

'My father once tried to do that when I was a youngster,' he was saying. 'I climbed out of the window and jumped onto the shed roof, and tore the backside out of my jeans doing it.'

Dad, Veerle wanted to say, but it felt too strange. The blood tie between them had long since shrivelled up and fallen away like an umbilical cord. She hesitated, and then she said, '*Geert.*'

In the startled pause that ensued she said, 'It's not like that. The way she goes on – it's not normal. It's—'

'Veerle,' said her father, and there was an edge to his voice that she had not noticed before, although whether it was annoyance or concern or bitterness she could not tell. 'I know your mother can be difficult. It must have been annoying, not being able to go out when you wanted to. But that's all, isn't it? She's not physically hurting you, is she?'

Veerle closed her eyes in frustration, drawing in a great breath. It was the same story as it had been with the doctor. *Is she a danger to you or yourself?*

'No,' she said tightly.

'There's really not much I can do,' continued Geert, and already Veerle could hear from his tone that he was disengaging, dropping away from her like an escape capsule jettisoned from a spaceship. Leaving empty space where there had been contact. A trail of smoke.

She heard him telling her that it was not worth him trying to talk to Claudine, that she wouldn't listen to him anyway, that Veerle must realize that.

He doesn't understand, thought Veerle dismally. *She wasn't as bad when he left, nothing like as bad, and now he just doesn't see it.*

Eventually Geert must have realized that his words were dropping into silence, like pebbles tossed into a well.

'Veerle?'

She roused herself. 'Yes.'

'I'm pleased that you called me . . .' Geert hesitated and then he said, 'I used to send cards and presents, you know. But your mother always sent them back.'

So you gave up.

'I'd like it if you called me again – as long as it won't make things difficult with your mother.'

She won't know about it if I do, thought Veerle. 'OK,' she said non-committally.

'Maybe you could come and see me and Anneke in Ghent one of these days.'

'Maybe.'

Veerle didn't listen to any more. She let the hand holding the mobile fall to her side. After half a minute or so she touched the red END CALL icon without bothering to check whether Geert was still on the line or not.

She slid the phone into her jeans pocket and went over to the window. The street below was deserted; there was no sign of Claudine returning yet. She leaned her forehead against the cool glass and let out a long sigh.

36

By rights, Egbert should have lain undisturbed in the wood until he seeped and finally crumbled away into the dense soil. The stretch of woodland where he lay was so rarely disturbed by the sound of human voices. It was not unknown for a year to pass without a single person walking through here; the last time anyone had done so was the day of Egbert's burial.

Even when foxes attempted to dig out the body, scraping the earth away from the dome of the forehead so that it appeared from the dark soil in a repulsive parody of birth, the head crowning out of the mud, still it might have remained undiscovered by human beings. A young dog fox trotted away from the mauled remains with part of Egbert's left hand in his mouth; he actually crossed the track while still carrying it, secure in the knowledge that there were no people about – his ears and nose told him he was alone. When he had gnawed all that was edible from the hand he left the bones lying in the undergrowth, where they remained, as though grasping ineffectually at the earth, long after Egbert's disintegrating remains had been laid on the autopsy table.

The unfortunate person who discovered the rest of Egbert was eleven-year-old Alexandre Lambert. Alexandre was a skinny, thin-faced, rebellious boy who bore something of a resemblance to Kris Verstraeten at the same age, although where Kris's hair was dark, Alexandre's was the colour of dirty straw. Alexandre was a member of a local French-speaking Scout troop, which he hated – at least, he hated it today. The troop had met in the forest to play a wide game, but in the first five minutes Alexandre had managed to get into a fight with two of the other boys. The Scout master had broken it up, but Alexandre could see in the other boys' eyes that the affair was not yet at an end; once the troop had dispersed in the woods, he was dead meat. The other boys were bigger than he was; it was probably madness to have started something with them but he just couldn't seem to keep his mouth shut.

There were, he decided, two options available to him once the broad blue shoulders and large denim-clad rear of the Scout master had vanished into the forest. He could stay and fight, which probably meant lying in the muddy under-growth with his arms wrapped around his head and his knees up protecting his balls, or he could make himself scarce for the entire ninety minutes of the wide game. He opted for the latter just too late. They had seen him, and were making their way towards him with grim determination.

Alexandre thought about it for a split second, and then the desire to survive the next hour and a half with his most sensitive parts unbruised won out over the desire not to appear yellow. He turned and ran.

He was not entirely surprised when he heard them crash-ing after him through the undergrowth. They were making so much noise that an image floated unbidden into his head, of a pair of rhinos crashing through the forest after him. He felt a wild desire to laugh. He was pretty confident he could outrun them; they were taller than him, but also a lot fatter. He hurdled a log and sprinted onwards, threading his way between the trees.

Merde, but they were persistent. Alexandre kept running, and they weren't catching him up, but they weren't giving up, either. From the whoop he heard behind him, he guessed that they were enjoying this a whole lot more than he was.

He ran out of the undergrowth and onto a path, and now he could see a notice board ahead, one of those ones with a map on. He knew that he had reached the outer rim of the area allowed for the game. The Scout master had been pretty firm about that; the forest went on for kilometres and he didn't want anyone getting lost. He had described the territory they had to keep to, and the path with the notice board marked the border on this side. They all knew it; every one of them was a local boy. Any further than the notice board and you were off limits, and in deep trouble.

Alexandre passed the notice board at a sprint. It occurred to him that he was going to have difficulties making it back to the meeting point at the agreed time. He was getting further and further away from the start. He could have doubled back, but he wasn't entirely sure where his pursuers were. Sound was deceptive in the forest; you could hear a crack or a rustle and you couldn't pinpoint the source of it at all. He put his head down and kept running. As he ran, he touched his pocket, checking for his mobile phone. If he ended up too far away at the end of the ninety minutes, he'd have to call someone and face the music for overstepping the boundary. If, that was, the two boys didn't catch him and smash the phone along with most of the rest of him. He was committed now.

Eventually he had to slow from a sprint to a trot, and from a trot to a walk. He had a stitch in his side and he was breathing heavily, and his straw-coloured hair was stuck to his face in sweaty strips. He kept to the path for a bit, where the earth was soft and there were fewer leaves to rustle or sticks to crack and give away his position. He was exhausted and he wished he had brought something to drink with him. Mostly he was desperate to stop moving for a few minutes, to flop down somewhere and catch his breath. He didn't dare stop in the middle of the path, so he listened for a moment to be sure that no one was close enough to hear him, and then he left the path and pushed his way through the undergrowth, looking for a place to lie low.

If he had been a little less weary, or a little more interested in the time-honoured Scouting activity of tracking, he might have noticed the footprints of the fox here and there in patches of mud. He might even have noticed a lone human boot print. But Alexandre didn't notice it at all; as he picked his way through the undergrowth, the mix of burgeoning spring green and the rot of the past winter, he managed to tread right in the boot print, turning his foot a little in the mud as he did so, obliterating it completely.

He paused, listening, but all he could hear was the wind in the trees and the cry of a bird. Gratefully he sank to his knees, head down, the damp ends of his hair hanging over his eyes. Slowly his breathing and heart rate slowed. The unpleasant feeling of tightness in his chest subsided. His fists, clenched on his thighs, relaxed. He closed his eyes for a long moment, then he shook back his fringe and raised his head.

At first he thought that what he was seeing was some sort of smooth rock breaking the surface of the earth. That was what it looked like, in a superficial sort of way, if you didn't study it too closely. A rock, or the dome of a great fungus pressing up through the earth, except that he had never seen a puffball that big. It didn't exactly invite the eye; there was something ominously suggestive about it, something strangely tainted, as though whatever it was belonged on a rubbish dump. Now that he came to think about it, there was a subtle odour on the air too, a whiff of something less than pleasant.

His gaze traced the shape of it, the two circular depressions below the hemisphere, the outline of the other shapes breaking the surface of the earth like the spars of a wrecked ship protruding from a black sea. He stared and stared, and then suddenly it was as though he were viewing one of those weird pictures, a stereogram, where you looked at a pattern and suddenly you saw something in it, in three dimensions, something you couldn't see at first glance.

A body.

The thought passed through Alexandre's mind like a blip on a cardiogram, and all of a sudden he was scrambling to his feet, his heart thumping and his eyes wide with shock, and he was brushing at the thighs of his jeans with frantic hands as though he might have got some of that disgusting taint on himself, because it *smelled*, it really smelled, and that meant there were tiny particles of the thing in the air he was breathing.

He backed away, and then he turned, and then he ran, no

longer caring whether he met the boys who had been pursuing him. He fled back to the path, inadvertently leaving another print from the sole of his trainer on the smear of mud where the single boot mark had been, and then he ran on, wide-eyed and revolted, until the yellow of his hair and the patch of blue that was his Scout shirt and the dark shapes of his jean-clad legs, opening and closing like scissors, were swallowed up by the forest.

37

After school, instead of taking the bus back to her village, Veerle walked into Tervuren. She had a scrap of paper in her pocket with the address of the hairdresser scrawled on it. She knew the town well but she wasn't familiar with the name of the salon, and when she found the street where it was located she knew why; it was the sort of place you could easily miss – so nondescript that your eyes slid past it, looking for something more interesting. There was a shiny awning, faded to beige, and a large window full of sun-bleached studio shots of models with big hair. KAPSALON read the letters on the awning, which was just as well, because otherwise you might have taken the place for a funeral parlour.

Veerle stopped on the other side of the street and looked at it. The moment she had laid eyes on the place, she had decided one thing: she wasn't making an appointment there just to speak to Hommel's mother. She didn't want to risk coming out looking like one of Claudine's friends.

I have to have a reason for going in, though, she reminded herself. *Kris said Hommel's mother just works in the salon, she doesn't own it. If the owner's in there, she probably won't take kindly to stray girls coming in to question the staff.*

I'll buy a bottle of shampoo. She glanced doubtfully over at the salon again. *Or maybe a packet of hair grips.*

She crossed the street and approached the salon door. Even before she opened it, she could see that the place wasn't exactly heaving with customers. There was a single old lady seated at the back of the shop; a stout middle-aged woman with a great confection of back-combed hair dyed an improbable shade of dark brown was putting dozens of little curlers onto the old lady's head, rolling the grey strands tightly, as if aiming for a face-lift, reeling in the flaccid skin along with the hair. The dark-haired woman was clearly not Hommel's mother; Kris had described her as blonde.

As Veerle entered the shop she saw that there was another woman inside, but just as the salon itself tended to blend into the buildings around it, so she seemed to be doing her best to melt into her surroundings. She was sitting behind the little reception counter, and when Veerle came in she did not look pleased to see a new customer; rather, she appeared full of trepidation, as though Veerle were likely to make some un-reasonable demand. She got to her feet, and Veerle realized that she was half a head shorter than herself; evidently Hommel got her height from her father. There was some family resemblance there in the faded face that might once have been pretty; Hommel's mother was fair too, but the blonde had turned to salt-and-pepper.

'What can I do for you?' she asked Veerle, and out of the corner of her eye Veerle saw the dark-haired woman turn slightly. Listening, probably.

On impulse she decided to forget about buying anything and get straight to the point. She had a feeling it wouldn't be long before the other woman came over to interfere, and it was Hommel's mother she wanted to talk to, not her. Veerle recognized a cast-iron harridan when she saw one. Time was short.

'Are you Mevrouw Coppens? Homm— I mean, Els's mother?'

The woman started, and that told Veerle that she *was* Hommel's mother, but she didn't admit to it, not immediately, and the look she gave Veerle was odd, nervous, almost afraid.

'Who are you?' she asked.

'I'm Veerle.' She didn't give her surname; if there were any trouble it was as well to provide as little information about herself as possible. 'I'm a friend of Els's,' she said.

Mevrouw Coppens leaned forward over the counter. Her shoulders were hunched in a permanent cringe; Veerle suspected that she was also anticipating interference from the other woman.

'Is she all right?' she asked Veerle in a low voice. 'Did she ask you to come here?'

'No.' Veerle saw the woman's face fall and found herself wishing she could have said yes. She lowered her own voice. 'Look, I haven't seen her for a while and—'

'Can I help?' said an acid voice behind her.

Heart sinking, Veerle turned round and was unsurprised to see the dark-haired woman standing there. She actually had her hands on her hips; the effect was so pugilistic that Veerle half expected to see a curler in one of those fists, with grey hair still attached to it.

'Do you want to make an appointment?'

'No.'

'Do you want to buy something?'

Veerle looked her directly in the eyes. 'I don't think so.' It was tempting to add something tart simply to annoy the woman, but she had a feeling there would be fallout for Mevrouw Coppens if she did that, and Hommel's mother looked so timid that Veerle hadn't the heart to drop her in it. Instead she simply glanced at Mevrouw Coppens and said, 'Thanks anyway,' and then she left the salon.

As she closed the door behind her she checked the opening times. It closed at five p.m. today. She put her chin up and walked away up the street.

I'll be back at five.

She went to the local library in the intervening time, and attacked her school work, but it was hard to keep her mind on it. There were so many questions she could have asked about Hommel, but the main one had been answered.

Is she all right? Mevrouw Coppens had asked.

So she doesn't know where her daughter is, doesn't know whether she's OK or not.

Veerle thought about Hommel's mother, about the way she looked so cowed and downtrodden. *She's completely under his thumb*, Kris had said, meaning Hommel's stepfather. It looked as though she was pretty much under the thumb at work too. She didn't look like the sort of person who would wade in to defend her daughter if it came to a confrontation. You could imagine her standing on the sidelines wringing her hands and looking agonized, but not actually *doing* anything.

Hommel could have run away, you know. Especially if it's that bad at home.

That didn't feel right though; Hommel was old enough to move out without anyone's permission. If her stepfather was that much of a bastard, she might not want him to know where she had gone, but . . .

Surely she'd have let her mother know she was OK. Or her friends. Veerle's brow knitted. *And her ex-boyfriend?*

It was no use; she wasn't getting any work done. She looked at her watch and saw that she only had twenty minutes to wait before the salon closed. It had looked pretty dead, anyway; no point in leaving it until five sharp, in case they closed a few minutes early. She packed her books back into her bag and stood up.

When she reached the street where the salon was, it was five to five. She was hurrying along, her eyes fixed on the dreary-looking awning, when she nearly cannoned into someone coming the other way. She looked into the person's face and realized that it was Hommel's mother.

'Mevrouw Coppens,' she said.

The woman gave her that look again, like a frightened rabbit, and then she glanced over her shoulder, instinctively looking back towards the salon as though she thought its domineering owner might see them speaking to each other and object.

'Sorry,' she said, and made as if to step off the pavement and into the road so that she could pass.

'Can I talk to you?' asked Veerle. She subtly shifted her stance to block the woman's escape, but dared not be too overt for fear of scaring her off altogether.

'What about?'

'Els.'

'You said you hadn't seen her,' said Mevrouw Coppens. She was looking past Veerle at the street ahead, as though dying to make her escape, as though she had sighted a route and was waiting for an opportunity to bolt.

'I know. But I'd like to get in touch with her.'

'Why?'

Well, because her ex-boyfriend asked me to. Because she's got the key to a house that doesn't belong to her, and someone wants it back. Because maybe – just maybe – something bad has happened to her.

'I'm . . . worried about her. I haven't seen her for a while and she's not answering calls.'

'She's left,' said Mevrouw Coppens. She was shifting her weight uneasily from foot to foot. 'I have to catch a bus,' she said.

'I can walk with you,' said Veerle, and again she saw that look of nervous dismay. As Mevrouw Coppens began to walk she kept pace with her. 'Look, when did you last see Els?' she tried.

'Before I went away,' said the older woman. She seemed impatient now to get the words out, to shake Veerle off. 'I had to go and see my sister for a couple of days, and when I got back, Els had gone. Jappe said she went out one night without saying where she was going, and she didn't come back.'

Jappe. The stepfather.

'Have you contacted the police?'

'Jappe said it wasn't necessary.'

'But . . . has she phoned or anything since then?'

'Jappe said she was angry . . . in a sulk. She'll come back when she's calmed down. She can be . . . difficult. They fight a lot.'

Jappe sounds like a klootzak, thought Veerle. 'When did you go to see your sister?'

'I suppose it was last month. She has a lot of ill health, she—'

Veerle didn't want to get sidetracked by Mevrouw Coppens's sister's health. 'Last month? And you haven't heard *anything*?'

'No,' said the other woman. She had stopped walking, but she was looking away from Veerle again, gazing ahead with longing at the bus stop, desperate to escape.

'Look, it's not up to me, but I think you should call the police,' said Veerle.

Mevrouw Coppens was shaking her head.

'Why not?' persisted Veerle. It was frustrating talking to this woman. *She's so vague and passive, it's like trying to grasp smoke.*

'She's over eighteen. She's old enough to move out, have her own place. Jappe says—'

'Screw what Jappe says.' Veerle was beginning to lose her temper. She reached out and tried to grasp Hommel's mother by her upper arm, to stop her moving away. 'She's *your* daughter.'

'Let go of me.'

To her astonishment Veerle felt a blow on her hip and realized that Mevrouw Coppens had taken a swing at her with her handbag. She released her grip and stared at the woman.

Mevrouw Coppens's faded features were finally suffused with colour. She was trembling with nervous indignation.

'You're just as bad,' she blurted out. 'Arguing, causing

trouble, never taking no for an answer. You're just as bad as she is.'

She began to walk away from Veerle, walking as fast as she could go without actually breaking into a run.

Veerle bit her lip, and then set off after her. She had to jog to keep up. *One last try*, she told herself, although she was pretty sure it was useless.

'Look,' she said, 'your daughter's been gone for weeks and you don't know where and you haven't heard anything. I don't want to upset you but I think you should call the police.'

It was like talking to a stone. She couldn't believe that the wan, indefinite-looking face could conceal such stubbornness; she suspected that it had not flowered from within but been caught like an infection from the objectionable Jappe. Mevrouw Coppens was afraid *not* to believe him when he said Hommel had simply gone off in a sulk.

'Please,' she tried.

'Go away.'

Veerle stood still then, and watched Hommel's mother scurry away up the street with her head down.

Hommel, she thought, and in that moment she felt more sympathy for the other girl than she ever had, as though her thoughts could somehow stretch out like questing fingers and find her, wherever she was. *Hommel – whatever has become of you?*

She sighed deeply, and then she reached into her pocket for her mobile to call Kris.

38

That *verdomde* rabbit was back on the bed again.

Veerle was moving around the bedroom like a whirlwind, lifting cushions and discarded T-shirts and magazines, opening drawers and then only half closing them, sweeping papers onto the carpet as she brushed her hands over the flat surfaces, searching for her wallet.

She glanced at the clock above the door and thought, *Lieve God – the bus is going to leave in four minutes and at this rate I'm not going to be on it.* In spite of the fact that time was running out she still grabbed the rabbit. This time she stuffed it head down in the bin by her desk. She had no doubt that Claudine would fish it out again but she was beyond caring. It gave her a kind of savage pleasure to see those floppy stitched legs protruding from the bin.

Where is it?

She was almost one hundred per cent sure that she had left the wallet on her desk when she went to take a shower, but it wasn't there now and she had exhausted all the possibilities. She'd opened cupboards and drawers that she hadn't touched for a week. She'd even got down on her stomach on the floor and peered under the furniture, but the wallet wasn't anywhere to be found.

She still had her phone, she could call Kris, no problem with that. She never let it out of her sight these days, not since the time Claudine had locked her in her room.

Claudine.

A horrible certainty filled Veerle's brain. She ran out of the room, leaving the door wide open, and thundered down the stairs.

Claudine was in the kitchen, clearing up the remains of supper. She had her back to Veerle, and she didn't turn round.

'*Maman?* Have you got my wallet?'

Claudine still didn't turn round, and she didn't give Veerle a yes or no. 'Why would I have your wallet?' she said. Her hands were busy with a plate, polishing it with a tea towel until it shone, but Veerle saw the colour rise in the back of her neck.

She took it, she thought, and the wave of anger that swept through her was dizzying.

'I don't know why,' she snapped. 'Did you go in my bedroom when I was in the shower?'

Finally Claudine did turn, although she held the plate in front of her body in both hands, as though holding up a shield.

'So I'm not allowed in my own daughter's room now, is that it?'

Veerle bit her lip to stop herself actually screaming.

'Have you got my wallet?'

Claudine put down the plate and the cloth and stretched out her hands. 'Do I look like I have your wallet?' Her voice had a slight tremor in it, but there was a faint air of suppressed triumph about her.

Veerle ground her teeth. 'Did you *take* it?'

Claudine looked at her for a long moment, and then she turned and picked up the cloth again. She said, 'You don't need your wallet. You should be staying in.'

Now Veerle did let out a little shriek of frustration. 'I *need* that wallet. How do you think I'm going to get to school tomorrow without my bus pass and my money?'

'I'm sure it will turn up in the *morning*,' said Claudine.

'I'm going to find it,' Veerle told her in a tight voice. She spun on her heel, scanning the kitchen surfaces, but she didn't really think for a minute that it would be as easy as that, that Claudine would have left the wallet lying out in plain view. She ran to the nearest unit and began opening drawers, rummaging through them with her fingers, slamming them shut so that the contents jumped and rattled. She opened cupboards and finally she even looked in the refrigerator, swinging open the ice box.

All the time Claudine kept working, drying dishes and wiping down the work surfaces. There was a self-conscious air of calm about her that made Veerle want to grab her by the skinny shoulders and shake her. *You'll never find it*, said that smug air of composure. *I'm sure of that.*

Veerle ran into the hallway and pulled out the drawer of the little telephone table with such savage force that it came right out and overturned on the floor, spilling pencils and old till receipts. *No wallet.* She went into the sitting room and began pulling the cushions off the sofa and running her hands into all the narrow spaces in the upholstery, but she came up with nothing apart from a fifty cent piece. She was breathing heavily now, her chest heaving, and her hair was hanging in her eyes. She had to fight the desire to scream with anger.

She looked at the clock on the mantelpiece and saw that it was far too late now, the bus would have gone, bearing with it an empty space that should have been filled by herself, speeding towards Kris, who at this moment was assuredly waiting for her at the bus stop in the town.

Ring him.

She touched the phone in her pocket as though it were a talisman, and then she strode out of the room and ran up the stairs. The crash as she slammed shut her bedroom door made the windowframes rattle. She dragged her phone out of her pocket, but before she did that she gave the bin with the rabbit in it a massive kick that sent it skidding and rolling into the corner of the room.

Kris's mobile only rang twice before he answered it.

'Veerle? Where are you?'

'At home.' Veerle found that she was so breathless with fury that she could hardly speak. She swallowed, brushing the hair out of her eyes with a shaking hand. 'She didn't lock me in this time, she hid my *verdomde* wallet.'

'Do you have any money on you? Could you get the next bus?'

'No. Nothing. It was all in my wallet.'

Kris thought for a moment. 'I'll come to you on the next bus back.'

What?!

Veerle gasped. 'Kris – you can't.'

'Why not?'

'You can't come here. She'll go mad.'

'Let her.'

'Kris—' But Veerle was speaking to thin air. She looked down at the phone in her hand with disbelief. Then she went and sat on the bed, still staring at the little screen as though it could tell her something, but she stood up again almost as quickly, her stomach prickling with apprehension.

He's really going to come over here.

He can't.

He's going to.

She could have called him back, but what was there to say? She had no idea where the wallet was, so unless she walked four kilometres she couldn't get into the town herself. She wondered when the bus would arrive. The trip only took about ten minutes but the buses went every half-hour or so. If he had just missed one, it could be a long wait.

She looked down at the silent phone in her hand again.

He can't really be doing this.

But he was. Exactly seventeen minutes later she heard the doorbell ring.

Veerle didn't bother to look out of the window. The one thought in her head was to get to the front door before Claudine did, to somehow avert the coming scene. She rushed out of her room and down the stairs, but before she had time to run the length of the narrow hallway she saw that her mother had beaten her to it.

Claudine was sliding back the bolt – naturally, she had locked the door, even though it was nowhere near dark yet – and then she was opening the door, and there was Kris.

Kris looked into the hallway, past Claudine, saw Veerle and smiled.

Claudine, however, standing behind the door, saw a stranger in a black leather jacket and jeans, a tall young man with sharp features and bold dark eyes, his shoulders filling the doorframe. She panicked and tried to shut the door.

Kris stopped her easily, bracing his arm against it. '*Mevrouw?*' he said mildly. 'Can I come in? I'm a friend of Veerle's.'

'*Non,*' said Claudine in a shrill indignant voice, but it was too late. Kris had eased himself inside and closed the door behind him. He held out a hand to her. 'Kris Verstraeten.'

Claudine looked at the hand as though it were infected with some frightful disease. '*Non,*' she said again. She glanced back at Veerle and then again at Kris, looking from one to the other as though she couldn't believe her eyes. 'Go away,' she said in French, and it was not quite clear whom she was addressing.

Veerle saw that her mother was actually trembling. 'She doesn't understand,' she said to Kris in Flemish. She approached Claudine and laid a hand gently on her arm. '*Maman?*' She spoke to her mother reassuringly in French. 'It's OK. I know him.'

'What is he doing here?' demanded Claudine. Her tone was belligerent but her eyes were wide and fearful. Her gaze kept sliding back to Kris as though she dared not take her eyes off him for an instant for fear of what he might try.

'He's my friend,' said Veerle. She sighed. 'He came here because I couldn't go and meet him like we had arranged . . . because you hid my wallet.'

'It was time we met anyway,' said Kris in French. Veerle shot him a glance. She had never heard him speak French before; there had never been the need. He spoke well but with a slight accent, and in a calm, amiable voice that she suspected was intended to get under her mother's guard. It crossed her mind that it was just as well Claudine hadn't seen the pair of them clinging to the outside of Tante Bernadette's apartment building in the freezing dark.

'Why?' asked Claudine querulously. She held her arms close to her body, hands clasped together, knuckles white, as though she were afraid that if she unclasped them Kris might try to shake hands again.

'Because I understand you're not happy about your daughter being with someone you don't know. So here I am.'

Veerle listened to this with her mouth open. The whole situation was beginning to take on a distinctly surreal tinge. Partly it was the way that Kris managed to make himself sound so stupendously *reasonable*, not to mention respectable, presenting himself like a suitor asking his intended's parents for permission to address her. Mostly, though, it was the fact that he had gone for a strategy she would never have tried herself in a million years: the direct assault.

She wondered whether it could possibly work. Her own instinct was to keep from Claudine anything that might provoke another maelstrom of anxiety, and besides, she hated the feeling that her mother was obsessively cataloguing every detail of her life, just as she would have hated it if Claudine had spent her days in Veerle's room, fondling every one of her possessions with her bony fingers.

But where has trying to keep things hidden got me? she thought. *Locked up once, and now minus my De Lijn pass, my ID card and all my money.*

They were still standing in the narrow hallway, as close and static as a bunch of statues in an auctioneer's storeroom. Kris was waiting for Claudine's reply, which from any reasonable person would have consisted of an invitation to come into the living room and sit down. For one startling moment Veerle really thought that this was what her mother was about to do. Claudine moved swiftly between her and Kris and opened the living-room door. For a second there was a glimpse of sofa and armchairs, coffee table and television, and then Claudine was through the door and had closed it in their faces.

Kris and Veerle looked at each other. *What now?* he telegraphed at her, but before she had time to respond, the door had opened again, and Claudine came marching out. She ignored Kris entirely. She went up to Veerle but she didn't look her in the eye; she stared over her shoulder.

'Take it,' she said, pushing something at Veerle so roughly that Veerle was forced to take a step back. It was her wallet. She was still looking down at it in her hands when her mother hissed something at her, pushed past her and vanished into the kitchen. The door shut with a resounding bang.

Veerle looked at the closed door. Then she went up to Kris, took his arm and pulled him towards the front door.

'Let's go,' she said grimly. 'Before she changes her mind.'

Out on the pavement, she took a huge breath of spring air, as though she wanted to clear her nostrils of an evil smell. Then she looked at Kris. 'Can we still go to that house?'

'Of course.'

'Then let's.'

They walked to the bus stop. There was a bus due in ten minutes. Veerle sat on one of the chilly plastic seats; Kris leaned against a poster for Carrefour.

'So, what did your mother just say to you?' asked Kris, crossing his arms comfortably.

Veerle looked up at him. '*T'es vraiment une garce, fille ingrate!* She said I was an ungrateful cow.'

39

The house was stunning in an idiosyncratic sort of way, if you liked period buildings. It was a large white stucco mansion in the Art Deco style, dating from the 1930s, with curved corner windows and startling blue roof tiles. It was also directly on the main road. There was a reasonable-sized front garden, as you might have expected for such a large house, but there was absolutely no cover. The garden fell away from the front door in steps, and the front wall was low and purely decorative. A couple of metres in front of that was the kerb. The front door was in full view of the road, which was a busy one. To make matters worse, it was now mid-April and the evenings were no longer so dark. It would be completely impossible to enter the house without perhaps a dozen drivers seeing you doing so.

Kris and Veerle stood on the other side of the road by the De Lijn stop. There were overhanging trees here, and anyway, anyone who saw them would think they were waiting for a bus. If they crossed the road, however, that would be quite another matter.

'That's *it?*' said Veerle incredulously.

'Uh-huh.' Kris seemed unconcerned.

'We'll be seen.'

He grinned at her. 'We'll be seen if we march up the front steps.'

Veerle looked back at the house again. 'Have you got the keys, or do we have to stand there and pick the lock with everyone watching us?'

'I've got keys,' Kris told her. He fished them out of his pocket and dangled them before her eyes. 'Nobody else wants them. This place only tends to get done in the middle of winter when it's pitch dark, and not often even then.'

'And apart from the challenge, why are we trying to do it?'

'Because of who lives there.' Kris leaned close and whispered the name in a conspiratorial tone.

'The TV guy?' Veerle stared at him.

'Yep.'

'This is insane.'

'Insane . . . but worth seeing. You know that actress he used to go out with, the blonde one?'

Veerle nodded.

'There are matching studio portraits of them, one either side of the living room. Not a stitch on.'

'Tasteful,' said Veerle. 'But not exactly worth getting arrested for.'

Kris laughed. 'There's loads of stuff like that – well, not all naked photos. Signed pictures of all these celebrities, and stuff from the shows he did. You know that giant fibreglass horse they had one year for Sinterklaas? That's in the corner of the dining room.'

'OK,' said Veerle drily. 'That I have to see.' She studied the front of the house. 'Is there an alarm?'

'Normally there is, but it hasn't been working the last

month or so, according to the guy's dog walker, who's one of us. He's getting it fixed but he hasn't done it yet. Well, I hope he hasn't because if he gets a new one the number will probably change.'

'And where's the dog right now?'

'Kennels.'

'OK, well, that's one less thing to worry about. So are we going to just march up to the front door, then?'

'That depends on you.'

'On *me*?'

Kris nodded. 'There's a back garden and that's much better protected than the front. Trees and a high hedge the whole way round. I guess that's where he does his nude sunbathing in summer.'

'Don't.'

'There's a back door there too, but I don't have a key for that. There is, however, one other way in.'

'Which is?'

'First-floor bathroom window. There's some problem with it . . . I think they put in a fancy jacuzzi or something and he spends so much time in it that the steam did something to the windowframe. It's antique, dates back seventy or eighty years, so it's not that easy to get it replaced. It more or less shuts but you can't latch it.' He looked at her thoughtfully, as though assessing her. 'If you can climb up and get in through the window, you can come down and open the back door. There's normally a key inside it, but the dog walker doesn't have one.'

'OK.' Veerle shot another glance at the house. 'Let's go then.'

'Hang on.' Kris caught her by the arm. 'It's not an easy climb.'

Veerle shrugged. 'We'll see.' She gave him a sly smile.

They walked about a hundred metres down the main road before crossing, then went up a narrow path between two properties and onto a small road parallel to the main one. All the houses here were surrounded by tall hedges or walls and there was little danger of being seen unless anyone actually drove down the street.

After a couple of minutes they found themselves behind the house they were targeting; Veerle glimpsed the distinctive blue roof tiles over the hedge. There was a tall narrow gate between two stout posts, and she could just see the thin grid of a security fence embedded in the thick foliage. The gate did not present much of a problem. *Really*, thought Veerle as she climbed over, *they might as well not have bothered.* She jumped down onto a gravelled path and gazed up at the back of the house.

Shit. Kris was right. This is going to be a bitch.

The back door was in the centre of a kind of square pillar that ran right up to the roof, and on either side of that there were round-ended balconies. *If I can get far enough up to reach the lip of one of those I'll be fine. The problem is how to get that high.*

The ground-floor windows were large and curving and unshuttered; indeed it was difficult to see how you could fit shutters onto anything that shape. A single slip or accidental swing and you could put a foot straight through one of those glass panes, causing damage that nobody could fail to notice.

I'd probably cut myself to ribbons too, thought Veerle, with an inward shudder.

The windows were about the only architectural feature at ground-floor level, she noticed. Everything else was white stucco, as smooth and featureless as cake icing and about as much use to her.

'So? What do you think?' said Kris in her ear.

'I don't know,' said Veerle. She shaded her eyes, staring.

I'm never coming out without my rock shoes ever again. She had on Converse trainers, which were better than the boots she had worn to climb Tante Bernadette's apartment block, but still nothing like as good as her rock shoes with their high-friction rubber soles.

In the end she just shrugged. 'OK, I'll try.'

She walked up the gravel path, taking her time, studying the problem.

'That's the bathroom window, the middle one,' said Kris, pointing, but she had already worked that out; you could tell that the frame wasn't quite closed – at least you could if you were looking out for it. You could also tell why the owner wasn't panicking about repairing it; you'd have to be Spider-Man to reach it.

When she got to the ground-floor window, things weren't much better than expected. Tante Bernadette's apartment had been a breeze compared to this: all those conveniently worn stone blocks with chunks of mortar missing, creating perfect finger-holds, the railings, that useful metal bracket.

She stood for a while looking at the window, head back, standing close enough to examine every centimetre of the frame. There were plenty of horizontal pieces, although none of them looked terrifically robust. The most difficult bit would be reaching the point where she could stand at full stretch on the top of the window and grasp the lip of the balcony.

There's not much to hold onto, she thought grimly. *If I come off I'll drop straight onto the gravel below, which is going to be like landing on a cheese-grater.*

When it came down to it, though, there were only two options: *I can give up, or I can start climbing.*

She started climbing. Before she did that, though, she took off her jacket and unwound her scarf from around her neck. She had a bangle on, and she slipped that off too. Then she stepped up to the window and began.

After the first couple of moves she had forgotten Kris, she had forgotten the scene with her mother, *and* the celebrity and his fibreglass horse. She had been absorbed into the problem, her entire consciousness focused on questing fingertips and the subtle shift of weight from side to side.

There was a narrow projection running along the top of the window. It was only a couple of centimetres deep but she thought that she could stand on it, if she could get up there. It was a convenient finger-hold too when you started out, but once you got to a certain height you needed something further up the wall. She leaned out and looked upwards.

The wall itself stretched upwards, as featureless as sheet ice. *No help there.* She could see the underside of the balcony from here though, and there was a small rim running along the edge of it. It would be no use for taking any actual weight – she'd have dropped off it in a second – but she might be able to use it for balance. Once she was standing on the top edge of the window she would be home and dry.

She moved up the windowframe and now she was able to

reach out for the bottom of the balcony. She ran her fingers along it, grasped, found her equilibrium, stepped up with her right foot, moved her weight to the right and stood up, feeling her stomach graze the stucco through the fabric of her T-shirt. The next second she was able to grasp the top of the balcony wall.

No point in hanging about there congratulating herself until she dropped off like a coconut plummeting from a palm tree. She scaled the balcony easily, using the horizontal railings set into the top of the wall, and then she slid over the top rail and sank down on the floor.

Thank God, she thought.

Her heart was thumping, and when she wiped her face with her hands she discovered that she was perspiring. She looked over the side of the balcony at the route she had taken up and thought, *I'd better not have to climb down this time.* She saw Kris staring up at her and gave him a cheerful grin, hoping she looked more nonchalant than she felt.

It was tempting to sit there for a bit, relishing the safety of the balcony and the view of the garden, but she made herself get up and start moving. First, however, she wiped her hands on the thighs of her trousers, ensuring that they were as dry as possible. The next moves didn't look technically difficult but it was a long drop now if her hands slipped off the holds.

Veerle climbed up onto the balcony wall, and over the railings. It was relatively easy to step out onto the façade; the sill of the nearest window was less than a metre away. There were two windows, of which the left-hand one was the poorly closed bathroom window. Clearly it was impossible to open that window outwards while standing on the sill, so she crossed to the right-hand windowsill. She was very aware now of the open space behind and below her. There was a very gentle breeze, almost imperceptible, and yet it made the hair on her arms stand up.

There was very little to hold onto as she leaned over to try the left-hand window. Standing on the sill and holding onto the windowframe was fine, but leaning over one-handed felt horribly insecure. Veerle had a hot, tight feeling in her chest and her mouth was dry. She had to turn her elbow out and bend her left hand almost backwards to get a grip on the edge of the window. When she managed it, she had to pull, but she was afraid to tug at the frame too violently in case the force of it swinging open pulled her off the windowsill.

Her right arm was beginning to ache with tension. Standing like this with her legs slightly bent was putting a strain on her thighs too. She gave a slightly more assertive tug at the window, and suddenly she felt it move. She let go, let it swing open, then pushed it the rest of the way with her fingertips.

Now she could step back onto the left-hand windowsill and climb in through the bathroom window.

This time Veerle didn't bother glancing down to give Kris any cheeky grins. It was simply a relief to be inside the house. She climbed down over the lavatory and sat down on the bath mat with her back against the bath, catching her breath, massaging the fingers of her right hand and looking around.

Tacky, she decided. Evidently immense amounts of money and even a feel for period décor didn't guarantee good taste. The bathroom was done out in black and white geometric designs that almost hurt the eyes. The white suite had been selected for its Art Deco styling but you could tell it was modern; Veerle doubted anyone had had an enormous jacuzzi like that in 1930. All the fittings were gold. Above the tub there was an enormous mirror. When Veerle eventually got to her feet she saw herself in it but she didn't look for long; the effect of those black and white tiles reflected in the glass was dizzying. She was glad to get out of the room.

She went downstairs to let Kris in. It was difficult not to be distracted on the way downstairs: the wall that followed the curve of the staircase was lined with glossy celebrity photographs. The guy who owned the house was in quite a few of them, Veerle noticed; she wondered whether Barbara Sarafian had minded him putting his arm so familiarly around her shoulders. A couple of steps further down and she found herself face to face with a black-and-white shot of Kevin Janssens.

He's met everyone, thought Veerle. She was itching to look for the dining room, to see if it was true about the fibreglass horse, but first she had to find the back door and let Kris into the house.

It wasn't difficult to orient herself; she knew the back door was under the bathroom window. She went through a kitchen that was enormous and expensively equipped but smelled cold and faintly antiseptic; clearly the owner was not an enthusiastic cook. Kris was waiting at the door. The glass was patterned in an old-fashioned style but she could see his dark silhouette, leaning idly against the doorframe.

Veerle unlocked the door and he stepped inside, pulling her into an embrace.

'Is there anything you can't climb?'

Veerle grinned delightedly. 'The Atomium, maybe.' She put her head on one side. 'Do you want to leave the same way, like we did when we went to my aunt's place?'

'No, thanks.' Kris sounded amused.

'This place is amazing,' Veerle told him. 'And amazingly *tacky*. Have you seen the bathroom?'

'The one that looks like a crossword puzzle?'

'Yes, that one. I felt dizzier in there than I did climbing up the wall. God knows how he stands sitting in the jacuzzi in there. Anyway,' she added, 'I want to see this horse.'

'We'll do a tour if you like,' said Kris. 'The only thing to remember is, stay away from the front windows and don't put any lights on. There aren't any shutters, remember.'

They wandered into the hallway, Kris's arm comfortably draped around Veerle's shoulders.

Now that the adrenalin rush of the climb was behind her, Veerle found her mind slipping back to the scene with her mother, the way Claudine had simply thrust the purloined wallet at her, hissed an insult and slammed the kitchen door in her face.

That wasn't the end of it. I'm going to pay for that later, she thought, although the idea seemed horribly unfair, as though she had been in some foreign country, some alien culture, and was going to be punished for transgressing a law she had not even understood. Claudine had *hated* not knowing where her daughter was going and with whom; logically, she should have been *pleased* that Kris had taken the initiative and introduced himself, but the fact remained that she had been first fearful and then furious. She had thrust the wallet at Veerle as if to say, *Go to the devil if you like; I wash my hands of you.* To Kris she had addressed not one civil word.

Dimly Veerle perceived that her mother was angry about being outmanoeuvred. Veerle could not see the matter resting there. The whole thing made her feel tired. She leaned her head against Kris's shoulder.

I wish I didn't have to go home at all.

She remembered once he had asked her if she wanted to spend the night at a house they had visited; it had been the night the two of them had dressed in borrowed evening clothes. She had said no almost instinctively, knowing that it would cause an immense row at home and – if she was honest – not knowing precisely what it would have meant for her and Kris. Now she wished she *could* stay over somewhere. She would have liked to step out of her old life entirely, shed it as a butterfly sheds the sticky cocoon in which it has transformed itself.

I wonder if it could be done, she thought dreamily. *Are there enough empty houses on the Koekoeken books that we could just go from one to another for ever?* She imagined herself and Kris moving from one splendid property to the next, dressing in expensive clothes fresh from the dry cleaner's wrappers, skimming off a bottle of champagne here and there from overstocked cellars, plundering the stacked contents of enormous chest freezers for food. Bathing in enormous claw-footed tubs or corner baths with golden taps, the steamy air heavy with perfumed salts. Sleeping on Egyptian cotton or raw wild silk. Sleeping each in their own high-ceilinged room in separate wings of the house, or . . . perhaps—

She blinked.

'There really *is* a horse.'

40

The horse was dappled grey and it stood about two metres tall. Rather unseasonably, it had a snow-white saddle and crimson saddle blanket and a red-and-gold bridle. It also had a long white mane and a rather savage expression. Standing in front of it was distinctly unnerving.

The dining room was very large; it would have been quite possible to seat a party of twelve or fourteen around the enormous polished dinner table without any of them being overshadowed by the horse; indeed, had it been a live one, it could quite easily have cantered around the perimeter of the room without so much as clipping the back of anyone's chair with a hoof.

Kris and Veerle sat at the far end of the table eating pizza from the TV presenter's freezer. Kris had reasoned that there were so many in there he would hardly miss one. Veerle's surmise that very little cooking went on in the extravagant kitchen was evidently correct.

There was no cellar crammed with champagne, but there was a bar in the corner of the living room, stocked with every single type of drink that Veerle had ever heard of, and quite a few she hadn't. She thought most of them looked toxic. In the end she chose plain iced tea.

Outside, night was falling. A couple of lamps had come on, clearly on a timer, but the light they threw was very soft. The unlit parts of the house would soon be as dark and un-navigable as a catacomb.

Veerle looked at Kris, his face half in shadow, half bathed in soft yellow light. She was irresistibly reminded of the night she had met him in the castle.

If I hadn't had the row at the climbing wall, she thought. *If I'd sat on the other side of the bus and looked out of the other window, and never seen the light in the castle. If I'd stayed on the bus . . .*

It was strange, the thought that her meeting with him had rested on so tenuous a chain of events. If they hadn't met that night, he would have remained in her memory for ever as that skinny nine-year-old with the shock of dark hair; the one who was nice in spite of his unpleasant older brothers. The one who had dared her to climb the bell tower with him that day all those years ago, when they had stared out over the village and seen a killer.

Fate? she wondered, but she pushed the idea away as though it were a dish she had tasted and hadn't liked. Veerle hated to feel that anything was pushing her around – especially not Claudine, but not anyone or anything else either. The future was like some great rock face stretching up and up until it vanished into the obscurity of the clouds. She intended to set to and climb it with all the skill and energy she possessed. *No fear of falling,* she told herself.

'Kris?' She reached out and touched his hand, wanting to

feel the warmth of his skin under her fingers. 'Tell me about the day we saw Joren Sterckx.'

Kris put his head back, studying her. 'You really don't remember?'

Veerle shook her head. 'I don't remember seeing him. What did he look like?'

'Tall.' Kris shrugged. 'Big. But OK, I was a kid then, and he was a lot older. And fair hair, I remember that. And he had blood all down him, from here to here.' He gestured.

Veerle shivered. 'And did you realize what he'd done? I mean, he could have been in an accident.'

Kris nodded. 'Oh yes. He was carrying the kid in his arms.'

'In his *arms*?' Veerle stared at him.

'Yeah. Well, that's how they got him so quickly. If he'd hidden the body, it might have been ages before they found him. But . . . he just walked into the middle of the village carrying it like a hunting trophy.'

'Why?'

'Why? Nobody really knows why. He was just crazy.' Kris shook his head. 'The weird thing was, he wouldn't ever talk to anyone about it. Caught red-handed, I mean, it looked like he *wanted* to be caught, but he wouldn't say why he did it. I guess now no one's ever going to know.'

'Why not?'

'He's dead.' Kris looked at her. 'You didn't know? He died in prison. It wasn't that long afterwards.'

'How? Did someone attack him?'

'No. He was sick. Cancer, I think. I remember my mother going on about it, saying it served him right. She was glad to move away, even though Joren Sterckx was in prison. She said it could easily have been me or my brother Ronny he attacked.' Kris grinned humourlessly. 'We drove her nuts, going off on our own for hours without saying where we were, getting up to God knows what.'

'I bet,' said Veerle. *Look how my mother reacted*, she thought. She considered for a moment. 'So nobody has any idea why he did it? Joren Sterckx, I mean?'

'Oh, there were all sorts of rumours going round afterwards. People saying he'd hunted the kid down like he was a wild boar or something. A lot of people said he'd been hunting animals in the village first – pets had vanished, stuff like that.'

'And that was *our* village.'

'Yeah. Well, the bad stuff doesn't just happen in the big city. It's just more of a shock when it happens in a small place where everyone knows everyone. If you know someone, it's' – he shrugged – 'more real.'

'Like Vlinder.' Veerle remembered how she had felt when she had heard the news, that the body in the park had been Vlinder. She'd never even met Vlinder, and yet the slender connection via the Koekoeken group had made her feel as though she and the dead girl were somehow linked.

That's how it started with Mum, she thought. *When the stuff that normally just happens in the news happened in* our *village.*

'Yeah, like Vlinder. Like I said, bad stuff doesn't just happen in the city.' Kris leaned forward, his face serious. 'Look, you know there's still been nothing from Hommel?'

Veerle stared down into her iced tea, not wanting to look him in the eye. She thought he was right to be concerned about Hommel. *Even if it's just because her own mother doesn't care enough about her to contact the police.* Still, whenever Kris talked about Hommel it always provoked an instinctive reaction, like the raising of hackles on a dog.

'Are you sure her mother didn't say anything about where she might have gone?' Kris was saying.

'No,' said Veerle. She made herself look up, made her voice deliberately neutral. 'She went on a lot about this guy Jappe, the stepfather. Said Hommel was always arguing with him. She seemed to think that's why Hommel had gone. She was just churning out stuff Jappe had said, about Hommel being over eighteen and not having to live at home any more. She wasn't going to call the police because Jappe said it wasn't necessary.' She grimaced. 'I think you're right, I think Jappe's a *klootzak*, but she's not much better. She's so busy worrying about keeping Jappe happy that she's stopped caring about Hommel.' Veerle looked away from Kris, down to the end of the room where the fibreglass horse stood in the gathering shadows, still snarling its frozen snarl. 'You know,' she said, 'it's possible she *did* just take off somewhere. Jappe doesn't sound like the sort of guy you'd want to live with, not if you could avoid it.'

'It doesn't feel right,' said Kris. 'Mevrouw Coppens told you Hommel went out one night and didn't come back, right?'

Veerle nodded.

'Well . . .' He hesitated. 'Supposing she went out to one of the Koekoeken houses, and something happened to her there?'

'I guess,' said Veerle. 'But her mother just said she went out. It could have been anywhere.'

'None of her friends have heard from her. If she didn't go to any of them, where did she go?'

'I don't know. But that doesn't mean it had to be one of the houses.'

'No, it doesn't.' Kris frowned. 'But it could have been. And Horzel's still missing – you know, Egbert, the lock-picking guy.'

'Well, that could be completely unconnected.'

'Maybe.' Kris fell silent for a moment, thinking. Eventually he said, 'It was the same with Vlinder, you know. It was in the papers. She went out one evening, supposedly to meet friends, only her family didn't know who or where, and she never came back.'

Veerle looked at him and she had a cold sensation in the pit of her stomach. 'What are you suggesting?'

'I don't know what I'm suggesting,' said Kris. 'I'm not even sure there's a pattern.' He sighed. 'Maybe Hommel's just gone off somewhere like her mother says. Maybe she and Horzel will show up next week or the week after, both of them. Or maybe Horzel won't show up again at all. Maybe he's had enough. That happens sometimes – people get bored or lose their nerve.'

'And they just vanish?'

'Yes. Well, nobody's going to chase them up. That's the whole point of the Koekoeken – you don't keep tabs on each other. You don't know most of the others, except by their user names. If someone stops posting, you don't go round to their place and check up on them.'

'So in theory . . .' said Veerle slowly, 'other people could have disappeared.'

She and Kris stared at each other.

'No,' said Kris, but Veerle was not sure whether he meant, *No, that couldn't have happened* or *No, I don't want to believe that.*

There was a silence. Then Veerle said, 'Let's wait and see. Maybe one of them will turn up in the next few days, or maybe they both will. They're probably both fine.'

But all the same, she wondered.

41

On Silent Saturday Veerle woke up late. Since babyhood she had slept through the sound of the church bell, and she was hardly conscious of hearing it any more, and yet it seemed that it intruded upon her sleep more than she thought. In its absence she slept longer than she normally did, and awoke feeling refreshed but somewhat disorientated, as though she had been under a general anaesthetic.

The house was unusually silent too; Claudine had driven off in her little car on Good Friday, to visit her family in Namur. Veerle had avoided going by promising to accompany her mother when she went again on Ascension Day. She strongly suspected that this would entail a number of sideways looks from her elderly relatives, who would no doubt have digested all the complaining remarks Claudine made about her at Easter, but for the present that particular problem was a comfortable distance in the future. She rolled over, luxuriating, taking the duvet with her, and came nose to nose with the stuffed rabbit.

'*Verdomme!*'

She sat up in bed and threw the rabbit across the room.

I ought to burn that bloody rabbit, she thought. *Only she'd probably buy another one. Or find some way to raise that one from the dead.*

She looked at the clock above the door. *Time to get up.* In fact, she was going to have to get a move on. She ran to the bathroom, showered, and went back to the bedroom to get dressed. Looking out through the window, she could see it was a fine sunny morning. The sky was a clear blue without a single cloud; there was a brilliant crystalline stillness to it, as though the silence of the bells had allowed it to set and harden around the spire of the Sint-Pauluskerk.

No time to make tea. She scavenged a glass of orange juice and a cellophane-wrapped frangipane tart from the kitchen. Five minutes later the front door was banging shut behind her as she bounced out into Kerkstraat.

She saw Kris before he saw her. He was leaning against a battered-looking black Volkswagen parked in the square. She guessed he had borrowed it, since there were no buses running today.

She crossed the street and went up to him. 'Nice car,' she said ironically. Now that she was closer to it, she could see that there was an enormous dent in the front wing.

'Jeroen's second best one,' said Kris, patting it. 'The cleaning business is booming, and he's got himself a BMW. He wouldn't lend me that, though.'

'Mean of him,' said Veerle, smiling.

Kris folded his arms. 'So, where are you taking me? Please tell me we aren't climbing up the outside of it, wherever it is.'

Veerle turned and pointed. 'There.'

Kris followed her gaze. 'We've done that one.'

'That was ten years ago.'

They stood side by side and studied the church. Like many Flemish churches it was built of brick, with the tower at the west end stretching its spire to the skies like a swan stretching its neck upwards, the sloping slate-tiled roofs of the north and south aisles forming the wings. Nearly nine hundred years old, the ancient building still dwarfed all those around it. Veerle had not been into the bell tower since the day she and Kris had gone up there as children and seen Joren Sterckx approaching across the allotments with his ominous burden, but even without going up there it was clear that the upper section would offer a splendid view of the entire village.

Kris put an arm around her. He said drily, 'It's not going to be much of a challenge getting in there. It's probably open.'

'The church is,' said Veerle. 'But the bell tower isn't. It's locked nearly all the time now. I'm not sure anyone's been up there since . . . well, since we were.'

They began to walk slowly towards the church. Veerle was scanning the street, checking for anyone who looked as though they were heading the same way, but no one was about. There was no reason why they shouldn't go into the church if it was open, although she thought that Kris in his black leather jacket and jeans made an unlikely proselyte. Going into the bell tower was another matter, however, and she was relying on the fact that the church would probably be deserted at this time of day. There was a service scheduled for the evening but nothing for the middle of the day.

As they went up the steps to the church she put her head back and gazed up at the bell tower. This close, it looked gigantic and you had the uncomfortable feeling that it was leaning forward over you; that with very little encouragement the whole lot would fall upon you, crushing you in a mountain of worn and aged bricks.

As they entered the church they were greeted by a familiar smell, the dusty scent of incense and furniture polish and old books. Veerle went to the wooden door at the back of the vestibule and peeped into the interior of the church, but it was deserted. Then she went back to Kris, digging into her jeans pocket.

'How did you get the key?' he asked her as she fitted it into the lock of the bell-tower door.

'I didn't,' she said, turning the key carefully. It took a little work but then she heard the lock click open. 'Mum has a box of old keys at home. It used to belong to her father or something. I brought all of them in here and tried every single one of them out.'

'And one of them worked?'

'The second to last one. It's a bit stiff, but it does open the lock.'

Veerle opened the door. She could have sworn that there was a change in the air as she did so, a subtle alteration in the musty odour of the church, as though the locked-up tower had been holding a pent-up breath and had exhaled at last. There were the stone stairs, curling away upwards, the treads a little worn in the middle from the passage of feet over the centuries. When Veerle began to climb them, they seemed somehow less steep than she remembered.

But I was smaller then, she thought. She tried to remember Kris as he had been ten years ago, but the memory was sliding away from her. The more solid a part of her present life he became, the more indistinct were the memories of his younger self; it was like glimpsing a ghost growing ever more transparent until it had altogether faded into the background.

She followed the curve of the stairs until they opened out into a room floored with wooden boards. She remembered the ladder that went up into the next floor but she did not recall it being as rickety as it now appeared.

Were there really as many bird droppings as this?

Every surface seemed to be encrusted with them, like the calcified excrescences inside an underground cave. Veerle didn't like to think what they were inhaling when they disturbed the dry white residue on the floor; she did her best to breathe through her nose.

It's cold, she thought; something else she had forgotten. It was bloody cold in the bell tower. It was cool to start with within the thick stone walls, and the windows had louvres instead of glass. The birds flew in and every bit of warmth leached out.

She went up the ladder carefully and emerged in the upper room. It was, if possible, even filthier than the one below. This was as far as they had gone last time, and even if they had dared to try to go further up now, it was no longer possible. The ladder that had led precariously to the upper reaches of the bell tower now lay in two pieces on the floor.

Veerle heard Kris's footsteps on the floorboards behind her, and turned.

'Nice,' he commented ironically. 'A bird sanctuary, right?'

Veerle laughed a little at that. 'I wanted to come back here – with you.'

'I'm touched.'

Veerle looked towards the west window. 'I thought perhaps I'd remember – if I came up here.'

'And do you?'

She shook her head. 'Not really. Nothing important. I recognized everything – the stairs and the ladder. Even the mess.'

'That's got worse. Nobody ever comes up here, you can see that.'

'I know.' She looked up at him. 'But I still don't really remember seeing Joren Sterckx. I can remember being scared, really scared. And looking out of the window. But I don't remember seeing him carrying anyone, anything like that.'

Kris shrugged. 'Would you want to?'

Veerle glanced away again, towards the window. 'I don't know. It just seems so odd, that I saw something like that and I can't remember it.'

'Well, come and look out. Maybe it'll jog your memory or something.'

Veerle approached the window with a faint sense of unreality. The interior of the bell tower was at once familiar and yet unfamiliar, as though she were now visiting a place that was very like another place she had known in the past, but not quite identical.

The window, she thought. *It isn't as high up as I remember it.* She began to have a stronger sense of her younger self, the seven-year-old Veerle, although it was impossible to recapture the child's perspective. It was more as though she were accompanying that child, the ghost of her seven-year-old self, or as if she had stepped back into the past herself, the shade of things yet to come.

Where the child Veerle had had to stand on the narrow ledge under the window to peep out, she was now tall enough to rest her elbows on the sill. She leaned forward, peering between the slats of the louvres, and looked out.

The view took her by surprise. *The apartment block,* she realized. That was relatively new; she could still remember them building it. The last time she had looked out of this window there had still been an ugly gap in the street, and a free line of vision through to the allotments beyond. You could still see some of the open ground behind the apartment block, and beyond that a distant row of houses, but if Joren Sterckx had been close enough to recognize, he must have been nearer than that, in the area now blocked from sight.

Veerle fought to recreate the view in her mind's eye. She knew the layout of the allotments: she could envisage the rough path that ran down the middle of them, towards the street and the church and now the back of the apartment block. Yet her mind refused to complete the picture, to fill in the shape of Joren Sterckx stumbling towards her with his arms full of his dreadful burden. He was as absent from her memory's landscape as though he were a figure snipped out of a photograph in a magazine, leaving nothing but jagged edges.

'No,' said Veerle eventually. She glanced at Kris. 'It's weird.'

She had the sense of something escaping her, something twisting away into darkness.

Why is it so important? Joren Sterckx has been dead for maybe nine years.

She stared down at the apartment block.

It's just so strange. That day – what happened – it could be the thing that set Mum off, that made her so scared of everything. In which case it's huge to her – and I can't remember it at all, seeing Joren Sterckx.

After a while she felt Kris's hand on her shoulder. 'Veerle? It's great up here, but . . .'

'It's full of bird shit.'

He smiled. 'Look, I've got Jeroen's car for the weekend. We could go somewhere. There's a place I've been once before, about half an hour's drive from here. A little chateau. It's empty, has been for a while, but the inside is amazing. There are paintings on the ceiling . . . and the security's crap. You won't even need to climb anything.' He looked at her expectantly. 'Want to come?'

She took one last look out of the window.

'Course I do.'

42

Veerle had only been in the house for thirteen minutes when Claudine arrived home from Namur. Veerle saw the head-lights of her little car sweeping round the corner into Kerkstraat. Normally at this time of day the roller shutters would already be down, sealing the house against the outside world; Veerle had deliberately left them up, savouring the feeling of openness and freedom. She suspected that Claudine would shut them all the minute she got inside.

She saw the lights slow, pause, and then begin to retreat as her mother backed into a space outside the house. Veerle went into the sitting room and sat down on the couch. She judged that it would be advisable to be found lounging safely in front of the television; if Claudine found her restlessly wandering the house it would simply make her nervous and suspicious.

As she heard the sound of Claudine's key in the front door lock she picked up a newspaper that was lying on the coffee table. Claudine always took a French language newspaper – *Le Soir* or *La Libre Belgique* – and so Veerle rarely read them, preferring to pick up the news from one of the Flemish TV stations. Even then, she didn't watch every day; there was only so much you could take of features about how long Belgium had been without a government.

The newspaper – she saw it was *Le Soir* – was only window-dressing, an attempt to make it look as though she had been on the couch for ages, and it wasn't even a convincing cover, since she saw now that it was Wednesday's edition.

All the same, when Claudine opened the door of the sitting room and stood there in her camel-coloured jacket with an expectant expression on her face, as though disapproval was waiting to sweep across it in a tidal wave, she seemed surprised to see Veerle so deeply engrossed in the paper that she didn't even look up.

'I'm back,' she said, and saw her daughter give a slight start. Veerle looked a little pale, she thought, although she was barely aware of the slight thrill of satisfaction the thought gave her. Evidently the girl had spent the day lounging about the house. She probably hadn't had a proper lunch, Claudine decided; she was blissfully unable to conceive of her daughter eating service-station sandwiches under a peeling rococo ceiling.

'Hi,' said Veerle, but she gave the impression of only half realizing that her mother had returned. Her gaze kept creeping back to the newspaper lying open on her lap.

Claudine advanced into the room. The first thing she did was go to the window and let down the shutters, hiding the mellow evening street outside.

'Have you eaten?' she asked Veerle. Her gaze darted around the room, sharp and swift as a pullet pecking seed. She was only half listening to Veerle say that she had had some soup, nothing more, as she moved behind the couch to get a clear view of what her daughter was reading. BODY FOUND IN WOOD.

That was enough to put anyone off eating. Claudine remembered reading the article; she found such headlines both compulsive and repelling. These things only fed the terrible feeling of dread that constantly churned in the pit of her stomach, and yet she felt driven to read all of it, every detail, as though she were searching for something, some hidden meaning – perhaps the single fact that proved to her that the victim was not like herself, had done something that she would never do, never in a million years; that they had asked for it in some way.

She remembered the body-in-the-wood story very clearly because, horrifically, it had been a child who had found the corpse. Admittedly it had been a boy, but a boy *Scout*: in the mental Venn diagram that Claudine drew of young people, this one existed in the very small intersection between Boys and Well-behaved Children. He had been taking part in a game in the forest (and that made it all the more appalling, since who goes hunting for their playmates and finds the decomposing remains of a murder victim?) and had stumbled over the body, almost literally. *He'll be scarred for life*, thought Claudine, imagining nightmares and therapy and an obsession with death, and further down the line an inability to form relationships.

'That's a terrible story,' she said aloud, nodding at the open newspaper.

'Yes,' said Veerle automatically.

She really did look pale, Claudine decided; perhaps she was a little anaemic. A trip to the GP might be in order. Veerle would probably have to take iron tablets, and spend a lot of time resting.

Claudine felt her spirits rise. 'I'll make us a cup of coffee, shall I?' she said.

Half an hour later, Veerle escaped to her room. She had listened to Claudine's description of her trip to Namur, which sounded terrifying; as far as she could tell, all the female members of the family (and they *were* nearly all female, the men having mostly died, perhaps in self-defence) had spent the day sitting around the chokingly formal parlour of Claudine's older sister's house, drinking coffee and gossiping. Veerle could imagine the scent of furniture polish and the ticking of the ormolu clock on the marble mantel. The scene it conjured up in her head was reminiscent of an afternoon spent in the Museum of Africa in Tervuren, amongst the cases of stuffed animals – all glassy eyes and moth-eaten fur and frozen in attitudes that were almost but not quite lifelike. Her aged relatives always seemed a little like that, as though they had stopped properly living some time ago. Now they lived vicariously on other people's lives, like a group of elderly vampires. More than about twenty minutes of their polite prying questions and Veerle always wanted to run screaming from the room, or else say something outrageous.

She listened anyway, to some long rambling anecdote about what one of her older cousins had said and done, but all the time her thoughts kept sliding back to the article she had read in the newspaper.

BODY FOUND IN WOOD.

There was no special reason to think that it was anyone she

knew of, much less a specific person, namely Egbert . . . or Hommel. All the same she was itching to get at her laptop and check the news sites.

The paper's three days old, she thought. *Perhaps by now they've published a name.* So she listened to Claudine's tales until she judged that she had made herself attentive enough that she could reasonably escape, and then she said she felt exhausted and wanted to lie down.

Claudine did not demur at this; physical ailments had an almost sacred quality as far as she was concerned. She began to offer fruit tea and soup and aspirin, but Veerle turned them all down and escaped.

In her room, she booted up the laptop and began to search. As her fingers flew over the keys she was aware that her heart was thumping.

Don't be stupid, she told herself. *There are, what, eleven million people in the country. What are the chances of it being one of them?*

And then there was the fact that she might not recognize Egbert even if it were him; she didn't know his surname, didn't even know if Egbert was his real name. He used that other name too, Horzel, but that didn't mean that Egbert was a genuine name, the one on his ID card. People in the Koekoeken group had every reason to keep their personal details to themselves. She only knew Hommel's name – Els – because Kris knew her.

She told herself all that, but the minute she saw the photograph she knew with heart-sickening conviction that it was him.

It wasn't a very good photograph; it had been taken for the

security pass at the company where he worked, so it had that kind of police-mugshot quality to it. The background was beige and institutional-looking. Egbert himself looked geeky and rebellious. He had a pale, rather angular face and very untidy brown hair that stuck up in clumps, and was wearing some kind of leather thong around his neck. You could see his shoulders and the top of his chest, and although you couldn't see much of the T-shirt he was wearing, Veerle was pretty sure she could work out what it said.

HORZEL.

You could only see the tops of the letters, but if you knew what the word was to begin with, it was obvious.

He put his Koekoeken name on his T-shirt?

Veerle stared at the photograph in disbelief. She couldn't take in the sheer audacity of it. The whole point of the user names was to bury your own identity under an additional layer of subterfuge, as though you were painting over it on a sign; and here was Egbert advertising his alter ego on his chest.

She began to scan the text underneath the photograph.

Egbert Visser. *So his name really was Egbert.*

Egbert Visser, aged twenty-six, software engineer. Older than Veerle, and Kris too, older by a long way, but he hadn't outgrown his taste for adventure, she guessed. Or perhaps it was his taste for anarchy that he had been indulging.

It was thanks to Egbert's taste for anarchy that he was in the picture at all. It wasn't his family who had reported him missing – he was a Dutch citizen and no close family had been traced at all – but his employer. Some weeks before, Egbert had failed to turn up at the office where he worked;

since this followed an incident in which his boss had disciplined him for playing online games during office hours, nobody was that surprised at first when he didn't appear. After a few days, however, questions began to be asked, and after ten days someone else was having to cover his work. Scenting an opportunity to rid himself of a difficult employee, Egbert's boss, Paul De Bock, had made redoubled attempts to contact him. It swiftly became apparent that Egbert had vanished altogether, not simply from the company where he worked, but from the unkempt studio flat he called home. The downstairs mailbox was stuffed full and the flat stank of mouldering food cartons and the contents of the overflowing kitchen waste bin.

By the time Alexandre Lambert came sprinting through the early spring forest, with his eyes wide and the back of his blue Scout shirt coming adrift from his jeans, Egbert was already considered a Missing Person.

The article said nothing about *how* Egbert had died, or *why*. Clearly it was not an accident, or natural causes; Egbert had hardly dragged himself dying into the depths of the woods and pulled the dark soil over himself like a blanket, turning his weary face to the bosom of Mother Earth before falling asleep for ever. Someone had carried or dragged him there, just as someone had carried Vlinder down to the over-grown pond in the park and let her lifeless body sink into the dark scummy water.

There was no indication that anyone had made a connection between Vlinder's death and Egbert's. Vlinder had been found in Flemish Tervuren; Egbert's body had been discovered in the depths of the Wallonian Ardennes. Egbert had been a software engineer; Vlinder, so far as Veerle knew, had still been studying. They hadn't known each other in 'real' life, only on the Koekoeken site, where each of them hid behind an insectoid user name, one a butterfly, the other a hornet.

The only connection between them was the Koekoeken, she thought sickly.

Veerle stared at Egbert's photograph with a cold hollow feeling in the pit of her stomach.

And the only people who know that are the Koekoeken.

She wondered how many of them would even connect the two deaths. She and Kris, and certainly Fred – but perhaps no one else, unless Fred posted something on the website.

Like what? Supposing he posts something warning the group but doesn't tell the police? If they ever do find out about the Koekoeken, we'll have been concealing evidence.

Useless to conjecture what Fred would do; she'd never met him. But the fact remained that none of the Koekoeken, Fred included, could involve the police without dropping every single member in it, up to their neck.

And if we do nothing?

She bit her lip.

Then who's next?

43

The following morning, Easter Sunday morning, Claudine went to mass. As usual she went to the French-speaking church in a neighbouring district, rather than the Sint-Pauluskerk opposite the house. She asked Veerle whether she would like to go with her rather than staying alone at home, but when Veerle said no she didn't press it. Clearly Veerle was not going to go anywhere (Claudine reasoned to herself) or get into trouble of any kind, since there were still no buses running. She went into the sitting room to say goodbye to her daughter, buttoning up her good coat as she did so, and found Veerle still lying indolently on the couch in her dressing gown, with a mug in her hand.

'Won't you be bored here?' she asked, but Veerle simply shrugged.

'I'm fine,' she said.

'I'll be gone two hours,' Claudine warned her.

'That's OK.' Veerle stifled a yawn. She lay back and listened as the front door closed. A minute later she heard the engine of Claudine's little car firing up, and then the sound of it pulling away from the kerb outside the house. Veerle looked at the ceiling, holding her breath.

Gone, she thought.

She put the mug down on the floor and jumped up. With Claudine's departure a deadening atmosphere seemed to have lifted. The very air felt cleaner, colder, sharper. Energizing.

Veerle ran upstairs to her room. In between dressing at lightning speed and brushing her teeth with savage briskness she phoned Kris on her mobile, as arranged. Three minutes later, as she was fastening her dark hair in a loose knot at the back of her head, she heard the doorbell. She pulled on her jacket as she ran down to answer it.

She had thought that she would instantly feel calmer when she saw Kris, but she didn't. The burden of knowledge about Egbert was too much; it was like a tumour in the heart of her, hot and heavy and toxic. She didn't invite him in, even though she knew Claudine was long gone. Instead she pushed past him, out of the front door.

'Where did you park the car?'

'A couple of streets down, like you said.'

They began to walk quickly. It was a cool morning but Veerle felt too warm, as though she were running a fever. She was desperate to reach the car, to get away, somewhere well out of earshot of any other living person.

'Where do you want to go?' asked Kris. 'We could go to the castle, if we're careful.'

'Anywhere.'

They passed an older man walking a couple of little dogs. Veerle returned his friendly greeting but inside she was seething with an impatience so intense that it was like rage. As soon as they were inside the car with the doors closed, and

Kris was sliding the key into the ignition, she said, 'What are we going to do?'

Kris paused, his fingers still curled around the key. 'We're going to think carefully before we do anything.'

'Did you see the photograph?'

'Yes.'

'He had his name on his T-shirt. Horzel, I mean. He had his Koekoeken name on his T-shirt.'

Kris said nothing. He started the car, and pulled away from the kerb.

'We have to do something,' said Veerle. She put her hand to her forehead, as though checking for a temperature. She was looking out through the windscreen but not really seeing the street as it slid past. Houses, a single shop, the yellow-painted façade of a bar, more houses, then at last an open expanse of grass. All of it as distant as a dream. It was Egbert who kept intruding into her consciousness: Egbert with his rumpled-looking hair and rebellious expression. Seeing his photograph for the first time had been like meeting him; she had to remind herself that he didn't exist any more, at least not like that. *What does someone look like after a month in the ground?* She shuddered.

Anywhere, she'd said, but the castle was too far, the conversation wouldn't wait. Kris drove until the last house was half a kilometre behind them and they were passing fields, and then he pulled over. When he turned off the engine the silence was startling.

'Let's think about this,' said Kris seriously.

'It can't be a coincidence,' said Veerle immediately. 'Two of them; three if—' She was going to say, *if you count Hommel*, but she stopped herself just in time. 'Two of them,' she repeated more firmly. 'And the only thing they had in common was the Koekoeken.'

'The only thing we *know* they had in common,' said Kris.

'It's a pretty big thing,' Veerle pointed out.

'Yeah.' Kris slumped back in his seat, thinking. 'I just don't see how the deaths are connected. I mean, Vlinder went missing ages before Egbert did, and nobody seems to know exactly when or where she died. She might have gone to one of the houses, or she might have run into the wrong person on the street somewhere. There's no way of knowing.'

'Maybe she broke into somewhere when there was some-body there, like that time we went to that place near Oudergem Woud.'

'What, she ran into the owner and they thought she was a burglar and whacked her, but a bit too hard?' Kris shook his head. 'It's possible, but it doesn't feel right. OK, so maybe that was what happened, and then the person who whacked her panicked and dumped the body. But I can't believe the exact same thing happened to Egbert. That really is too much of a coincidence.'

'Supposing it was the same house?'

Kris shot her a glance, eyebrows raised.

'No,' said Veerle, relenting. 'That's too far-fetched.'

'Vlinder normally did the old places,' said Kris. 'And Egbert – the last place he did was one over in Sint-Genesius-Rode. I checked through his posts last night. It's a big house, really modern. Not Vlinder's thing.'

A dampening silence fell between them.

Think, Veerle said to herself.

After a moment a thought came to her, chill and un-welcome. She said slowly, 'Maybe it's not the houses. Maybe it's the Koekoeken themselves.' She looked at Kris, her expression grim. 'Maybe someone's working their way down the list. Picking people off. Hunting them.'

Kris stared back, and she could see the horror on his face as the idea sank in.

Hommel, she thought.

'Who has a list of everyone?' she asked him.

She could see him consciously shaking off the images that were passing through his brain.

'Fred,' he said. 'Although' – he thought quickly – 'in theory anyone could make one by looking at who's posting on the website.'

'That's just user names. You couldn't track anyone down from those.'

'Fred doesn't have much more information. I mean, he knows names and he must have their email addresses, but not everyone's actual street addresses. Nobody has those.' Kris shrugged. 'Some people have some other people's addresses, if they've sent keys through the post. But nobody has *every-one's*. There's no point. It would be needlessly risky.'

'Well, if it's not the houses,' said Veerle slowly, 'and it's not the website . . .' Her voice trailed off. An idea was burgeoning in her mind, pushing its way up through the topsoil of her consciousness like a strange and toxic weed, opening up into ugly glory.

She heard the words running through her head two or three times before they found their way onto her tongue.

'Maybe it's both,' she said.

Her mouth was dry and the words came out more quietly than she had intended.

'What?' said Kris, his brows drawing together in a frown.

'Maybe it's both.'

They stared at each other, her hazel eyes searching his darker ones.

'You mean . . .'

'Maybe someone's using the houses *and* the website. Checking who's going where and when . . . and turning up there themselves.'

There was a silence.

'They'd have to have access to the website,' said Kris slowly. 'Unless someone could hack it.'

'Why would anyone bother?' asked Veerle. 'It looks like a bird-watching forum.'

'Well, either someone hacked it, or . . .'

'Or it's one of us,' finished Veerle. 'One of the Koekoeken.'

'No.' Kris was shaking his head. 'This is crazy.'

'I'm not so sure,' said Veerle grimly.

'How would they get into the house if they did that? There's only ever one set of keys going round.'

'Maybe they've been to that one before and made copies. Or maybe they can lock-pick, like Egbert can.'

'Could.'

Veerle shivered. She said, 'It's pretty horrible to think of. You turn up at some place and there's someone already in there.'

'Like that place near Oudergem Woud,' Kris pointed out.

Veerle stared at him open-mouthed. 'Oh God. *No*,' she said.

Kris looked alarmed. 'Veerle, I was just thinking out loud.

We still don't know what we saw there. Maybe it was nothing. Just someone messing about.'

'But the house was empty and it said so on the website. If there was someone monitoring the posts . . .'

'Then what?' Kris sounded almost fierce. 'Supposing you did see a dead body. Supposing it *was* the girl who vanished . . .'

'Clare,' supplied Veerle.

'Suppose it was Clare, then. She wasn't one of the Koekoeken, was she?'

'How do you know?'

'She was *British*.'

'Well, Egbert was Dutch,' Veerle pointed out.

'That's different. Egbert was here pretty much permanently. Anyway, he was up to his neck in it, picking locks for Fred and stuff. You couldn't invite some spoiled little expat girl to join. She'd be there for maybe two years and then she'd be off somewhere else, boasting about what she got up to in Brussels, and sooner or later there'd be trouble. Anyway,' added Kris, 'how many of them do you actually know?'

'British people?'

'Any of them. Them and the Americans.'

Veerle shrugged.

'And how many of them are at your school?'

Veerle thought about that. 'There's one.'

'One. One out of hundreds, maybe thousands. They don't mix, Veerle. There's no way Clare was one of us.'

'She's still disappeared, just like Vlinder did.'

'Well, maybe that's just—'

Coincidence. Veerle waited for him to say it.

But Kris was putting a hand to his forehead, tugging at his dark hair as though trying to uproot some unwelcome idea that was sprouting inside his head.

'Kris?'

'She wasn't meant to be there,' said Kris, and Veerle had the feeling he wasn't talking to her at all, but to himself, following some script she couldn't see. 'And he came to scope out the house and she was already inside, or maybe he was inside when she came in.' He exhaled slowly, a long sigh. 'Wrong place, wrong time. She *wasn't* one of us, but maybe he thought she was. It all fits.'

Veerle stared at him and she had a cold feeling in the pit of her stomach. *It all fits.* Kris was right. And now she was realizing that she didn't want any of it to fit, she had been relying on him to be the sceptic, to prove that none of it was connected, anything that *seemed* connected was a coincidence. A coincidence, rare as a Spix's macaw but undeniably still in existence. *Because if it's all true, if it really all fits together the way Kris say it does . . .*

'We can't walk away from this,' said Kris grimly. His hand was on her arm, the fingers digging into her flesh. 'We have to do something now.'

Veerle found her tongue. 'Supposing we're wrong?' She looked into his eyes, and although she was afraid of hardly anything she could feel the fear seeping into her now, like freezing rain soaking through her clothes. Veerle thought she would rather have solo-climbed the sheerest rock face in the world, the most featureless façade – she would rather have climbed the gleaming surfaces of the *Atomium,* for God's sake, and risked falling off and landing on the tarmacked surface of the Eeuwfeestlaan, splattering passing tourists with her blood and brains – anything rather than this. The consequences of making the wrong decision at this point were so enormous that her imagination could hardly map them.

If Kris is right, and one of the Koekoeken is behind what happened to Vlinder and Egbert and even that British girl, Clare, we can't let it go, we have to do something. To ignore what was happening was to walk heedlessly through a darkened catacomb, deaf to the silent reproaches of the massed dead. But acting . . .

That means involving the police, it means exposing dozens of other people. It means placing ourselves at a crime scene. It means confessing before everyone that we – possibly – saw a murder and didn't report it. We'll probably top the list of suspects, Veerle realized sickly. *As for the people who owned the houses we visited – those great big palaces with their pools and jacuzzis and home cinemas – every single one of them is rich and powerful and well-connected. They aren't going to write off those clandestine visits to their houses as the result of youthful exuberance. They're going to want blood. Mine and Kris's.*

Kris said, 'I don't think we're wrong.'

Veerle looked at him and saw it in his eyes.

He's going to act, whether we're wrong or not, because the consequences of not doing anything if we're right are too terrible. Blood on our hands, she thought.

She looked at him, taking in every detail of him with a painful intensity, as though she were seeing him for the last time. The dark hair falling over one side of his forehead, the dark eyes, the nose that was a little too big and the mouth that was a little too wide for perfect good looks but which somehow combined to make her heart leap whenever she saw him. She had the sense of something immense and terrible thundering towards them, like a dam bursting, tonnes of brown and stinking water bearing everything before it, shattering trees and buildings like matchwood, scouring clean the face of the earth, sweeping them both away. Crushing them.

She said nothing. Anything she could have said would have sounded like a farewell.

'Veerle?' said Kris at last. 'Are you *sure* Mevrouw Coppens didn't say anything about *where* Hommel might have gone – to a friend, or a relative or something? Anything at all?'

Reluctantly Veerle shook her head. 'No. She asked *me* if her daughter was all right, and when I talked to her in the street she just kept saying that Jappe had said this or that, and that she was old enough to move out.'

She hated to see the way the look in Kris's eyes darkened. 'It's still possible she did just move out, you know,' she said. 'We don't *know* anything's happened to her, not for certain.' The words sounded empty even to her own ears. Still she wished that just by saying them she could somehow breathe life into the possibility. On the single occasion she had actually met the girl the air had practically crackled with the enmity between them, but Veerle thought about Vlinder, suspended face down in frozen pond water, and Egbert mouldering under the forest trees, and she was truly afraid for Hommel.

'I don't believe that,' said Kris.

Veerle looked at him for a long moment and then she sighed.

'No. Neither do I.' She looked away, out of the window, as though there might be some comfort to be found in the familiar view of fields and sky and the distant roofs of the village. Then she looked back at him, because it had to be done, the medicine had to be taken.

'So,' she said, 'what are we going to do?'

44

Kris and Veerle sat side by side on the tram as it swayed and rattled through the woods, heading for Brussels. The trees were clothed in the bright light green of springtime. It was a very fine evening, mild and sunny, but Veerle took no pleasure in the beauty of the woodlands. She could not look at that burgeoning foliage without reflecting on the fact that it made the bare winter wood opaque; it created a thick canopy of leaves that could cover all manner of things. Egbert had lain hidden in such a place, and Vlinder had been found just a few kilometres away from the tramline, at the border of forest and park. It was impossible not to speculate about the others – the British girl, Clare, and Hommel. Were the green shoots of spring weaving a concealing carpet over disturbed earth, vacant eyes and pale dead skin? She shivered.

Kris had his arm around her, but she was tense; she wasn't relaxing against him. He followed her gaze and saw that she was staring fixedly out at the passing trees.

'Hey,' he said in her ear. 'Relax. She was probably just putting it on to stop you going out.'

His words seemed to recall Veerle to herself, but they didn't lighten her mood.

'I don't know,' she said. 'She seemed really ill. She sounded sort of . . . weak.' She bit her lip. 'I offered to call the doctor but she wouldn't let me.'

'Veerle,' said Kris patiently. 'Of course she didn't want you to call the doctor. Look, think about it. She's tried arguing, she's tried locking you in. She even tried taking your wallet. This is just the latest ruse.'

At the word *ruse* he saw Veerle's eyes widen, and he added, 'I don't mean *ruse*, I mean—'

'She's not doing it on purpose,' Veerle told him. '*She* thinks she's sick, even if it's all in her head.'

'Well, you offered to call the doctor,' Kris pointed out.

'I know.'

Veerle lapsed into silence. *If I could tell her*, she thought. *This is important. I'm not leaving her on her own to go off and mess around. This is about people's lives.* She knew the impossibility of it. She couldn't even tell her school friends.

She glanced up at Kris. *It's him and me.*

And Hommel?

That was the question: whether the connection she felt to Kris was a straight line between the two of them or one side of a triangle.

The tram had left the woods behind and was now passing a large park. A few minutes later they passed the tram museum. After the stop known as *Chien Vert* – the green dog – they left the parkland behind and the streets of Brussels closed in upon them.

There was a tight knot of tension in the pit of Veerle's stomach at the thought of the meeting ahead.

We have to talk to Fred, Kris had said, and she had seen the determination in his face. It made sense, of course it did; it was either that or go directly to the police, but that was the equivalent of weighing into a war with a nuclear bomb; it might stop the war but it would take everyone with it, yourself included.

We may still have to do that. What if Fred's no help? That seemed like a frightening probability. Veerle couldn't imagine that Fred was going to be able to suggest anything they couldn't have thought of for themselves, the two options being: do nothing, or tell the police. She supposed that in some ideal fantasy world Fred would take the whole horrible problem off their hands and offer to contact the police himself while leaving them out of it altogether. She knew that wasn't going to happen, though. She had no personal knowledge of Fred but she knew perfectly well that he didn't owe them anything. He wasn't her father, he had no obligation to protect her.

Play with fire, and you can't complain if you get burned, she thought grimly. Still, there was nothing to do but see what happened when they actually got to the meeting. She stared out of the windows at the apartment blocks sliding past and tried to distract herself by imagining how she would attempt to climb them. On an iron balcony far above her she saw a middle-aged man come out to water his plants and thought how shocked he would be if he stared over the ornamental railings and saw Veerle moving up the façade of the building towards him.

The tram cornered twice and then began to descend into the earth towards Montgomery station. They had to take the metro from here; Fred's gallery was in Ixelles. When they got out of the tram Veerle could smell the city in the air; she could almost taste it on her tongue, a slightly gritty, smoky essence of traffic fumes and dust and closely packed bodies. It had been sunny up above but down here it was never daytime, it was always a kind of unhealthy yellowish twilight.

Kris and Veerle stood slightly apart on the platform, both too full of nervous energy to entwine themselves round each other. It was too serious an expedition anyway to embark upon it holding hands like a pair of children skipping through a meadow. When the train arrived it was nowhere near full but neither of them sat down; it would have been impossible to relax. They stood up, holding onto the pole and swaying with the movement of the train, staring sombrely into each other's eyes like a pair of aristocrats in a tumbril, heading for the guillotine.

They changed at Arts-Loi, travelled a couple of stops, then left the train and took the escalator back up to ground level. The metro station of Porte de Namur was on a major intersection and the constant sound of traffic was like white noise. All the same it was welcome to feel space and air around them after the windowless environment of the metro.

Kris set off at a fast pace, threading his way through the commuters heading for the nearest station or tram stop. His legs were longer than Veerle's, and although she was not unfit she was soon flushed and breathing hard. She didn't ask him to slow down, though.

Let's get this over with.

After a few minutes they turned down a side street; now the incessant sound of traffic was behind them, muffled but still audible, like the sound of water thundering down a distant canyon. Kris had checked the address and the route beforehand and he moved swiftly and confidently.

'Down here,' he said, cocking his head to indicate that they should take a right turn down a narrower street.

Half a minute later Veerle saw the gallery. The building was old, perhaps as much as a century old, she thought, with a façade of white stucco and elegant mouldings around the upper windows. The ground floor had been modernized; there was a glass front polished to such reflective brilliance that it almost sparkled. It was not possible to see right inside the gallery from the street; behind the glass were single items spot-lit against a black background, so that they appeared almost to glow, like items of gold jewellery offset against ebony velvet. As Veerle approached the gallery she could see that one of them was a gigantic dish made of white and gold glass spun so finely that it looked like candyfloss. It was also perforated like lace; you could not have put a grape inside it without it rolling through one of the holes, or an apple without breaking those delicate glass filaments. It gave Veerle the same faint sense of unreality as the houses she had visited with Kris; it was hard to conceive of anyone being so affluent that they could fill their home with things like this, so rivetingly beautiful and yet ultimately so useless.

On the other side of the window was a cube of what looked like sandstone, the corners smoothed and the different faces pockmarked with carved symbols. Veerle thought that it was quite staggeringly ugly.

Kris tried the door of the gallery but without much conviction: places like this one didn't allow just anyone to wander in off the street. Sure enough, it was locked. He leaned against the doorframe and pressed the buzzer.

After he had pressed it for the third time, there was a crackle and a male voice said '*Oui?*' Even in that single syllable the speaker had managed to convey a curt, disapproving tone.

Kris did not react to this. He leaned close to the speaker and said in French, 'We have come to see Fred.'

There was a pause and then the voice said, 'We don't see students.'

Veerle looked around at this; she guessed correctly that the unseen speaker was looking at them on a security camera. She spotted it, high in the upper corner of the doorway, its dead cyclopean eye trained on them.

'We're not students,' said Kris. 'Can we speak to Fred?'

'The gallery is closed,' said the voice irritably.

'We don't want to see the gallery,' Kris told him. 'We want to see Fred. Tell him it's Kris Verstraeten and Veerle De Keyser.'

'*Monsieur,*' came the reply, in tones of festering dislike, 'the gallery is only open to serious enquirers. If you will kindly—'

'Look,' interrupted Kris. 'Tell him it's Schorpioen and Honingbij. OK? Schorpioen – and Honingbij.'

There was a silence so long that Veerle began to wonder whether the person at the other end of the intercom had decided to disengage from the conversation altogether and wait for her and Kris to go away.

When the voice spoke again the tone was quite different; the contemptuous edge had gone and the speaker sounded anxious, almost furtive.

'What did you come here for?'

Kris opened his mouth to reply but the voice went on, 'No, don't say anything. I'll come down.'

There was a *click* and then silence. Kris straightened up, shooting a glance at Veerle. They waited, and after about a minute they saw the silhouette of someone approaching the door.

The door opened inwards and Veerle saw a man of perhaps forty with a smooth face and grey eyes and thick dark hair with the first stripes of silver in it. *He probably blow-dries it*, she thought. She took in the expensive tailored shirt in a bold shade of papal purple, the Italian shoes, the gleaming aviator watch. The armour of wealth. In spite of it, he was clearly ill at ease, the gaze of those grey eyes dancing nervously over the pair of them and flickering towards the street behind.

'Come in, come in,' he said hastily, flapping at them with a well-manicured hand.

Kris shouldered his way past, Veerle following, looking all around with interest.

We don't see students, he'd said. She wondered whom he *did* see, what sort of person dropped into a place like this to pick up an ornamental chunk of sandstone or a gossamer dish.

The narrow space between the two display windows opened out into a large room with white walls and a polished wooden floor. There were rows of spotlights, but most of them were off, so that the various sculptures and artworks loomed eerily in the half-light. Veerle saw what looked like a horse's head on a pedestal, and something else that looked vaguely architectural. The effect was reminiscent of an over-sized chess game, the pieces abandoned in the dark. There was no time to take a closer look; Fred – at least she assumed the dark-haired man was Fred – was leading them towards a flight of stairs going to the upper floor. He was moving quickly and nervously, his hands carving shapes in the air, and it sounded as though he were carrying on one half of an argument, complaining about their sudden arrival in a rather rhetorical manner; he clearly expected no reply and no sympathy.

The upper rooms had a distinctly businesslike atmosphere that contrasted with the sleek elegance of the gallery below. The office into which Fred led them was cluttered with files and papers. There were no finely spun gilded glass bowls or horses' heads here, although Veerle noticed several large black-and-white photographs on the walls. They were close-ups of architectural details, chunks of carved masonry and inlaid wooden panels. *One of the Koekoeken places?* she wondered, but there was no way to tell.

'Sit,' said Fred, indicating a couple of spindle-legged chairs. He moved behind the desk and sat down, and Veerle noticed as he did so that he never took his eyes off them. There was a large chrome coffee machine in the corner of the room, but he didn't offer them anything, nor did he take anything for himself. He looked at Kris and Veerle and said, 'How did you get this address?'

Kris leaned forward. 'I called people. Seven people, to be exact. The sixth knew someone who knew you, and the seventh gave me the address.'

'Persistent,' commented Fred.

Kris shrugged.

'But unwise,' Fred went on. 'If you ever have to contact me again, and I strongly advise against it, kindly do it through the website.'

'The website's the problem,' said Kris curtly.

Up went Fred's eyebrows.

'Look,' said Kris, 'there's something going on, and we think it has something to do with the group. First Vlinder vanished—'

'You think that had something to do with the group?' interrupted Fred. 'They don't even know where it happened, poor girl.'

Why do I think he sounds insincere? thought Veerle.

'No,' conceded Kris. 'But now there's Egbert – Horzel – too.'

'Schorpioen—' began Fred in a faintly ironic tone.

'Kris.'

'Kris, don't imagine that this has not occurred to me. But what do we have? Two people, unfortunately both dead, found in completely different locations, both of them outdoors. Not in a house, no; certainly not in one of the houses we visit.' Fred saw that Kris was about to interrupt and put up a hand. 'This may seem like a coincidence. Certainly it is a coincidence. But let us think about those two people. Members of a group like ours, they are unusual people. If they did not enjoy taking risks they would do something else with their spare time.' He shrugged. 'They would go to the cinema, or press wild flowers – who knows?' Fred leaned forwards, across the desk. 'But people like Vlinder and Horzel, they enjoy danger. And therefore, by necessity, there is more likelihood of something happening to them than there is to the population at large.' He shook his head. 'After all, who knows what else they were mixed up in?'

He's brushing us off. Veerle could feel her temper rising. 'It's too much of a coincidence,' she told him hotly. 'Both of them Koekoeken—'

323

'Nevertheless—' began Fred, and then Kris interrupted both of them.

'Vlinder and Horzel, did they know each other outside the group?'

Fred gave him an outraged look. 'How should I possibly know that?'

'Well, who introduced them to the Koekoeken? Did one of them introduce the other?'

He won't remember that, thought Veerle, but to her surprise he did.

'No. Gregory introduced Vlinder, and some friend of his seconded it. I don't recall who. Egbert – I introduced him myself.'

'Who seconded him?' asked Kris.

'No one.' Fred's pale gaze rested on him for a moment. 'It was not necessary, since he was personally known to me. And Egbert is a very useful person. *Was* a very useful person.' He sat back. 'Unfortunately, he was also a rather unpredictable person. It's impossible to say what else he was involved in.'

'You knew him?' blurted out Veerle. 'He was your friend?' She could feel indignation bubbling up again from some magmatic chamber deep inside her. *How can he sit there arguing so coolly when one of his friends is dead?*

'Friend?' repeated Fred. 'No, it wasn't really a friendship. More of a' – he thought for a moment – 'symbiosis. Egbert was able to access properties for me, you see. Not the sort of places you two probably visit.' He sniffed. 'Beautiful, ancient buildings. Sometimes I do what small things I can to maintain them. Sometimes all I can do is record their beauty before it crumbles.' He nodded at one of the black-and-white blow-ups on the wall.

'And what did Egbert get in return?' asked Kris.

Fred shrugged. 'A chance to break the rules. To break the law, in fact, since all these places are private property.' He glanced from Kris to Veerle. 'He wasn't, as you two appear to be, involved in it for the social aspect.'

Veerle saw a stormy expression cross Kris's face, but he didn't rise to the bait.

'So as far as you know,' he asked levelly, 'Vlinder and Egbert didn't know each other?'

Fred dipped his head. 'So far as I know.'

'So the only connection between them is the Koekoeken,' persisted Kris.

'Still a coincidence,' commented Fred. He put a hand on the desk, palm down, as though laying down a deck of cards. 'Look, people die. We are all going to die – one day. It is tragic that this has happened to Vlinder and to Egbert, but you cannot assume there is any connection.'

'Well, what about the British girl, Clare?' asked Veerle. She felt very tempted to stand up and lean over the desk with its highly polished surface and watch her reflection reach out and slap Fred very hard around the face. When she looked at that cool, unruffled expression she could almost feel the smooth skin of his cheek under her open hand. With an effort she kept her seat.

'Clare?' repeated Fred.

'Yes, the girl who vanished from the house near Oudergem Woud.'

Of course, Fred knew whom she meant; hadn't he posted a

warning on the website, that everyone should avoid that house? Now he was looking from her to Kris and back again with apparent incomprehension.

'If you mean whom I think you mean, she vanished from England,' Fred pointed out.

'But the police think she came back to her parents' house,' said Kris.

'We don't know that.'

'The media were filming outside it,' Kris pointed out. 'They must have had some reason for doing that.'

Fred looked at him. 'Nevertheless, I don't see what this has to do with Vlinder and Egbert. You have been trying to tell me that what happened to them was something to do with the group. This girl, Clare, wasn't one of the Koekoeken.'

Kris didn't look at Veerle, he kept his eyes on Fred, but Veerle could almost sense the words *Told you so* drifting towards her. He was silent for almost half a minute, thinking. Then he said, 'Something may have happened to her in that house. A Koekoeken house.'

Veerle held her breath, waiting for Fred to ask the inevitable questions, for Kris to reply.

This is it. This is where we tell him we saw her.

For a long moment Fred said nothing at all. Then: 'Why do you think that?'

'Because we went there. To that house.'

'When?'

'February. Before they reported her missing on TV and you warned everyone off.'

'A precaution,' said Fred.

'We got to the house and we were about to go in when

we realized there was someone already inside,' said Kris.

'How?'

'A light was on. So we went round to the back of the house to see if we could see anything.'

'And you saw this girl?'

'We saw *something*. Veerle looked in through the kitchen window and saw someone lying on the floor.'

'The girl?' Fred sounded shocked.

'We don't know. All she saw was a hand.'

'A girl's hand,' Veerle cut in. 'And it was still. Completely still. I thought at first maybe she was sick, maybe she'd collapsed. But we looked again and then we saw someone standing up.'

'So she was all right?' Fred sounded a little mystified, as though he wondered where this was going.

'It wasn't her. It was a man,' Veerle told him.

'So let me be clear,' said Fred. 'You saw a hand and thought it belonged to a girl, but then you saw a man?'

'It wasn't the same person,' said Veerle firmly.

'I see. And did you see this man attack the other person? Is that what you are saying?'

'No—' *How can I tell him what I saw?* She recalled the strange, vague feeling of dread that had come over her when she saw that figure unfold to his full height behind the kitchen unit. It had been more than just the realization that he was tall and broad-shouldered, hulking, probably strong enough to knock her down with a single blow. There had been something *wrong*, something that had made her hackles rise instinctively; she had felt that as strongly as if she had been leaning over the concrete rim of a big cat enclosure, watching tigers rending a side of beef, the air thick with the pungent yellow scent of jungle animal.

'There was just something wrong,' she said, wishing that she could think of some better way of expressing it.

'What did you do?' asked Fred. 'Did you call the police?'

'No,' put in Kris.

'Why not, if there was "something wrong"?'

'Because we weren't sure what we'd seen.'

Fred's eyebrows went up.

'But look,' Kris went on, 'the house was supposed to be empty. The people who owned it, Clare's family, they were away. While they were away, Clare vanished, and we saw a girl lying on the floor in the kitchen.'

'But you didn't feel concerned enough to call anyone,' Fred pointed out.

'That was before Egbert,' said Kris.

'You see a pattern,' said Fred. 'But there is no pattern. This British girl, she had nothing to do with us. Maybe you saw her. Who knows? But I don't see what that has to do with Egbert – or Vlinder.' He glanced at Veerle and the expression in his grey eyes was unreadable. 'Two quite separate deaths and a disappearance. Tragic, yes, but there is no pattern.'

'It may be more than those three,' said Kris grimly. 'There's Hommel. Her real name is Els Lievens.'

'I know,' remarked Fred. 'And what is the problem with *Mademoiselle* Lievens?'

Out of the corner of her eye Veerle saw an almost imperceptible movement. She glanced down and realized that Kris's right hand had curled into a fist; the knuckles were white.

When he spoke, however, his voice was quite neutral. 'She's vanished too.'

'What makes you think that?'

'Nobody's seen her for weeks.' Kris looked Fred straight in the eye, challenging him to try brushing this aside. 'She doesn't answer calls, either to her home or to her mobile. Veerle went and talked to her mother and she doesn't know where Hommel is either.'

Fred glanced at Veerle and she was irritated to see an assessing air about the look. She glared at him.

'Has the mother reported the disappearance?' asked Fred.

'She's under her husband's thumb,' said Kris shortly. 'Hommel's stepfather. He's not reporting it, partly because she's over eighteen but mainly because he's a *klootzak*.'

If Fred was taken aback by this piece of Flemish invective tacked onto the end of a stream of French he gave no sign of it.

'If her own family aren't concerned, why should you be?' he asked Kris, and Veerle was infuriated to see his gaze flicker back to her for a moment. 'Are you one of the friends trying to call her? Maybe she doesn't want to speak to you.'

'It's not just me,' said Kris tightly. 'Koen has been trying to contact her to get back the keys from the last place she visited. He's left half a dozen messages. It's clear he's not going to give up. It's more trouble than it's worth for her to ignore him.'

Fred eyed him for a moment. Then he said, 'I think we can clear up the question of Hommel. She returned the keys to me a few days ago.'

Veerle heard Kris say, '*What?!*' but she was too stunned to even look at him. She stared at Fred as though she could not believe what she had just heard.

'You saw her?' Kris was saying.

'No, of course not. You think I encourage people to come here? She sent them in a padded envelope.'

'Was there a note?'

'I don't know.' Fred threw up his hands. 'No – well, I believe there was a label attached to the keys.'

'Do you still have it?'

'No. I sent them on to Koen.'

'How long ago was this?' asked Kris.

'A few days. A week perhaps – or ten days.'

'So,' said Kris slowly, 'you don't actually know that it was Hommel who returned the keys.'

'Who else would it be?' demanded Fred. He shook his head. 'Why look beyond the obvious?'

'Because we can't afford not to,' snapped Kris. The colour was rising in his face.

'It's a fairy story,' said Fred. 'No – a horror story. You have created a horror story.' He leaned forward again, his grey eyes bright and ironic. 'What is your theory, then? You think that someone inside the group is making people disappear? There is absolutely nothing to base that upon. Two deaths – regrettable, yes, but neither of them was found indoors, much less in one of our houses. A completely unconnected disappearance of some spoiled expat girl who is probably in Ibiza with an unsuitable boyfriend. And Hommel, who has also vanished, according to you, but apparently not to any location lacking a post office.'

There was a sharp screech as Kris stood up, pushing back his chair. Veerle had the satisfaction of seeing the ironic expression drop from Fred's smooth features in an instant.

Now he was leaning back in his own chair, his hands clasping the arms so tightly that the knuckles were white, and his mouth was open.

'What if you're wrong? What then?' Kris barked at him. 'Someone else could be next.'

'Calm yourself,' said Fred faintly, but Veerle thought that in truth he was the one who needed to calm down – the colour had drained from his face, and when he stretched out a hand as though to ward Kris off she saw that his fingers were trembling. Kris had noticed too; he drew in a deep breath and backed off, sinking back into his chair. But he didn't take his eyes off Fred.

'Why did you come here?' Fred asked him querulously. 'If you think your friend has disappeared, why didn't you go straight to the police?'

'Because we're all involved,' Kris told him. 'How many of us are there? Twenty-five? Thirty?'

'Over forty,' said Fred.

'Once we tell the police, they're going to want to see everyone, all forty. They're going to want names, and they're going to want a list of houses. Maybe they won't care too much about the old ones, the ones where nobody lives, especially if you've been doing them up. But what do you think the owners of the other places are going to say – the big smart houses in Auderghem and Tervuren? We'll be dead meat.'

If Fred had looked grey before, now he looked as though he were about to faint.

His hands moved convulsively and Veerle saw his gaze flickering about the room, panic-stricken, dancing from Kris to herself to the black-and-white pictures on the walls.

She could see quite clearly what he was thinking, could almost pick it up like a radio signal: *They can't touch me, I didn't do anything, I only did the old places. I renovated them, for God's sake. Oh God, oh God, let this be a bad dream.*

'So . . .' When he spoke his voice was feeble, as though he had aged thirty years in an instant. 'You came here to get my permission?'

Kris shook his head. 'Maybe I hoped you'd talk us out of it. But nothing you've told us changes anything. There's no proof Hommel sent those keys – in fact if she didn't, it pretty much proves that someone else inside the group knows what happened to her.'

'It will destroy all of us, you realize that?' said Fred, his voice trembling. 'And for what? You know most of this is your . . . your imagination. That, and a coincidence. Vlinder and Horzel. You could put all of us in prison for a coincidence.'

There was a long silence.

He's right, thought Veerle. *There's no proof. Maybe it was just a coincidence, a horrible one, but all the same . . . Maybe there's no connection between what happened to Vlinder and what happened to Egbert. Maybe Hommel's just moved on. Maybe Clare . . .* But she couldn't go on with that line of thinking. *Maybe Clare just happened to be lying inert on the floor of a house we visited, and it has nothing to do with us . . .* There wasn't any pattern to it, there was no logic, and yet she still felt that slow welling of dread inside her.

'I will tell you what I will do,' said Fred suddenly, and there was a new tone in his voice; he sounded almost defiant. 'I will go to Gregory, since he set up the website for us in the first place, and tell him to take it down. It is of little use to me anyway since Egbert is no longer with us. I will remove it, and that will be the end of the Koekoeken, and the end of these dangerous ideas.'

The end of the Koekoeken?

Veerle was shocked. She shot a glance at Kris and saw that his reaction was much the same as hers. This was unexpected; there was no time to think it through.

Kris opened his mouth but he had barely had time to say, 'But—' before Fred interrupted him.

'If there is any basis for this theory of yours, we will put an end to it.' He raised a finger as though he were a school teacher about to lecture the pair of them, and Veerle saw Kris's jaw tighten. 'The Koekoeken will be gone, as though they never existed.'

I doubt that, thought Veerle. *You can't wipe out all traces of yourself on the Internet as easily as that.*

'That's not the answer,' said Kris shortly.

'It solves the problem.'

'It doesn't solve anything. If you take down the site there's no way of finding out who's doing this.'

'You're assuming there's something going on in the first place.' Fred had recovered his confidence. 'There is no proof of that. This is the best solution. We take down the website, the group ceases to exist, and if there is anything going on, it ends there, without us having to involve the police. No trouble for anyone.'

'And what about Vlinder? And Horzel?' demanded Kris.

Fred looked at him levelly. 'We cannot do anything for them now.'

Veerle was unable to contain herself any longer. 'What about justice?' she said angrily.

'Justice?' Fred repeated the word almost thoughtfully, as though he were savouring an entirely new taste in his mouth. He turned to look at Veerle. 'And if we go to the police with this story, where is the justice for the forty people who suddenly find themselves under investigation? You said so yourselves: they would be dead meat.' He shook his head. 'No. This is really the best solution.'

'You're going to take the site down? Immediately?' asked Kris.

'As soon as possible,' Fred told him. 'Gregory is away. Another week, ten days, then he will be back and I will tell him to take it down.'

'If someone's stalking the group, they're going to get away with it,' said Veerle.

'They are also going to stop,' Fred told her coolly. The gaze of his grey eyes rested on her for a moment. '*If* someone is doing that, and it is not all a figment of your imagination.'

This time it was Veerle who got to her feet, the legs of her chair uttering a screech of protest as they scraped the floor.

'Let's go, Kris,' she said, but her eyes were on Fred and the expression in them was fierce. As Kris stood up she touched his arm, wanting them to get moving before she lost her temper altogether and took a swing at Fred.

I won't give him the satisfaction, she thought, looking at that cool, complacent face, the expensive shirt and the even more costly watch under the purple cuff.

All the same, she didn't trust herself to stay in the room with him a minute longer. The atmosphere was suddenly stifling. She thought she could smell the stale aroma of old coffee from the machine in the corner and it reminded her of ashes. Veerle wanted to run downstairs and into the street, where she would have the open sky over her head, but even that would not be enough because the streets were full of people and cars and trams, crowded with them, and right now she wanted space. Space, and loneliness to run off her anger. She chafed under every moment spent in the gallery.

Fred rose too; it seemed he would not trust them alone in the building, even just as far as the entrance. He followed them down the stairs and unlocked the door for them. As he held it open, he said, 'Don't come back here. Ever. You understand?'

Kris passed very close to him, and as he did so he turned and looked directly into Fred's eyes. Their faces were a handspan apart. Kris said nothing; he didn't need to. Fred fell back against the wall, but as soon as Kris and Veerle were outside he was locking the door behind them with trembling hands.

After she had gone a few paces, Veerle turned once and glanced back at the gallery, but Fred had already vanished into the dark interior, fading away like a ghost into its shadowy recesses. There was nothing to see but the useless white and gold bowl and the ugly chunk of carved sandstone, inert under their spotlights, and the dead eye of the security camera glaring at them.

Kris put an arm around her shoulder, pulling her away. 'Come on,' he said in her ear. 'Let's go to the Warandepark. We can talk there.'

45

There was a bench free beside the pond but Veerle found herself unable to sit down. She was too restless even to stand in one place. Instead she and Kris walked up and down together under the trees, giving other strollers a wide berth. It was not possible to walk comfortably at that pace with their arms around each other, but after a while Kris took Veerle's hand. It was a strangely comforting feeling, his long fingers entwined with hers. She could feel the warmth of his skin, the roughness on the pads of his fingers from working outdoors. Veerle imagined that if she looked closely at those fingertips she would see that the whorls of the skin were finely marked with the dark soil, a faint tattoo that even scrubbing would not remove. She didn't want to stop and look though; she wanted to carry on walking beside Kris, with the warmth of his hand in hers, not speaking, just being together. Putting off the moment when they would have to talk about it – about what they were going to do.

The trouble was, she didn't have a clear idea about it herself.

It's too much, she thought. *Vlinder in the frozen lake, and Egbert lying in a forest in Wallonia, and whether we did see*

Clare – and if so what was happening to her – and whether it was Hommel who returned the keys or not.

All of it was swirling around inside her brain and she felt as though she had been woken late at night in pitch darkness by flood water pouring into the house, and she was fighting her way through a maelstrom of unrecognizable objects that struck her and each other before whirling away into the freezing blackness; she was unable to grasp a single one of them before it was torn away from her.

Veerle had no idea where they were walking; she could have continued making a circuit of the park for hours. At last Kris stopped before the pedestal of one of the park's statues, seemingly a hunter with some unidentifiable beast, man and animal gazing vacantly out of blind, blank eyes. Neither Kris nor Veerle gave the statue more than a cursory glance.

Kris pulled Veerle into an embrace. From a distance, if one of the well-dressed ladies walking a lapdog or the homebound commuters taking a short cut through the park had happened to glance their way, they looked like any other young couple stealing a kiss under cover of the drooping tree branches. There was no joy though; Veerle felt a cold burden of dread coalescing inside her, as though ice were forming around her heart. *What are we going to do?*

When Kris spoke she almost jumped.

'I'm not letting it go,' he said in her ear.

She put back her head and looked up into his dark eyes. 'Me neither,' she said.

'So Fred's shutting down the group,' said Kris. 'He's probably right. But what about the people who vanished? What about—'

'Hommel,' said Veerle.

They looked at each other and Veerle thought she could read what he was thinking in his eyes.

This doesn't have to be your fight.

It's my fight now, she telegraphed back.

'And Clare,' she said aloud. 'I'm not letting that go either. If she died in that house and I saw it . . .'

Then I've already walked away once. I'm not doing it again.

'Fred said Gregory would have to shut down the website, and he's away,' said Kris. 'So that means it's going to be active for at least another week. Long enough to do something.'

'But what?' Veerle could have screamed with frustration. 'Supposing we tell the police and then it turns out Fred was right, and what happened to Vlinder and Horzel had nothing to do with the Koekoeken? We'll be in so much trouble we'll never get out of it again, and so will everyone else.'

Kris was silent for a moment. Then he said, 'But if we knew for certain someone was monitoring the group we'd have a readymade list of forty suspects. And Fred must have their email addresses. If we knew it for sure, I'd tell the police.'

'But how can we be sure?' Veerle said, and before the words were out of her mouth she knew. 'We could leave a message on the forum. One that he would understand but nobody else would.'

'And if he responds,' said Kris, 'the list of forty is narrowed down to one. We could get the email address and maybe even the name from Fred – I don't care what he says about not going back to the gallery, he'll co-operate if it's that or drop everyone in it. And then the information could be passed on to the police anonymously, without involving anyone else at all.'

'Unless the stalker tells them,' Veerle pointed out.

'Then we have to hope that Gregory knows his stuff and buries the website deep.' Kris shrugged. 'It's a risk. They say once stuff is out there on the web it's never really gone, even if you delete it. But I'd say it's a risk worth taking.'

'We'll have to do it soon, before Gregory gets back,' Veerle pointed out.

'Yeah.'

'What are we going to say? In the message?'

They stared at each other.

'You know,' said Veerle, 'we can't say, *Whoever murdered Horzel, please identify yourself.*'

'I realize that.' Kris looked away, gazing into the distance, thinking. Then he said, 'We have to offer him something. An incentive to show himself.'

'If he exists.'

'Yes, if he exists. And it has to be something that only he will want. We don't want anyone else replying and messing things up.'

'Information?' Veerle felt her spirits flag. She couldn't think of anything a person capable of hunting others down in the way they suspected could possibly learn from her or Kris.

'No,' said Kris slowly. 'I'll tell you what we'll offer him. Bait.'

46

Even from the end of Kerkstraat Veerle could see that something was wrong.

Lights, she thought. *Why can I see lights?*

She was back later than she had planned, and although it was not yet properly dark the daylight was fading and the street was slowly sinking into shadow. Normally Claudine put down the roller shutters before nightfall, sealing the house so that not one chink of light escaped.

Now, however, yellow light was pouring out of the front windows, and as Veerle approached the house she could see that the front door was ajar and it was pouring out of that too, as though the house were haemorrhaging light. She picked up her pace a little, and then she slowed again, feeling the first stirrings of apprehension, as fleet and subtle as mice scurrying under straw. When she came to the stretch of pavement in front of the house, she paused altogether for a moment and stood there looking at the open front door.

Something's wrong.

She pushed the door wide open and went inside.

'*Maman?*'

For one long moment there was silence, and unpleasant

ideas flickered at the edges of her mind. Then she heard someone stirring in the sitting room and she thought, *I've spent too much time thinking about Vlinder and Egbert.*

Veerle went to open the sitting-room door, but before she could do so, it was opened from the inside and she found herself face to face, not with Claudine, but with someone else entirely. The expectation of seeing her mother was so strong in her mind that for several seconds she stared quite blankly at the person in front of her. Then she recognized the woman: it was a friend of Claudine's, a French-speaking woman who lived in the next village.

What's she doing here?

Veerle couldn't recall the woman's name. She was about Claudine's age, but that was the only thing the two women had in common. Claudine had a worn and faded look, as though life were wearing her thin; Madame Whatever-her-name-was had a considerably more solid appearance, with a large-featured face, big hands and a bosom that jutted alarmingly. She did not look pleased to see Veerle.

'So there you are, miss,' she said in French.

Veerle tried to look past her but there was no peeping around that meaty shoulder. 'Has something happened?' she asked. 'Is my mother all right?'

'Now she asks.'

Veerle's patience unravelled. She pushed past and went into the sitting room. She could hear the woman's indignant remarks behind her but she ignored them.

Claudine was sitting in the armchair, propped up with cushions. There was a blanket over her knees. Her head was thrown back, her eyes closed, but when Veerle came into the room she opened them, blinking as though waking from a deep sleep.

'*Maman?* What happened?' asked Veerle, but it was not Claudine who answered, it was her friend.

'You know perfectly well what happened,' she snapped. 'Your mother is very ill.'

Veerle opened her mouth to say something, to say *I didn't know she was ill,* but it occurred to her that she *had* known; at least, she had known that Claudine was claiming to be ill. She simply hadn't believed her – or at least, not enough to abandon her expedition with Kris.

Claudine's friend was sweeping on anyway. 'You should not have gone out leaving your mother alone. She had to call me! Of course I came at once, but I couldn't be here immediately because I had to come from home. It's four kilometres, you know.'

Veerle's hands closed into fists, so tightly that she felt her nails digging into the palms of her hands, but she did not rise to the bait.

It's true, she thought. *She told me she was ill and I still went out. And I can't tell either of them why I had to go.*

She tried to make herself think of Kris, of the pressure of his hand on hers, the warmth of his fingers entwined with her own. *Stay calm. Don't lose it. You can't tell them anything.*

The creeping fear that perhaps the woman was right, perhaps Claudine really *was* ill, wasn't helping.

I wouldn't have gone if I didn't have to, she thought.

Aloud, she said, 'We should call the doctor, *Maman.*'

'Call the doctor?' said her mother's friend contemptuously. 'The doctor came and went an hour ago.'

Veerle faced her. 'What did she say?'

'It was a male doctor,' came the reply, swiftly and with an unmistakable note of satisfaction in it; the woman was *enjoying* this, Veerle realized. 'But I cannot tell you what he said,' continued her mother's friend. 'I would not have dreamed of intruding. I went into the kitchen while he was speaking to her.'

'Fine,' said Veerle. 'Well, I can ask her when you've gone.'

She had made herself speak levelly, without any audible trace of malice, but she saw the other woman stiffen anyway.

'Of course, you want me to go now. But I wouldn't be here at all if you had stayed at home.'

Veerle briefly closed her eyes. *Don't lose your cool.* She could feel the weight of the evening's excursion into Brussels, the frustrating conversation with Fred, the dangerous proposal Kris had made. There was a feeling growing inside her chest, as poisonous and pressurized as an abscess; just a gramme more pressure and she thought something would rupture. *Keep your temper*, she urged herself.

The woman's attention had shifted to Claudine now, anyway. She was leaning over her, fussing with the pillows and the blanket, making a show of ensuring that Claudine was as comfortable as possible before abandoning her to the dubious custody of her neglectful daughter. She spoke to Claudine as she did so, reassuring her, but she did not address another word to Veerle until the pair of them were at the front door, Veerle holding the door open, waiting for her to go, and the woman standing on the step, buttoning up her coat against the cool evening air.

'Don't leave your mother alone again when she's sick,' she

told Veerle, then turned abruptly and walked towards her car, without further farewells.

Veerle watched her go for a moment, and then she went back into the house and closed the door. She went to let down the shutters, as she knew her mother would have done, first the ones in the kitchen, and then the ones in the sitting room.

She re-entered the sitting room somewhat unwillingly.

I don't know what to think. What to feel.

Her feelings about her mother were huge and incomprehensible, a great unscaleable slab carved with hieroglyphics she could never understand. Veerle was indignant and angry, and she was afraid – afraid that all the substance of her own life was going to be used up for the war effort that was her mother's life, struggling incessantly against unseen enemies, foes that perhaps existed only in her mind. Guilt and resentment were so closely entwined that she could not have unpicked them even if she had wished to, but most of all she felt sorrow. As she crossed the room to the window she glanced at Claudine, lying limp and wan in the chair, and the pain she felt inside was a physical ache.

Why can't I do what she wants?

She let the shutters down slowly and the darkening street outside was reduced to a square and then a flattening rectangle, and then it was gone altogether and she was faced with the blank slats. They were sealed in together, she and Claudine. Already Veerle felt as though she were suffocating.

47

The old lady looks her age, thought Veerle as she picked her way through the overgrown grass to the castle, shielding her eyes against the spring sunshine. In the winter dark, the old building had had a certain sinister grandeur; now the bright light showed the effects of the passing years and the damp Flemish climate all too clearly. The pointing between the castle's red bricks was wearing away, leaving the spaces between them as deeply graven as wrinkles on an ancient face, and there were slate tiles missing here and there, as though the ridged roof were the back of some sleeping dragon, millennia old, moulting scales as it slumbered its way towards the sleep that never ends.

Veerle kept glancing back towards the road as she approached the castle door with its stone canopy. There was a good deal more foliage at the border of the grounds than there had been in winter, but she was acutely aware that without the cover of darkness she could easily be spotted. Her school bag swung against her shoulder as she walked. There were no books inside it; instead she had packed her torch and screwdriver and also her rock shoes. *After that Art Deco place, I'm never going anywhere without my rock shoes.*

Even before she got to the castle she was eyeing the windowframes and the stone bosses and the ornamental ridge that ran along the top of the ground floor. It was a habit; she couldn't stop herself doing it. In her imagination she was already scaling it, curling her fingers around the stone ridges, fitting the toe of her rock shoe into a crumbling hole in the brickwork and launching herself upwards in defiance of gravity, as though she wanted to take flight. She looked at the tower with a critical eye and thought that even that might be climbed; the walls sloped slightly.

Veerle supposed that the owners of the castle – if it even had owners – might one day decide to improve the security of the site, fix new locks on the door. If that ever happened she probably *would* have to climb the walls to get inside. That was not necessary today, however; the door opened easily. She slipped inside, inhaling the familiar scent of brick dust and ancient wood. Shafts of sunlight pierced the hallway with its panelled walls and tiled floor; Veerle could see dust motes floating in them, as though the very fabric of the building were dissolving away into the air.

'Kris?' Her voice sounded strangely dead in the stillness of the castle's interior.

'Here,' he said, and stepped out of the shadows.

Veerle had expected him to be in his work clothes but he was dressed as he always was for their excursions to the Koekoeken places, all in black – black jeans, leather jacket, boots – so that when he appeared it was as though part of the deep shadow had detached itself, budded off like an amoeba. Veerle looked at him and felt that familiar feeling, as though something inside her *jumped*.

She went over to him, and when he kissed her she closed her eyes, thinking, *I wish it could be like this for ever. I wish I didn't ever have to go back.*

When she opened her eyes the castle sprang back into being around her, and with it the knowledge that they had work to do; this wasn't just about having fun any more.

They went upstairs, the wooden treads, polished with age, creaking beneath their feet. It was safer up there; if anyone happened to approach the castle they could be spotted from the front windows, and if anyone looked inside the front door they would see only empty hallway. Veerle followed Kris into a large wood-panelled room dominated by a reddish marble fireplace, the stone shot through with lighter veins. Above the panelling was a greenish wallpaper, so faded in places that the pattern could barely be picked out any more; it could have been ripples in stagnant water. A sudden flash of reflected sunlight amongst the muted colours caught Veerle's eye and she crossed the room to investigate. Standing on the marble mantelpiece was a single empty brown beer bottle.

'Someone's been here,' she said. She looked at the bottle but didn't like to touch it.

'A tramp,' said Kris, with a shrug. 'We can take it with us when we go.'

'How do you know?'

'It wasn't one of us. We're supposed to improve the places we visit, not leave rubbish. It's not the first time, anyway.'

Kris's attention had shifted already; he was examining the mantelpiece itself, running a finger along the worn carving. He didn't seem bothered by the bottle's presence.

Veerle looked at it again. *I wish that wasn't there.* The bottle was a reminder that others visited the castle, that it was not just hers and Kris's. It was faintly disturbing, as though they had found strange footprints on territory that belonged to them alone. *As though we're sharing the jungle with animals we never see.*

'Let's go somewhere else,' she said impulsively. 'Let's go and look at the tower. I've never been in there.'

She turned her back on the mantelpiece and the bottle winking in the sunlight, and went back into the corridor. The tower was at the very end, she thought, and began to walk along it. The floorboards creaked gently under her feet, as though the old castle were sighing.

Like a mummy, she thought. *Ancient and dry*. She remembered the night she and Kris had met here, how he had lit a candle at the top of the stairs. You'd have to be careful doing that; the interior was so desiccated that it could easily go up, as though committing suttee for its long-dead owners. There was a window at the end of the corridor, and as she watched, the sun came out and turned it into a dazzling rectangle of white light, as bright as an acetylene torch, as though the old castle really had caught fire.

She blinked once, twice, and then the effect was gone; clouds had drifted across the face of the sun. The window was simply a bright oblong once more.

Kris appeared at her side. 'The tower's through there,' he said, pointing, and Veerle saw that there was a narrow doorway to the left of the window. The heavy wooden door stood open to its fullest extent, pushed back flat against the wall.

Kris had to duck his head to enter the room. It was immediately apparent that the tower was considerably older than the rest of the castle. There was no carved wood panelling here; the walls were coarse textured and white-washed and a metre thick; you could see that from the depth of the window openings. The floorboards were rough and unvarnished, the wood grey with dust and age.

Veerle went to the nearest window and pushed at the windowframe; it opened easily and she stuck her head out, looking down at the wall as it sloped away.

You could climb down here, she thought, *but it would be difficult.* She didn't like to say *dangerous* to herself; the very word made her think of Claudine, always seeing hidden hazards in everything. All the same, when she looked down at the wall she could very well imagine how easy it would be to lose your grip with nothing but the slight slope and the gaps between the bricks to support you, and once you started to slide and then to fall there would be nothing large enough to grab as you shot past.

If I ever have to climb in or out of the castle I'll choose another route, she decided.

She drew her head back in and closed the window.

'Is there a room under this one?' she asked Kris.

He nodded. 'It's just a storeroom or something. There's no way down to it from here – you have to go back downstairs.'

'Strange.'

'This part is older than the rest. Maybe there was a staircase when it was first built. Not now, though.' Kris lounged against the wall, studying the room. After a moment he said, 'So how did you get away?'

'I just didn't go to school. I'll write a note and take it in tomorrow.' *And pray nobody phones my mother.*

Veerle hadn't dared enlist Lisa's help this time; it would have led to too many questions. She was already aware of a certain coolness between her and Lisa and her other school friends. She'd never breathed a word, never said anything that might suggest she had anything to hide, but people knew. They could tell when you were shutting them out of something.

Veerle looked at Kris and thought, *I don't care.* It would be useless caring about that now anyway; the pair of them were in too deep.

Aloud, she said, 'What about you? Did you bunk off work?'

'I took a day off. They didn't like it, but' – he shrugged – 'this is important.'

'Kris . . . the things Fred said, about Hommel sending the keys, and Clare disappearing being a coincidence . . . he could still be right.'

'He could. But I don't think he is. I think there's someone doing it. Don't you?'

Veerle sighed. 'Yes. I do.' She rubbed her arms as though she felt chilled. 'If there is, you know he's probably a crackpot and definitely dangerous.'

'I know.'

'If he's clever enough to get away with killing people it's not going to be easy to get him to show himself.'

'I've thought about that,' said Kris. 'No matter what we say, he's not going to just post something on the forum. Once he does that, we've got his user name and we can get his email address from Fred and then he's not anonymous any more. We need to get him to show himself, physically. Then we know he exists, we know what he looks like, maybe one of us will even recognize him.'

'You mean, confront him?' Veerle asked. 'Kris, we don't even know what he did to Vlinder and the others. He might be armed.'

'No, not confront him,' said Kris, but he didn't catch her eye.

He's going to wait and see, thought Veerle. *He's going to see whether he can take him on or not.* It was not a reassuring thought. Kris was lean, hardened by working outdoors, and he was tall, broad-shouldered too. But this other person, this shadowy person whose presence they deduced from a pattern of events, as an archaeologist reads changing hues in the earth when all proof has mouldered away, what about him?

'We just have to know whether he exists or not,' Kris was saying. 'If we contact him through the Koekoeken and he shows himself, he's one of us. If we know who it is, we tip off the police. If we don't, we go to the police and tell them everything. There'll be trouble, but at least we know they'll get him.'

Veerle stared at him. Kris still wasn't catching her eye. He was looking out of the window, and his profile was turned to her so that she saw his aquiline nose, one cheekbone, one dark eye gazing out into the castle grounds as though he thought the unknown killer might come strolling across them.

'OK,' she said eventually. 'But how do we do that without confronting him?'

Now Kris did turn and look at her. 'We hide,' he said simply. He pushed away from the whitewashed wall and began to move around the room. 'Here,' he said. 'We get him to come here. It's the obvious choice. We know this place; we have to know it better than he does. Some of the others come here, but not many. It's too far out of Brussels, too far away from the metro and the tram. He won't know his way around. We will. That's the first thing. Second, we know it's going to be empty. Most of the other places, they're only empty if the owners happen to be away. We can't control that; there's no way of picking one we know well. Thirdly, there are a lot of ways in and out of this place. OK, we normally come in through the front door, but we could leave any of the downstairs windows unlatched, in case we need to get out in a hurry.'

'That makes sense,' said Veerle, watching him. 'So where do we hide?'

'The upstairs gallery? No; if he spotted us we'd be trapped up here. The middle room at the back of the castle, downstairs. It's got doors through into the rooms on each side and a huge window. If we need to, we can get out of there and run for the trees.'

Simple, thought Veerle. *He makes it sound so simple.*

Aloud, she said, 'So what do we put in the message?'

48

De Jager sat at the kitchen table with the laptop open in front of him. The sleek silver machine looked out of place in the kitchen, like an alien artefact uncovered in an archaeological dig. Everything else dated from around 1970: the orange and cream tiles, the brown work surface, the curtains with their yellow and white floral design. De Jager was uninterested in updating the kitchen or any other part of the house. He himself had other things to do, and it would have been impossible to allow workmen into the place; you couldn't trust them not to poke their noses in where they were not wanted. Besides, the outdated décor gave him a certain sense of time streaming past, a sense of having survived and triumphed. The house he had grown up in had looked something like this, old-fashioned and drearily respectable, and all the family members who had peopled it were dead now, all of them except him. The martyred-looking, defeated mother with her hunched shoulders and grey face, the blustering, bullying father – gone.

De Jager knew that he was not as other people are; he was as different as if he belonged to an entirely new species. He knew too that anyone who tried to analyse his behaviour (had anyone been able to observe it, which was unlikely, since those who saw his real self invariably died shortly afterwards) would search for something in his relationship with his family that had shaped him. The idea made him angry. He was himself, uniquely himself, his own creation, without any contribution from his genetic parents. That was why the rest of his birth family were dead, and he was still alive, free, pursuing his own savage impulses like a shark moving through the dark ocean, following the scent of blood. Because he was different. *Better.*

He stared at the illuminated screen, re-reading the text carefully to ensure that he had understood the message correctly, that there was no mistake. He'd spotted it the minute he logged on to the Koekoeken website, using his member name of *Wolfspin*, the wolf spider. The message subject was an address and a date. The address was in Sint-Genesius-Rode. The Koekoeken visited a number of houses in that district but De Jager recognized the address immediately. He didn't need to check the date either; he knew immediately that it was the night in early March when he had sent Egbert to meet his maker in the wet room. He remembered the event with crystal clarity: the pursuit through darkened rooms, the tracking of the prey to the cellar, the sudden blaze of light and the satisfying sound of the crossbow bolt puncturing flesh. Afterwards he had grasped the bolt and used to it pull Egbert's lifeless body away from the wall, so that he could check there was no damage to the tiles.

Not so much as a chip. He had removed the body and let the shower run for a long time, until the vivid red on the walls and floor had streaked and turned pink and finally run clear. Next time the owner of the house used his fancy gym and showered afterwards, he would have no idea that the gleaming tiles under his bare feet had run crimson with blood. Someone did though. The poster of the message. Schorpioen.

You left something at the house. If you want to get it back, come to Het Rode Kasteel, Kasteelstraat, on Saturday at 9.30 p.m. Your friend.

De Jager looked at the message. He knew better than to think that Schorpioen was his friend, or indeed that he had left anything at the house in Sint-Genesius-Rode. What the message was really telling him was that his time was up, he would have to move on.

It was not the first time that this had happened to De Jager. He had moved several times before, always evading discovery, always tying up loose ends. There was a drowning in Brugge, apparently accidental, and a house fire in a suburb of Antwerpen, neither of them traceable to him. De Jager thought that Schorpioen would have to be dealt with in the same way.

Fire, he thought. It was clean and final.

He went out of the message and began to look for previous posts by Schorpioen. He had a vague remembrance that Schorpioen went about with someone else; for that reason De Jager had rejected him (or her) as a possible target in the past. He was quite confident of his ability to handle two subjects at once, but less sure that it could be done without noticeable damage to the hunting environment. The search did not take long.

Honingbij.

De Jager sat back and considered. He judged that they were a couple, male and female, and that Schorpioen was the male,

Honingbij striking him as a female name. So Schorpioen's signing off as 'your friend' (singular) was disingenuous; there was a good chance that two of them would be waiting at the castle.

So much the better. Taking down both of them would present a challenge, and require meticulous planning, but De Jager excelled at planning.

And fire will clean it all up.

It was perfect that Schorpioen had selected the castle for the proposed rendezvous. A fire in an old and derelict building would excite far less comment than one in a luxurious villa. When the bodies were found – assuming that the charred remains were even identifiable amongst the blackened beams and bricks and tiles – people would assume it was a prank, an act of vandalism, gone tragically wrong. There would be nothing to connect the fire to a harmless web forum about bird-watching.

There was another option, of course. He could ignore the message altogether and simply move on. Schorpioen had no idea of his identity, that was plain. The post was not addressed to Wolfspin but to the group in general. De Jager could simply withdraw from the Koekoeken, either for ever, or perhaps with a view to resuming his activities at some future point when he deemed it safe to do so. The idea had its merits. The Koekoeken group was an almost perfect hunting ground, after all, the best he had ever had. Also, taking out Schorpioen and Honingbij was not without its risks, especially since they would be on their guard.

De Jager gazed at the screen, his blunt features bathed in its cold light, and considered.

49

There was a horrid inevitability about it. On Saturday afternoon, Claudine was sick.

Not today. Please, not today.

Veerle shut herself in the downstairs bathroom. She felt the need to barricade herself in, to get away, to think, before she was engulfed by the bitter panic welling up inside her. If she stayed in the living room a second longer she was afraid that she would lose control, that she would start screaming in sheer frustration, venting the feelings that threatened to burst forth like the noisome contents of an overflowing sewer, but . . .

Supposing she's really sick?

So what? she wanted to shout. *She won't* die *of it. And I have to meet Kris – I have to.*

The room was small, only a couple of square metres, and she hadn't bothered to flick the switch on the wall outside the door, so the only light was from the small window with its patterned glass. Everything had a grey, almost bluish hue to it, even her reflection in the mirror: dark hair, pale eyes, skin tones so drained of warmth that she might have been looking at a corpse. A drowned girl. Vlinder, suspended under the ice. Veerle shivered.

She looked at her dead self and thought, *What am I going to do?*

There was no question of not going. She was meeting Kris no matter what.

How am I going to deal with her?

She had to find the answer to that question very soon because this was going to be their only chance, this rendezvous tonight at the old castle. Veerle knew that because she had tried to log on to the Koekoeken website that morning before Claudine was up and about, and all she had got was a *URL not found* message.

It was possible that it was some sort of temporary glitch but she didn't think so. Either Gregory had come home sooner than Fred had expected, or he'd found someone else to do the job. The Koekoeken had vanished. She imagined them all, precipitately disconnected from each other, like the thread of a necklace suddenly snapping; what had been an elegant pattern suddenly dissolving into a hail of individual beads, bouncing away on their own into the dark under the furniture, in corners, between the cracks in the floor . . .

Gone, she thought. *And if there really was someone out there, reading people's messages and lying in wait for them, we only have one chance left to know it. Just one chance. Tonight.*

The thought of it made her feel slightly queasy, but she was resolved on one thing: Kris wasn't doing it on his own.

I have to go. I have to be with him.

She thought she could hear her name, feebly called from the other side of the locked door: 'Veerle, Veerle, where are you, Veerle?'

Veerle sighed so heavily that her breath misted the mirror

in a great circular patch. Now the drowned girl looked as though she were gazing out through a thin glaze of ice. She put up her finger and wrote *K*.

Her mother was still calling. Veerle didn't reply. She said nothing, even to herself; she didn't even let herself *think* about what she was going to say, because then she would want to discuss it further with herself; she'd never open the door.

She slid back the bolt and opened the door, crossed the hallway into the living room.

'There you are,' said Claudine reproachfully. 'Where did you go?'

Veerle didn't reply to that. Her mother was on the couch, propped up on cushions, her stockinged feet outstretched. Veerle sat on the armchair opposite.

'*Maman*, do you want me to call the doctor?'

Claudine looked at her. 'It's Saturday afternoon.'

Veerle leaned forward. 'I know, but if you're really ill, I can try to get someone to come. There's usually a number you can call out of hours.'

Stubbornness was seeping into her mother's face like a dark stain, setting the lines. 'Of course I'm really ill. I don't know what you mean by saying that.'

'Well, let me call someone.'

'There's nothing the doctor can do for me. Just stay with me.'

'*Maman*...'

'Just as long as there's someone in the house.' Claudine looked at her and Veerle thought she detected something sharp in that glance, hidden under the flaccid layers of reproach like a spiked burr in the blameless pelt of a rabbit. She saw that this was almost certainly going to end in a fight.

She glanced at the little clock on the mantelpiece. *Almost six o'clock.* Kris wanted to meet at the castle at half past seven; he didn't trust their quarry not to turn up early. *Assuming he exists.*

There was a bus shortly after seven; if she took that one she would be at the Kasteel stop shortly before half past. If she took the one before, she would have a wait at the other end but at least she would minimize the risk of being late.

Veerle looked back at her mother and saw a flicker in her expression that meant Claudine had noticed her checking the time. There was nothing for it. *I have to be firm.*

'*Maman*, I have to go out tonight. I wouldn't go if it wasn't—'

'Out? Where, out?'

If you're going to lie to her, now is the time. But Veerle couldn't do it.

'It's private.'

She felt something snag her sleeve and realized her mother had reached out with one thin hand and was clutching at her wrist.

'You're meeting that man. The one who came to the house and frightened me.'

'His name is Kris,' said Veerle.

'I don't want to know what his name is. You're meeting him, aren't you?'

'It's not against the law, *Maman*.' As soon as she had said that it occurred to Veerle that much of what she and Kris had done together was entirely illegal, and she felt her face grow warm. She prayed that she wasn't actually blushing, that her mother would not notice anything, but when it came to misdeeds Claudine had the almost uncanny sense of the shark that can detect a single drop of blood in a million drops of water.

'Not against the law, possibly, but it's wrong,' she snapped. 'Your own mother is sick, and you want to go off God knows where with someone like that?'

'*Maman*, I have to. I don't want to leave you, of course I don't, but this is really important.'

'Why?'

'I can't tell you.'

'I'm your mother.'

'I know.'

'I need you here.'

'*Maman*, I can't be here all the time.' The question of whether Veerle *wanted* to be there all the time loomed in the background like some dark spectre. She did her best to ignore it. 'I have to go to school, I have to—'

'School, of course you have to go to school.' Claudine looked at her balefully.

'I mean, I can't always be here. If you're sick, we have to find some way—' Veerle was running out of words. 'You have to manage without me.'

No. No. That was the wrong thing to say. Now she's going to go nuts.

'Manage without you?' Claudine looked outraged. Spots of colour were appearing in the dull papery skin of her cheeks. 'I have to manage without you?'

'I didn't mean it like that.'

'Well, what did you mean then?' Claudine's hold on Veerle's wrist was like the grip of some gigantic bird of prey, the nails digging into her skin like talons. 'Manage without you? What does that mean? I have to do without food or drink if I can't get up? I have to crawl to the telephone if I need the doctor?'

'No.'

'What then?'

'That's why I wanted to call the doctor. So we could see what she said. I don't want you to do without anything, *Maman*. I just— I really, really *have* to go out tonight.' Claudine's grip on her arm was becoming painful. Veerle had to force herself not to shake off her mother's hand. She made herself look at Claudine, look her in the eye in spite of the resentment that smouldered there like hot ashes. 'If you won't let me call the doctor, why don't I call that friend of yours, the one who came before?'

'Berthe? You want to bother her again?'

No, thought Veerle, remembering the woman's stout, intimidating body blocking the hallway and her strident, indignant voice, *I'd rather never see her again in my life*. But time was passing – she could hear the ticking of the clock on the shelf and she *had to go*, no matter what it cost.

'Just this once,' she said. 'Maybe she could come and sit with you. We could ask her.'

But Claudine was shaking her head. 'And tell her she has to drop whatever she's doing and drive over here because my daughter wants to go out and meet a man? No.'

'*Maman*—' Veerle saw her mother flinch and realized that she had finally been goaded into shouting. With an effort she made herself lower her voice. 'It's not like that. I really wouldn't go if it wasn't important. I'll stay here all day tomorrow with you,' she added recklessly.

'And I'm not important?'

There was no reasoning with Claudine, and yet Veerle felt she had to try.

'Look, I'll get you anything you need before I go. I'll go over to the chemist in the village if you want something. There are still a few minutes before it shuts. I'll make you coffee – or something to eat – anything—'

'I don't want coffee, or something to eat.'

'What do you want, then?'

'I want my daughter to stay here.'

There was a long silence.

'I can't,' said Veerle.

Claudine looked at her and said nothing. Her mouth was working as though she wanted to say something but no words came.

Very gently Veerle unpeeled her mother's fingers from her wrist. 'I'm sorry,' she said simply. Then she got up and left the room.

There was still plenty of time to go before the earlier bus, at least half an hour, and yet already she was anxious about missing it. She was acutely aware of the passing of time: the ticking of the clock on the shelf in the living room, the slow track of the sun down the sky, the imperceptible, relentless turning of the world itself like the rim of a great wheel rolling towards nightfall and whatever awaited her at the castle.

I want to go now, she thought as she ran upstairs to her room to get ready. Impatience sparkled through her like electricity; her skin crawled with it; she thought that every hair on her body must be standing on end. *Now*, she thought. She knew that part of her eagerness was fear, but that only made her keener to face up to what was to come. Waiting was what made you feel slightly crazy; it charged you up like a dynamo with tension. *If it were trial by fire*, she thought, *if I had to pick up red-hot iron, I'd want to do it now, right away. The pain is not the torture, it's the waiting.*

It was a warm day but still she chose winter clothing: dark, drab colours, matt fabrics, nothing that would show up in the gloomy interior of the castle. Black jeans, a black jumper with sleeves so long that she could pull them over her hands. The winter boots she rejected: she could see those thick soles clattering on the castle's hard floors. She went for her Converse trainers instead.

Veerle dragged her little rucksack out from under the bed and stuffed her rock shoes into it, together with a screwdriver and her torch. *Ready for anything*, she told herself unconvincingly. Then she sat on the bed and reset her mobile phone, so that it would vibrate but not ring. *The last thing I need is for* her *to phone me at nine thirty wanting to know where I am.* Appalling thought: herself and Kris lying concealed in the middle room at the back of the castle, peering cautiously round the doorframe at the deserted hallway, the shadows deepening as night slowly suffocated day. Hearing footsteps in the stone porch, the sound of the great door opening, its hinges groaning – and then the sound of her mobile phone trilling out like a canary in a coal mine. The thought of it made her a little queasy, as though she had narrowly avoided a nasty accident.

When the phone vibrated in her hand she jumped and almost dropped it, but it was only an incoming text from Kris. *OK for tonight?*

Yes, OK. V x, she typed back.

She was sliding the phone into the pocket of her jeans when she heard it. A thump from downstairs; a definite thump, as though something heavy had fallen onto the floor.

Veerle stood up and went over to the door, the rucksack in her hand. She stuck her head out. Silence.

'*Maman?*'

She listened again and there was nothing, no sound at all from inside the house except the creak of boards under her feet as she shifted her weight and the tick of the clock above her bedroom door. Outside she could detect the faint sound of a distant car passing through the village, but inside everything was still and silent.

'*Maman!*'

No reply. Veerle began to feel a sense of foreboding pressing in on her like a fog, thick and clammy and disorienting. She went out onto the landing, and still there was no sound from below, no reply to her call.

Did I shut the living-room door?

She couldn't remember. Even if she had, she thought Claudine should have heard her. Veerle looked down the staircase at the patch of hallway visible below: the familiar tiled floor, the worn rug.

Terrible feelings were rising up inside her, feelings so searingly hot and toxic that she thought they would choke her; her chest was tight with them, her throat was closing up painfully. Her heart was racing, its beat so frantic that she was afraid she might faint.

If she's fallen – if she's hurt – I can't leave her.

I have to go. I have to.

It was impossible – she was being pulled two ways, and it felt as though something inside her were tearing, ripping apart in two great ragged pieces. She went down the stairs, her knuckles white as she gripped the banister, and it was as if she were seeing herself from the outside, as though some grinning demon with red-hot iron tongs had dragged out her soul and it was hanging uselessly in the dead air above her body, watching it go down to Claudine.

I can't leave her.

You have to.

The living-room door was open, and as she rounded the doorframe she saw her mother lying on the couch, perfectly motionless, her eyes closed and her mouth gaping open. She looked like a carved cadaver on a tomb.

Oh God. What if . . .

Then she saw the little table that normally stood at the end of the couch lying on its side on the rug.

'*Maman?*' she said, and now Claudine opened her eyes and looked at her. 'Didn't you hear me?' asked Veerle.

'Yes.'

'Well, why didn't you reply?'

'I feel too ill.'

'I thought you'd fallen,' said Veerle. She advanced into the room. 'What happened to the table?'

'I don't know,' said Claudine.

Was it Veerle's imagination, or did she see something pass

swiftly and almost imperceptibly across Claudine's weary expression, some brief glint of cunning?

Don't be horrible, she berated herself. *She's sick, or anyway she really believes she is.*

But all the time the sense of urgency, the need to get away, was growing. *Maybe I should have gone even earlier. Supposing the bus is late? Supposing it gets held up somewhere between here and Kasteelstraat?*

'Let me call someone,' she said. 'Please.'

Claudine's lower jaw tensed; her mouth became a thin, rigid line. She looked at her daughter with eyes that were bright with mutiny.

Veerle could feel her own breath coming quickly, hissing in and out between her teeth like steam. She looked at her mother and she looked at the fallen table. There had been nothing on the table that Claudine could have wanted, no hand control, no telephone, no pill-box. She looked at it and she saw her mother pushing it over, knowing that Veerle would hear the noise upstairs. She saw her lying there on the couch with her lips closed in that hard line, listening to Veerle calling down from the upper storey, knowing what Veerle would think when she got no reply.

The desire to leave flamed within her like a fever. She was acutely aware of the living-room clock but was trying not to glance at it, knowing that Claudine would notice and that it would upset her even more. Then she did look and it was already twenty past six.

'I have to go,' she said.

She waited for Claudine to say something, even for her to relent and say that, yes, Veerle could call someone for her before she left, but her mother said nothing at all. It was not until Veerle had turned and was halfway to the door that she heard a soft sound like a groan. When she looked back, she was horrified to see that Claudine was crying.

'Oh, *Maman*,' said Veerle. The need to leave was clutching at her, goading her, and yet when she saw her mother crying she felt a pain so sharp that it was almost physical.

'You don't understand,' wept Claudine. 'To feel so ill, to have so much worry all the time, to be alone . . .'

Veerle went back to her. 'You're not alone, *Maman*.' She put her arms around her mother, pressed her lips to the papery cheek. She could feel Claudine shaking as she sobbed. More words were leaking out of her now, barely coherent words of loneliness and anger and fear. She clung to Veerle like a child clinging to its mother.

When at last she had run out of words she subsided into gentle coughing and then into silence. The sound of the clock ticking filled the air. Veerle looked at it and saw that she had missed the first bus.

50

Kris reached the old castle at twenty past seven. He didn't need to look at his watch to know that he was early; he had done it on purpose.

Kris had no doubts about involving Veerle. She wasn't stupid and she had plenty of nerve; he'd seen that pretty plainly the first time she had scaled the front of a building. The memory of their climb *down* it still made his flesh crawl.

All the same, he thought he'd try to get to the castle ahead of Veerle, so that he could take a quick look around and make sure that there were no surprises. He slipped over the wall at a spot where the top layer of bricks had crumbled away, paused for a moment in the safety of the shadows under the trees, and then began to wade through the grass towards the old building.

It was a warm evening, unseasonably warm even for May, and there was no wind, so that the air had an unnatural feeling to it, as though it were exactly the same temperature as his skin. It didn't feel like being outdoors; he had no sense of the air moving against his face and hands as he walked. He kept his eyes on the castle; he was pretty well shielded from the road by the thick spring foliage, and anyway, there was nothing more he could do to hide himself. He had learned long ago that if you worried about the tiny risks, about the freak occurrences, you couldn't do what he and Veerle and Hommel and the rest of them did. You had to trust that things were going to go your way.

He was getting closer to the castle now, he was perhaps twenty-five or thirty metres away, and he could see no cause for alarm. The evening sunshine was reflected in the windows, the flash and wink of sunlight on the glass the only movement. The great wooden door was shadowed by the stone canopy above it, but even from this distance he could see that it was closed. The castle looked as though it had lain undisturbed for a hundred years, and would probably remain so for another hundred.

Kris strode towards the door, and as his boots whispered through the grass he thought about Hommel, wondering whether the answer to the question of her disappearance would come strolling through it at nine-thirty with the dying rays of the sun, or whether she was destined to remain no more than an unsolved absence, a Hommel-shaped rent in the fabric of life. He didn't want to consider that possibility. If the road she had taken ran one way only, he wanted to know who was responsible. He wanted to settle it with them. Unconsciously he clenched his fists.

Ten metres from the castle, and he could make out the details of the door, the panels, the drift of old leaves and litter blown into the stone porch by the wind. Five metres, and the old building was looming above him, the dormer windows of the attics like heavily lidded eyes frowning down upon the interloper.

Kris slowed his pace, not wanting to burst precipitately through the door. He had gravel under his feet now, and even though it was heavily choked with weeds it was difficult to move silently. He approached the stone canopy overhanging the door.

Everything was silent and still. There was no movement anywhere, not so much as a sparrow hopping about the porch. Kris had to step through leaves to reach the door. He grasped the iron handle, feeling the metal cold under his skin in spite of the evening sunshine, and very cautiously turned it, wary of the telltale squeal or creak of hinges that would give away his presence. Then he pushed gently and the door began to open.

Kris's nostrils flared at the familiar scent of ancient wood and accumulated dust, decay and mould spores. A thin sliver of interior wall became visible – battered panelling and some worn wall covering so faded that its pattern was indecipherable. The sliver became a long rectangle, and now Kris could see the edge of the nearest windowframe and the evening sunlight casting a golden tint on the worn floor tiles.

He stopped pushing and listened. Silence. Outside he could hear a car passing and the chirping of birds in the trees; inside the castle there was nothing. All the same he remained there, motionless, for perhaps half a minute before resuming his stealthy pressure on the door. Now he had a clear view of the shabby entrance hall and the wooden staircase, the banister worn smooth and gleaming by years of hands running up and down it. He scanned it and saw nothing moving. Even the festoons of grey cobwebs suspended from the ceiling hung limply with not so much as a breeze to make them tremble.

Kris relaxed. His shoulders went down. He was not aware of it, but his heart rate began to slow. He let out a pent-up breath. He took a step further forward into the castle. The sound of his boots on the tiled floor almost obscured the tiny rustle from above.

Kris looked up and saw a flicker of movement in the shadows at the top of the staircase. He stepped back at the same moment as he heard a hard brittle *snap*.

For a moment Kris thought he had been punched. He staggered on his feet and his mind was flailing too, trying to make sense of an assault by an invisible assailant. He looked down at the front of his jacket and there was something sticking out of the leather, so close to his face that he could barely focus on it. Red and yellow. It looked like the feather fletching of an arrow, if the arrow-maker had been able to find a bird with red-and-yellow plastic plumage.

Kris's nervous system caught up with his eyes and it was as though a bomb had gone off in his shoulder. The pain was huge, a great red fist that hammered him to his knees. He wanted to cry out but the agony was too intense; all that came out was a wheeze, and now he was on the floor, the patterned tiles so close that he could make out every scratch and chip on their surface, and his mind was too full of the all-encompassing pain even to form the thought *Please God let it stop*. He slumped onto his left side and there was another explosion of agony through his shoulder. Kris realized that whatever was sticking out of the front of his jacket had gone right through him; the new kick of pain was the other end of it scraping against the floor, pulling at the rim of the wound. Nausea roiled over him in waves. The air seemed to be getting thicker; he was struggling to draw breath, as though the pain itself were some thick poisonous gas filling his lungs. He coughed helplessly, and the agony it produced was seismic.

He lay on his side, and the world was fading in and out in grey pulses, and he could not work out why he was seeing the staircase and the worn tiles at this angle, as though the soles of his feet were on the wooden panelling and he was trying to walk along the wall in defiance of gravity. He heard a series of thuds, a heavy tread coming down the wooden staircase, but he could not untangle the sounds from the thumping of his own heart.

Kris closed his eyes, and for a second – or perhaps a minute, or much longer – there was thick velvet blackness, as comforting as a blanket, and then he opened them again and he was staring at a pair of boots. He could not look up at their owner; he was too preoccupied with the mind-blowing pain. He felt as though he had fallen into a lake of fire. *Hell*, he thought. His mouth opened and closed uselessly.

He waited for whatever would come next, carried limply on the ebb and flow of agony.

'Schorpioen,' said a voice, and something wheeled into view like the weight of a pendulum swinging down, a thing the shape of an anchor, taut with ugly probabilities. Kris knew what it was, but even the single word *crossbow* was unable to coalesce in the seething cauldron of his brain.

'Schorpioen,' said the voice again, and it was urgent and terrible, the sound of a blacksmith's hammer striking an iron anvil. 'I am the hunter. Where is the other one? Where is Honingbij?'

51

At five to seven Veerle left the house and ran to the bus stop. It was a clear dry evening and the air was very still but she felt as hectic as if she had been running through a tempest, fighting her way through high winds and rain. She had had to leave Claudine alone; there was nothing for it. She had missed the first bus and she had avoided looking at the clock as she put her arms around her mother and tried to comfort her, but all the time a terrible urgency had been building up inside her. She had been horribly aware of the long hand making its stealthy way upwards, moving all too quickly. She looked at the clock once and it was on the seven, and it seemed as though she had barely blinked and now it was on the nine. Veerle thought of the bus barrelling along the road that led to the village, drawing closer and closer; if she were not at the bus stop when it arrived it would simply sweep past, and all it would carry to Kris would be broken promises and empty intentions. At last she had disentangled herself from her mother, gently removing the hands that clung to her arms, shaking her head.

'I have to go, *Maman*. I promise I'll be back as soon as I possibly can.' She felt a pang at that; she wasn't nipping out on a five-minute errand. Claudine would be alone all evening whatever happened. Impulsively she went back to her mother and kissed her. 'I love you,' she said. Then she looked at the clock and she ran.

The front door banged behind her but she didn't look back.

When Veerle got to the bus stop there were theoretically five minutes to spare, but that didn't make her any less anxious. If the bus arrived early and there was no one at the stop the driver was quite likely to pass it by instead of waiting, she knew that from experience. She leaned out into the road, peering into the distance, looking for the familiar white-and-yellow bulk of a De Lijn bus.

Calm down, she told herself. *We're meeting two whole hours before the time, remember? It's not going to matter if you're five minutes late.*

If the hands of the living-room clock had seemed to hurry before, now the bigger hands of the clock on the tower of the Sint-Pauluskerk seemed to creep along with agonizing slowness. Veerle pulled her mobile phone out of her pocket and checked for messages. Nothing.

That's good, isn't it? But it didn't feel good. She leaned out into the road again. Still no sign of the bus.

Five minutes later she was still waiting, and the itch of impatience had turned into a raging fever.

Where is it? Where is the verdomde *bus?*

She began to pace up and down.

I should have got the earlier one, I should have just left her.

Veerle looked up at the church clock and saw the hand move ponderously on a minute. *What if it doesn't come at all?*

She began to calculate when she would arrive if she had to take the next bus. She'd be more than half an hour late, even assuming the next one was punctual to the minute.

What other option do I have? It was too far to walk – if you went as the crow flies it would be shorter than going by the road, especially by the circuitous bus route, but even at a run it would take far longer than half an hour. Even if she took out her old battered bicycle it would take longer than that, and what if the bus turned up while she was wheeling the bike out of the back gate?

Veerle rocked forwards onto her toes, poised for flight. *Go for the bike – run – wait?* Still no bus, but here was a car, and for a second she considered trying to flag it down, beg for a lift. Then it was almost level with her and she saw the driver's face, unshaven and unsmiling, and thought better of it.

It was twenty past seven now, and she was definitely going to be *very* late. She took out her phone again, meaning to text Kris, and then she glanced down the road, and there was the bus, finally. She slid the phone back into her pocket and thrust out her arm.

A minute later she was swinging herself into a window seat as she watched Kerkstraat and the Sint-Pauluskerk slide away behind the bus. Veerle glimpsed the façade of her own house for a moment before the grey stone bulk of the church obscured it.

Don't think about it. You have to concentrate on what's ahead.

She sat in her seat and hugged herself and waited for the bus to reach Kasteelstraat.

52

De Jager stood in the hallway of the castle with the crossbow in his hands, looking down without pity. He recognized the expression on Schorpioen's face; he had seen it a score of times on other faces. Shock. Schorpioen couldn't believe what had happened to him, how quickly it had all gone bad. He couldn't believe that he was going to die. The pain, though, that would convince him. Pain was persuasive; it needed no interpreter.

De Jager felt nothing for Schorpioen, but he felt a certain irritation with himself. His plan had been to take out whoever entered the castle first, and then pick off the second person at his leisure. He had shot to kill, but Schorpioen had moved at the last minute, seeing movement above him, and the bolt had penetrated his shoulder.

He had reloaded the crossbow – it took time but Schorpioen wasn't going anywhere – and now he aimed it at the figure on the floor. At this range it would punch through any part of the body with no more resistance than a skewer going through a marshmallow. He didn't fire, though, because he was thinking, *Where is the other one? Where is Honingbij?*

He had asked Schorpioen that and had received no useful reply, but if he put a bolt through Schorpioen's chest or his eye cavity there would be no information forthcoming ever again, and De Jager still needed to know the answer to the question. It was tempting to shoot him in the leg or the hand to try to force the information out of him, but De Jager could see that Schorpioen wasn't handling the pain too well already. If he cranked it up any further he thought Schorpioen might pass out or actually die of shock. He lowered the crossbow so that it was within Schorpioen's range of vision.

Let him see what he's getting if he doesn't talk to me.

'Schorpioen.'

He wasn't getting a response to the name, not a flicker, so he leaned over, pulled open Schorpioen's leather jacket and extracted his wallet from the inner pocket, ignoring the groan of pain this elicited. The ID card was tucked into a clear plastic pocket, Schorpioen's face, shrunk and reduced to monochrome, staring out as though trapped behind glass.

Kris Verstraeten, read De Jager. He dropped the wallet on the dusty tiles next to Kris. It would be ashes by morning anyway. He prodded Kris in the hip with his foot.

'Kris. Wake up, Kris.'

This time he got a reaction. Kris flinched and tried to turn his head. His mouth opened but nothing came out.

De Jager was terribly tempted to shoot him. Instead he made himself crouch next to the huddled figure. *Patience*, he told himself.

Aloud, he said, 'Kris, where is Honingbij?'

It took him some time to understand the reply, and even then it wasn't much use.

'Don't know,' Kris choked out. His voice sounded ancient, ravaged, the voice of a seventy-year-old who has smoked thirty a day for decades. He was beyond lying, De Jager judged. He really didn't know.

De Jager considered. Then he said, 'Kris,' and waited until he was sure he had what little attention Kris had left to give him. 'Honingbij was supposed to be here, but hasn't come. Is that correct?' He waited. 'Is that correct?'

After a minute De Jager stood up, still cradling the cross-bow thoughtfully. Kris wasn't telling him anything – he seemed to have floated off into a grey world of his own – but De Jager was pretty sure the answer to his question would have been *yes*.

So Honingbij had failed to turn up, which meant that either he or she had had cold feet and wasn't coming at all, or he or she (and De Jager thought it *was* a she) had been held up and would be arriving at some unspecified point during the evening. She (if he was right) would know that she was late and would be on her guard. She might even bring reinforcements. Not the police; if she and Schorpioen were going to do that they would have done it already. Maybe a burly friend or two. Either way De Jager had to be ready.

First of all he closed the castle door. It opened inwards and it was heavy. Kris wasn't going to be standing up on his own any time soon, and certainly not pulling the door open. It was safe to leave him where he was. It was also tempting to pin him to the floor in another couple of places just to make sure, but De Jager didn't waste the time. He could do it later, perhaps in front of Honingbij.

He strode down the long hallway that ran almost the

length of the ground floor, to the room at the end. He had entered the castle through the window here, a window deeply overshadowed by the branches of a tree that grew too close to the wall. He had simply broken a single small pane and reached in to turn the latch. Even if Schorpioen had had the common sense to check the building before he entered it, looking for access points, there was a chance he would have overlooked this one.

The room itself was dingy, the sunlight filtered through the dark green leaves clustering against the windowpanes. It was like being at the bottom of the sea, in the green-black depths where light barely penetrated.

In a corner stood two metal cans, as ominous as depth charges. De Jager put down the crossbow and went over to them. When he unscrewed the cap of the first one the air took on a poisonous taint, the sharp oily reek of petrol. Honingbij would smell it the moment she opened the front door, but that couldn't be helped. She'd have to come inside anyway if she wanted to know what had happened to her friend.

It did not occur to De Jager to speculate on the bond between her and Schorpioen, any more than a hunter considers the feelings of the hare or the vixen. To take a buck and a doe at the same time, that would be an experience. Other than that, he was mainly concerned with tying up loose ends.

He lifted the can easily, even though it was full, and carried it out into the hallway. He tilted the can and petrol came out in spurts with a sound like vomiting, and splattered onto the tiled floor. De Jager moved methodically down the hallway, the muscles of his arms working as he swung the can back and forth, sowing the seeds of the conflagration to come.

He hoped that Honingbij would come alone. He would take his time with her, and then he would burn the castle to the ground.

53

Veerle thought she would explode with frustration. Wasn't it enough that the bus was late? It had stopped moving altogether, midway between stops, because someone up ahead had rammed the back of someone else's car, and now everyone was out in the road arguing with each other and the traffic wasn't going anywhere. She swung herself out of her seat and strode down the aisle to the front of the bus. The driver, a stolid grey-haired man in his fifties, didn't even look at her.

'Can you let me off here, please?' Veerle made herself be polite.

'At the next stop.' He didn't take his eyes off the road.

'We've stopped. Can't you just open the door?'

'No. Not until the next stop.'

'Why not?'

No reply.

Veerle took a deep breath.

It's not worth it.

She almost went back to her seat, but then she thought about how late it was.

It's nearly eight, and I was supposed to be there at seven-thirty.

Up ahead there was no sign of the blockage clearing. Now not only was their own lane blocked by the car accident, but someone had stopped in the lane coming the other way, and was leaning out of the window dispensing advice, or perhaps abuse. Horns sounded like angry geese.

Veerle swung her little rucksack off her shoulder and rummaged inside it until her fingers closed around the screwdriver she habitually carried with her. She pulled it out of the bag, holding the metal shaft so that she was wielding the handle like a club.

'Look,' she said loudly, and he must have glanced her way, though she didn't see his head turn, because he flinched back as though she had taken a swing at him. 'If you don't open the door I'm going to break the glass on the safety hammer with this and then I'm going to smash a window.'

There was a silence, and then Veerle heard the sigh of the hydraulic doors opening.

'Thank you,' she said as courteously as she could, and bolted down the steps and off the bus.

'Fucking kids. I should report you to—'

The rest of his words were cut off as the bus doors closed again. Veerle wasn't listening anyway; she was running along the pavement, her rucksack banging against her back, dodging round other pedestrians. The road was long and straight and the distance between herself and the stop called Kasteel seemed far greater than she remembered; the familiar landmarks of petrol station, blue-painted apartment block and doctor's surgery that lay ahead seemed like peaks in a mountain range she had to scale. She had thrown herself into the run without trying to pace herself;

very quickly she was breathless and her side was aching.

Veerle glanced behind her and the bus still hadn't moved.

Keep running. You did the right thing.

Veerle looked ahead and she didn't seem to be any closer to Kasteelstraat than she had been before. She came to a side turning, and there was a car approaching the junction but she ran across anyway, ignoring the angry bleat of the horn.

There was the petrol station on her left. Her lungs were a tight mass of agony; she was sucking in air but it didn't seem to be doing any good, it was like breathing soup. Still she forced herself to keep stumbling on.

When she passed the doctor's surgery she could see the bus stop quite clearly. There was nobody waiting.

Thank God, thought Veerle. She couldn't imagine how agonizing it would be having to wait for the people to be picked up before she could enter the castle grounds unseen, or having to waste time looking for another way in. When she was twenty metres away from the stop, she cut diagonally across the road, looked around once to make sure that there was nobody watching, and then dodged in between the fence panels that covered the castle gateway.

With the cover of unkempt foliage at her back she felt safe from prying eyes. All the same, she didn't want to approach the castle at full tilt, arms flailing, breath sawing in and out like a bellows. Veerle slowed to a walk. She looked at the old building standing silent, an island in its surrounding sea of overgrown grass, seemingly deserted, the ancient brickwork gilded by the evening sunshine. She was filled with a sudden foreboding.

Don't be so stupid. You think Kris is going to stand at the front door waving a flag?

Obviously he would be inside, out of sight. *Obviously*. All the same she fished her mobile phone out of her pocket and checked it, just to make sure there were no messages, no last-minute changes of plan.

Nothing. Veerle slid the phone back into her pocket and kept walking, letting her ragged breathing become slower and more regular. She kept watching the front of the castle, but there was nothing to see; this late in the day the low sun was reflected dazzlingly in the windows, obscuring what lay behind the glass.

Like mirrored sunglasses, Veerle thought. She had always disliked those – the way the wearer could see you but you couldn't see their eyes, couldn't see where they were looking.

Now she was stepping off the grass and onto the over-grown gravel of the drive. The front door was visible under the stone canopy. Veerle could see that it was closed.

Shouldn't it be open, if Kris is already inside?

But she supposed he might have closed it after him, not wanting to advertise his presence if anyone else turned up.

Get a grip, she scolded herself. *You're already late. Stop speculating and just get inside.*

Veerle crossed the last few metres as swiftly and quietly as she could, and then she was standing outside the heavy wooden door with her fingers on the metal handle. On impulse she put her ear to the wood but she could hear nothing from inside, nothing at all. Silence. *Peace.*

Veerle opened the door and stepped into Hell.

54

The door begins to swing open and the first thing that hits Veerle is the acrid stink of petrol, so thick on the air that it is like a hand around her throat. Even before she realizes what it is, her imagination blooms with orange fire; she can almost hear the roaring of the flames. Conflagration is only a spark away. It is a dangerous smell, a fatal one, and every instinct in her body is telling her to run, but she overrides the urge because she has to know what has happened to Kris.

His name is running through her head – *Kris Kris Kris*, like the throbbing of her own blood through the veins – and she is very afraid that it is no longer a name at all but an epitaph.

Veerle takes a step forward, and now she is inside the castle, fully enclosed in its space, in the poisonous fume-ridden air, like an insect in a killing jar. She feels light-headed, slightly sick. Drawing breath is disgusting – she imagines the oily residue of the petrol fumes coating the inside of her throat, the labyrinth that is her lungs. Her gaze is darting about like a trapped bird, beating at the walls and the windows, and now she sees Kris lying on his side on the dusty floor and she feels a great jolt of shock, like a kick to the chest.

Three long strides and she is crouching over him, hands

outstretched, wanting to touch but not daring to, silently praying that this is unconsciousness and not death. Then she sees it. For half a second she can't make sense of it, the flash of red and yellow that has nailed the black leather to his shoulder, and then she sees that it has gone right through him and is protruding from his back. Something like an arrow. Someone has shot Kris.

Briefly she thinks she will vomit. The toxic stink of petrol and the sight of that gleaming rod with its pointed tip piercing Kris, spitting him like a piece of roast meat – it's too much.

He's dead, she thinks, pressing her hand to her mouth, and it is just beginning to occur to her that she may be dead too, that she needs to get out of here, when she sees Kris move. His face is a terrible grey colour, the lips almost blue, and she thinks he looks like something out of a zombie movie, the living dead, but still he moves. His eyes flutter open and his mouth is working, though nothing audible comes out.

Kris is paralysed by shock; it has hardened around him like cement overshoes, weighting him down as he drops into the endless freezing dark, drowning in it. He sees Veerle but he is not sure whether she is really there or not. There is something he must tell her, something terribly urgent, but the left side of his body has imploded. He is choking with the heavy stifling pain of it and he thinks perhaps he really *is* drowning; perhaps her pale face leaning over him is glimpsed on the dock as he slips down into the black water.

Veerle hears something then, something stirring deep within the old building, like claws scrabbling within a nest, the dragon uncoiling as he prepares to take flight, to explode into the air on leathery wings. Time is short, the passing seconds flee before the dragon like a flock of shrieking bats. If he finds the pair of them here like this, they are both dead.

Veerle is afraid to move Kris, afraid of what the working of the arrow-thing will do to the inside of him, but she is more afraid of what will happen if she leaves him here. A single spark and the whole castle will go up. She takes hold of Kris under the arms, wincing away from the point of the thing protruding from the back of his jacket, and pulls. Kris is taller than she is, heavier, and he is a dead weight. The muscles in Veerle's back flex; she bites her lip. Tomorrow her back will hurt her – if she is still alive tomorrow. Right now there is no pain because adrenalin is running through her like an electric charge, but still she is not moving him fast enough, she knows that. She has dragged him over the threshold where the evening air is blissfully clean and sweet, but she can't drag him all the way to the road before the person who is in the castle catches them.

Veerle's head comes up as she hears a new sound, a metallic clank. She thinks she knows what that sound is: the sound of an empty petrol can being cast aside.

Now he's going to come for us.

She starts to shake Kris's shoulder, tentatively at first, and then as hard as she dares.

'Kris! Wake up!'

Veerle looks over her shoulder into the interior of the castle. Nothing to see yet, and anyway her eyes are blurring with tears, the fumes are so strong. She thinks she hears footsteps. In desperation she grabs Kris's hand. She can't think of any better way to bring him round than to bite him. She sinks her teeth into the soft flesh at the base of his thumb, bites down hard.

Kris's eyes open, and now Veerle thinks she sees some recognition, some awareness in them in spite of the fog of pain clouding his consciousness. He looks at her like an animal staring out between bars.

'Kris, you have to get away from the castle,' she tells him, and when he looks at her uncomprehendingly she slaps him on the good shoulder. 'Go!' she screams at him.

She is sure she can hear footsteps now. Time has run out. Her mind is wheeling, a bird circling a desolate crag. What to do?

No time no time no time—

In a split second she makes up her mind. It's a desperate plan, it's an *insane* plan, but since she can't get Kris away any faster it's the best she has.

Veerle steps back inside the castle and closes the door. She is aware of someone approaching rapidly, of footsteps ringing out like a series of shots on the tiled floor, but she is focused on the polished wooden staircase, measuring the distance between her and it as she races across the hallway. There is a roar of rage – or perhaps it is jubilation as the hunter sights the prey – and a sharp brittle sound like something snapping. Veerle tries to duck, still running, and something passes by her, so close that she thinks she feels the air parting, cloven in two as the bolt streaks over her shoulder and punches into the wooden panelling.

It takes up to thirty seconds to reload a crossbow but Veerle doesn't know this. She flails and scrambles her way up the staircase, expecting a second bolt at any moment, one that will puncture her flesh as mercilessly as the one that has skewered Kris. There seem to be more stairs than she remembers. It takes for ever to get to the top, and even though she isn't standing in petrol any more, in that conflagration-to-come, her flesh is still wincing away from the pain she expects to come screaming at her on red and yellow wings.

Veerle reaches the top step and scans the wooden floor of the landing. She sees what she was looking for – *Thank God, thank God, it's still there!* – and lunges for it. Then she runs to the carved wooden banisters that form a kind of balcony on the first-floor landing and leans over, making sure she's in his line of vision. She's waving the thing she snatched up from the floor. A box of matches, the ones Kris used to light candles when he came here at night. Her best, her most desperate plan: a threat. He is standing in petrol; she isn't.

Then he turns and she sees him clearly and she nearly drops the matches altogether. She knows who he is.

Time has turned inside out. The years are streaming past her, running backwards. She is seven again, and the cool sensation under the palm of her hand is not wood worn smooth by the years but stone. The stone window ledge. Seven-year-old Veerle De Keyser looks out of the bell tower of the Sint-Pauluskerk, looks down from her eyrie, and far below her she sees a killer.

She screams, and the scream echoes down the years to where the grown-up Veerle, seventeen years old, leans over the wooden banisters in the old castle and sees a dead killer standing below her.

It's impossible. The hairs stand up on the back of her neck. *Nine years dead,* she thinks. But there he is.

He has aged, but not as much as you would think. He still reminds her of a shark, with that blunt head of his, the hair close-cropped, and that great cruel mouth, and the eyes so small and dark and *dead*. She can see nothing of humanity in those expressionless eyes, just the blind instinctive drive to hunt and kill. He is powerful too – you can see it in the broad, muscular shoulders. Fight him? She might as well throw herself into an industrial machine and hope to come out whole.

Veerle thinks her mind is giving way; she thinks she is dead. She cannot possibly win this one. You cannot fight a dead man; you cannot fight Satan. You cannot fight . . .

'Joren Sterckx,' she says, and she is surprised at the loudness of her own voice. Veerle looks down at him and she still has the matches in her hand, held aloft, but he has something else in his hand. A knife. She can see how big it is, even from here, how wickedly serrated the blade. The sun is low in the sky now; it streams through the dusty windows and turns the metal to flashing gold. So clean, that blade, so very sharp. She does not know how Joren Sterckx can be here, in the castle, when Kris has told her he is dead. Perhaps Kris has lied to her, perhaps he was mistaken, but none of that will occur to her until much later. She simply sees the incomprehensible, the impossible, a dead man walking. She looks at the knife though, and she knows what *that* means.

De Jager does not bother to try to run at her. He knows he will get her in the end. He begins to move towards the bottom of the staircase.

'Stop!' screams Veerle, and when he glances up at her, his expression almost uninterested, she lets him see the matches. She takes one of them out of the box and flourishes it.

'I'll light it,' she tells him. She wishes her voice wasn't wavering so much. She wonders whether fire can even hurt him. *Dead nine years*, she thinks, sickly.

De Jager looks up at her, his eyes blank and reptilian. In the dying sunlight his skin is almost golden. Veerle thinks of a mythical creature. A basilisk.

'Go away,' she says, and her voice rises to a scream. 'Go away or I'll light it.'

De Jager takes another step. 'You won't do that,' he tells her. It is the first time he has spoken, and suddenly he becomes more real. Whatever he is, however he can be here when Kris has told her he is dead, he is not a ghost. He is solid, a living man.

'I will do it,' Veerle shouts down to him, and for good measure she adds, 'Fuck you.'

The invective bounces off De Jager as uselessly as a pebble off plate armour. He would not bother to argue with her, but he sees some merit in pointing out her mistake to her, watching her pathetic attempt at resisting him turn to panic. It will add a certain piquancy to the hunt, which will be lacking if she just stands there and lets him cut her down.

'You won't do it,' he tells her, 'because you're trapped up there. If this floor burns, you burn too. And so does Kris.'

He sees her react to the name *Kris*. She is losing her nerve. He takes another step towards the bottom of the staircase, watching for the moment when she will break and run. If she is corralled up there with no way out, there may even be time for him to reload the crossbow.

'That's crap,' shouts Veerle. Her chest is heaving; she is a hair's-breadth away from bolting. All the same, he keeps an eye on the match in her hand. If he can get onto the bottom stair before she tries it—

'I'm not trapped!' she screams at him. 'There's another way out.' She sees him pause, taking this in. 'Didn't you check?' she shouts. '*Klootzak!*'

De Jager stops walking. He looks up, looks at the dark-haired girl leaning over the banisters, her face alight with savage jubilation. Doubt crosses his mind. This is a new experience for him; he examines it as though it is a strange alien artefact that he holds in his hands. He *did* check the castle, but now he wonders. A building of this age is a maze, a patchwork of architectural features of different periods. Is it possible that he has missed something: a door, a concealed staircase? The question is important. He does not want the girl to escape. She has seen his face.

De Jager stares up at Veerle and she stares down at him, her expression defiant. This is what it comes down to: his will or hers. Is she bluffing? If there is no way out from her wooden eyrie he can walk away, throwing down a lighted match behind him, and let her be consumed in the inferno. But if she is telling the truth, if she *does* have another way out – that is a very different matter. She could make good her threat to light the petrol that coats the floor under his feet in a rainbow slick. And even if she isn't quick enough to do that before he reaches the staircase, she could get away from him.

All this passes through De Jager's mind as he stares up at her, although none of it shows in his expression.

Is she bluffing?

De Jager decides that Veerle is not bluffing. She has another way out. He must move before she can burn him, and he must stop her getting away.

Things happen very quickly. De Jager lunges for the staircase. He focuses all his energy on that, on getting his feet off the tiled floor with its deadly slick of petrol. He's still not home and dry because the air is full of it, that poisonous stink. If she lights a match now he'll be crisped like a moth flying into a barbecue.

She doesn't light it, though. He charges up the stairs at her and she just stands there with the match in her hand and her mouth open. It is darker up here than it is on the ground floor and her face is a pale oval in the dim light. In another moment she will have to abandon her threat and make a run for it. De Jager wants her to do that. He wants to smell the fear, he wants to feel the ancient floorboards thundering under his feet as he bears down on her with the knife. The hunt, that is what he wants. He towers over her, and now he has the satisfaction of seeing her back away, turn to run.

Let us finish this.

De Jager takes something out of his inside pocket, something small and square that glints dully in his thick fingers. A wind-proof cigarette lighter – considerably more reliable than a match. He flips the cover open, letting the girl see it, letting her know what he thinks of her empty threat. Then he runs his thumb down the wheel, and the instant he sees the tiny flame spring up he hurls the lighter down, over the banisters, towards the tiled floor below.

He has taken two steps towards Veerle when the air catches fire below them, with a flash that lights up the dusty interior like a lightning strike. A split second later the liquid petrol on the tiled floor ignites with a sound like something infinitely vast settling upon the castle, smothering it. By that time De Jager is halfway down the first-floor landing, driving his prey before him. Behind him, bright flame fills the air, dazzling and rapacious, sucking in oxygen, seizing upon the dry wood, the ancient castle's desiccated parts. Against the backdrop of yellow fire the man Veerle knows as Joren Sterckx appears as a dark silhouette, grim and hulking. A troll. He brandishes the knife.

55

Veerle flees, dropping the useless box of matches on the floor. Her heart is racing, her breathing is ragged with panic, juddering in and out like an engine misfiring. She sprints down the long corridor that runs the length of the first floor, and already she thinks the air is becoming thicker up here. How long before the boards start to blacken under her feet? How long before the smoke billowing up from the ground floor coalesces into a solid grip about her throat, squeezing shut her airways?

There is no time to think about how it has all gone wrong: the bluff that Joren Sterckx believed all too well, the threat that she could not at last carry out. No time to consider the all-consuming question of how a dead man can be hunting her down. No time even to worry about Kris, to pray that he has managed to crawl or drag himself away from the castle, from the greedy suck of the flames. There is no room left in her mind for anything other than the urgent question, *How do I get out?*

She glances back, and Joren Sterckx is close behind her, too close. The blade in his hand carves chunks out of the air. A handspan closer and he would be able to take one out of her shoulder, her arm, her cheek. Fear ratchets up the adrenalin kick another notch, and if her cardiovascular system were a motor it would be smoking now, it would be a few revolutions per minute away from exploding. Veerle feints left and the knife slices through the air to her right. The big window at the end of the first-floor landing is fast approaching. She is running out of space to run. Her head turns from side to side, the dark hair flipping back and forth, but when she looks at the doorways on either side of the corridor she can see only traps. Dead ends.

There is no way out.

De Jager is trapped too but he doesn't realize it yet; he still thinks she is heading for some secret escape route of her own. He is not worrying about saving himself; he is only thinking about catching Veerle before she slips away from him, out of his reach. Veerle is hampered because she doesn't have that confidence; she knows it is the fire or the knife, and she doesn't even have a split second in which to decide which she would rather face. It is her body that has control now, not her mind; her body does not know that there is no escape – it simply wants to stay out of reach of the searing flames and the slicing blade.

For a moment Veerle looks at the window ahead of her, the panes reflecting leaping flames and the dark shape pursuing her, and she almost keeps running at it, straight at the brittle glass and the long drop on the other side of it.

Then she sees it – the narrow doorway leading to the tower room, the heavy door standing open. She doesn't think about it, there is no time to debate anyway; she feints right, then darts to the left and through the doorway, ducking her head just in time.

Shut the door shut the door shut the door . . .

Veerle fights with the door, shoving it closed just as De Jager begins to apply pressure on the other side. There is a bolt and she slides it across but she can see it isn't going to hold for very long. The metal is rusted, flaking off in places. A few hard kicks and he will be in the room with her.

Veerle backs away from the door. A strange calm descends on her. When there is only one option open to you, there is no need to panic about whether you are doing the right thing. In every meaningful way Veerle is dead already, she knows that. She has one chance to climb back out of Hades, back towards the light, and she may as well take it, tenuous though that chance may be.

She takes the rucksack off her shoulders and drops it on the dusty floor. Her rock shoes are inside it; she has been carrying them around for weeks in case she ever has to do this, has to climb up or down something unexpectedly, but now she doesn't have time to put them on. Joren Sterckx would be through the door before she had finished tying the laces on the first shoe. So she leaves them there for the flames.

As Veerle opens the tower window she hears the first mighty kick shake the wooden door. The evening air feels cool on her face; it is getting warm inside the castle, even up here. She hears distant shouts, the bleat of a car horn from the road. Someone has seen that the castle is on fire. She hopes that Kris has managed to get away, that he has crawled out of reach of the conflagration, but she doesn't look for him. There is nothing she can do for him now. She climbs onto the window ledge.

There is another titanic blow on the door, as though a giant

fist were slamming into it. Veerle turns her back to the sinking sun, to the great empty expanse of open air, to the
unkempt grass stretching away to the trees and the roadside
and the few faces that have already gathered there, staring at
the leaping flames. She climbs out of the window.

She clings to the window ledge, the toes of her Converse
trainers braced against the brickwork, and looks back into
the room she has vacated. It looks unnaturally empty; she
should be in there, not out here, clinging precariously to the
wall. Her rucksack is lying on its side in the middle of
the floor. Veerle looks at the door and sees it jump in the
frame with the force of another blow. She lets go of the
window ledge with her left hand, instantly feeling the strain
on her right, and grasps the edge of the windowframe. She
has to lean back, ducking her head, to close the window, and
even then she can't fasten it because the latch is on the inside,
but she thinks perhaps it may fool him for a few moments. It
might buy her time to get further down the wall – if she
doesn't fall off first.

Veerle is used to heights – the mere fact of empty space
behind and below her doesn't worry her – but still she has to
steel herself to let go of the window ledge. Once she is below
the window there are few decent holds; she has to rely on
the worn spaces between the bricks and the slight slope to the
tower walls. She wishes she had her rock shoes on. She wishes
she had her chalk bag; her hands are perspiring. She steps
down with her right foot and feels the toe slip; a chill wave of
vertigo sweeps over her. Veerle rests her forehead against the
brick. She is pinned to the wall like a butterfly in a museum
case. She wishes she could stay here until the emergency

services come with a ladder to rescue her, but she knows that if she doesn't keep moving she won't last that long. She has heard the crash inside the room as the door gave way; now something is raging about in there like a bull, bellowing with incoherent rage. She steps down with her left foot now. Her fingers roam the bricks like spiders, looking for crannies in which to wedge themselves.

Down below her, to her right, a window blows out. Smoke and flames billow out into the evening air. Suddenly glass is pattering down around her and at first she is confused, thinking, *How can it be falling on me when the window is below?* but then she realizes that it isn't coming from the downstairs window. Joren Sterckx has thrown open the tower window with such force that one of the panes has shattered. When she's sure no more glass is falling she risks a glance upwards, and through the drifting smoke she sees him leaning out, a bulky shape that fills the windowframe completely, proving (as if she needed showing) that there is no turning back now: the only way is down, either slowly or, if she is unlucky, in one swift dive.

Has he reloaded the crossbow? If he has, he will be able to shoot her at point-blank range from there. Veerle moves down again, putting a few more centimetres between herself and the open window. It's not enough. She tries to speed up, almost loses her footing again. Her breath is coming in great whoops now. She draws in smoke and begins to cough. Her body spasms; her grip on the brickwork is weakening. She forces herself to take another step down, but the ground is still too far away. If she falls from here she will break something for sure, and then he can shoot her at his leisure.

Veerle tries hard to control the coughing. She tries to

breathe through her nose, hoping to filter out some of the smoke. Her fingers are in agony. She is clutching the tiny holds between the bricks so hard that it hurts. A storm is building in her arms, a dull ache like thunder rolling through them, muscle spasms like lightning strikes. She moves down again. Each time it is getting harder to make her limbs, her digits, do what she wants them to do. When her right hand lets go of the bricks the relief is so enormous that it doesn't want to clamp down again on a lower hold; it rebels, the fingers numb and useless. Now the strain is on her left hand and her legs are beginning to shake uncontrollably, as though she were a novice climber, for God's sake.

Dimly she wonders whether Joren Sterckx is going to shoot her or not. She glances upwards again, but she can see nothing through the strands of smoke that unfurl above her, blotting out the open window with its broken pane. Then she hears something so shocking that she almost lets go of the wall altogether. A scream bursts out of the tower room above her, a scream so raw and savage that it is barely human – the sound of a soul ripped brutally from the bloody rags of its body. It goes on and on, rising and falling raggedly, a symphony of pain, building to a crescendo and then suddenly – horribly – ending in a guttural choke.

The fire has Joren Sterckx, thinks Veerle. She moves down the wall again, but she can hardly feel the bricks beneath her fingers and toes any more; she thinks perhaps she is floating close to the wall, borne up on the wings of the smoke. She inhales, begins to cough again, and then she peels slowly off the wall and drops into the dark.

56

Veerle passed through a vague and confusing period of time in which strange, grim faces hung over her, washed with blue light that pulsed rhythmically like blood pumping out of a beating heart. There were voices, and she could hear them but she couldn't seem to listen to them, she couldn't grasp a single word or phrase and draw it into her. She was dimly aware that there was someone else, that the activity buzzing about her had a second focus. It was important to look at this other person, but Veerle could not remember why. She thought about turning her head but the effort was too great; if she thought about doing it for a century she might at last summon up the energy, but for now she could do nothing more than consider the idea in some abstract way, as she might consider trying to flap her arms and fly away. The pulsing blue was soothing; it was like waves lapping over her. She tried to concentrate on keeping her head above the water but her body was not responding; its weight was dragging her down. In the end it was easier to give up the struggle. Veerle closed her eyes and let the water close over her head.

When she opened her eyes again the soothing waters had withdrawn like the ebb of a tide, leaving her broken on the jagged rocks. Veerle tried to move, and the pain was sharp and brittle and all over, as though her body were a sack of diamonds, glittering and sharp, scraping viciously against each other. She gave up and let her eyes explore instead, taking in pale green walls and a cream ceiling and Venetian blinds, thin shafts of brilliant sunshine stabbing through them. At the corner of her vision was a grey metal arm but she couldn't see what it was attached to. There was a second bed in the room, a couple of metres from the one in which Veerle lay, but it was empty. Someone had made it up with such savage efficiency that you could have bounced a twenty-cent piece on the tightly stretched covers.

Veerle looked at the empty bed and felt a cold stab of foreboding.

Kris, she thought. *Kris* . . .

She wanted to call out, to attract someone's attention, but her throat was horribly sore, or perhaps she *had* called out and nobody had heard her, or perhaps she *thought* she had called out but she had dreamed it. She glanced at the empty bed again and the light had changed. There was no more sunshine slanting through the blinds, only the yellow of artificial lights.

Veerle managed to turn her head on the pillow, though her neck felt like a hinge that has almost rusted into place and she felt hot sparks of pain. There were two people by the bed – a woman perched on a plastic hospital chair and a man standing behind her, with a hand on her shoulder.

The woman was in her thirties, with blonde hair pulled back into a knot at the back of her head, a thin nose and rather small grey eyes. The skin of her face was a little reddened, as though she spent a lot of time outdoors. She was wearing a cardigan over a blue dress with a fine white print on it, flowers or trefoils, and she had folded her hands protectively over her stomach.

The man was older, in his early fifties perhaps, well-built though not actually fat. A lumbering bear of a man. He had heavy, sleepy-looking features and a thick shock of hair in which there was still much more light brown than white.

Veerle did not recognize either of them. She lay there and looked at them, feeling the sharp diamond edges of pain prickling up and down her body.

'She's awake,' said the woman.

'Veerle?' said the man. He leaned forward, bending over her, and Veerle felt him take her hand. When he touched it, she felt sparkles of pain scamper up her arm to the shoulder. 'How are you feeling?'

'Who are you?' said Veerle, or at least that was what she intended to say. Her throat felt horribly dry; the words crept out of it like dying things crawling across a desert. She saw non-comprehension on the two faces and she tried again. 'Who are you?' she managed.

'I'm Geert,' said the man, surprise in his voice. 'I'm your father.'

My father. Veerle stared at him. She remembered Geert as taller, thinner. His hair had been darker, or perhaps it was simply that there had been no grey in it before.

'This is Anneke,' said Geert, patting the blonde woman's shoulder.

'Hello, Veerle,' said Anneke, and she smiled, but the smile

didn't reach her eyes. Her gaze remained cool and steady, her hands neatly folded over her abdomen.

Veerle said nothing. She lay in the bed and she could feel reality solidifying around her.

I'm not dreaming. My father is here.

She remembered the empty bed across the room.

'Kris,' she said.

Her father frowned. 'What?'

'Kris. Where's Kris?'

'Kris? Is that the young man they brought in with you?'

Veerle nodded, feeling screams of protest from her neck as she did so.

'I think he's on another floor.'

'He's all right?'

'All right? He had a crossbow bolt through his shoulder. A *crossbow bolt*!' Geert shook his head. 'What in God's name were you mixed up in, Veerle?'

'Geert,' said Anneke in a warning tone. To Veerle she said, 'He's OK. I'll try to find out exactly how he is, if you want.'

'He's not . . . ?'

Veerle felt a cool hand on the side of her face. Anneke had reached out to touch her.

'He's not dead, if that's what you're worrying about.'

Thank God. Veerle would have liked to let go then, to hug her relief to her and slide back into the welcome oblivion of sleep, but something was nagging at her. A sense of something wrong.

My father is here. My father is here from Ghent.

Seeing him standing by the bed, when she hadn't seen him for ten years, not since she was a little girl, felt faintly unreal.

He had changed so much, and that was odd too, and he had a girlfriend with him; she had known about Anneke ever since she called Geert at home, had actually spoken to her, but that was different from *seeing* her. It felt strange.

It was more than strange, though; it made her feel uneasy.

They shouldn't be here, thought Veerle. She closed her eyes, frowning, trying to recollect. *They shouldn't be here in my room because* . . .

That feeling was growing, that feeling that something was really very wrong.

They shouldn't be in my room, because Mum will go mad if she finds them here.

Veerle opened her eyes. She looked at Geert, at the harried expression on his face. He looked drawn. Anxious. Shocked.

She looked at Anneke, and saw a cool smile that concealed something else, something being held back. Reluctance.

'Where's Mum?' she croaked.

'Veerle . . .' began her father.

'Where's Mum?' she demanded again. 'Claudine. Where is she?'

Silence. Veerle stared at her father as the seconds trickled past. She waited for him to speak, until at last she realized that she did not want to hear what it was that he had to say. She squeezed her eyes shut then, cutting off the sight of him trying to think how to frame it.

She heard Anneke begin to say, 'I'm sorry—' and she had to cut her off, because when people said they were sorry to you in that particular way, in that pitying tone, it only meant one thing; it meant that someone was—

'Go away,' she said, and finally she had her real voice back; it sounded strong and angry.

'Veerle,' said her father again.

'Go away.'

'Veerle—' That was Anneke chiming in.

'Go away!' She screamed the words out so loudly that her throat began to hurt again; the sound seemed to have torn off bloody strips of flesh with it.

Veerle lay with her eyes closed and listened to Anneke getting up from the plastic chair, the legs scraping on the hospital linoleum, the two sets of footsteps moving towards the door, the muttered scraps of words drifting like smoke on the air. She heard the door open and close, movement in the corridor outside.

She kept her eyes shut, tight shut. There were too many things out there, on the other side of her eyelids, the other side of the door. Information she didn't want to face yet. Questions. Recriminations. Explanations. Veerle decided that she did not want to go there.

Kris, she thought, and in her mind's eye she saw him at the bottom of the staircase in the house with seventy-three bottles of champagne in the cellar. First she saw him in his usual uniform of black jeans and black leather jacket. No; that was wrong. He was supposed to be wearing evening dress. She dived back into the well of memories and clothed him in black and white, complete with bow tie. He was smiling at her, that lopsided smile that went to her heart.

Veerle looked down at herself and saw that she was wearing the red silk dress with the spaghetti straps and the matching shoes. The shoes still had ludicrously narrow pointed toes and towering heels, but she glided down the staircase without difficulty. Her feet didn't even hurt. *Anything is possible in a dream.* Veerle touched her earlobe and felt the diamond nestling there. She reached the bottom of the staircase. Kris was offering her his arm, an old-fashioned courtesy. She smiled up at him.

Someone was knocking on the front door. Veerle paused for a moment. The knocking was growing more persistent. Someone was out there and they were very keen to come in. She knew that there was no dark moonlit garden on the other side of that door, no glittering black ornamental lake. There was a well-lit corridor with a number of people in it, and she thought that some of them had uniforms on. They wanted very much to wake her up so that they could talk to her.

They were persistent, the people on the other side of the door. It took an effort of will to ignore them, but Veerle had plenty of that. She turned her back, the red silk dress rustling as she did so, and took Kris's arm. Together they strolled out of the hallway, into the heart of the house.

ACKNOWLEDGEMENTS

I would like to thank Camilla Wray of the Darley Anderson Agency for her honesty and enthusiasm. I would also like to thank Annie Eaton, Fiction Publisher, and the team at Random House, for their energy and vision.

Particular thanks are due to Tom Alaerts and Rebecca Benoot for their advice about various aspects of Flemish culture and language; any mistakes are mine. Thank you also to Gaby Grabsch for her support and friendship, and for providing transport and accommodation during my research in Belgium. And as always, I would like to thank my husband Gordon for his unfailing support and for all those cups of tea!